A PEARL BUCK READER

A PEARL BUCK READER

*Selected
and Condensed by
the Editors of
Reader's Digest*

Volume Two

The Reader's Digest Association, Inc.
Pleasantville, New York
Cape Town, Hong Kong, London, Montreal, Sydney

The credits and acknowledgments that appear on
page 504 are hereby made part of this copyright page.

Library of Congress Catalog Card Number: 84-6784
ISBN 0-89577-195-0 (Volume Two)
0-89577-196-9 (Set)

Printed in the United States of America

Contents

THE PROMISE

A CONDENSATION OF THE BOOK BY

Pearl S. Buck

ILLUSTRATED BY STEVEN STROUD

World War II found Pearl Buck
living in an old stone farmhouse
in Pennsylvania.
Her beloved China had been
invaded by the Japanese in 1937
and, though many thousands of miles
away, she was nonetheless
deeply concerned about the
events unfolding there.

The Promise opens in a small
Chinese village just before
the bombing of Pearl Harbor.
The war-weary villagers think
the Japanese forces will surely
be defeated now that the men
of Mei (the Americans) have
entered the fight alongside the
Chinese armies and the men of
Ying (the British). But once
again they learn the bitter lesson
that foreign friends do not always
act in China's best interests.

I

IN THEIR DESPAIR men must hope when a promise is given, though it be only a promise.

And though his second son, Lao Er, always shook his head when Ling Tan spoke of the promise, still the old man believed in it. Ling Tan believed the men of Ying and Mei to be the strongest and fiercest of all men on earth, and he hoped daily that the enemy would overstep himself and enrage those foreigners across the sea and force them to come into the war and bring an end to it. For, evil and strong as the enemy was, none believed even this enemy could conquer the foreigners, the men of Ying and Mei.

Nor would Ling Tan listen to his sons when they told him that these foreigners were not so strong as they had once been. In Nanking one day, where Lao Er had gone to sell some duck eggs, he saw an enemy guardsman spit into the face of a foreigner, and the foreigner did no more than wipe it off with a white cloth he took out of his pocket.

"All of us who saw it were amazed," Lao Er said to his father

9

when he came back. "It used to be that when a foreigner was given an insult, men with guns came down from foreign warships that always lay ready in the river."

"Where are those warships now?" Ling Tan's eldest son, Lao Ta, asked. "There are only enemy warships in the river these days."

But still Ling Tan hoped, for where was there hope in any other place?

All through that evil autumn the times grew steadily worse. Located outside the south wall of Nanking, the village of Ling lived as though it were in the middle of a silent world. There was no news except such as could leak in by the whispers of men hastening through. From them Ling Tan and his sons heard that war was now being made on the enemy in five provinces at once. They heard, too, that though the capital had been moved far inland, even there the enemy had sent down the great bombs like those that had torn up the earth near Ling Tan's village.

In the eighth month of that year Ling Tan finally heard some news of his third son, Lao San. The word came through a traveling priest, who took from his gray robe a paper in which there was a piece of curly black hair. The priest said, "This was given to me by the tallest young man I have ever seen. He told me to go out of my way to pass this house and that you would give me food when you saw this piece of hair."

When Ling Sao heard this, she was sure it was from her third son, who had gone away many months before with some of the hillmen. "Whose hair curls like this except my third son's?" she cried.

"Where did you see him, good priest?" Ling Tan asked.

"Near the city of Long Sands," the priest said. "He was on the way to battle, as all young men were in those parts, for it is expected that the enemy will gather there for a new attack on that city."

Ling Sao took the hair from the priest's hand and wrapped it in a bit of red paper that she had kept in a drawer. Ling Tan

told his eldest son's new wife, the widow whom he had
married after his first wife, Orchid, had been killed, to prepare
food for the priest. This the woman did, for she had become in
this house a willing, faithful soul whom all called upon. Even
the work once done by Jade, the wife of Ling Tan's second
son, this woman now took for her own. If Jade mentioned it,
she laughed and said, "If you suckle those two boys of yours,
what else can be asked of you?" And it was true that Jade's
twin sons were always hungry, and it seemed that however
much Jade ate or drank, she could never turn the food into
milk fast enough for those two thirsty boys.

Not long after this Jade received a letter. It was from Mayli,
and it came from the city of Kunming in the province of
Yunnan. It was a short letter, seemingly full of playful talk,
and yet it ended with this question: "How is it your husband's
younger brother has not brought me back my little silk flag?"

Now none but Jade and Lao Er knew that Mayli had given a
small silk flag to Jade to give to Lao San as a sign that Mayli
was going to the free lands, if he cared to follow her.

More than a month later there was another letter to Jade.
This time Mayli said, "Tell your parents that their third son
has come here to this city. He has fought in the battle of Long
Sands, and he is full of the great victory we won there against
the enemy."

They all were greatly cheered to know that somewhere
there had been a victory and that Lao San was alive. Only Ling
Sao fretted because there was nothing in the letter to tell her
whether her third son and this Mayli were to be married or
not. "I wish I had that third son of mine here so I could jerk his
ears!" she said. "When did a son of mine ever go near a
woman when she was not his wife? If he is hungry for her,
why does he not marry her?"

"Perhaps she will not marry my brother," Lao Ta said. "You
must remember, Mother, that she is full of learning and my
brother does not know his name on paper when he sees it."

But Ling Sao flung up her head at her son. "If she has her

belly full of ink, she is not the woman for him anyway," she said, "and all the more he ought not to go near her." By this time they were all laughing at her and she seized one of the twins from Jade's arms and bore him away to comfort herself in the kitchen.

These were the small things of Ling Tan's house with two of his three sons at home and his daughter, Pansiao, safely away at school in the inland mountains. Somehow the house went on, but the family never for one moment gave up their hope that, when Heaven set the day, the people would sweep the enemy into the sea.

"On the day when we hear that the men of Mei have come into this war on our side," Ling Tan said to his sons, "we shall all be given strength to rise up and fall upon the enemy and drive them out. Then we shall all be free."

It was on a cool night that he said this—so cool that Ling Sao had bade her two sons move the table from the court and set it inside the main room so that they could eat their meal in warmth. She lifted her head and sniffed the air before she shut the door. "I smell winter tonight," she said.

"The fifth winter of this war," Ling Tan said gravely. "But next winter we shall be free again."

None spoke when he said this, not wanting to take away his hope. There was still not one word of news from the outside world to tell him that the promise would be kept by the men of Mei and Ying. Even the random news they used to hear from their old cousin in Nanking had stopped, for that old scholar had taken too much opium one night and had not waked again. Thus Ling Tan was not ready for that evil day when the enemy took the men of Mei by surprise. They fell upon the ships as they lay side by side in the harbor, and set fire to the airplanes on the ground. And those who had the keeping of these ships of sea and cloud were sleeping or finding their pleasure on a day when all were idle. The enemy cried their victory in the streets. It was written upon the walls, and voices took it over the land faster than the winds could carry it.

So the news reached the village of Ling. A young fellow, the son of a neighbor, came running to Ling Tan and told him that in the early morning of that day the enemy had fallen upon the ships and the airplanes of the people of Mei, thousands of miles across the sea, and had destroyed them utterly. The men of Mei were full of rage—but helpless.

Hearing this black news, Ling Tan said, "I will not believe it." But his mouth went dry, for he saw it might have happened thus if the men of Mei were unwatching. He made the young man tell his sons the story, and when it had been told again, Ling Tan turned to Ling Sao and said, "Mother of my sons, get my bed ready. I must lie down, and I do not know whether I shall ever get up again."

He lay in his bed with eyes closed for eleven days and would not eat. On the twelfth day Ling Sao came in with ashes on her hands and face and a length of coarse white mourning cloth in her hand. "If you die, I will swallow the gold earrings you gave me," she said, weeping. "I cannot live on without you, old man."

Then his sons came in with their wives and children, and they wept and begged him for the sake of all to rouse himself.

But it was Jade who said the words that made him finally move. "Will you let the enemy kill you at last, when in all these years you have been the one to give us courage?" she asked him.

He thought for a moment as she looked at him shrewdly. Then he dragged himself up. "You would find the right words to make me live when I long to die," he said feebly.

His sons leaped forward to help him. The women went away, and with his sons' help he washed and dressed and ate a bowl of broth with two eggs in it. And so he began to live again.

But he was never what he had been. His withers were weak, and when he walked, he clung to the shoulder of a son or he leaned on Ling Sao. He never mentioned the war again, nor the enemy, nor the hope he had lost.

A THOUSAND and more miles away from where this old man fretted, his third son, Lao San, sat in the courtyard of a home in Kunming. He had another name these days. Lao San, or Lao Three, is well enough for a farmer's son, but after the victory of Long Sands he had been made a commander and his general called him Sheng from that day on.

He was sitting at a small porcelain garden table talking to the woman he loved who would not marry him. It could be said, rather, that she persuaded him to talk, drawing out of him all that he had been doing since they last met, more than two months before.

"You look beautiful in that uniform," she said. "But why do I tell you? You know it."

He did not answer.

"How many characters can you write now?" she asked.

"Enough for me," he said.

"Then why did you not write me a letter?" she asked.

"Why should I write when I knew I was coming here?"

"If you see no reason for writing to me, then there is no reason," she said. She took up her tea bowl in her hand and held it and he looked at her long narrow hand, its nails painted scarlet.

When Mayli had left Jade six months before, she had given Jade the small bright flag and said, "Tell Lao San I go to the free lands—tell him I go to Kunming." To Kunming he had come after the victory. But she was still not willing to marry him.

Over the wall of the courtyard behind Sheng's head were the high tops of the mountains that surrounded the city, bare mountains, purple against the clear winter sky. The day was not too cold and the light of the sun fell upon Mayli's face and his, and each saw the other's beauty.

"I ask you again if you will marry me," he said.

Her eyelids fell. "You are very bold these days."

"I have little time now," he said. "A soldier must go by the straightest road to what he wants. I ask you this—will you marry me before I march to my next battle?"

She lifted her lids again. "Is this the last time you will ask me?" She put the question to him as playfully as a kitten tosses a ball.

"No," he said. "I shall ask you until you yield."

"At least wait until you come back before you ask again," she said.

Each of them thought the same thought—what if he never came back? But neither would speak it aloud.

He stood up. "I have said what I came to say. There is no reason for staying longer today."

She rose too. "Do you go?"

"Yes," he said.

She felt her heart pull at him to stay. She stood near him, tall for a woman, but still only a little beyond his shoulder. "I swear I think you are still growing," she said willfully. "Can you blame me that I do not want a growing boy for my husband?"

"I do blame you for not wanting me," he said gravely. "I blame you because you know we are destined for marriage."

The air around them was so clear, so still, the sunshine so pure, that their two shadows lay on the white stones beneath their feet as though they were one. She saw the closeness and stepped back from him and the shadows parted.

"Go away," she said. "When you are finished growing, you may come back."

He gave her a long look, so long and fierce that she stamped her foot. "Don't think I am afraid of your eyes!" she cried.

"Don't think I am afraid of you," he said. He turned and went away without another word.

And she, left alone in the courtyard, walked back and forth. When would she be sure of this man for whom her flesh longed? She would not marry a lout, and was he more than a lout? Who knew? It had taken him months to prove that he could lead something more than the handful of ragged men who had escaped with him out of the hills near his father's house. For those months he had drilled in the common ranks of soldiers and at night he had learned to read and write like a schoolboy. Marry him she could, but she wanted to marry a man whom she could love until she died, and to keep her love he must have the power to be great. Had Sheng that power? She did not know.

LATER THAT DAY Sheng stood at attention before his general, a man still young and hearty who was in command of the armies in the Kunming region. He made a motion to Sheng. "Sit down," he said. "I have something to say to you, not as your superior but as man to man. I have had an order from the One Above that our two best divisions are to march into Burma. But I cannot obey without letting you know that I do not approve of this thing. Sit down—sit down!"

At this Sheng sat down. He took off his cap and held it silently to show his respect. There were two guards in the room, standing like idols against the wall. To these the general lifted his eyelids and they went out.

"Your father is a farmer, you told me once," he said to Sheng.

"I am the son of farmers for a thousand years," Sheng replied.

"Are you your father's only son?" the general asked.

"I am the youngest of three," Sheng replied. "And all are living."

The general sighed. "Then I may send you out to an unlucky war without cutting off your father's life." Picking up a writing brush, he asked, "Where is your father's house and what is his name? I shall write him myself if you do not come back from this battle."

"Ling Tan of the village of Ling, to the south of the city of Nanking, in the province of Kiangsu," Sheng said.

"But that is land held by the enemy," the general exclaimed.

"Do I not know that?" Sheng replied. "They came in and burned and murdered wherever they could."

The general quickly brushed the name of Ling Tan and where he lived, then he put down the brush and fixed his eyes upon Sheng's face. "It is against my will that I send these two divisions to Burma," he said. "I have reasoned with the One Above. I have told him that we must not fight on soil that is not our own, for two reasons. In the first place, the people of Burma will not welcome us. They do not love the men of Ying who have been their rulers, and when we come to aid the men of Ying, they will hate us, too. In the second place, the men of Ying despise those not of their own pale color, and even though we come as allies, they will look on us as servants."

"What does the One Above say when you tell him these true things?" Sheng asked.

The general leaned forward. "He says the men of Ying must know how small their chances are of holding Burma. He says that since they need our help, they will be grateful to us and we will fight by their side and win a great victory over the enemy at last."

"Is the One Above so sure that we can win?" Sheng asked.

The general fell silent and sat like a man of stone. Then he began to speak in a low thick voice. "I say the men of Ying are doomed. If we go with them, we are doomed. We ought to stay on our own earth and fight only from our own land. The men of Ying have treated us like dogs and lorded it over us since they won those wars against us—the Opium Wars, they call them. They took land from us, they refused to obey our laws, and when one of them killed one of us, there was no justice."

Suddenly he leaped to his feet and his wrath burst out of his eyes like lightning. He paced back and forth in the long narrow room. "And I am commanded to send my best young men to fight for these men who have despised us and trodden us down for all these years!" he shouted.

Now Sheng himself had always lived in his father's house outside the city. The few times he had ever seen these foreign men whom the general so hated could be counted on the fingers of his right hand, and he himself did not know of all the hateful things they had done to his people. He waited to see what the general would tell him to do.

"What must be done must be done!" the general said loudly. "For many days I have resisted the One Above and I have held back my men. Now his commands have come down to me, and either I must obey or take my life."

Sheng rose and stood to receive his orders for battle.

"You will prepare your men to go to Burma with the others," the general said harshly. "I myself will lead you. When we are at the edge of Burma, we are all to encamp on our own soil until we receive orders to march on."

Sheng put his heels together and saluted, then waited. The general sighed and leaned forward. "We go to fight in a battle already lost," he said. "I know it, but what shall we do to make the One Above know it?"

"Let your heart rest," Sheng said. "If the battle has not been fought yet, how can we have lost it?"

The general sighed again. He lifted his head and looked at Sheng's brave and honest face. He remembered this man when he first came from the hills, wild as a tiger, his hair long and shaggy, his garments ragged blue cotton such as peasants wear. Had he been a smaller man, none might have noticed him, but Sheng was a head taller than most men, and the strange thing was that he was still growing, though he was more than twenty-two years old. Wherever he went, men's heads turned to stare after him, and because he was so large, he was the more easily a leader. Had he been stupid or timid, he would have been only a bigger lump of clay. But he was sensible and he learned eagerly. And while all his men liked him, still they were afraid of him, as men should be of the one who leads them.

There was yet another reason why Sheng had risen so quickly to be a commander. In the battle of Long Sands it was he with his men, and those of another officer who had fallen, who had driven the last of the enemy out of the city. When the battle was finally won, the men left alive sent messengers to the general and begged him to give them the young giant for their leader. This wish was granted and the general saw to it that these men had the best food and the best guns.

And then there was Mayli. She knew the general and had taken the trouble to speak good words for Sheng, gay words, half in fun, so that none might think she cared whether this tall fellow lived or died. But she praised him and told of the brave things he had done in the hills. "I came from the city near where he lives," she said to the general. "He is famous there for his strength and his bravery."

And so this was where Sheng stood with his general when he was told to prepare to lead his men to Burma to fight by the side of the men of Ying.

"How shall we get to Burma?" Sheng asked.

"There is no railroad. We go by the Big Road," the general responded.

"And when do we go?" Sheng asked.

"In four days."

As soon as Sheng had received these orders, he saluted and turned and went out. It would take two days to prepare his men for the long journey, but not more, for they were hard and ready. But they ought to have some hours in which to tell their women good-by and do all the things that men must do when they prepare for a journey from which they may not return.

And then, when he came out of the room where the general was, it suddenly came to Sheng that he, too, might never return. For he knew very well that this would be the bitterest battle that he had ever fought. To lead his men a thousand miles by foot over mountain and river, then to fight on foreign soil, this was gravest hazard.

He stood for a moment outside the gate and the people passed him. The street was bright with the hard, clear sunshine of winter. It would be a long time before he could see again the woman he loved. What if he never saw her again? He turned to the left instead of the right and strode through the crowd, head and shoulders above them, toward where Mayli lived.

II

MAYLI'S HOUSE was very still when Sheng entered it. It was midafternoon. In a corner of the court under the scattered shade of a clump of bamboos, an old woman in a black coat and trousers sat sleeping. On the flagstones beside the old woman was a small dog, also asleep, which Mayli had found one day on the street and had brought home with her. It opened its eyes at Sheng and, seeing who he was, went back to sleep again.

Sheng smiled at the two and tiptoed across the court and into the main room of the little house. Perhaps Mayli was asleep, too, for the house was as quiet as the court. He was about to sit down and wait for her when his eye fell on the door into Mayli's room.

The door was open, and through it he saw her standing before the window. She had washed her hair and was tossing it, long and wet, into the sunlight that streamed in, and she did not see him. He stood watching her, and his heart beat hard. How beautiful a woman she was, how beautiful her black hair! "Mayli!" he called.

She parted her hair with her hands and looked and saw him. She leaped forward and slammed the door between them. He heard her push the wooden bar into place. "Oh, you big stupid!" he heard her breathe through the cracks of the door. And in a moment she was calling for the old woman.

Sheng sat down quickly at the right of the table, laughing. The old woman stumbled across the threshold, rubbing her eyes. "How did you get in, Big Soldier?" she asked crossly. "I swear I did not see you come in."

"What would you say if I told you I have a magic dagger?" he asked to tease her. "I carry it in my girdle, and when I say 'Small!' I am so small I can blow myself over the wall in a particle of dust."

But she thrust out her lower lip at him and would not smile. "We ought to have a better watchdog. Our dog is no better

than a cat," she said as she went into the kitchen to make tea.

The little dog appeared, wagging its tail, and Sheng leaned over and pulled its long ears. "Of what use are you?" he inquired of the dog. Its large brown eyes hung out of its small face like dark glass balls, and its body quivered.

At that moment Mayli opened the door. She had put on an apple-green robe and her hair was bound in a coil on her neck. On her finger was a ring of green jade. She came in, picked up the tiny creature and sat down with it on her knees.

Sheng watched her. She moved so swiftly and gracefully, and seemed as foreign, he thought, as though she had no blood of her people in her body. "I came to tell you that I am to be sent with the armies to Burma," he said.

At the sound of these words she forgot the dog and stopped petting it. "When do you go?" she asked.

"In a few days," he said. "Two or three—four at most."

The sun shone down on her fine smooth skin, and he saw that her eyes had flecks in them, like light. "You have gold in your eyes," he said. "Where did it come from?"

"Do not talk about my eyes," she said. "Tell me why it has been decided that you should go so quickly?"

"It only seems quick to us," he said. "It has been talked of for weeks. My general is against it. But the One Above is for it. And when that one says 'yes,' what 'no' is strong enough to balance it? We go."

He said the words we go so firmly that Mayli saw in a moment what her life would be without this man with whom she quarreled every time he came. But when had she ever wished for a quiet life?

"So now we go to ally ourselves with white men," Sheng said.

"Why is your general against this?" she asked.

"My general says that the white men will fail," he said.

"Oh, why?" she asked. Her mind flew across the sea to the land where she had spent most of her life. Her mother had died when she was born, and before she was a year old her father had taken her to America. The first words she had spoken were in the language of that land, and now Mayli thought of those great cities and factories and the rich, busy people, and all the wealth and the pride everywhere. "How can they fail?" she asked.

"My general says that wherever white men have lived among the peoples near us, they have held them as dogs, and that now those peoples will join with an enemy they hate because they hate the white man even more than this enemy."

This Mayli heard without understanding it. How could she understand it when most of her life she had lived in a country of white men where all had been kind to her? Her father held an honored place in Washington and she was his daughter. "But the people of Mei do not despise us," she said.

"Well, we are not going to Burma to fight beside the people of Mei," Sheng replied. "It is the people of Ying who rule there, and it is the people of Ying the Burmese hate."

"If the people of Ying are against the Japanese, then we must be with them," she said.

"If we can win with them," he said gravely.

"Who can conquer the peoples of Ying and Mei together?" she cried, remembering again the great factories, shaping out iron and steel as though they were wood and paper.

"The enemy has conquered thus far," Sheng said.

Then he rose and she was filled with the sense of his power. As he stood there looking down on her, she felt the blood run to her face. She rose quickly and walked back and forth in the room, then she sat down and put her arms about her knees.

"All that you say is true," she said, "and yet, when I remember them, I know they cannot lose. No, whatever has happened, and whatever will happen, they will be the victors in the end, and for this we must stay with them."

"What do you remember?" he asked.

"It is the most beautiful country," she said. "I do not love it as my own, and yet I can say that."

"Beauty will not win a war," he said sternly.

"No, but there are the factories," she said quickly. "The factories make ships and automobiles and airplanes."

"It is strange they have not been able to send us a few," he said bitterly.

At this moment the little dog raised its tiny head and howled. They stopped their talk and both looked at the beast.

"What does this dog hear that we do not?" Sheng asked. He looked out into the court.

"Listen!" Mayli whispered.

They listened and heard the rising wail of a siren.

"It is the enemy!" he shouted.

In all the time that Mayli had been in Kunming no enemy planes had come over the city. She had heard talk of their coming and she could see the ruins from earlier raids, but still it was only hearsay to her.

Now the noise grew louder and louder and the old woman came running out, wiping her hands on her apron. "Now, now—where shall we go?" she cried. "Big Soldier, think for us—be of some use to us—we are only two women!"

Sheng ran to the gate and threw it open. In the street the people were already running, some here, some there.

"If we were outside the city! To be caught in the city is like being in a pen!" he shouted over his shoulder. And he remembered how, when the first bombs had fallen in the city near his father's village, he had grown sick at the sight of men and women and children crushed and scattered into scraps of meat and bone. But Mayli did not move from where she stood. She could not fear what she had not seen.

He considered quickly. It was perhaps a mile to the south gate of the city. If the gate was not closed, they might gain the countryside before the enemy came. Then they could take refuge in the bamboo groves, where at least the beams of roofs and the masonry of thick walls could not fall on them and crush them.

"Come!" he shouted. The two women ran to follow him. But Mayli remembered the little dog and she went back to pick it up. When Sheng saw what she had done, he wrenched the dog out of her arms and threw it on the ground. Then he pushed her out of the gate and held her to his side.

"Oh, you daughter of an accursed mother!" he shouted. "When your two feet must run faster than a deer's four feet, you stop for a dog—a worthless dog!"

She was wrenching and twisting to be free of him, but the more she wrenched and twisted, the more he held her, and all the time he was hurrying her down the streets to the south gate with the old woman panting behind them.

They could hear the drone of planes coming nearer. The great gate was ahead, and in a moment they had entered the cold shadows of the city wall, which was thirty feet thick and arched over the road. At the end of the long arch was the gate.

The moment they entered the shadows Sheng saw that the city gate was closed and the darkness under the wall was full of people who had come there for shelter. In this chill dimness stood a beggar whose cheeks had rotted away from leprosy. He drew as far back as he could. Mayli cried out at the sight of this wretched man and turned to run out again.

The airplanes were over the northwest corner of the city and already the heavy thunder of the bombs had begun. Sheng put out his arms and held Mayli, though he, too, was torn between his horror of the leper and his fear of the bombs. "Wait," he cried, and he put himself between her and the man, though he was careful not to touch him.

Voices cried out against the leper, saying he ought not to have come in where other people were. One voice after another complained.

"Is your life worth saving, you rotted bone?"

"Are we all to escape from the devils outside only to come upon another here?"

"Stay far from us, turtle's egg!"

Through all this the leper said nothing. Then from the far end of the tunnel came a young Buddhist priest in a gray robe, carrying his begging bowl. Without speaking, the priest put the leper against the wall and stood between him and the others. So they all stood, their heads bent, while the fearful rain from heaven came down.

The air in the gateway under the wall grew thick with dust and once or twice the old wall shook around them. Then it was over. Sheng stepped out of the shelter and climbed quickly up on the wall. He leaned over the inner side and shouted to Mayli to come up. Now the people whose homes were in the city went back and the travelers went on their way. Before the priest left, he took some coins from the bosom of his gray robe and dropped them into the palm of the leper.

Mayli climbed up the wall and soon she was beside Sheng and he saw distress in her eyes. Four great fires blazed, and the coils of smoke rose against the fair evening sky. She cried out, "I am so angry! We wait for them to come and kill us and we can do nothing but hide ourselves!"

He reached for her hand and they stood watching the fires. Then the old woman's voice came scolding up to them from the street. "Are you staying there? It will soon be night. I go home to cook the rice."

They came down and followed her, and their hearts were cold with what they had seen.

"I must go back to my men," Sheng said.

"Will you come to me again before you go to Burma?" she asked.

He did not answer. For where the street forked to the north a house had fallen under a bomb, and a young man, weeping aloud, was digging at the ruins with his hands.

"My house, my silk shop and all I had are buried underneath it," the man said, sobbing. "My wife and my old father and my little son!" At this moment he came upon a small piece of red-flowered cloth. "It is my little son's jacket!" he screamed.

Sheng took a stick and began to dig, and Mayli fell to her knees on the rubble stones when she saw the flowered cloth and dug with her hands.

Soon the child was uncovered, and the young father cradled him in his arms. But the child was dead. No one spoke, and the young man lifted the child up and sobbed to the heavens until none of them could keep back the tears.

"If this child is dead, be sure all the others of your house are dead," Sheng said, "and you alone have been saved for some will of Heaven. Come with me. I will give you a gun for revenge."

"Give the child to me," Mayli said. "I will buy him a coffin and see that he is buried for you."

So the young man gave her his dead boy. When Mayli took this little creature, he lay against her so helplessly that her heart swelled in her breast and she could not speak. Over the dead child she and Sheng looked at each other, and though neither of them had ever seen him in life, this dead child made them tender toward each other again.

"I will come to you as quickly as I can," Sheng said.

"I shall await your coming," Mayli said. It was only a courteous sentence, but she made her eyes speak it too.

So he understood, and he went his way, the man following, and she went hers.

Mayli carried the child home, and there the house was as they had left it, though on the south side ten houses had fallen in a row and a cloud of dust was everywhere. Inside the court her little dog stood trembling and waiting. She went in and laid the child on her own bed.

He was a fair little boy, about three years old, and his face was round and smooth. So far as the eye could see, he was not injured, and she took the little fat hand in hers, wondering if by some chance there was still life in it. But no, she could feel the stiffening of death already in the delicate fingers, dimpled at the knuckles. For the first time it came to her what this war was and what it meant in the world when a child could be murdered. Anger grew in her like a weed. "I wish I could put out my hands and feel an enemy's throat," she muttered.

At this moment the old woman peered in and asked, "Shall I go and buy the coffin?"

"Yes," Mayli said. "We will find land for a grave outside the city. A farmer will sell me a few feet somewhere for the body of a child."

"To rent it will be enough," the old woman said. "A child's body does not last long, and this child is not even your own blood."

"Every child whom the enemy kills is my own blood!" Mayli cried with such passion that the old woman went away quickly. After a while Mayli rose and drew the curtains about the bed. Then she went out into the court and lay down in a long rattan chair. She lay with her hands over her eyes and the dog came and curled beside her. The little dog was alive and the child was dead. There was no meaning to this. Now she understood Sheng's anger that she valued a dog so much.

When the old woman came back in a ricksha with the coffin, Mayli helped her to carry it in, and together they laid the child in it. Then they went outside the city wall, the old woman and the coffin in one ricksha and Mayli in another.

A mile or two beyond the city they found an old farmer who dug a hole at the far end of a field for some silver, and they laid the coffin in the earth.

Then Mayli and the old woman stepped into their rickshas again and went back to the city.

In the night Mayli woke. For a moment she listened to hear what had wakened her. But there was only silence. As she lay listening, she suddenly became aware of everything, of her body and her breath, of the room and the bed she lay upon, where she had earlier laid the dead child. All was real, and yet nothing was real. She had waked to the blackest melancholy she had ever known, a sadness so heavy that it stifled her.

"Did I dream an evil dream?" she asked herself. But no, her mind was empty of everything except this desperate sense of loss. Everything about her seemed suddenly foreign and she longed for some home she did not have, where she might escape the disaster that was everywhere around her. But what home? She had no one except her father in America.

At the thought of her father all her longing welled up. She thought of the cheerful rooms where he lived, of the clean bright curtains, the blue carpets on the floor. Why had she left him? Why had she left that good place? She had left it because she had wanted to share in the war in her own country.

"You will be sorry," her father had warned her. "You will wish you had not gone. You are not used to troubles."

I cannot go back to America, she thought. The red line of her full lips grew straight. I will not go back.

But there was no place for her in her own country. There was no place here for such a woman as she was. Peasant women tilled the soil, as the young men did, or if they had been to school, they made themselves into nurses and caretakers of the wounded. But what could she do, she who had never done work of any kind?

In a few days Sheng would be gone. Then what would she have left except the old woman and her dog? Her lips curled at the thinness of such a life. She threw off the quilt and began to walk about the room. Suddenly it came to her what she would do. She would go west, too. When Sheng went to fight, she would go to do—anything. Yes, there it was. She would go with the armies, but how?

Now she wished she had learned something about the care of the wounded, but she knew nothing even of the sick. Well then, she must have another reason to go. As her brain went flaming on and as her will grew firm and stubborn, she was her old bold self. "Why should I not go to the One Above?" she asked herself. "I could ask him, and if he will not let me go, then his lady will. I daresay she is like me. We both grew up in the same foreign country. She will know what I want and how I feel. She is an impatient woman, too."

I will tell Sheng nothing, she thought, for she knew he

would forbid her. I will go and get my way. Whether he likes me to be there or not I shall not care.

When she had made up her mind, she lay down on her bed again and fell asleep as sweetly as a child does.

III

"WHERE HAS SHE gone?" Sheng asked the old woman two days later.

"How can I tell you when she did not tell me?" the woman said. "When I asked her where she was going, she laughed and said that she would not tell me because you would ask and pull it out of me."

"When is she coming back?" Sheng asked.

"She put some money in my hand and told me to feed myself from it, and that before I had eaten it all up, she would be back," the old woman said.

"Show me how much money she gave you," Sheng commanded her.

So the old woman put her hand in her bosom and brought out ten silver dollars wrapped up in brown paper.

"How many days can you eat from that?" he demanded.

"I can eat it up quickly if I eat well," she said. "Or I can eat poorly and make it feed me for a month."

Sheng stared about the empty court and then angrily turned away. But at the gate he paused to shout at the old woman, "If she comes back, tell her I have gone away to war."

At that moment Mayli was high above the mountains in the general's own airplane, and the general was beside her.

She had gone straight to his headquarters, and because the guards knew her, they had let her pass them. The general was at his breakfast when she came in.

"Will you be going back once more to see the One Above before you go to Burma?" Mayli asked.

He looked up from his bowl. "Who told you we go there?" he asked.

"I know," she said, smiling. "And I want to go, too."

He put down his bowl. "But what would you do?"

"You are taking women with you," she said.

"Only those to care for the wounded," he said. "We take some doctors and with the doctors are the nurses."

She sighed and said gently, "Well, at least take me with you to the capital when you go to see the Ones Above. I must do something. If I go to the capital, perhaps I can help. I can work in their orphanages, or use my foreign language for them."

"That I will do," he said.

And this was how it came about that she went with him in his own plane. She felt the sweetest pleasure now in thinking that Sheng did not know where she was, nor would he dream of this. When would she see him, where would they meet again? When she saw him, what would be their first words?

Now these Ones Above were no strangers to Mayli. The lady had been her mother's friend, and the One Above was himself her father's friend, the man to whom her father looked for direction and command. Therefore the meeting was granted easily enough. Mayli sent a message and the lady herself returned a message in English, which said, "Come and breakfast with us tomorrow."

So the next morning Mayli put on her favorite gown of apple green and bound back her long black hair in a smooth knot and hung plain gold rings in her ears. Then she left her hotel and set off in a ricksha that was waiting at the door.

The streets were lines of ruin, and there was scarcely a whole house to be seen anywhere, so heavy had the summer's bombings been in this city of Chungking, but nobody seemed to see it. Indeed, the war had been going on for so long now that there were children able to talk and run about who had never seen a roof whole over their heads, and who considered bombings as natural as thunderstorms and hurricanes. Pleasant curses and laughter and the shouts of people at their everyday life filled the air. There was liveliness everywhere and no sign of fear or sadness, and Mayli found herself smiling out of simple satisfaction that she was alive too and on her way to have breakfast with the Ones Above.

She came to a plain brick house, no palace, and yet here was where the One Above and his lady lived. The guards at the gate knew of her coming, and let her pass, and she walked across a small garden. Once inside the house, a serving man took her to a plain room, furnished half with Chinese goods and half with foreign, nothing rich or costly.

She had not long to wait, for in a moment or two she heard quick footsteps, and there was the lady herself, very fresh and pretty. She put out both her hands to Mayli.

"Let me look at you," the lady cried. "Yes, you are your mother's daughter! You look like her. Your mother was very beautiful." She sat down on the long foreign couch, all her movements quick and full of grace, and she pulled Mayli down with her.

For the first time in her life Mayli was shy and speechless. She sat and stared at the lady, who was dressed simply but richly in a dark blue silk robe. Over this she wore a little velvet jacket of the same color, and the dark hue set off her clear skin and red lips. It was a very handsome face, but what made it most remarkable was the proud intelligence in the eyes and the fearlessness of the head carried high upon the slender body. She was not a young woman, this lady, but she looked imperishably young.

"And tell me about your father," the lady said, smiling. "My husband thinks very highly of him, you know. Yes, it is true. He listens to your father's advice, and then I grow jealous." She burst into clear laughter as she said this. "He will not always listen to me," she said with a pretended pout. "Oh, what a disadvantage it is today to be a woman! Do you not feel it so?"

"I cannot think of any disadvantage it is to *you* to be a woman," Mayli said.

"Oh, but it is," the lady said quickly. "I long to do this and that—anything and everything—I see so much to do. Then my

husband says to me, 'Remember that you are a woman, please.'"
She laughed.

Mayli had no wish to talk but only to listen and watch the
laughter and the earnestness play like light and shadow over
this most lovely face. Then suddenly the lady fell silent. They
heard a footstep at the door. The lady rose. "It is he," she said.
Mayli rose, too, and into the room came the One Above
himself, with no guard or servant to announce him.

He was a slender figure, seeming taller than he was. He had
the carriage of a soldier and a face such as Mayli had never
seen before. First she saw the eyes and she felt him looking at
her so clearly that it seemed two shining dark blades were
passing through her brain. And yet she did not feel he saw her
at all, but only what she was thinking. That she was young or a
woman or beautiful meant nothing. What she was thinking
meant everything.

"This is Mr. Wei's daughter, Mayli," the lady said to him.

He came forward and took her hand. His hand seemed like
steel to her touch. Then he turned to the lady. "We must
breakfast," he said. "The generals are waiting for their orders.
They must return at once to their posts."

He led the way and the lady followed, taking Mayli's hand.
They sat down at a small table and food was brought, half
foreign, half Chinese. The lady had bread and coffee and an
egg, and the man ate rice and salted foods. The woman spoke
as easily in English as in Chinese, thinking now on one side of
the world and now on the other. But the man spoke only
Chinese. He said very little, but she pressed Mayli with many
questions. "Did the Americans think the enemy would attack
them?" the woman asked, and then she answered her own
question swiftly. "Of course the Americans never think anything at all. They are so busy." She frowned and bit a crust of
bread. "I need money for my war orphans. I have not enough.
And it is absurd that we have not more planes."

The man looked up, his face mild for the moment and kind.
"The planes have been promised us," he said.

She made a pretty face of laughter at him. "Oh, you who always believe!"

"I believe our allies," he said.

"Those who ask receive," she retorted. "Does it not say so in the Bible?"

"We have asked," he said.

"There are many ways of asking and we have only asked as gentlemen ask—with our words."

This, it seemed, was an old argument between them, for stubbornness settled between the man's brows. "I still believe in my allies," he said to the lady, "and I am sending my best divisions to Burma. If we fight side by side, we will win the campaign to keep the Big Road open."

The man rose, having finished his meal, nodded to Mayli and went away, and the two women were left alone. For a moment there was silence. The woman sat with her long eyes downcast.

When she lifted them, Mayli saw fear. "I am afraid of this campaign," she said. "He is sending our very best fighters, the ones he ought to keep for our own country. What if the enemy advances upon us while these divisions are in Burma? And he values them so much that it is like sending his sons. I dread the effect upon him should the campaign not go well."

"Why should it not go well?" Mayli asked.

The lady shook her head. Her beautiful face was very sad now. "There are reasons," she said. "I wish I were a man and could go and see what happens from day to day, so that when the campaign is won—or lost—we might know the truth and be misled no more."

Mayli's heart leaped. "Send me in your place," she said. "I will go and watch and tell you all that happens."

The lady lifted her head and fixed her beautiful powerful eyes upon Mayli's face. "It is too dangerous," she said.

"The one thing that matters today is that each does his duty. If other women can fight in the army beside men, and walk thousands of miles beside men, I, too, can do these things."

"Yes," the lady said,"you could. But there are no women in these divisions except for the nurses."

"Let me be the one who takes care of the nurses," Mayli said. "I will see to their food and their shelter and what they need, and I will stay with them at night and see to their protection in the strange country."

"Yes," the lady said again slowly,"you could do that."

"And wherever I am," Mayli said quickly, "I will be your eyes and your ears."

The lady sat reflecting on this for some moments as the sunlight streamed through the window, then she lifted her eyes and said,"I can trust you and you shall go. Now leave me and I will prepare your way."

MAYLI RETURNED to her hotel and waited. She soon received a note from the lady saying, "That which we planned is done. You will return to Kunming by plane tonight. I hope your mother looks down and approves."

Mayli did not go out of her room all that day, but rested. When at last near midnight she stood beside the small plane, she felt refreshed and ready for whatever was ahead of her.

On entering her little house the next day, she found nothing but stillness and peace. It was so quiet a spot after the excitement of her visit that she could scarcely believe it was there. In the court the bamboos were motionless and the little pool was clear and still under the blue sky of the fair day. Then the little dog heard her and began to bark wildly with joy that she had come back. In a moment the old woman came out of the kitchen. "You have come!" she cried and made haste to fetch tea and food.

"Did the big soldier plague you while I was gone?" Mayli called to her in the kitchen.

And the old woman shouted back, "Did he not? He roared like a tiger because he did not know where you were."

"And you could tell him nothing!" Mayli cried gaily.

"Nothing, nothing!" the old woman cackled. Now that her

young mistress was back, she felt excited and alive again and tried to do everything at once.

As Mayli sat throwing bits of bread to the dog, her mind was leaping across the miles of land and mountains. Surely we will succeed at stopping the enemy, she dreamed, and our allies will honor us for it and redeem their promises.

So her great thoughts went on, making the hardships of the battlefield easy and the armies victorious, and in those armies would not Sheng be the bravest and the best of all the young leaders? She and Sheng together, could not they be like the Ones Above someday? Then she laughed at herself and pulled the dog's ears. "You will be ill if you eat any more bread, you mouse," she said.

She rose and paced about the court restlessly. Should she tell Sheng that she was going or let him find out for himself? There would be pleasure in telling him, and yet she was a mischievous creature and she delighted to think of his face when he saw her the first time on the march with him. This so tempted her that she decided she would not tell him.

Then she remembered the general. She knew he had come back before her. Would he not tell Sheng immediately when he saw her name on the lists? She must go quickly and beg him to keep her secret.

So Mayli took a ricksha and went to the general's headquarters. She gave her name to the guard at the gate, who took it in. The general was alone, and he bowed when he saw her.

"I come to ask you to help me," she said.

"I am always glad to help you," the general said, smiling.

"You know the lady has appointed me to go as the one in charge of the young nurses," she said.

"The lady does what she likes," he said. "But are you not young to be put in such a place?"

Mayli smiled a most mischievous smile. "I am young, but I can walk for miles, I can endure heat and I can eat whatever there is to eat."

"A good soldier," he said. "Well, what else? Your work will

not be under my direct command, you know. You will report to one of my commanders, Pao Chen."

She put the name into her mind securely. "Pao Chen," she repeated. "But that is not why I have come to you."

He leaned back and looked at her, still smiling. "When will you tell me why you have come?" he asked.

"I will speak quickly," she said. "It is a short thing and yet difficult for me to say. It is this—please tell no one that I am going."

"Why should your name be kept so secret?" he asked.

"The young commander—the one you have newly promoted—of whom I have spoken—"

"Sheng," he interrupted.

"Yes," she said. "I do not wish him to know that I go."

"Ah," he said.

"He has some silly thoughts of me," she went on, her cheeks burning, "and—and—it is better if we do not meet—that is, we have a grave duty and I do not wish to—to—"

"In other words, he loves you," the general said.

"But I do not wish to be loved," Mayli said hotly. "This is not the time for such things."

The general shook with mild laughter for a moment. Then he wiped his eyes. "You shall have your own way," he promised.

She prepared to leave. At that moment a soldier came in to say that the commanders of the divisions were outside.

"Tell them to wait a moment," the general said.

The soldier went out, and Mayli thanked the general and went out, too. She was afraid that Sheng might see her, so she drew the collar of her cape high and bent her head and hurried. She did not see him anywhere, and she thought herself safe.

And so she might have been, if the soldier had not been a fellow who loved to joke about women and men. He went back sniggering and told the three commanders that the general had a woman visitor. They looked at one another and said nothing, out of respect for their superior. But when the soldier was gone, Sheng said plainly, "I did not think that he was such a one."

Then they all stepped to the door and saw the tall slender woman wrapped in a cape for one quick moment, too quick to catch her looks. But Sheng knew who it was. A rush of terror and fear and anger swept up his body. Was this where she had been all these days, here in this house? Was his own general his rival for her?

But Sheng was compelled to move forward with his fellow officers and march into the room where the general was. There they stood at attention and saluted, and Sheng smelled the faint sweetness of Mayli's perfume in the air.

EARLY THE NEXT morning Mayli was summoned by messenger to go to her superior, Pao Chen, and receive her orders. When that message arrived, she deemed it time to tell the old woman what lay ahead. This old woman had come to her when she had returned from overseas and told her that she once was her wet nurse. "Your dead mother put it into my mind to find you," she had said. "I knew it was she because I smelled the cassia flowers she always used to wear in her hair."

"My father still loves cassia flowers," Mayli had replied. One reason she had wanted the old woman near her was so that she might hear these small stories about the mother who had died when she was born.

So when she had eaten and when the old woman came in to fetch away the bowls, Mayli said, "I have something to tell you. I am going away. I have received a command from the Ones Above to do a certain work I cannot tell of, but I must do it."

The old woman's jaw dropped and she stared at Mayli.

"What day I go is not yet known," Mayli said, "but that messenger this morning brought me an order to see my superior. I want you to stay here until I return and keep the dog and this house. If you are lonely, you may find another woman to stay with you."

Hearing whence the commands came, the old woman did not dream of crying out. But because she could not protest the larger, she protested the smaller. "Why should I want another woman here to be fed and spoken to and noticed all the time? I would rather stay alone with the dog, whom I know."

"You shall do as you like," Mayli said with good humor. "All that I ask is that you keep the house for a home for me."

"I do not know whether it is well for me to do even that," the old woman said, wanting to feel peevish. "How shall I know whether you will come back or not? You may change your mind, and here I shall be waiting for you until I die with nothing but a dog beside my bed."

"Now you are being an old bone," Mayli said, laughing. "Stay only if you want to, and in all things do only as you wish." Thus she took away all cause for discontent, and this made the old woman more peevish still, but she held her peace and went on about her work, though she sulked and thrust out her lip.

Mayli went on foot to the place where she had been told to go, and when she reached it, she saw other women gathering there, too. She joined them and entered a large room where two men took the women's names and told them to wait.

When Mayli's turn came, she was not sent with the others but straight ahead through an open door, and there she found Pao Chen, a young officer with a large, plain face. She stood before him until he bade her sit down, and waited while he looked at a paper before him. Then he put it down.

"You have been told your duties?" he asked.

"I have been told only part of them," she replied.

"Here." He took the sheet of paper and handed it to her. "Read it," he commanded. "It is your duty to see to each of these things. Your co-worker will be the head doctor, Chung Liang-mo. Together you will be responsible for all that concerns the sick and the wounded, and the nurses will work under both of you. He will be responsible for the medical matters, and you for the nurses' food, quarters and supplies."

He struck a bell on the table and a soldier came in. "Invite Dr. Chung to come here," he said.

Pao Chen sat silent and without moving until in a few minutes the doctor entered the room. From the moment he came in, Mayli liked him. He was a short, strong man with intelligent eyes.

"This is your co-worker, Wei Mayli, of whom you have been told," Pao Chen said. "She has received her orders and you have received yours, and it would be well for you to draw apart and talk alone in the next room while I proceed with what I have to do here."

Mayli rose and followed Dr. Chung into the other room, and there he sat down and she also. He looked at Mayli kindly, examining her face. "You are very young, I think," he said. "Have you ever endured any hardships?"

"I have not," she confessed, "but I am ready to."

"We shall have great hardships on this campaign," he said gently. "The One Above has laid down a very stern order. We may die, but we may not surrender. Many will be wounded, and we must be ready, day and night, without sleep or rest, once the battle begins."

She bowed her head. "I can eat and sleep or I can go without," she said simply. "I have only one question—when do we go?"

"That one question no one can answer," he replied. "It is locked in the mind of the One Above. When he gives the sign, we go. One division is already gone. The rest of the men will go within the next few days. Perhaps we will go with them."

When she heard this, her heart immediately asked if it was Sheng's division that had gone and if that was why he had not come near her. But who could answer a question her heart asked? She sat silently, her eyes upon the doctor's face.

"I will ask you to come each day to my office and help me prepare the boxes of goods that must accompany us," he said. "In the meantime, be ready to leave at any moment."

"I shall be ready," she said.

AND SO MAYLI went to Dr. Chung's office each morning thereafter for eleven mornings and came home late at night. Her life fell into a pattern. She rose early, ready for the day's work. When she had eaten her breakfast, she walked the mile to the house where the hospital supplies were gathered together. However early she arrived, the doctor was there before her, his hands, red with cold, piling goods into bundles and tying them himself if no one else came as early as he. But soon the long room was full of nurses and soldiers and clerks checking lists and nailing up boxes. These boxes began to grow into a great heap at one end of the room. None could be heavier than one man could carry on his back.

On the very first day Chung had assigned to Mayli the task of overseeing the goods that the nurses must use and he had thrust into her hands a sheaf of lists.

"Check them yourself, please," he said in English. "If there is anything missing, supply it." He always spoke to her in English, for he had spent more years abroad than he had in his own home, and French and German were as quick on his tongue as English. Yet his short, squat figure was common looking enough. Only his hands were the fine hands of a surgeon. The time was to come, however, when she would see them explore the tendrils of a man's life so often that she would run to save those hands whenever he touched a coarse or heavy thing, lest their lifesaving delicacy be harmed.

Slowly the mass of goods, the crowd of men and women, grew into order and readiness. She came to know her nurses one by one. There were several score of them, and some were dull and slow. But all were going because they were glad to go, and felt that what they did was a necessary thing. Three she soon knew because they were always near, ready to take her commands. One of these was Han Siu-chen, a student whose family had been killed in the sack of Nanking, which she had escaped by being away at school.

The second girl was a thin, pale, small one from Tientsin, a city girl accustomed to wealth, whose parents had fled before the enemy. Her mother had died from hardship, and her two brothers had been killed in battle. Her father besought her to avenge herself for her brothers. When he found that she was unwilling because he would have no one to care for him, he took a peaceful poison. She found him dead and knew that now his command upon her could not be denied. This girl's name was Tao An-lan.

The last girl was no girl at all but a young widow who had suffered from the enemy in ways she would not tell. She had been a soldier in the army in the northwest, and had been captured and had escaped. Her name was Mao Chi-ling.

Besides these three, there were many others who began to look to Mayli as their leader, and this made a change in Mayli. She, who all her life had thought of no one except herself, now found that she must think and plan for these young women. She worked all day and in the night she woke fearing that she had forgotten something. The country through which they would march was full of sickness and ill fortune. So she searched out those who had been there—truck drivers, coolies, soldiers and traveling merchants.

"What is the climate there?" she asked.

"So hot that hot tea is cool," one said.

"So rainy that the clothes mildew and fall from your back," said another.

"The insects consider you a gift from Heaven."

"The snakes rise up in the middle of the path before you and greet you as their daily rice bowl."

"The poisonous vines reach out their arms."

"The sun peels off your scalp, hair and all."

"The rivers lie smooth and small until you come, and then they rise into seas and swallow you. The river gods there are very strong and evil, and they have all been bribed by the enemy," one old man said. He had fallen into a river somewhere and his leg had been bitten to a stump by a crocodile.

Medicines Chung would take, but she bought extra leather shoes for her women. She rolled wide strips of heavy cloth to wrap around their legs to protect them from insects, and she found yards of coarse linen and tore them into veils, to keep away the flies and mosquitoes. She packed small boxes of dried bean curd, salted meat and rock sugar for each woman. And she made sure that all the packs were light, for there was talk of foreign soldiers who had carried so much that they could not march quickly enough to catch the enemy.

Meanwhile the general was swearing impatiently that there must be some trick to delay their going, for why did they not go, seeing that the enemy was growing stronger every day? Then suddenly one day the order came down, and within an hour all knew that the next morning at dawn the great march would begin.

That night in her little house Mayli could not sleep. Several times she got out of bed and examined her garments. Everything lay ready for her upon a chair: heavy shoes, a uniform that was like a soldier's, a pistol, her pack. She had opened the pack and was counting everything in it when the door opened and the old woman came stealing in. She had a bag in her hand, not much bigger than her own palm, and she gave it to Mayli.

"What if a button tears off?" she whispered solemnly. "A small thing may cause great trouble."

Mayli took the bag and inside she found short Chinese needles, yards of fine strong silk thread, a pair of very sharp small steel scissors, two brass thimbles, some foreign bone buttons and six foreign closing pins. Who could tell where the old woman had found these luxuries?

"I had not thought of this," Mayli said. "But indeed it is what I might need very much."

"Why should you think of a small thing when I do all your sewing?" the old woman said. "But now who knows whether you will ever need me again?" Then she burst into loud tears.

"I shall be back," Mayli promised her.

"Only Heaven can fulfill promises," the old woman said, and went away wiping her eyes on the corner of her jacket.

THE MARCH began the next day at dawn in confusion and shouting. Mayli, in her stiff cloth uniform, her pack strapped to her shoulders, stood ready at the head of her young women. They were dressed alike, and in its gravity each young face looked strangely like the next.

"Watchers of the wounded—this way!" a little lieutenant shouted and waved a sheet of paper at them, and they began to climb into their trucks. Mayli took her place beside the driver, a big common-faced fellow. A moment, a scream or two, some excited laughter, and they were ready to start.

Mayli's truck was the first of the four that carried them, but when the driver pushed a certain handle, it would not start. He stamped both feet and pushed another handle, and still it would not start. At that he cried out to Heaven and beat the sides of his head with his palms. "You!" he roared. "Have I not stuffed you full of foreign oils and burned incense for you to the gods? Now what more will you have?" But still it did not move.

Then Mayli, who had often ridden in foreign cars abroad, pointed to a small handle. "Let that fly back," she told the man.

He grinned at her and pulled it back, and the truck moved forward at once. The man drove the vehicle like a wild animal, and Mayli was thrown from side to side and up and down. All she could do was cling to her seat and brace her feet against the floor.

"Can you—can you—not go a little slower?" she gasped.

But he shook his head to this. "This accursed son of a foreign mother," he shouted. "If I let him go slower than this, he thinks it is time to rest. I must keep him going until I myself am too hungry and must stop for food."

Mayli shook her head, for by now what breath she had was not for talking.

How welcome was noon of that day! "I feel I have already marched a hundred miles," she said to Siu-chen.

"This afternoon I will change places with you," Siu-chen said, "for I saw how your driver paid no heed to any clod in the road. Now the man in our truck is a student and very clever at escaping the ruts and clods." But the truth was that Siu-chen, being a hearty young woman, liked the heartiness of the soldier who drove Mayli's truck. This Mayli divined and let pass with a smile.

So when they had eaten their noon meal, Siu-chen climbed in beside the big-faced driver and Mayli found herself beside a pale, thin young man who nodded to her without smiling. This was a very different fellow. He handled his vehicle with care and it moved along as smoothly as a cat. Mayli said, "You drive this truck as though you knew it."

"I do," the young man said. "I am an engineer. I have a degree from an American college."

"Then why are you doing this?" she asked in English.

In English he answered her: "I couldn't go on. I had to come home and get into it. Well, I went to Chungking and waited and waited. Months. Nothing happened. This chance came and I took it."

He was silent for a long time. Then, without moving his eyes from the road, he began suddenly to talk to her. "Ours is the most beautiful country in the world. Look at those mountains! They are the most beautiful in the world. I was sick to get back home."

Indeed all around them was very beautiful. The hills, bare of trees but covered with ruddy winter grass, were purple in the evening, a rich purple against a gilded sky. Farmhouses clustered in villages in the valleys, and the hills were terraced into fields. Blue-clad farming folk stood at their doors to watch the trucks go by, and little children ran to the roadsides to wave at them. Now and then a temple roof lifted its high pure curve.

"This is what I came back for," he told her, still in English. "I came back for this land and these people."

They rode another half hour in silence, and he drew up

smoothly outside the gates of a small town. "Here is where we camp tonight," he said and leaped out.

Tomorrow I must ask him his name, she thought, and she wondered that she had not asked it today. But names seemed meaningless. They were all moving forward together, and the name of anyone was nothing.

SHE SLEPT THAT night in the back courtyard of a temple. The men were in the front, and the back room was so small that half of the women slept outside on the ground, and she had chosen to be among these.

For an instant when she woke in the morning she could not find herself. Upon the gray morning air, very chill and damp, she heard the thin, struggling crow of a young cockerel. Then she saw lights already lit in the temple, and lying a moment longer, she heard the deep, droning chant of the priests at morning prayer.

At her side Chi-ling lifted her head. "Are you awake?"

"I am awake," Mayli replied. She put back her blanket and sat up. All about her heads lifted. They had been waiting, and when they saw her awake, the young women rose and silently folded their blankets and packed their knapsacks.

Mayli went to the temple kitchen. There she found an old priest feeding grass into a great earthen stove. On it was a caldron of very hot water.

"Dip in, lady," the old priest said, not looking at her because she was a woman. "That is water for washing."

She filled a tin basin and took it to the courtyard where she washed herself and combed her hair. She had kept her hair long but at this moment she thought, What will I do with this hair? What can it be but a care to me? She thought of Sheng and how he had liked her hair long, but only for a moment. Then she went to where she had slept and opened her pack and took out the little scissors that her old woman had put into her sewing bag. Holding her hair in her left hand, she cut it off at her neck with the scissors. Then she went with the long hair

in her hand into the kitchen where the old priest was crouched at the stove, and before his astonished eyes she thrust her hair into the fire like grass.

Out in the courtyard again she shook her head, and the wind was cool in her short hair. She felt light and free, and from that day on, she held her head higher than before.

The young engineer was in the truck when Mayli was ready to leave. He was very neat and clean, his hair smooth. He looked at her with the smallest of smiles as she took her place beside him and said, "My name is Li Kuo-fan. Called Charlie by the Americans."

"Charlie?" she repeated. "It suits you better than Li Kuo-fan. Let it be Charlie. And I am Mayli, surnamed Wei."

He nodded and started the truck.

She could see the excitement in his eyes. "I've looked for this day," he said. "I have wanted to travel the Big Road since it was made. This is my first chance."

They had come by small roads so far to escape the enemy's bombing. But as they had neared the border, the order had come down to move south on the Big Road. Who had not heard of this road? They all knew that it had been made by men and women whose tools were the spades and hoes with which they had tilled the fields. Those who had no tools had used their hands. The road now rose very rapidly, clinging to the sides of the steepening hills like a trail.

"See how it follows the footholds on the hills," Charlie said proudly. "It was made by men who had walked these hills so long that they knew where each foot could cling. Foreign engineers were asked how long it would take to make this road with their tools. They said, 'Years.' But the One Above said, 'It must be months. We will use our own tools.' So it was months."

In the middle of the morning they passed a great hole in the road from an enemy bomb, and there they saw such men and women as had built the road. They were now mending the hole, and when Mayli's vehicle stopped, she stepped down and went over to a woman who sat flat on the earth, pounding rocks to pieces with a harder, larger rock. The woman was young, but the rock dust had made her face and hair gray. Near her in an old basket a little child slept under a torn quilt. The woman looked up shyly. Mayli spoke to her politely. "Have you eaten?" she asked.

Now this was the salutation of the north, and the woman answered it as a question. A wide bright smile came over her dusty face. "I have worked all night," she said. "And I eat while I work."

"And the child?" Mayli asked, astonished.

"He sleeps here well enough," the woman said, laughing.

"But your family?" Mayli asked.

"There is my man and me and the older two, and we all work here on the Big Road," the woman said with pride. "We live not far from here, and when they call for the road to be mended, we lock the door and all come together. Let the enemy blow their holes—we can mend them." She laughed and her white teeth shone out of her gray and dusty face, and she began pounding. Men and women, they worked with the unhasting speed they were used to, and in less than an hour more there was a bridge of earth and rock across the hole.

The road soon soared so high that traveling on it was more like flying than riding. Once when the road marched along the top of a high ridge, Mayli looked back. She saw An-lan, her pale face set in terror. She called to her, "An-lan, can you go on?" The girl could only nod her head.

"All right?" Charlie asked.

"An-lan is green with fear," Mayli said. "But this is no place to stop."

It was indeed a dangerous spot. At the foot of the precipices on both sides of the road they saw the wrecks of trucks and cars. The wrecks were surrounded by men who were taking them to pieces and packing the metal into bundles that they could carry.

They stopped for their noonday meal in one town where this

metal was particularly precious. This town had for hundreds of years been famous for the making of scissors and Mayli and her women were very curious to see them. Mayli could not resist a small shining pair with butterflies on it.

"How sharp they are," she said to the old man who sold the scissors to her.

"It is the foreign steel," he said. "The steel is from the trucks that slide over the side of the Big Road. These trucks are made in the Mei country. The steel there is mixed with many metals and it is very hard—harder than any iron we can make."

"I have been in the Mei country—America, they call it," she said, smiling. "And I have seen the great steel furnaces in Pittsburgh where the metal is mixed."

He listened with wide eyes and then he shook his head gravely. "Those foreigners," he said, "they know everything, and they can fly their airplanes as though each man had made his own. I see them sometimes fly over our heads. How the enemy shrieks and flees when they come! Who are these men who drive such monster machines? I thought, once, that such men must be ten feet tall and winged like eagles. But no, I see them sometimes, for there is an airfield not far from here. They are only young men full of temper and noise like any other young men." He laughed quietly. "Children," he said gently. "Children—playing with magic!"

He looked so wise that she felt humble before this old man who had done nothing but make scissors all his life, and she took her purchase and went away.

The next afternoon they were winding along a very hazardous part of the road when seventeen enemy planes suddenly appeared out of the sky. The planes rushed out like dragons and the valleys roared and crackled with their noise. Mayli gripped the side of her seat and braced her feet against the floor.

Then as swiftly as the enemy had appeared, four other planes came and attacked the enemy, weaving in and out so fast that the eye could not follow them. The enemy turned against the four planes, but who could catch those skillful creatures of the sky? Six enemy planes crashed into the valleys.

Charlie had stopped his truck, as had the whole long line of vehicles. "The Flying Tigers," Charlie said.

It was over in less than ten minutes, but when the skies were clear again, Mayli's body still ached from tension. She felt her hand and saw she had pressed the metal side of the seat so hard that she had cut into her flesh. But before she could speak, she heard a sudden roar of wings, and there, at her side over the emptiness that fell away to the plains below, was a plane very near her, and out of it leaned a laughing American face. She saw him wave before flying away over the mountains. Then she remembered what the old man had said yesterday when he sold her his scissors. Children—playing with magic!

THEIR EYES were filled now with the beauty and grandeur of the mountains. When night fell, they camped in majestic sleeping places, in little towns high above the crags, or in temples built in cuplike hollows on the mountaintops. Then slowly, as the days passed, the mountains sank to hills and the chill, dry air softened. Bamboos appeared, and lilies and ferns, and now they were coming down the mountain walls into the lowlands that led to Burma.

And yet nothing was so strange as the thing that happened toward the end of their journey on the Big Road. A certain town, scarcely more than a village, lay waiting for them at the end of the day. Mayli had settled her young women in and had a little time for herself. Being eager to see new things, she went to the gate of the temple that they had hired for a stopping place. There she saw a handful of young women who were not hers come by. Among them was one she did know, and who was it but Sheng's younger sister, Pansiao, who had been for many months in the school in the mountains where Mayli had taught for a while.

She stared at the girl and thought, It cannot be Pansiao, for how could she be here?

The young women were all in uniforms and they were laughing and talking. As they came near, Mayli said in a low voice but very clearly, "Pansiao!"

The girl stopped, turned and stared at her with rounding eyes. It was indeed Pansiao.

"Oh," she cried. "You!" She sprang out and seized Mayli's hand in hers and stared at her and laughed. "Oh, how I've missed you," she cried. "This is my friend," she said joyfully to the other girls, who were standing fixed with astonishment.

"Come inside, all of you," Mayli said.

So they came inside and sat down on the marble steps in front of the temple, and there Pansiao told how she had run away from the school in the mountains. She looked so naive, so fresh, with her red cheeks and her soft brown eyes, so much a child, though thin and hard-fleshed with walking, that Mayli could not but smile. It was Pansiao who had first told her about Sheng, and had, childlike, wanted her to be his wife.

"Do you know your brother is somewhere on the way to Burma?" she now asked Pansiao.

"You mean my third brother?" Pansiao said, then leaned close. "You are not—are you?"

"I am not married," Mayli said.

"Nor is he, yet?" Pansiao asked gently.

"No, he is not," Mayli said, feeling her face very hot under the young girl's clear gaze. "Where do you go now?" she asked Pansiao, changing the subject.

"I don't know," the girl replied.

"Would you like to join us?" she asked.

"Oh, I would like to go with you," Pansiao cried.

"Then I will see what I can do," Mayli replied. "Come tomorrow morning with your things," she said. "Tonight I shall talk to those who are above me and ask them to let you come with us."

Pansiao jumped up. "I will go and pack now," she said.

Then, dropping to her knees before Mayli, she pleaded, "Let me come back tonight!"

"Very well, tonight," Mayli said. "It will be best, for we start the day at dawn."

V

SHENG HAD BEEN waiting, his men gathered grimly about him, on the border of Burma. They had walked a thousand miles and more, a steady march of thirty miles a day, each man carrying his rifle and bayonet, a bamboo rain hat, a helmet, three days' food, a second pair of shoes, a water bottle, a spade, twenty bullets and two hand grenades. Carriers marched beside them, each with eighty pounds of rice. Sheng and his men were the vanguard of the long, steady stream of strength coming out of China. They had reached the border of Burma on the exact day that Sheng's general had set. The men were mud-stained and weary, but not one rifle had been lost. For these rifles were new weapons that the One Above had ordered to be given them, and each man felt his rifle a personal gift. If his own head lay in mud while he slept, at least his rifle was laid high and safe.

Sheng's men had often asked him, "What is our plan when we reach the border?" and always he answered, "The foreign commander under whom we are to serve will tell us when we reach the border. The man of Mei will send word what we are to do."

For so great had been the faith of the One Above in his foreign allies that he had given over these, his best veteran troops, to the leadership of an American.

"Why has the One Above put us under a foreign leader?" Sheng had asked his general.

"There are things not to be understood in this war," the general had replied. "Put it this way—the men of Ying will deal more easily with him than with us." His lips had curved with bitter meaning.

"This white man," Sheng had asked after a moment, "is he a good heart?"

"I have seen him twice and I have talked with him," the general had replied, "and it seems to me his heart is good. He is tall and thin, not young, and his temper is reasonable. Nor does he hold himself above his men or above us."

"And how shall we understand the American when he speaks?" Sheng had asked.

"He speaks our language," the general had replied. "It is my belief that we can follow him and trust him. But he is not the highest in command," he had warned. "The men of Ying have put another over him. He is in command of us, but they are in command of him."

Sheng was now exceedingly anxious to know how the war was in Burma. Where was the enemy? Had the white men held the port city of Rangoon?

But there was no news. On the Burma border all was as peaceful as though there were no war anywhere in the country. He led his men into the suburbs of a small town. It was a mixed place, made up of Chinese and Burmese and tribesmen. The Burmese were of darker skin than the Chinese and their ways were full of childlike gaiety and merriment. Chinese and Burmese lived together here well enough, but the people of China were shrewder and better at trade than the Burmese and this often made the Burmese angry.

Sheng saw this the very first evening when he sauntered out upon the streets of this strange town and stopped at an outdoor inn to ask the price of a sweetmeat. The innkeeper, a Burmese, scowled at Sheng and muttered the price so low that Sheng could not hear. Sheng asked him outright, "Do you want to sell me your wares or not?"

The Burmese said, "How do I know you have the money? I have been cheated before by a Chinese."

At this Sheng grew angry and he threw down his coin on the counter.

Then the Burmese was good-tempered again, and as he

wrapped the sweet in a twist of newspaper, he said, "Do not be angry with me. When a man is twice bitten by a dog, he is a fool if he does not expect it the third time."

"How a dog," Sheng inquired, "and how a bite?"

The Burmese shrugged. "The farther you go into the land, the more you will see what I mean. Between the Chinese and the English, we Burmese are pinched as a louse is pinched between the thumb and forefinger of a beggar."

"English?" Sheng asked, not understanding the foreign word.

"You call them the men of Ying," the shopkeeper said. "The English! They govern us for their own good, and the Chinese steal away our business. The truth is we hate you all."

That night Sheng studied the map of Burma the general had given him. He had gone over it often enough before, but tonight he looked at it with new care. For this day had taught him that when they marched deep into Burma, it would not be to the welcome of the people of the land.

For a long time he pondered the map with its small, closely printed names. When he folded it away at last and lay down in the darkness under his blanket, a great weight of fear fell upon him. What would befall them in this unknown country where the jungles were deep and the roads few?

He heard the whine of mosquitoes about his head, and he covered his head with his blanket. He had heard that mosquitoes brought malaria, and though he doubted it, having all his life been bitten by mosquitoes, yet it might be true that these mosquitoes so far from home had poison in them.

He lay sweating under the blanket, sleepless, his mind sifting fragments from his past: himself in his father's house, his brothers, Jade and his mother, his sister-in-law Orchid who had been killed so mercilessly in a bombing, and Mayli, again and again. She was doubtless at this moment in her little house in Kunming, playing with her dog. He remembered her as he had seen her that day at the window of her room, tossing her long black hair in the sunlight. He ached and suffered, and then he put the thought of her out of his mind. He might never see her again, and he had sworn to himself that he would not think of a woman until the victory was won. Soon his longing passed, and he fell asleep.

WITH THE NEXT day word came that the general himself had arrived, and Sheng made haste to report to him in a small room in the inn that had been rented for headquarters. When he saw Sheng, he motioned to him to wait for a moment while he read a letter he held in his hand. Then he folded the letter, put it into his pocket and sighed.

Sheng waited for the general to ask him his business. But the general did not ask. Instead he sat there, his face distraught, and he was silent, as though his mind were full of troubles. Then he took the letter out again. "I cannot understand this," he said to Sheng.

He threw the letter to Sheng, who saw that it was from the American. It was written in Chinese and said the general was to hold all the divisions at the border until further word.

"I cannot understand this," the general repeated. "I came here expecting to find my orders to march tomorrow. Instead I find the command to wait until further word. What word— whose word?"

They looked at each other. "I suppose, if I can guess, the word of those above the American," Sheng said very slowly.

"That," the general said clearly, "is what I also guess."

Sheng went away troubled and doubtful, leaving the general sitting as though he were made of stone.

In the next few days there was scarcely an hour when some of the men did not come to Sheng and ask him when they were to march again. What could Sheng say but the truth, that he did not know? The men went away staring and muttering, for they were free men who had not been taught to be silent beasts before their leaders.

None of this was made better by the news leaking in from the south. The foreigners, the Englishmen, were massed along the Salween River, but the enemy had already crossed that river below them and had taken the town of Martaban.

"It is not that Martaban is important," a peddler of small goods said to Sheng one day. "But the place is a crossing point for the enemy coming from Thailand."

"Why do the English not let us come in?" Sheng asked frankly of this stranger, who was a man of India.

"The English do not want the people of Burma to see you armed with foreign weapons and fighting under your own leaders," he said. His face changed into a mask of hatred. "The English will lose Burma," he hissed. "The people of Burma will turn against them. It is our chance everywhere to rid ourselves of the English."

The general heard such words, too, and one day he called his officers to him. "We can be defeated by our own selves, if we allow it," he told them. It was an evening in February, but the air was hot. On the wall of the room where they had gathered, a lizard licked its delicate quick tongue at mosquitoes. Sheng watched it as he listened to the general. There was a new officer among them, a young man whom Sheng had never seen before.

"I have asked our brother from Kwangsi to come and to bring us some direct news of our foreign allies so that we can wait more patiently," the general said.

Upon this the young officer rose. His voice was low and firm. "We came, my men and I, on foot, dragging what artillery we had. We crossed the border and went to the Englishman in command there. I gave him our greetings, and said what the One Above has said: 'If Burma wishes help from us, we will send thousands of soldiers at once.'"

"What did the Englishman say?" the general inquired.

"He said there were already many Chinese forces in Burma, and he was glad to know that more could come—if necessary."

"Is that all?" the general asked.

"It is all," the young officer replied. "Except that he assigned us to the mountain territory and there we wait."

They had all sat immobile, listening to this young officer, until he had said the word wait. Then the same look passed over their faces. They were all hard young men, seasoned soldiers, and to wait was torture. The lizard fell to the floor and scuttled away. The young officer sat down again and began to speak from his seat, his eyes fixed on his tightly clasped hands on his crossed knees.

"I asked the Englishman why they did not invite us to come in quickly. He said that we would be invited in when all was ready. He said that his brothers were fighting a delaying war in the south in order to gain time for the ground bases and the airfields to be prepared for us, and that the main war would be fought in the central plains."

The general gave a sharp, loud laugh. "We can fight without these mighty preparations," he shouted. "We are used to fighting without any preparations!" He rose and began to pace the room. Then suddenly he stopped and looked at them. "If orders to march do not come within a few days, I shall tell the One Above that I must be relieved of my command here. I protest this waiting." He motioned dismissal with outflung hands and they rose and went away, their faces grave.

The general watched the young officers as they went out of the room, then unlocked a closet in the wall and took out a small radio. It was his most precious possession, for it needed no wires or machinery to link it to the air. He set it on the desk and turned the knobs on its face. Music came out, sweet and wild to his ears, along with voices speaking languages he did not understand. But now and again there came words either in his own language or in the language of the enemy. He understood the enemy's language very well, for as a boy he had lived in Japan for five years

Now, over the evening air, there came an enemy voice, shouting harsh syllables. "Rangoon burns! Today our forces bombed the city without mercy. The British locked thousands of coolies on the docks, fearing they would run away under our bombs. They perished a cruel death, unable to escape, and the British are safe. Our forces are only eighteen miles from Rangoon. Do not flee, people of Rangoon! You are about to be saved.

"Take heart, people of Burma! We are your brothers, men of your race. Asia for the Asiatics!"

He turned the voice off. It was impossible to endure it, lest there be even a fragment of truth in it. He sat heavily by the table, his two hands clenched and motionless. Who could tell? Had the Japanese not been so cruel, had they not invaded, had they used other means than death and destruction, they might have been right. But now, whom could his people trust? There was nothing to do but to fight on, one war at a time. And today Japan was the enemy.

Late that night, when the general could not sleep in his room because anger and concern still burned in him, he heard a commotion in the inn yard. Being still full of impatience, he leaped from his bed and, stopping only to pull on his under-garments, burst out of the door, impetuous with rage at this new noise.

"Mother of my mother of my mother—" he bawled, and then he stopped short.

The inn yard was full of women, and they stared at him, astonished. Nearest was Mayli, who saluted him and said, "We have only just arrived, sir. Where are we to be billeted?"

Then he came to himself and in one leap and two steps was in his room again, pulling on his uniform and buckling his belt around him. A moment more and he opened the door. Looking very stern, and as though he had seen none of them before, he shouted, "Have you come? Where is your superior?"

"The doctor lost himself, I think," Mayli said gently. "We were following him until about fifteen miles back, and then we could not find him and came on alone."

"Ha!" the general shouted and his aide came to his side. "Take these women to the Confucian temple that was set aside for them," he said.

The general stood very straight, waiting, while the girls fell in behind Mayli. Then he went back into his room and it came to him how he had looked bouncing into the inn yard. Suddenly he began to laugh and he sat down and laughed a long while. When at last he went to bed again, he felt eased and ready to sleep, until something came into his mind. Here were Sheng and Mayli, and Mayli had told the general that Sheng was not to know where she was. Should he tell Sheng that she had come? He pondered this for a moment and weighed the pleasure of surprising Sheng so joyfully and of teasing Mayli. Then he thought, No, this is war, and it is better that they do not meet, lest they forget their duty and think of love.

This he decided, and after yawning loudly two or three times, he fell asleep.

IN THAT PART of the town where the women were quartered Mayli was busy. She who had never had to work hard in her life was now finding it a pleasure. If there was a filthy room to clean before they could use it, she commanded her women, "Fall to, every one of you, and clean away this filth!" But even as she commanded it, she led the way, and from morning until night she did not take off the cotton uniform she wore. And always close beside her was Pansiao, who was happy and complained of nothing if she could be near Mayli.

Pansiao was one of those who would never be anything but a child. She had almost forgotten her old home and her family, so Mayli took care to speak of Ling Tan and Ling Sao and the others. Pansiao's round, pretty face lit itself with smiles whenever Mayli spoke of them, but soon the smiles gave way to a strange listening gravity.

"Do you remember," Mayli said one day as they stooped together beside a pond to wash their clothes, "how there is a pond near your father's house? They told me it was made by a bomb."

"Was there a pond?" Pansiao asked, puzzling. "Did I see it?"

"Ah well, perhaps you did not," Mayli said quickly. "But do you remember the little pool in the court where there are goldfish?"

Pansiao did not answer. She stopped beating out her coat on the stone and looked quietly at Mayli.

"Do you not remember how cool the court is in summer?" Mayli asked her.

"Of course I remember," Pansiao said slowly. Then a look of pain stole out of her eyes. "I cannot remember their faces," she said in a low voice. "I remember my third brother's face, but my father's face—I try to think how it looks. I know my mother is a strong, thin woman, but I cannot remember her face." The young girl's eyes strained through the distance as she forced her memory.

"Someday you will see them all again," Mayli said gently, "and then it will come to you."

Pansiao laughed with sudden childlike laughter. "Of course it will," she said, and she fell to beating the garment again so that little droplets of water fell everywhere and glistened on her pretty eyebrows and hung on her cheeks like tears. "But I remember my third brother well. We used to ride the buffalo together when we took it to the hills for grass and he used to tell me that one day he would run away from home."

Mayli rinsed her blue coat. "Run away and do what?" she asked.

"I don't think he knew," Pansiao said, laughing.

"It is just as well," Mayli replied, "since all young men now have the same work to do—fight the enemy."

"Yes," Pansiao said gaily, for she had no feeling or knowledge of the war. She busied herself cheerfully with whatever Mayli told her to do, but let the war be mentioned, and blankness came over her face like sleep.

THE DAYS SLIPPED past, one after another, and not once did Sheng and Mayli meet or know that the other was within a mile or two. But each in his own place dreamed of the other, though not with great longing. For war is to the heart like pepper upon the tongue—it dulls everything else. The sour and the sweet alike are lost in the mere sharpness.

But the restlessness of the armies began to filter through even to the women. To while away the days Chung, the doctor, began to see the sick and diseased in the town. He said to Mayli one day, "It chafes me very much to have so little to do, and I see so many children with bad eyes and beggars with ulcers. We have no right to give them the medicines we may need when the battle begins, but we could brew some medicines from herbs and at least wash the sores we see."

"It would be a good thing," Mayli answered.

Thereafter each morning for three or four hours she opened the gate and let in the sick, and Chung treated them.

One night during this time of waiting and working Li Kuo-fan, called Charlie, came to Mayli and said, "Tomorrow I shall be gone, but I shall be back in seventeen days or so."

"What if we march before you come back?" Mayli asked.

"There is no danger," he said grimly. "I think we are stuck here like camels in a snowstorm."

Now these two had kept up a sort of rough friendship ever since the days when Mayli had ridden over the mountains in his truck. "Where are you going?" she demanded of him now.

"The general is angry with waiting, so he sent for fifty of us to go out and see what is to be seen." Then suddenly he said in English, "Keep an eye on that little sister of yours."

"Little sister?" Mayli repeated, wondering. Then she saw his eyes go to Pansiao, who sat on a bench sewing. "So that is why you come here!" she said saucily. "And I thought it was to see me!"

"I would not dare to come and see you," he said impudently. "You are a lady and I am a son of common people."

At this she kicked up the dust from the ground at him with her right foot and took the apron she wore and shook it at him and he went away laughing. But after he was gone, she thought over what he had said. Her eyes fell on Pansiao. "Do you see Charlie Li when he comes here?" Mayli asked her.

"Sometimes I see him," Pansiao said, and blushed deeply.

"Ah ha!" Mayli cried softly.

"He looks a little like my third brother, I think," Pansiao whispered, to excuse what she had said.

Mayli stopped. "No, he does not," she said quickly. "Sheng is much better-looking than Charlie."

"Is he?" Pansiao murmured. "Then I have forgotten him, too." And she sighed. But Mayli only pulled Pansiao's little nose gently and laughed again.

SEVENTEEN DAYS later Charlie Li came creeping back through the border post where an English sentry stood guard. To deceive this man was easy enough. No Englishman, he had discovered in those seventeen days, knew the difference between Chinese, Burmese and Japanese if their clothing was the same. Charlie had disguised himself by darkening his skin and wearing a priest's saffron robe. He was about to pass when the Englishman stopped him, pointed his gun at Charlie's breast and said, "Take your bloody hand out of your chest! What's that you've got there?"

Charlie brought out the alms bowl with which he had begged his way.

"*Thabeit*," he said with a false smile, for that was the name of the begging bowl in Burma.

"Get on, you beggar," the Englishman said, and let him pass.

Charlie went straight to the general's headquarters. It was midnight but he saw a light streaming out of the window and the general bent over a map on the table. Around him were Sheng and Pao Chen and his other young officers.

"Halt!" the soldier at the door cried when Charlie came near.

"Do not halt me," Charlie said. "I have news."

At the noise the general came to the door himself. "What is this noise?" he shouted into the darkness, and then the light fell on Charlie and he told him to come in. A cry of laughter went up from all, for indeed Charlie looked like any traveling young priest of Burma.

"You are the sixteenth to come back out of the fifty," the general said. "Now, let me hear what you have."

"I went to Rangoon," Charlie said, "because there is the heart of the battle."

The general nodded, and his face tightened. "Go on," he said.

"But the white men have left the city with their families," Charlie said. "They are in the hills, safe—waiting for a few weeks until the war is over."

A loud laugh went up from the young men at these words.

"Go on," the general said. "Tell us about the harbor. Is it well defended?"

"It is scarcely defended at all," Charlie said. "Along the docks I saw barbed-wire barricades. I supposed that these were defenses against the landing of the enemy but was told they were against the coolies who carry the cargoes off the ships. The white men feared that when the city was bombed, these ignorant workingmen would flee into the hills and there would be no one left to carry the goods. So they ordered these barricades made, and when the enemy did come over the city, they had the gates locked, so the coolies on the docks could not escape and were killed."

At last the general said, "Go on. Did you see goods piled up for our men on the airfields?"

"Hundreds of tons of goods from America," Charlie said.

The general lit a cigarette and his right hand trembled. "It will never get here," he muttered. "It will all be lost—that precious stuff we have been waiting for all these months! The enemy will take Rangoon first. Of course they will take Rangoon first. It is the heart of Burma."

"It will cease to be in a few days," Charlie said in a low voice. "The white soldiers will not hold. They will retreat!" he cried.

Groans and curses broke from the listening young men. The general put his head between his hands. "Go away," he said, "go away all of you, and leave me to think. Pao Chen, come tomorrow to write down a message to the One Above. I will beseech him once more."

The young men rose and saluted and went away, but the

general called Charlie back. "I shall not forget you," he said with meaning.

"Then send me out again," Charlie said, and he saluted, his priestly robes fluttering.

The general laughed. "Get on your soldier's uniform," he said. "You deceive no one who knows the difference between a priest and a soldier!"

THE GENERAL SAID to Pao Chen the next day, "Write something that will move the heart of the One Above and make him see what he asks us to do. Tell him I will fight where he tells me to fight, but in the name of all our people, tell him to give me freedom to fight our own war and not go into battle tied to an ally who gives up before we can get there. Put your strength into words, Chen, and let them eat their way through the paper. Ask him where the American is. Tell him we sit here on our tails like treed monkeys, waiting while the enemy takes what he will. Tell him—"

Pao Chen's pen was rushing across the paper, and the sweat was pouring down his face.

"Make it as black as you can and you cannot make it black enough," the general said passionately.

"I make it black," Pao Chen muttered, and for a while, the only sound was his pen, scratching out the bold characters. "Shall I read it?" he asked when he was through.

"Read it," the general replied.

But at that moment the door opened and a seventeenth spy came running in, his garments torn and his feet bleeding. "Rangoon!" he gasped. "Rangoon has fallen!"

The general leaped to his feet. "Put that in the letter!" he shouted. "Rangoon has fallen and we are not yet allowed to cross the border!"

When Pao Chen had set these words down, the general snatched the letter and shouted for his aide.

"Let me!" Pao Chen cried. "Let me take it to the One Above! I will carry the letter for you and I will speak for you."

The general paused, his brows working above his angry eyes. "Well enough," he said shortly. "Take the small plane. I will wait long enough for you to come back but no longer. We march, one way or the other."

VI

THE ONE ABOVE put down the letter that Pao Chen had written for the general. He had read it carefully and without haste, and his lady had stood behind him, reading as he read. He lifted his head and the two exchanged a long look. Then he said to Pao Chen, who stood waiting, "Do not think I am ignorant of what you have told me. I know and I have known, but this war is a war in which we are only one among others."

At this the lady said impetuously, "We fought it alone for the others all these years. Are we to go on fighting it alone?"

He silenced her with a look. "I know what I do," he said.

She rose at that, her eyes very bright, and with a proud grace she left the room. When she was gone, the One Above turned to Pao Chen. "Go back to your post," he said. "I will come and see for myself."

Thus it was that in a very few days the whole waiting encampment of the armies was thrown into turmoil. With what care each made the best of what he had, every soldier furbishing up his uniform and polishing his gun, and the women gossiping among themselves about the lady and asking Mayli if she was as lovely as everyone said she was.

At noon on the appointed day a plane descended bearing the Ones Above, and with them the American.

By midafternoon all were ready for inspection, and Mayli stood very straight before her lines of young women. They all saluted as the One Above and his lady came by with the American and the general. The lady stopped and said in her easy way, "You all look beautiful, and you will never be more beautiful than you are now, ready to serve your country." And to Mayli she said, "Are you happy?"

"Yes, lady," Mayli replied, not moving.

Then the lady added in a low voice, "You may come to me in half an hour."

When Mayli went to headquarters, the lady kept her there for nearly an hour with piercing questions. "I told you to be my eyes and ears, so tell me now all that you have seen and heard."

She listened while Mayli talked, and every now and again she thrust in a barbed question. When the hour was nearly spent, she put her hands before her eyes and sighed deeply. "Go back to your women," she said to Mayli. "You have been faithful eyes and faithful ears, but you have told me heavy news, heavier than you meant to tell."

After the Ones Above had departed and Mayli had dismissed her women, the courtyards were full of admiration for the two who were more than leaders to these simple girls. They saw in them all the dream of love between man and woman that they themselves might never have. Even Mayli thought about Sheng that night. Had the One Above been uncouth when he was young like Sheng? He, too, had been the son of plain people, not much schooled, accustomed to hardship and work. She sighed and wondered where Sheng was now. She rose from her bed and went to the window and stood looking out into the starry sky above the roofs, and suddenly, without thinking, she felt him very near.

Not too far away Sheng lay flat on his back on a pallet in the barracks, one in a long row of men. Behind the lids of his eyes he was seeing her face. He had stood at the head of his own men while the Ones Above had passed, and the lady had given him a look that had made him think of Mayli.

He might never see her again. For after the inspection was over, the One Above had called all the commanders to him and said, "Tomorrow you shall lead your men across the border. We will wait no longer."

And then his profound eyes had singled out Sheng. "You, tall fellow," he had said kindly, "you are one of my best men. I have told your general that if there is any task too hard, he is to choose you for it."

At these words Sheng's pride had risen in him like a banner. "And I will do it," he had said.

MAYLI WALKED across the border at the head of her young women. We are on foreign soil, she thought, and a dread rose through her bones and marrow. On this soil who knew what would happen?

It was a morning without clouds, and all were on foot, since the roads of this region of Burma were too twisted and narrow for vehicles. Ahead of them were the carriers, bearing weapons and food. Ahead of those were soldiers. She could see the men in their blue uniforms winding like a huge long beast. She wore the same uniform and so did her women and so did the general, who had nothing to tell he was different from the soldiers save his badge of blue enamel with the white star of China. Behind them were more soldiers, winding as far as the eye could see.

She smiled at her women. They looked fresh and strong, their skins brown, their eyes clear. Not one wore paint on her lips or cheeks, as such things were forgotten nowadays. Mayli had put away her own foreign lipstick and powder and now washed her face with soap and hot water, as they all did. Sometimes at night they rubbed a little mutton fat into their windburned cheeks, but that was all. Yet never had she felt so strong or looked so well.

She lifted her eyes. To the north, the land broke into uneven hills that grew quickly into mountains, but southward the land leveled toward the sea. It was rich country. The rice fields were green even now, and she saw the farmers bent over them. At noon they halted along the road and ate the fried rice that was their ration. The sun was hot and the road dusty, and as they sat, a horde of small children came running across the fields and stood staring at them.

"How pretty they are," Chi-ling sighed. "I had a little boy

once—" She rose and turned away. But no one spoke, for who in those days had not lost one dearly loved?

Then the order came to march again and they all rose and fell into the long swinging step that carried them thirty miles a day. The afternoon wore on and the sun fell before their eyes as they marched toward the Sittang River. All knew that the allies had withdrawn from the enemy and that the Chinese armies were to meet them and engage the enemy.

Engage the enemy! These words were said as easily as if they meant going to a rendezvous, a party, but Mayli dreaded the certain hour ahead.

That night, their first upon alien soil, a deep uneasiness swept over them all, the men and the women. They encamped at sunset in a shallow valley between low hills. Above them the sky was pearl and pink for an hour, and then the color changed to purple. Mayli and her women were gathered together, their blankets spread, but none was ready to sleep.

Why are we restless? Mayli wondered to herself. Then suddenly she heard her own name murmured, and standing outside their circle was Pao Chen. Mayli rose and went toward him.

"The general sends me to you," he said. "He says, Can you and your women come out and amuse the men—sing, perhaps? Or talk to us? Or make a little play? The men are disturbed. They say the air here is full of strange spirits."

"Yes, we can," she said quickly. "We will think of something. Give us half an hour."

He nodded and left and she went into the midst of the circle of women and clapped her hands for them to listen to her. Then she said, "Who can do any small clever thing for the men? Let none be shy! This is for our country. The men must be eased of their weariness and made to laugh and so to sleep."

Then, as though they longed for laughter, too, such a giggling and chatter rose that Mayli had to smile—these women, how young they were! Were there no war, most of them would have been in schools and homes. Now here they were, part of an army, going out to engage the fiercest enemy their country had ever known!

One by one the women came forward.

"I know some foreign songs," Siu-chen said.

"And I have a sword dance," Chi-ling said.

"I know a juggler's trick my brother taught me once," An-lan said.

"I will tell a story," Pansiao said.

And so some twenty came forward, each with a thing she could do, and these followed Mayli to the camp of the men where they found a circle ready for them.

There in the brilliant light of the moon Pao Chen said, "Brothers, tonight we are far from home. We carry the battle into the land of other peoples. And because this is foreign to us, we feel restless and not sure what we do is right. Now, so that our hearts can be free, our sisters will sing to us, play before us and speak to us for an hour or two. What their names are does not matter. That they are our sisters is enough."

So saying, he bowed and stood aside, and Mayli came forward and in simple short words told what they would do.

When she began to speak, Sheng was sitting far toward the back. He gave a great start and stood up on his feet. Could two voices be so alike as this girl's and Mayli's, he asked himself? He stood listening, not catching every word she said because he was too far away. He could not see her face, and she wore the uniform they all did.

He sat down again. Of course it was not she. How could it be when he had left her many hundreds of miles away in a little house in Kunming?

The girl stopped speaking and began to sing a foreign song, her voice high and sweet. Sheng knew that Charlie, who sat near him, understood all foreign things. He leaned toward him and asked, "What is she singing?"

"Some song she learned in school," Charlie said. He translated it: "Drink to me only with thine eyes."

"Drink to me only with thine eyes," Sheng repeated. "What does that mean?"

"It means," Charlie said, "that when a woman's eyes look into yours, you need no wine."

Sheng did not speak again. He listened to the strange words and the clear, high voice. It is true, he thought, remembering Mayli's eyes. He rose when the girl stopped singing and went beyond the outermost edge of the circle. Under a little tree he took the blanket he had with him, rolled himself up in it and lay down to stolidly endure his inner loneliness.

HE WAS AWAKENED by someone stumbling over his body and he sat up with a roar, then staggered to his feet.

He glared at the man, who shouted, "You—an officer— asleep when the command has come down to march instantly! Our allies are in a trap. Where are your men?"

Sheng's jaw went slack. How long had he slept? Surely not more than an hour. The sky was glittering with stars, and he could still hear the echoes of music in his ears. I am an ox, he thought in shame. How did I fall asleep? He charged his way through a running crowd of men and in a few minutes he had reached the general's headquarters. There he found the other commanders gathered and waiting.

"You, Pao Chen," the general was saying, "are to form your men into the middle ranks." He looked up and his darting eyes caught sight of Sheng, and a flicker of laughter shone in them for a moment. "You look as though you were asleep in a briar bush," he said.

Sheng put his hands to his head and felt dried bamboo leaves in his hair. He combed them out hastily, his face scarlet. "I am a water buffalo," he muttered. "Let there be quiet around me and I fall asleep like a beast."

"There will be no quiet for the next days," the general said grimly. "The white men are trapped, with the enemy attacking on all sides. Unless we can reach them in time they will die like beasts. You are to be the vanguard, Sheng. You must

leave within this hour. You are to head south and then bear
west. You will cross the next river as soon as you can, for the
bridges farther down may not still hold."

Sheng saluted, turned and walked quickly from the room.
Outside he broke into a run and nearly overturned the doctor,
who was hurrying toward the general.

"Is the general there?" Chung shouted as Sheng ran past.

"Where else?" Sheng bellowed back over his shoulder. In
the darkness a woman stepped along behind the doctor, but
Sheng did not turn to look at her.

The woman was Mayli, and at the sound of Sheng's voice
she stopped and stared after the young man's hurrying figure.
But Chung turned and called back to her, "Don't delay! We
cannot start until we have our orders."

She pulled back her wondering mind. "I do not delay," she
said firmly and entered the general's room.

VII

THE MARCH was not to be made in one day or even two or
three. The terrain was their enemy, and the few roads were
rough and rutted with the wheels of rude farm carts. Sometimes there were only paths through the jungles, so they had
to walk singly. In the skies were enemy planes. "We are safer
in the jungle with the snakes," Sheng told his men.

They put on their green coats and wound branches of trees
about their heads so that from above they would be less easily
seen. Mayli bade her women wind branches about their hair.
They were very pretty, she thought, watching them, and so
young that they even made a game of this trick against death.

By now the whole countryside knew that the white men
were encircled and a sort of glee was upon every face. It was
an evil merriment, and Sheng took it as an enemy thing, for it
was against them, too, because they went to the aid of the
white men. The people in these parts of Burma also hated
the people of India who had come into Burma because they

thought these Indians had taken work and rice from them. Sheng found this hatred everywhere, and three or four times he had to save an Indian or a family of them.

One Indian left his comrades out of gratitude and followed Sheng for a whole day. But at the end of the day Sheng felt his devotion a burden and he called one of his soldiers to take him to live among the men. "I am not easy with his eyes always on me whenever I move," Sheng said.

Now the general had appointed Charlie Li to go with Sheng. Each day, disguised in his beggar's garb, Charlie went out, and each night he came back to Sheng and told him what he had found. "I hear everywhere that if it were not for us, the war would be won by now and the white men gone," he told Sheng sadly.

Sheng sat apart from his men to talk with Charlie. "If I had not seen what the enemy did in the city near my father's house," he said, "then I might have said that these people do well to say we have betrayed our own. But I saw and I will never forget. No, it is not to save the white men that I sit here tonight." Sheng rose and, looking out over the dark alien land, sniffed the night wind. "Even the winds smell evil here. There is a rotten smell to them," he said.

"It is the jungles," Charlie said. "The jungles are rotting."

THEY WENT in silence the last day of the march. By now the general knew to the third of a mile where the white men were. He was in touch by messenger with the American, but he did not rely on what he heard.

"I must trust to what wisdom I have of my own," he told himself and looked at the watch on his wrist. By dawn tomorrow they should be in sight of the white men—if those men were still alive.

Mayli was sleepless that night. All knew that tomorrow there would be battle. For the first time there would be men bleeding and dying and having to be cared for. Could she do her duty? And then it came to her that perhaps she might be killed, and she wept a little, secretly so her women would not hear her. But Pansiao did hear and put out her hand in the darkness. She touched Mayli's cheek and, finding it wet, was so startled that she burst into her own tears. Mayli had to speak sharply to her, knowing that reasonless weeping like this might sweep over all the women like a panic. "Stop!" she whispered to Pansiao. "Stop or I shall punish you like a child!"

And Pansiao did stop. Then Mayli lay down again, cured of her own sadness. What is there for me, she thought, except the one duty I see clear ahead?

THEY AROSE the next morning long before the dawn broke. They ate their rations cold and began to creep onward. Every foot fell softly and not a voice spoke, even though the air hissed and split with the sound of guns not far away. The general had sent down warnings that the enemy was thick around them. "Remember that here we have no friends among man or beast," he said.

As sunrise came nearer, their spirits lifted somewhat, for they had not been attacked by the enemy so far. If they could join their allies before the enemy found them, there was some hope that together they could stop the eternal retreat.

As for Sheng, he was eager to come upon the white men and see what they had for weapons and machines. He had fought for so long with nothing but his rifle that it seemed to him that if the white men had even a few tanks and planes, the tide could surely be turned.

He paused at the place where the general had told him to wait. They could clearly hear the sounds of battle, but there were no great guns and they wondered at this. Had the white men no great guns? Then Charlie Li came in. He had been scouting the countryside since three a.m., and he had found exactly where the white men were.

"The enemy attacked them in the night," he told Sheng, "but the white men are still fighting."

"Do they have their machines?" Sheng asked eagerly.

"They have some machines," Charlie replied. "But they are hard pressed. They are all gathered together in a shallow valley not above two miles from this spot."

Soon the general came up with his men, and all the commanders gathered while he considered the news. The enemy was advancing on three sides and was blocking all the roads with trees. While the white men struggled to push aside the trees to make way for their machines, the enemy attacked from the skies and the white men died by the score.

This was what the general heard from his spies, and he told himself he must press on, though his every instinct warned him it was a war already lost. But no one could read his inner hopelessness that day at dawn when he stood on a hillock above his soldiers.

"Men," he cried, and his voice rang over their lifted heads, "you have your duty to do. We are here to rescue our allies and to turn defeat into attack. Do not forget that this is the same war we have fought for years upon our own earth. The enemy is the same enemy. We must defeat him and restore the Big Road into our country. Fight, then, for your own!"

A low cry went up from the men, restrained but deep. Immediately they began to move out as a single body and Charlie Li went with the general to point the way. When the dawn broke, the sun seemed to set the air afire.

"They are west of the next hills," Charlie said at last in a low voice. The sound of guns was very near now, cracking the hot air about them, and every heart tightened with hope and dread.

Then the general led the column toward a hill. Not far away he saw two motor cars. The cars stopped in the road and the general lifted his glasses to his eyes and he saw white men looking up at them, their faces stiff with terror. "They are afraid of us," he said to Charlie in surprise.

He handed the glasses to Charlie, and after staring through them, Charlie began to laugh. "They think we are the enemy," he said. "The enemy also wears green uniforms—who but fools would wear another color in this green country?"

"Let them sweat," the general said dryly. "We have the sun on our blue caps. If they cannot tell by our faces, let them tell by that."

So he marched on, and true enough, when they came nearer, the faces of the white men changed and what had been terror was now joy. They stood up and waved their arms vigorously and shouted out the Chinese war cry: *"Chung kuo wan shui!"*

The general was moved by these white men shouting the war cry that his men had carried into a hundred battles and he felt his spirit come out of his heart like a bird from a cage. He shouted in a mighty voice, *"Chung kuo wan shui!"* and all his men caught the cry and shouted it, too, until it went up to Heaven itself.

"Where is the enemy?" he commanded Charlie to ask them in their own language.

"There—there!" the white men roared, pointing to the rear. Now they could see that these men were not soldiers, but civilians of some sort. "The enemy is there and our men are still fighting," they shouted.

The general marched on, the column following him. Sheng stared at the faces of these new allies. He had never seen a white man up close before. What faces these were—bearded, haggard, bony, the noses huge, the eyes sunken. White? They were dark with filth and burned red by sun. And far behind Sheng, Mayli trudged with her women. The spring was gone from her step and her hair was wet with sweat. But when she saw the white men and caught their grins, she waved her hand at them and called out in English, "Hello there!"

She knew well enough what power these words would have. Grimed and ragged though they were, the men leaned toward her and shouted joyously, "Hello, hello yourself! God! It's a pretty girl!"

She could not stop, for the general led on, but something young and laughing stirred in her heart. Oh, what good times she had had in America, talking and flirting with such young men! What good times the young could have together whatever their country! But not in times like these.

"Are they not very fierce, those hairy young men?" Pansiao asked.

"No," she said shortly, "they are not fierce at all. They are hungry and tired and have just escaped death." She was hungry and tired herself and she sighed and suddenly wished with all her heart that the war was over.

Where was the glory of battle? When the general surveyed the scattered weary men who were his allies, he knew that when he allied himself to these, he was adding weakness, not strength. Nevertheless he marched through their ranks steadfastly, for he must report himself to the American whom the One Above had put over him.

Soon he saw the lean American coming toward him. The two stopped and each saluted the other. "I greet you," the American said in Chinese. "But I fear you are too late," he added curtly. It was not perfect speech and it was learned from common men. But the meaning was clear.

"It is not my fault if we are late," the general replied coldly. "We were kept waiting on the border for many days."

"Whatever mistakes have been made," the American said, "it is better to remember that we are allies and to work together and not against each other. Are you prepared for attack?"

"We have nothing else in mind," the general retorted.

"Then," the American said, "I advise you to attack as soon as you can. The enemy is entrenched in the city whose pagoda you see over those hills. Under cover of your attack we can reorganize and straighten the lines with the English."

The general saluted sharply, turned on his heel and shouted to his waiting men, "Men! Fall in, to the left—march!"

They turned and marched across a little stream to the bank beyond. And the American stood watching them, sadness upon his exhausted face.

Sheng, marching past, stared at him curiously. So this was

the American! He looked too old for this life. So old a man should be at home among his children. Were there no young men in America? He was very thin, too, his face so thin that his ears looked big. But big ears were a sign of a kindly, wise man, or so Sheng's mother had always said.

The American, catching Sheng's bold young eyes, smiled suddenly and asked, "Have you eaten?"

"How is it that you speak our language?" Sheng asked.

"I have lived in your country for twenty years," the American answered.

"Almost as long as I have," Sheng said with a grin.

Then Sheng went on and the American stood there watching the long line of men. He let them all pass until the very last, which were the carriers of goods and hospital supplies, and then the doctor and the women. These he stopped. "Doctor," he said to Chung, "I would take it kindly if you could stay and tend our wounded before the flies eat the flesh off their bones."

The wounded lay in the bushes. Some were dying and many were dead. Mayli's heart beat in her throat as she commanded her women, "Here is our work. We will lift those wounded into the shade of that one great tree yonder. Then let each of you tend those who seem the weakest. Siu-chen, you gather some fuel and we will build a fire to heat water. Ten of you will care for the wounded and two will help Siu-chen. Pansiao will stay by me."

Chung put on his surgeon's garments and prepared to cut out bullets and sew up gaps in the bodies of those who lay wounded. And now for the first time Mayli found herself quarreling with him, for Chung said, pointing to this one and another, "Let that one die, he is doomed. That one's eyes are glazed. We must save only those who have the chance of life."

"How can you tell who will live and who will not?" she cried.

But he was ruthless and pointed with his finger to signify which ones were to live and which to die. And she felt tears come into her eyes while she worked. She took the time, nevertheless, to hold a cup of water for a dying man to drink and she stopped for the stained letters and pictures they held out to her of those whom they loved—their wives and mothers and children. Even as they drew their last breath they summoned strength to take out sweat-stained, bloody bits of paper and give them to her, gasping their last hopes: "Tell them—tell them—" Mayli saved all the poor bits of paper that had served those men as symbols of what they loved best on earth.

And without knowing it, she began to sob, not aloud, but inwardly, and her hands trembled. She would not weep aloud, for she knew there would be many days like this, but she was new and untried. Her women were far more calm than she, for they had done these same tasks before for men of their own kind. But Mayli had seen young men like these in their own countries, carefree and full of merriment, well beloved in comfortable homes, and they were not strange to her. It was piteous to see them here, outwitted and betrayed, cut off and trapped. Most piteous of all was to see their gratitude when they heard her speak to them in their own tongue.

"I haven't heard—a woman—speak English—in a thousand years," a blond young lad sighed. He closed his blue eyes and clutched her hand. "Couldn't you—sing?" he whispered. "Just—something?"

And she, her throat so tight that she could scarcely breathe, forced herself and sang the song she had been singing a few nights ago:

> *"Drink to me only with thine eyes*
> *And I will pledge with mine."*

She sang it low at first, but the singing eased her throat and in a moment her voice came more clear.

The dying boy smiled. "Why—it's an English—song," he whispered. "How did you—"

His voice ceased and his hand loosened and yet she held it,

tears streaming down her face as she sang, until the song was ended. And then she laid the heavy hand down, such a young hand, and put her head on her knees and wept, not caring who saw or heard her.

At that moment she felt herself lifted up. Two hands pulled her to her feet and she turned. "Sheng!" she whispered.

"It was you, then," he said. "It was you I heard the other night—singing that same song!"

Each took the other's hands, and they stood, their eyes searching each other's face, feeling a comfort that was beyond speech. Gladness there could not be, for they stood in the midst of defeat and death, but courage poured through their hands to their hearts.

In that instant Sheng understood why Mayli had been at the general's headquarters so many weeks ago. He saw her streaming with sweat, her hair hanging wet upon her forehead. She was bone-thin and her blue cotton uniform clung to her thinness. Her feet were bare in straw shoes, and her sleeves were rolled above her elbows.

And she saw a tall, gaunt young man, hard as leather, in a dirty uniform. Down his face the sweat poured like rain. Indeed the sun was merciless upon them both. Near them an Indian began to moan softly for water. They turned at the sound of his voice, and saw that his shoulder was torn away and that he was bleeding to death. Sheng dropped Mayli's hands and went over and put his own bottle of precious water to the dying man's lips and lifted his head so that he might drink more easily.

"Oh, he will die anyway," Mayli cried in a low voice. "Save the water for yourself—"

But Sheng let the man drink until the last was gone. Then he put the man's head down, and as he did, the man died.

"The water is wasted," Mayli said in the same low voice.

"It would have choked me had I refused it to him," Sheng replied. Then he took her hand in his again. "Where have you been?" he asked.

"Here with my women," she said,

"And I have been dreaming of you in that little house with the foolish small dog that you love better than me," he said.

These few words they said to each other in the midst of the men who lay wounded and dying, and each knew that this moment must end. Indeed, the women were stealing curious looks at them already, so they unclasped their hands.

"I will seek you out tonight," Sheng said.

"I shall be watching for you. Take care of your life," she said to him and her eyes pleaded. "Be sure that the night finds you safe."

His hot dark face seemed suddenly to flame. "Do you think I could die now?"

He turned and strode off. She watched the tall thin figure for seconds, until she felt a small hand creep into hers.

"Who is that tall man, sister?" Pansiao whispered at her shoulder. Mayli turned her head and stared down into Pansiao's eyes. Then she began to laugh.

"Why, that is your brother, child—your third brother!" she cried.

"Shall I run after him?" Pansiao asked.

Mayli shook her head. "There is no time now," she said. "We have our work to do. But tonight he will come back, after sunset," she said, "and you must help me to watch for him."

She drew Pansiao to her as she spoke, and together they stooped over an Englishman who was crawling on hands and knees to the shadow of a wrecked truck. "Can I help you?" Mayli asked.

With mighty effort he lifted his head at the sound of her voice and at her English words. Then she saw that the lower part of his face was gone. His frightful eyes stared up at her in agony. She bent and Pansiao helped her and they dragged the man to the shade of the truck and laid him down. Mayli let him clutch her hand. Then when she felt his hold weaken and saw his blazing eyes grow dim and dull, she put his hand down upon the dry earth and left him. There were others whom perhaps she could save.

VIII

WHILE THE WOMEN did their work, the great retreat went on and the enemy did not cease for one moment to harass them from the sky and from the jungles. Living and dying, they had to move and move again. Even as the doctor was operating in a truck under an awning, the order would be cried out that they must move still farther to the rear.

All through that hot day Mayli turned from wounded man to wounded man. New ones were brought continually to die or to struggle on with life. When she grew faint with weariness, she looked at Chung and knew that she must not rest because he did not. She watched her women carefully to see how they bore the day, and they bore it well, or so she thought. Pansiao, whom she had feared for most, bore it best of all. In the midst of the heat and blood and dead, Pansiao came and went, fetching and carrying, her small face always cheerful. Siuchen, the young girl who had been an orphan since the attack on Nanking, was crying as she worked. Mayli did not fear for her so long as she could weep. So long as they could shout or weep, Mayli felt her women safe. Only when they were as silent as An-lan and Chi-ling did she watch them. These two worked side by side without letup, and when at noon a little food was sent around, Chi-ling shook her head and would not eat. "I cannot," she said to Mayli, "even if you command me. I would vomit it up." Mayli let her alone.

So the long day drew on. By midafternoon all knew that the battle was being lost. Defeat was in the smell of the air, in the dust, in the heat. No one spoke the word, but the knowledge swept through them like an evil wind.

The general knew it. He had led his own men out to clear the road for the retreat. But whenever a road was cleared in one place, the enemy blocked it again in another. When the night came, they halted, knowing that the enemy would block the roads they must travel tomorrow.

Late in the day, before the halt was called for the night, Sheng, looking for a camp for his men, felt a sting in his left upper arm. He put his hand to his arm and to his amazement found the head of a nail as neatly in his arm as though a carpenter had hammered it in. He jerked out a three-inch-long nail and held it up between his thumb and forefinger. "See this," he said to his men. "This is what they fell us with now."

"That nail," an aide said, "is not from the enemy, but from one of the men of Burma who has joined the enemy against us."

Dark blood was now dripping slowly out of the nail hole. Sheng tore a strip from the tail of his coat and bound up the wound and went on with his work.

That night they encamped in the middle of the road, whence they could watch whoever came near on all sides. When they were ready for the night and the men had eaten, Sheng bade another officer take his watch and then he went down the road where the wounded were to keep his tryst.

As he came near, his heart leaping in his breast, he saw two figures instead of one waiting for him in the moonlight. He saw Mayli's head lift, listening, but clinging to her hand was a shorter, younger figure. His ardent heart chilled. Why had she brought a stranger to their first meeting? He grew angry and strode forward. She saw his face was surly when he came near. She did not speak but gazed at him and waited.

"Who is this you have brought with you?" he asked shortly.

Then she understood the cause of his anger and she laughed. "Sheng," she said, "you know her."

Pansiao lifted her little face timidly and looked with wonder at this tall harsh-voiced fellow. Was this indeed her third brother? She remembered when he had let her ride the water buffalo to the grasslands with him, and there upon the peaceful sunny hills he had not been surly but kind. And she could remember that sometimes he had sung to her.

"Do you remember the song you used to sing about farmers hoeing in the spring?" she now asked him suddenly, and she sang a snatch of it in a clear trill.

"Why, how do you know that song?" he asked her. "It is a song of my native hills."

"Because I am Pansiao," she said.

He stared down at her and drew in his breath. "What a thing I am," he said, "that I do not know my own sister!" Now his surly looks were gone and he was all eager and amazed.

"What is the name of my sister-in-law?" he asked.

"Jade," she said quickly.

"And what is the number of my brothers?" he asked.

"Two," she said happily, "Lao Ta and Lao Er. And our house is built around a court with a small pond in the middle and there are goldfish in it, and my elder brother's little boys run to and fro and—and—" She put her hand to her mouth. "Oh, poor Orchid," she whispered, "I have not remembered you for so long and you are dead!"

"Orchid's two boys are also dead," Sheng said shortly.

Pansiao gave a wail of sorrow. "Oh, but they were so pretty!"

There in that strange and lonely place, in a short hour of peace in the middle of the night, with the moans of the wounded in their ears, the brother and sister drew near to each other in longing for their home.

"Let us find somewhere to sit down," Mayli said gently.

There was a broken truck near them, turned on its side and blasted partly away by an enemy shell. Upon this they sat, Pansiao between Mayli and Sheng, and the memory of that farmhouse so many miles away crept into them.

IT SO HAPPENED that at that very moment Ling Sao was thinking of her third son as she lay sleepless upon her bed. She was uneasy because of a new evil that had befallen the house that day. Ling Tan could not sleep either and he lay at her side, still but wakeful. On this day he had heard from his two elder sons that the war was lost in Burma. The evil news had come many miles by secret voices in the air.

"What are the devils doing now?" Ling Tan had asked his sons, who had come back gloomy from the city.

"It is not the devils this time but the white men in Burma," Lao Ta told him, and he sat down on a bench at the door and lighted his little bamboo pipe.

Now Lao Ta had grown sleeker since he had remarried and fatter than he had ever been in his life because his new wife made him secret dainties. She always praised him and coaxed him with her praise. Indeed this woman could coax so sweetly and with so much love that it was a pleasure to yield to her. Therefore Lao Ta was cheerful enough these days, so gloom showed on him when he felt it. And all shared his gloom when he told them what he and his brother had heard that day. They sat late in the evening talking of it.

"Those white men," Ling Tan said again and yet again, "I never dreamed that those white men could fail. Why, with their guns—their weapons—how could it be?"

"It will be years of war for us if we are shut off from Burma," Lao Er said sadly, and his eyes sought Jade's.

"Are our children to be brought up as slaves?" Jade cried out and burst into tears and ran from the room.

Ling Tan looked at his second son's grave face. "What does she mean?" he asked.

"It is her great fear that our children will not know what freedom is," Lao Er answered. "So far she has been hoping beyond reason that the white men will vanquish the enemy quickly, and she knows that for this Burma is our last hope." Ling Tan spoke again to Lao Er. "If you want your sons to grow up free, then you must leave this house."

"What?" Ling Sao cried at this. "Am I to let my grandsons go out and be lost like my third son?" And she put her blue apron to her eyes and wept aloud and Lao Er made haste to comfort her.

"Now, my mother," he said, "have I said I am taking your grandsons away from you?"

"No," Ling Sao sobbed, "but if Jade wants to go, you will."

"How can we take two small children out secretly?" Lao Er urged. "It is only a dream of hers. We will not leave you."

But Ling Sao would not be comforted, and though Lao Ta's wife brought hot tea to soothe her, she would not drink it. So when at last they went to bed, no one was eased.

Now in bed Ling Sao lay and thought how great a sorrow it would be if there were no grandchildren in the house. It would be worse even than if she heard her third son was lost, and soon she fell to weeping softly.

Ling Tan heard her weeping and he spoke sharply from his pillow. "Give over weeping, woman. Your tears should be dry by now with so much trouble as we have had."

At this Ling Sao wailed afresh.

"Give over—give over," Ling Tan shouted, "lest you make me weak, too."

At these words she paused and put her hand to his cheek and found it wet. "You, too?" she whispered.

"Be still," he muttered, but his voice broke her heart.

AND IN THE hot night Sheng sat remembering, and Pansiao, beside him, remembered, too, and Mayli let them be.

Pansiao put out her hand and Sheng took it and held it. "Ah, my little sister," he said sadly, "why are you here?"

"It is very lucky for me to have found Mayli and now you," Pansiao said cheerfully, and she told him how she had come to be there by one chance and then another.

Over her head Sheng and Mayli looked at each other. Though they longed to be alone, they had not the heart to tell this young and trusting creature to leave them even for a little while, so they sat listening.

Then Pansiao turned to look at her brother with sudden thoughtfulness. "The moment I saw this elder sister in the inland mountains school I said she would be a good wife for you," she said.

Sheng laughed aloud. "So have I always said the same thing," he said. "But can you get her to agree with us?"

Pansiao was all eagerness. She took Mayli's hand and brought it to Sheng's, and she put them together and held them there. "Now you t-two," she said, stammering, "ought you not to agree?"

And as though to humor her, Mayli let her hand lie under Sheng's, and Sheng closed his right hand strongly over her narrow one. "Child," Mayli said, "is this the time for such talk? Who can tell what tomorrow will bring to any of us?"

"But that is why you should agree," Pansiao said. "If we were sure of tomorrow, there would be no haste."

"She is right," Sheng said in his deep voice.

Then Mayli felt her heart drawn out of her body. Would it not be strength to make her promise to Sheng and so be secure at least in that?

Then, as though Heaven would not give her even that much, she heard the sound of running footsteps and there was An-lan, pale in the moonlight, gasping with running, her eyes black in her pale face. She shouted to Mayli as though the other two were not there, "Oh, you are here—oh, I have searched for you everywhere! Chi-ling—Chi-ling has hung herself upon a tree! There!" An-lan pointed to the farther side of the encampment.

Mayli leaped to her feet and ran toward the place An-lan pointed, with Sheng behind her. At the edge of the jungle, they saw Chi-ling, a slender shape hanging loosely from a branch in a gnarled tree.

Sheng took out his knife and cut the cloth that held Chi-ling. He caught her as she fell and laid her on the ground.

But was her life quite gone? Mayli stooped and felt the flesh still warm. "Run," she bade An-lan. "Run—find Chung!" And she began to chafe Chi-ling's limp hands and to move her thin arms. In very little time Chung was there, and he stooped and felt Chi-ling's heart. He shook his head—the heart was still and she was dead. They rose.

"I saw her," Chung said slowly, "not above an hour ago. She came in to tell me that one of the Australians had died, as I had feared he would. There was gangrene in his wound and my sulfa drugs are gone. But he was a stranger to her."

"She always took every death too hard," An-lan muttered. "I told her—I said, 'We shall see many die, and what are we to do if you behave so each time?'"

"What did she say?" Mayli asked.

"She did not answer me," An-lan said. "When she saw the young man die, it must be that she came here to the jungle and died, too."

Mayli stooped and straightened Chi-ling's body on the ground, and there she lay peacefully, the white moonlight on her face. "We cannot leave her here," Mayli said. "The jungle beasts will have her."

So they stood a moment and then Chung said, "Let us bury her." So there at the edge of the jungle they dug a hole with sticks and a shovel that Sheng found. An-lan and Mayli put green leaves into the hole and they laid Chi-ling among them and then covered her with earth.

When all was done, Sheng said in his old rough way, "Now I must get back to my men and you back to where your duty is."

Pansiao had come up and was watching them silently, her eyes strange and startled. An-lan sat on the end of the log, her head in her hands.

"Let us meet as often as we can at night," Sheng said to Mayli. "Keep watch for me, and I will find you when I am free."

She nodded, and he went away, and when she saw him gone, she went over to An-lan and put her hand on the girl's shoulder. "Come," she said. And An-lan rose and now Pansiao came near and Mayli put out her hand and took Pansiao's. And so in silence the three went into the encampment to sleep, if sleep they could in the few hours until dawn.

BUT SHENG and Mayli did not meet the next night nor for six nights after that. For at dawn the next day they were attacked by low-flying enemy planes that strewed fire even on the rear where Mayli and her women were. Now the enemy made sorties over the retreating armies five and six times a day. Each time the dead were more than could be buried and the wounded more than could be cared for. There was no sleep and little time for food, and then no appetite for the poor stuff that was given them to eat. And over them and under them and about them like blankets of wet wool was the eternal heat, which did not abate night or day. Indeed there was no good thing to be said of these days.

But on the evening of the seventh day the retreat was halted because a heavy rain was clouding the skies too much for the enemy to fly. For the first time in all these days and nights Mayli took time to wash herself. She took out from her pack the last piece of soap she had saved since she left home. She called Pansiao a little apart and told her to hold up a piece of matting and behind that matting she washed herself clean in the rain.

It was while she did this that she heard Pansiao exclaim, "I see that third brother of mine coming near."

"Then I will dress myself quickly," Mayli said, and in a moment she was ready, for she had only to put on her wet uniform and bind her wet hair. The first thing she saw when she came out from behind the matting was that Sheng looked ill, and then she saw his arm tied into a rough sling. "Oh, you are wounded!" she cried.

"I don't say it is enough to call a wound," he replied. "It is a nail hole that I had seven days ago, and I thought the wound clean, but now I think there was poison on the nail."

"Let me see it," she cried, and she drew him aside into the little tent and made him unwrap the cloth he had torn from the tail of his shirt. There was indeed a very ugly wound, for pus was coming out of the hole and small red streaks ran up and down his arm and shoulder.

"Oh, you stupid!" she cried, her fright making her angry. "How could you not tell me about this before now?" And she turned to Pansiao, who was looking at them with anxious eyes. "Go and call the doctor," she said. And Pansiao went running to find Chung.

Now shyness fell upon Mayli and Sheng. They could only

be alone a few minutes, they both knew, and each quickly set about to think of some words to say in those few minutes that would last until they were alone again.

Sheng spoke first. "If ever we come out of this trap, I will not wait one day longer to know your true mind about me."

She had been making herself busy washing his wound, and now she looked up to smile. But the smile stopped on her face, for she saw that even her soft touch on that arm had made him sick with pain. "Oh," she cried, "this is very bad. Sit down. Now, I must hurt you—I cannot help it. It must be washed out. Then when Chung comes, he will know what to do—"

And he sat still, not speaking because her words were sweet to him and the tone of her voice warm. How close—how close they were. Could anything part them, even death?

But before they could grasp the moment, Chung was at the flap of the tent. "Now what?" he asked.

"This fellow," Mayli said. "A nail has poisoned him."

Chung stared into the hole, now cleaned, smelled it and shook his head. "This man should have sulfa," he said, "but I have none. I used the last days ago."

"Would they have some—the English?" Mayli asked.

"How do I know?" Chung answered. "I have not seen an English doctor for ten days."

"We can't keep up with them," Sheng said wryly. "They are always ahead of us in retreat. We get our orders each morning to hold. We hold at any cost. Then by midday the order comes to fall back to where the new line is."

"But where is the end of this?" Mayli asked.

"Who knows?" Sheng said. "The general is like a man gone mad. He has never retreated in his life."

"And the American?" Mayli breathed.

"The American is no god," Sheng said shortly. "He is like us—a foreigner, fighting on foreign soil. No, the battle is lost. We know it. The men smell defeat even in the rear and soldiers are deserting."

"Our men?" Mayli asked faintly.

"All men," Sheng said. "White, yellow, black—"

All this was said while he sat holding his arm stiff. "What to do with you I cannot tell," the doctor said.

Then Pansiao spoke. "Do you remember, Third Brother," she said, "that our mother used to make a poultice of wet yeast bread and put it on boils and it drew the boils and they went away? I have a piece of bread like that in my pack that I have kept a long time against another day when I would be more hungry than this one."

"It can do no harm," the doctor said, "though perhaps no good. Fetch the bread, child."

So Pansiao got her little pack and inside was the bread. She gave it to Chung, who took it and made it into a poultice, which he wrapped about Sheng's arm.

"Do not use your arm," he said.

"Luckily it is not my gun arm," Sheng said. Then he stood up. "I must not stay longer. The general has called us to a meeting tonight."

He gave Mayli a long deep look. "If I do not come for some days, it will be because the general has put a command upon me. I will come when I can."

Mayli smiled and said, "I shall not let myself fear for you."

And so they parted yet again.

WHEN SHENG left Mayli he went to the general's tent. Pao Chen and the others were already there, as was Charlie Li, wearing a ragged pair of trousers torn off at the knees.

"Sit where you can," the general said shortly. "I have called you here because I have orders from the American to move quickly and relieve the white men who are in yet another trap.

"The enemy holds a bridge over the river where the last of the white men must cross. We are commanded to fight our way through and force the enemy from this bridge and hold it while the white men cross. Then we retreat across the bridge ourselves and destroy it before the enemy can follow. It is a piece of work as delicate as an ivory maker's."

He said all this in a level cold voice. And when he had finished, no one spoke for a while. Then Sheng asked, "What will become of these white men when they have crossed the river?"

"They will continue the retreat," the general said. "And let us not deceive ourselves. The air support that we thought the white men would send, they cannot send. There will be no help of any kind. Now we have our orders. Who volunteers?"

There was silence.

"If it were not for the One Above and his pride in us," the general said slowly, "I would command you all to turn your backs upon this lost battle—lost before we ever set foot on the soil of this country. But how can I face him unless I have spent all he bade me spend?"

At these words Sheng sighed deeply. His arm ached and pain shot into his shoulder. "I will go," he said. "I will be part of what must be spent—if so it must be spent."

"Stay after the others have gone," the general said to him, "and I will give you maps and tell you what the road is."

"I ask only one price," Sheng replied. "I want this fellow to go with me," and he put his hand on Charlie's shoulder.

The general nodded, and the others went. Then the three talked for two more hours, with Charlie now and again putting his finger on the map to point out shorter paths to the river.

"In one day's hard march," the general said, "you should be there. Rest, then attack by night. Scatter your men as you march. But instruct them to meet at the given place at the given hour, and let none delay."

"No one will delay," Sheng said.

"When can you start?" the general asked.

Sheng did not answer for a moment. Under his uniform his shoulder throbbed with pain, but he hesitated for another cause. Should he go back to Mayli and tell her? Would she take it well or ill? Could he hide from her that his head swam with fever and that his eyes burned in their sockets? No, he could not trust himself against the power of her will upon him.

He had told her that it might be days before they met again—
let it be days, therefore.

"I will start at dawn," he told his general.

"Since you risk your life," the general said to Sheng, "I will
choose the best men for you to command."

Sheng heard these words, which at any other time would
have given him joy, but now his brain could not comprehend
them. He tried to fix his eyes on his general's face, but he
saw double.

"You hear me?" the general asked.

"I will do my—very best," Sheng stammered. He forced his
right arm to salute and turned and went back to his tent.

IX

SHENG COULD not sleep for the pain in his swollen arm. At
dawn he ripped off the sleeve of his uniform, for the skin was so
red and stretched that even the weight of the cloth on it was
too much. Then he took off the bandage and poultice and let
the wound flow. He was much eased, enough so that he went
out and met his men.

As Sheng stood before them, the clear still air of the dawn-
ing day calmed his feverish mind. "Are you ready?" he asked,
and the men shouted back in their various voices that they
were ready. So without more ado Sheng went at their head and
they followed behind, swarming through the valley. Among
them, although Sheng did not know it, was the Indian who had
followed the march to be near Sheng. Ahead of them somewhere was Charlie Li, who had gone to spy out the enemy.

They marched for some miles until it was full light. Sheng
stopped and put his men at ease. Then he sent down his
command: "Now that it is day, we will scatter ourselves
fanwise, but you are all to head for the Village of Three
Waters. Near it is a small lake, which is now nearly dried.
There we will meet. Do not keep together. Walk as though
you were travelers or pilgrims or straying soldiers."

Sheng chose a young lad to go with him because this boy was silent. For now Sheng's arm was painful again and his head was hot and giddy and he wanted no talking. Of half that day Sheng remembered nothing at all afterward except that he put one foot in front of the other. He did not stop for food or rest but only where he found water. Sheng and the lad kept to the fields and hills and passed around the villages.

The Burmese farmers stared at them and Sheng pointed to his wounded arm, as though he were in search of a doctor. Once they were stopped by a man who, when he saw Sheng's arm, shouted and pulled Sheng by his other hand into a monastery nearby. The man led Sheng into a room where a venerable old man in a robe sat.

That old one lifted Sheng's arm and stared into the wound. He shook his head as if to say it was very grave. Then he rose and moved slowly into another room and came back with a little pot containing a smooth black ointment. This he smeared over the angry wound. At first Sheng thought he must cry out with pain, for the ointment was like fire on the wound. But he held himself silent and soon the fire changed to coolness and then his arm felt numb. In a little while more there was no pain at all. Sheng took out his purse from his girdle to pay the old man, but no, the old man would take nothing. So Sheng went on his way, wondering that even here in this enemy country were those who could be kind.

Now that the pain had stopped for a while he could travel more easily. In the afternoon he and the boy met a man selling fried rice balls. They each bought four or five of these hot balls and sat down beside the road under a tree to eat. The fever made Sheng drowsy, and after he had eaten, he lay back and fell asleep. He was wakened by the pain throbbing in his arm again. He struggled up and resumed the march, with the lad falling in behind him.

At dark of that day they came to the lake, now dried into a big pond, and on the other side they found their comrades waiting, not together, so that men could see they were indeed an army, but a hundred here and a hundred there among the low trees. Charlie came forward with some food. On the ground nearby was a teapot full of hot tea. When Sheng saw the teapot, a mighty thirst fell upon him and he picked up the pot in his right hand and drank as long as his breath held, and then again until he had drunk his fill. When at last he put the pot down, Charlie said quietly, "Now I can tell you the news. It will not do to rest much tonight. The white men will all be dead unless we reach them by morning."

This Sheng heard, but his arm began to throb again. He sent word to his men that they were only to rest and not to sleep. Then he went alone to the side of the lake and dipped the muddy water up in his hands and threw it over his garments for coolness. But so great was his fever that when it was time to go he was dried and hot again.

ALL THAT night the division moved up. The men stopped after midnight to scatter again and rest for three hours before they attacked.

"Before you wake, I will be back to tell you where the enemy is closing in and where the white men are," Charlie said to Sheng, with his grin as wide as ever.

"Do you never sleep?" Sheng asked.

"I sleep on my feet," said Charlie.

Sheng would have said he had not slept, so vivid was the pain in his arm, and yet it was out of sleep that Charlie waked him at the end of three hours. Charlie touched Sheng's wounded arm lightly enough, but Sheng leaped to his feet with a yell and stood in the darkness shaking with agony.

"Elder Brother, what is the matter with you?" Charlie whispered in amazement.

"Nothing," he said. "I was dreaming of an evil thing."

"Well then, put it aside," Charlie said. "For I have found the white men. They are caught in a trap, indeed. The enemy is between them and the river. You must attack toward the bridge, where the enemy is stretched in a thin line not more than half a mile along the river. If you press through that half mile, you can relieve the white men, and they will push to the bridge. But it must be suddenly, so that the devils do not destroy the bridge, for then we shall all be trapped."

Charlie wiped his sweating face with the tail of his coat and continued. "Some of the white men are escaping by bribing Burmese with their guns for boats."

"Do they give their good guns to these Burmese traitors?" Sheng cried in rage.

"What else have they to offer as bribes?" Charlie said.

"But a good gun!" Sheng groaned. His head throbbed violently and he repeated the words: "A good gun—a good gun—"

"Are you drunk?" Charlie shouted.

Sheng's brain cleared again for a moment. "No," he said. He was drunk with pain, but how could he heed pain now?

He went back to his men and roared at them to follow him. He ran and they ran, and he felt his whole body filled with strength and fire. His brain whirled and his eyes burned, but he ran on, and there was strength in him beyond anything he had ever known.

Before the dawn broke, he saw the low tents of the enemy ahead. He bellowed like a bull when he saw them, and roaring together, he and his men fell upon the enemy while they were still half asleep and expecting no attack.

Sheng's men followed him as though he were a god. When they saw his madness, they became mad and they plunged their bayonets into the enemy wherever they found them. They stabbed and cut and tore. And ahead of them all was Sheng like a demon, his eyes red and burning and his mouth yelling. All who saw him were filled with fright, and his own men swore to each other that never had they seen any man so fierce as Sheng was in that battle.

His men swept aside the enemy, and into the breach the weary white men poured. Some waved their arms and shouted to their deliverers, but they were few. Most went on without heeding anything except saving their lives. As they pushed

and pressed each other, some fell into the swirling muddy water of the river, but none stayed to help those who fell.

Sheng rushed on. In his feverish confusion he had forgotten why he was here, except that he had been sent to defeat the enemy. He led on and fought until suddenly he felt a hand on him.

"You fool!" he heard Charlie shout. "Do you plan to fight straight through to India this day? Turn—turn. The enemy is counterattacking!"

Then Sheng turned, staggering and panting. "Have we—have we crossed the bridge?" he gasped.

"The bridge is a mile and a half behind you!" Charlie shouted.

Sheng began to run with the men whom he had led too far, and they raced like hounds that mile and a half back to the place where the bridge had been. There they stood and stared across the river.

"The bridge—" Sheng stammered. "The bridge—" But his giddy brain could not finish.

The young voice of the silent lad who had stayed with Sheng all along now rose in a clear and piercing scream. "Oh, my mother, my mother!" he wailed. "The white men have cut the bridge!"

At these words Sheng's blood rushed upward and filled his head. He laughed in a great howl of laughter. "Our allies," he howled, "our allies—"

He felt his head split in two, as though an ax had cleaved it, and he knew no more.

HE WOKE, where or how many days later he did not know. Then a strange voice began to speak in English. This sound, which he could not understand, made the place more strange to him. He could not lift his head.

Now he heard a voice he knew. It was Charlie's voice. He forced his eyes open and stared up into the dark face of the Indian. This fellow shouted with joy, and then it was Charlie's face and he heard Charlie's voice saying, "Sheng, are you awake? Can you hear me?"

Sheng made a mighty effort and his voice came out small, like a boy's voice. "Yes."

"Do you know me?" Charlie asked.

"Yes," Sheng said again.

"Now I know you will live," Charlie said gently and took out of his bosom an egg, cracked it open carefully and put it to Sheng's open lips. "Drink. I have been saving this hen's egg for you."

Sheng felt the soft smooth flow of the egg slip down his throat. He swallowed and drifted off again.

Charlie Li sat on his heels for a moment watching him. "He will get well," he said to the Englishman.

"Thanks to you," the Englishman said.

"It was you who gave him the sulfa," Charlie replied gently. He stared down into the empty egg and licked the inside clean. "I have not tasted an egg for months," he said. "But this morning I stumbled upon a black hen in her nest. She had not laid the egg yet, but I persuaded her."

"Midwife, eh?" The Englishman grinned. "What fellows you are, you Chinks!'

Charlie glanced up sharply at the word Chinks. No, the Englishman's haggard young face was kind. He had used the word without thought. "Here is the trouble with you damned English," Charlie said in his pleasant voice. "You do not even know when you insult us."

"Insult you?" the white man asked, amazed. "But how?"

Charlie decided to avoid the real issue. "We have been together two days and a half," he went on, "and you have not asked my name."

The Englishman sprang to his feet. "Sorry," he said, embarrassed. "I'm Dougall."

"I am Li," Charlie said quietly. But neither put out his hand.

Later, having gone off into the jungle by himself to think, Charlie cleared a small space about a fallen log and sat down. When he had seen Sheng fall, he had seized him under the arms, and even as he ran, a lithe dark figure had sprung out of the bush to share the burden of Sheng's body. It was the Indian. They plunged into the forest away from the riverbank, Sheng's inert body between them.

Charlie knew very well what was happening behind them. Caught between the river and the enemy, Sheng's men were being cut to pieces. If any escaped, it would only be by chance. They put Sheng down at last, and Charlie knew the moment he looked at him that he would die unless he got aid. Bidding the Indian to keep watch on Sheng, he crept to the edge of the jungle and stared out into a burning countryside. Fires blazed on the horizon like volcanoes. The Burmese, in madness, were firing their own towns and villages. He stared awhile and then he turned and made his way back again.

On his way back, he came upon the Englishman hiding in the jungle. He almost stepped on the fellow, and for a second he saw nothing but the muzzle of a gun, for Dougall had taken him for a Japanese. In a second he leaped on it and saved his life. They fell down together, and there, the white face not six inches from his own, Charlie Li cursed and swore and gasped out that he was Chinese. Dougall released him instantly.

"Good God!" he said. "I nearly killed you."

They went back together then. Sheng was still alive, and Dougall reached silently into his pocket and brought out a small sealed packet, which he unwrapped. Inside were some flat white pellets. "He'd better take these," he said.

That had been yesterday morning. Dougall had been kind again and again. He had made a better bed for Sheng to lie on out of broken ferns, he had washed his handkerchief clean and filtered the dark jungle water for Sheng to drink, and he had sat holding Sheng's wounded arm to the sunshine that fell in slanting beams through the trees. "The sun will heal this sort of thing," he remarked. "We learned that, over and over again."

Of the retreat neither had said a word.

Charlie rose, sighing. He hated these forests. There was no

peace for man in the jungle and no safety. What now? They must keep moving until they found the general.

He went back to the small clearing they had made for their hiding place. He found Sheng awake, his eyes sensible and clear. The Englishman had propped him up against a pile of small branches, and he was standing there, his hands on his hips, looking down on Sheng.

"I was hoping you'd be back soon," he remarked to Charlie with great cheerfulness. "He doesn't know a word of English, does he?"

"Not a word," Charlie said.

Sheng began to talk. "Where are my men?" he asked.

For a moment Charlie thought that he must shield Sheng a little longer from the truth. But he decided quickly that the truth must be told. "Those men are destroyed," he said.

"Destroyed?" Sheng repeated.

"The white men cut the bridge after they had crossed," Charlie said. "You remember that?"

Sheng nodded, his black eyes fixed on Charlie's face. "The Indian was there—he helped me with you and we escaped. But I saw the enemy fall upon the others with their guns and their bayonets."

Sheng lifted his eyes to the Englishman. "Does this long white radish say why they left us without a way of escape after we had rescued them?" Sheng asked.

Without further ado Charlie asked the Englishman, "Why did you fellows destroy the bridge behind you and leave us with no retreat, after we had come to save you?"

Dougall opened his blue eyes wide. "I'm sure we couldn't have done that," he said.

This Charlie told to Sheng.

"If he does not know what happened," Sheng declared after a moment, "then he is a deserter. Ask him why."

"Why have you left your army?" Charlie asked Dougall.

The young face of this Englishman burned red again under the thin white skin. "I was fed up," he said. "Anyone could tell we were licked. The commanders themselves didn't know what they were doing. It was every man for himself." He smiled, shamefaced. "Anyway," he said, "what's the use?"

This Charlie translated to Sheng and Sheng groaned in his weakness. "Ask him what he will do now," he commanded again.

"What will you do now?" Charlie asked.

"I?" Dougall lifted his head and looked from one face to the other. "Why, I'll simply come along with you, if you fellows don't mind. It was most awfully lucky my finding you—I mean, because you can speak English, you know."

"He says he will come with us," Charlie told Sheng.

Sheng closed his eyes and smiled bitterly. "Since he is our ally," he said, "let him come."

Two days later they set out again. Sheng was on his feet, weak but ready to live.

X

THE GENERAL looked at the American. He made his face blank. He wanted to say what he felt, that nothing this American could do would save any of them, that the battle here had been lost before they had ever trod upon the soil.

"I have sacrificed one division," he said. "Not one of the Fifty-fifth has returned. Where are they?"

"I have never heard of a division disappearing," the American replied, "but so it is."

"It is impossible for an army to fight this way, you understand," the general said, making his Chinese simple and plain for this foreigner. "You understand? I am given orders to hold a line. I hold. My men fight without regard to life. Then we find that while we have been fighting, our allies have been retreating without notice to us. Then we have to give up what we have been holding at the cost of our lives. Is this the way to fight a winning war?"

The American's thin cheeks flushed. He did not answer.

"You white men," the general said distinctly, "you are determined to save each other's faces."

He rose, saluted with sharpness and wheeled away. He marched to his quarters, passing his own guards without even seeing them. Suddenly he wished that he had a woman to talk to as he might talk to his wife. His wife was sensible and quick to think of a way out of trouble, but she was thousands of miles away. In his tent he sat down and closed his eyes, feeling really desperate. Sheng had never returned; meantime the enemy's rate of advance was thirty to forty miles a day.

He suddenly felt the impulse to weep and was surprised at himself. "It is this eternal retreat," he told himself. Sighing, he thought of his lost men. Sheng, that great brave fellow from the Nanking hills, was lost. It occurred to him that he should tell that pretty girl. He shouted and an aide ran in.

"Send Wei Mayli to me," he said. "Tell her I wish her to go as a messenger for me to the American. Her English is good enough—I can no longer understand his Chinese."

He thought with a sparkle of pleasure how it would shame the American to hear that his Chinese could not be understood. He smiled, and a little of his old quiet arrogance came back to him.

"YES, OF COURSE I will come," Mayli said to the aide. She wiped her hands as she spoke. "I will only change my coat—it is blood-spattered."

She hastened toward the operating room where a moment before she had been helping Chung deliver a Burmese woman of a large fat boy. The woman's husband, a Chinese merchant, was waiting now at the door and stopped her as she passed.

"Tell me," he urged, "has the child a mole on his left earlobe? I won't know this is my son if my mark is not on him." And he turned his head and showed her a round black mole on his left earlobe.

"But not every child you have will bear your mark," Mayli cried. "What—will you test your wife's virtue by a mole?"

She laughed but the man would not laugh. "Look for it, for I do not want to waste any red eggs on another man's son. My wife is pretty and young and I cannot always be at home."

She pulled away from him, promising, and in the room she found Chung carefully washing and polishing his instruments. "Chung, the general has sent for me," she said. She began to scrub her hands. "Is it Sheng, do you think? Why else should the general send for me? I have not seen him for weeks."

"Sheng should be back by now certainly," Chung said. It had been strange to see so many men march away and not one return.

The women came in and lifted the stretcher on which the new mother lay and took her away. Mayli reached for a clean uniform and in a moment she was at the door again, when suddenly the child wailed. He was still lying in a corner wrapped in a towel on some straw. Mayli paused, then ran back again. "Give him to me," she said to Chung. "I will tell Pansiao to look after him until I return."

She seized the plump little bundle and hurried toward the door once more. There outside was the father, and seeing him, she remembered what he had wanted. "Here," she said, "see for yourself."

She knew there was small chance that the child had inherited his father's birthmark, but she moved the end of the towel from the head and there was a tiny dot of black on the little left ear.

"It is here," Mayli cried with joy, "so small that it can hardly be seen, but then he is so small."

The Chinese merchant rose, felt in his bosom for his spectacles, which he put on to examine the tiny lobe. "He is my son," he said solemnly. A smile came over his face. "My first," he said. He put out his arms. "I will take him."

"But we have to wash him and put on his clothes," Mayli protested.

"I will take him," he repeated firmly. "I can wash him and put on his clothes."

She gave him the child and watched while he strode away, the child laid across his two arms like tribute being borne to an emperor. He disappeared down the street and she came to herself. How foolish was life, she thought, that in the midst of war and death and evil news of every kind, one could forget for a moment all except that a son had been born to a man again! She hastened on, smiling and sad.

"OF SHENG I have heard not one word," the general said. Mayli clasped her hands a little more tightly on her lap. "What there is between you two I do not know," he went on, "but I ought to tell you that not one man of his command has come back, and by now I ought to have had Charlie Li here at least to tell me that they were rejoining us." He paused. "I want you to go to the American, as my private messenger, and speak in his own language so that I can be sure he understands. Tell him that I will retreat no more. I will take my own stand and guard the borders of our own country, and let the white men do what they like."

"Shall I go to the American now?" she asked.

"Now," he answered, "for tomorrow we march."

She rose, and he lifted his troubled eyes to regard her.

"Do not give up hope," she said quickly.

"I have not given up hope," he replied. "Hope has been torn from me."

"I will go and come back quickly," she said and went away.

She knew, of course, where the American was. He lived in a little tent like that of any common soldier. When she came to the guard at the entrance of the tent she said in English, "I come as a messenger from the Chinese general."

"Righto," the guard replied and went inside. In a moment he came back. "The boss says to come in," he said.

She found the American sitting on a folding stool, eating a green-skinned melon. He looked up, smiled and rose, the melon in his hands. "Would you like a piece of this?" he asked.

"No, thank you," she said, sitting down on a second stool. "I have a message from our general. He wishes me to say that tomorrow he will march back to the borders of our own country."

The American sat down. "I'm sorry he's made up his mind. Try to dissuade him, young lady—I can't. He doesn't take my orders."

"He is discouraged," she said. "We are all discouraged."

He put the melon down on a small folding table and wiped his hands on a white handkerchief. "I know," he said gently.

She turned away her head and rose, having fulfilled her mission. But he delayed her a moment. "In spite of what your general may be thinking," he said, "I have never seen braver men than these British. They have known that they would have no reinforcements—no planes, ships or additional troops—nothing. They have been fighting what is called a delaying action. Their lives are the scraps thrown to the advancing wolves so that others might be saved."

"You defend each other, you and the British," she said, suddenly ablaze with anger. "You forget that we would have had allies here in Burma instead of enemies had you white men been human beings all through these decades of your possession."

"Do not forget I am American," he reminded her.

"I can only remember that you are white," she retorted, and she bent her head away from him and went out.

She hastened back to the general. "I have delivered your message," she told him, "and he advises against it."

"I will not heed his advice," the general replied.

"Then we march tomorrow?" she inquired.

"At dawn," he replied.

She nodded and made haste, for the severely wounded must be scattered among the homes of Chinese wherever they could be found and a hundred small things had to be done before they marched again. She bustled so much that at last she drove Chung to rebuke her thus: "You are as bad as a foreigner sometimes."

She paused at this and after a moment she said, "Well,

perhaps you are right." She grew quieter. Her step moved as swiftly, but the bustle was gone.

Pansiao asked in her soft voice, "Are we moving?"

"Yes, but this time nearer home," Mayli replied.

"What about Sheng," Pansiao said, "how will he find us?"

Mayli paused for one instant. "I have been thinking of that," she said. "See, we will leave a letter here with the husband of the woman who had the baby today. He is Chinese, and when Sheng finds us gone, he will go to the Chinese."

Still Pansiao was not satisfied. She hung her head and twisted her fingers and looked sidewise at Mayli as she worked, causing Mayli to say, "Speak what is behind your eyelids, for I can see something is there."

"Nothing," Pansiao faltered. "That is, something that doesn't matter. That is, it matters nothing to me. But if we leave a letter for Sheng—"

A guess darted into Mayli's mind. "We ought to leave one for Charlie Li," she said, laughing, sharpening her two forefingers at Pansiao like knives in the old childish gesture of derision, and Pansiao threw the end of her jacket over her face and ran away.

Mayli, left behind, ceased laughing and stood motionless for a long time. It was possible that she and Sheng would never meet again.

. THAT LAST NIGHT Mayli wrote a letter to Sheng that said:

> We leave tomorrow morning at dawn, under orders. The American will tell you where we go, if you cannot find out otherwise. If you can follow, I shall be watching for you day and night and so will your sister. I believe you live. Would I not know it if you were dead?

When this letter was written, she sat for a while thinking of Sheng's family in the village near Nanking. In quick, clear characters she wrote to Jade and told her that Sheng had not returned but she did not think him dead. Then she wrote:

I ought to tell you that our allies have not upheld us here. Do not have great hopes, for we are in retreat. Tonight is dark—who can see tomorrow? But I send good wishes to you all. If we live, Sheng and I will come home again someday.

Now this was as near as Mayli had ever come to saying to the family that she and Sheng would one day be wed, and as she wrote the words, a deep warmth came up out of her heart. She sealed the two letters and she mailed the one to Jade, but the one to Sheng she gave to the Burmese woman to give to her husband, saying, "Tell your husband to look for a tall fellow with a wounded arm and give him this letter."

The Burmese woman, pleased with her child, promised that she would do what Mayli asked in thanks for the healthy son she had. All this was on the last night before the new march began.

Now THE LETTER Mayli sent to Jade went by carrier and by plane and by carrier again, and then over enemy country by the hands of hillmen and then by carrier again until it came to Ling Tan's house.

No one in the village could read except Jade, and Jade, because of her learning, had come to be looked upon as a woman of great wisdom and skill. Under her calm face and behind her kind eyes Jade kept her own thoughts, and these thoughts hovered continually about Mayli and Sheng. They had done so ever since Lao Er had told her she must dream no more of leaving this home and going to the free country. She looked to Mayli and Sheng, therefore, with constant, unchanging hope that someday they and others like them would free the people from the hold of the enemy. If not, then indeed there was no hope, and her fine sons would grow up as slaves. Again and again this thinking woman would lift her eyes to the starlit night skies and her heart would swell and ache with the longing to be free. Then she would cry inside her heart where none but she could hear, "If we are not to be freed, I had rather my sons died now in their childhood."

To Jade, then, did Mayli's letter come, saying that Sheng had gone to rescue the white men and that he had not come back and no one knew where he was. Again and again Jade read the lines: "Our allies have not upheld us here. Do not have great hopes, for we are in retreat."

When Jade read this she was alone. The others lay sleeping after the noon meal, but it was her custom while the others slept to sit in the court and sew. There the letter had been delivered to her. She pondered for a while, the tears wet on her cheeks, whether or not to read the letter to the others and so destroy their hope. She thought to herself, It would be easier for me to hide this letter and keep the evil news in myself rather than to hear the wails of my husband's mother and the curses of my husband's father.

And yet she did not dare to keep from these two the news of their own son. At last she rose and went into her room where Lao Er lay sleeping. She sighed and laid her hand gently on his bare shoulder. "I have a letter from Mayli and it has bad news," she said when he awoke. "You must tell me whether we will keep the news to ourselves or tell the others." So she read him the letter and he listened and cursed under his breath and frowned as he sat on the edge of the bed.

He thought awhile, then said, "Of what use will it be to tell the old ones? You know how my old father still trusts that promise the white man made. What will he think if he hears the white men have betrayed us? No, let us keep all to ourselves, at least until we know whether my third brother is dead or not."

"I am glad you say this," Jade replied, "for it is what I wanted to do and feared."

She came to him and they clasped hands for a moment.

Then Lao Er said, "I must get back to the field."

She wiped her eyes and said, "I must see to your mother and father."

And so these two carried their despair secretly from that day on.

NOW THE BURMESE woman had put Mayli's letter to Sheng in her pocket and forgotten it for six days. First her house was dirty and needed cleaning, then her husband grew moody, and what with these matters, she forgot the letter. It was only when she came to wash her garment one morning at the pool that she found the letter still there. She put it into the pocket of the garment she wore and forgot it still another two days, and only then did she remember and give it to her husband.

It so happened that this man had heard that very day in town that three men from the Chinese army had strayed back dazed and lost and, after looking for their comrades, had left again. So he seized the letter and traveled on the main road on a small ass for half a day until he came upon not three but four men walking ahead of him: two Chinese, one Englishman and an Indian, all ragged and filthy and weary. One of these Chinese was so tall that the merchant put his hand in his pocket and brought out the letter and gave it to him, saying, "Are you this one?"

Sheng saw his own name. "I am," he said.

"Then my duty is finished," the merchant said and bade him farewell.

Sheng was full of wonder at receiving this letter from Mayli. He sat down under a banyan tree and he read it three times while the men with him waited. Then he said, "We must find the American and ask him where the armies have gone."

He rose as he spoke and put the letter into his girdle and the others rose with him except the Englishman, who continued to sit. When Charlie told him that they must go to the American to inquire where their armies were, the Englishman looked abashed. "I will not turn back," he said. "You go and I shall sit here and wait for you."

At this Charlie Li laughed and said to the others in Chinese, "Since this man is a deserter, it is only natural that he does not wish to see a white officer."

So they left the Englishman and walked for half a day to the encampment where the American was, with such troops as he still had left, a motley handful of Chinese and Indians. They found him sitting outside his small tent in his shirt and trousers like any common soldier. Charlie asked him where the Chinese armies were.

When the American saw the three ragged men before him in the uniform of the lost division, he asked, in wonder, "Where have you been?"

Charlie told him straightly and simply how Sheng had led his men to rescue the white men and how the bridge had been cut, so that they had all been hewed to pieces except for themselves.

The American listened with his blue eyes hard and he said not one word.

When Charlie saw that nothing was to be said, he asked, "Where are our men?"

"They have gone toward the border," the American said in English. "I told your general that it is a fool's decision to do what he is about to do—the Japs will get him for sure—but he wouldn't listen to me."

Charlie put this into Chinese for Sheng and Sheng said, "Tell the American I fear he is right, and let us hasten ourselves and tell our general so. Maybe it is not yet too late. Let us go quickly." So with their thanks to the American, they hurried on their way.

When they got back to the Englishman and told him what they planned to do, he was very reluctant. "We ought to get on to India," he grumbled to Charlie. "That's the only hope of saving ourselves."

"India!" Charlie cried, aghast. "Why, man, do you know what mountains lie between us and India?"

But the Englishman would not change his mind. "If I could get to India, I'd be all right," he said. "I know people there."

Nevertheless, since he was helpless in enemy country with the Burmese shooting Englishmen, he went with them.

When they had been traveling for some days, they perceived by many signs—villages half burned or flying enemy flags—that an enemy army was ahead of them. When Sheng saw this, he said to Charlie, "If we do not creep around the enemy somehow, the battle will be over by the time we reach our general, and if the American is right, we shall be too late."

XI

WITH GREAT care the general set his men out along a road, and when in the night he grew uneasy, he fortified himself with the thought that he and his men could vanquish any enemy attack.

Among the women none knew anything except to do each day's work as it came. And there was much to do, for the men's sandals were gone and their garments were in rags. They were bitten by spiders and snakes and some were poisoned by stagnant jungle water.

As Chung worked to heal them, he grew uneasy, for he heard rumors among the men. One evening he went to Mayli as she sat sewing and said in a low voice, "Should we be attacked, should we be defeated, what plan have you to save yourself and your women?"

Now Mayli had often thought what she would do in such a case, and she said, "We will stay by the armies if we can, but if we cannot, I have told my women to go straight into the jungle, choose a spot a mile or so inside and wait for me. What else can we do?"

"I want to give you a small gift," Chung said, and he put his hand into his pocket and took out a little compass. "Take this so that you will know how to walk west, away from the enemy."

She took it and put it into her pocket. "I thank you," she said, and went on sewing. Looking at her, he thought to himself how changed she was from the beautiful, impetuous girl she had been when he first saw her. She was as lean and hard now as a peasant. Her ways had changed, too. There was no time these days for coquetry and smiles.

She felt his gaze and looked up, but she did not speak nor

did he, for what was there to say? He rose and went away, not knowing that never again would he see this woman.

At dawn the next day, out of the seemingly peaceful countryside, the enemy came down upon them. The first to rise saw a cloud on the horizon toward the south. The mornings were often cloudy here until the sun rose full, but this cloud came from the dust of trucks and vehicles that carried the enemy army. Above them were airplanes, and these airplanes suddenly roared down out of the sky.

When the general heard the commotion, he leaped from his pallet and ran out of his tent. At that moment a small enemy plane swept downward and fired on the general. He fell and in one second his life was over.

The enemy was everywhere now, attacking and scattering and felling all as they ran. Chung flung up his arms and stood still. "I am caught," he muttered as the enemy dropped down on him and he died.

What the enemy in the sky did not do, the enemy pressing furiously from the earth finished. In so little time that the sun had scarcely crept above the clouds, the battle was over, and the enemy vehicles and airplanes were sweeping furiously northward to cut off the Big Road into China.

Who can tell why one is spared and another killed? Mayli lay motionless, her face upon her arms, and felt the heat of the enemy fire around her and heard the roar and whine of guns, and nothing touched her. She did not lift her head as she lay there. I am dead, she thought. This is death. I shall never stand upon my feet again, never speak a word. This thinking I now do is my last.

But she had never been so alive as she lay waiting for death. I wish I had married Sheng, she thought passionately. What waste to have lived lonely all these months! Sheng, oh Sheng! And this was what sorrowed her most, awaiting death.

But death did not come. The enemy went on and she lay in a field of dead. The noise grew less and the planes went echoing over the sky, then she heard them no more. The battle here was over and she lifted her head. The dead were all about her, but she—she was alive. She rose and stood staring at the twisted shapes about her. Then she turned and ran stumbling toward the jungle as she had told her women to do.

TRY AS THEY would, Sheng and his companions could not circle the enemy, for the enemy went in vehicles. When at last they did come up to where the enemy had been, there were only the heaped dead, rotting in the sunlight. The general they found dead in front of his tent, where he had fallen.

"Where are the women?" Sheng muttered to Charlie. "There was one among them whom I knew—"

"Was there?" Charlie asked. "There was one among them whom I knew, too."

The two men stared at each other in this field of death. "I mean that tall one—surnamed Wei and named Mayli," Sheng said to Charlie.

"That one?" Charlie exclaimed. "The one I know is a little thing, like a child, who follows Mayli all the time."

"Why, that is my sister!" Sheng cried. "That is Pansiao."

"Pansiao is your sister?" Charlie shouted.

And these two young men seized each other's hands in the midst of the death around them, and the tears came into their eyes.

Neither Sheng nor Charlie could leave the dead until they had walked among them to see whether Mayli and Pansiao were there. At last, when they could not find the two women, they went into the jungle for shade and to find water and to plan ahead. It was difficult to find a path, so the Indian led them. He searched out the only slight path he saw, which was the way Mayli had gone some four or five hours before.

STUMBLING INTO the jungle, Mayli had found only Pansiao, Siu-chen and An-lan, clinging together in fearful silence. A rain had begun to fall when Mayli came upon them. They put out their hands and drew her into their midst, tears streaming down their faces with the rain. And she put back her wet hair from her face and asked herself where they could go in this enemy country. How could a handful of women escape and find their own again? The trees about them were vivid green in the rain and monkeys parted the leaves like small humans to peer down at them. Mayli shivered to see those little dark faces, for so the enemy hid, too, in the trees like monkeys. They all felt the presence of the enemy, and this terror passed from one to the other until they seized each other's hands and ran in blindness toward the road. Mayli came to herself first. She pulled back and shouted at them, "Stop—stop—we are all fools—where are we going?"

At the sound of her voice they stopped and looked at her, and Pansiao began to cry because she was so weary and frightened. The rain had ceased and around them the wet green light shone soft and deep. At this moment they heard men's feet crashing through the jungle and men's voices. They shrank together, fearing enemy men more than all else. The noise came nearer and Mayli heard a complaining English voice speaking. "I say, you chaps, I shan't have any boots left on my feet for tomorrow if we keep this up."

She put her finger to her lips, loosened herself from the others and crept forward. Parting the tree branches a little, she saw three young white men sitting at the edge of the path. They were ragged and empty-handed except for the rifles each clutched. She crept nearer. Should she speak or not? They were pale, weary, lost-looking men, very young, little more than boys. Yes, she would speak. "Hello!" she said softly. "Hello!"

They leaped to their feet, their eyes staring, their guns ready. "You there," one said sternly, "are you friend or foe?"

She stepped out from the bushes that hid her. "I am friend," she said.

The three young Englishmen looked at Mayli. "Are you alone?" the first young Englishman asked. He had lowered his gun, but he still grasped it tightly.

"No, I am with three other women," she replied. "We escaped from the battle today."

"What battle?" he asked.

"Did you not come from the road?" she asked.

He shook his head. "No, we've been wandering through the jungle for days. We had an idea we were going toward India, but we may be entirely wrong."

She took from her pocket the little compass Chung had given her. "You are going southeast," she said.

"Good God!" he said in a low voice. "All this time we've been walking in the wrong direction. Are the Japs south of us or where?"

"They passed through here this morning," she said, "going north and east. How far they are now I cannot tell."

"If they were here only this morning," he said, "then we ought to move quickly. But where?"

"We must get out of this jungle," she said. "We cannot see anything until we are out of it. I will call my friends."

She lifted her voice and called, "An-lan—Pansiao—Siu-chen!"

At the sound of her voice the women came out timidly, Pansiao clinging to Siu-chen's hand. They looked at each other, English and Chinese. The men, Mayli could see, were not too pleased. Women, they were doubtless thinking—women would be a burden.

"We can walk as swiftly as you," Mayli said.

"Well, come along, everybody," the first Englishman said. "We'd better be on the march again."

And so the men took the lead and the women fell in behind, single file. Now these two kinds of people, men and women, light and dark, walked hour after hour in the sultry dusk of the jungle, each dubious of the other. Every now and again each kind muttered together concerning the other.

The Englishmen, glancing backward at the women, spoke in low voices:

"The little one doesn't look more than seventeen," one said.

And another one said, "They'd be pretty if you didn't remember your own girls."

"They're too yellow, too thin," the third one said.

"Still, they're girls," the first one said.

"I suppose you'd call them that," another answered.

The women spoke freely, knowing the men could not understand them in their own language:

"Are all Ying men tall and thin and bony like these?" Pansiao asked Mayli.

Mayli could still smile, hot and tired though she was. "Ying men come fat and thin, as any other men do," she said.

"They look like peeled fruit," Siu-chen said, and the women laughed. Yes, they could still laugh, looking at these Englishmen and seeing their knobby bare legs, tall, lean bodies and lank necks burned crimson.

With such talk they lightened some miles of walking, but it could not go on forever. They must think of food and shelter for the night. So when afternoon wore on to evening, Mayli called out to the Englishmen, "Had we not better talk together and decide what we should do about food and shelter? There is no end to the jungle. Yet we must eat and sleep."

The men stopped and waited for the women to come up. Then, since they were the leaders, Mayli and the tallest Englishman walked side by side to talk.

The more the Englishman looked at Mayli, the more he liked her. "It's great luck that we fell in with someone who speaks English," he said.

"It is not easy for women to travel alone here," she replied, and added, "I have been thinking what we could do. If we could find a main road that leads into India, it might be best for us to go in that direction."

He pressed his swollen lips together. "But there is no main road leading into India," he said.

"No road to India?" she exclaimed.

He shook his head. "That is why the retreat is so hard. The roads are narrow, old roads and they are clogged with people."

"What incredible folly of your generals," she cried, "to bring into this country armies too few for victory when they knew that there was no way for retreat!"

"You don't say anything that I do not myself say," he told her. "I've said it over and over. But that's the way it is. I was at Dunkirk and Dunkirk was easy compared to this. This isn't the place to fight. Why, we can sink men into this hole by the thousands and never win. It isn't a fit battlefield for white men!"

This she heard but did not answer. She looked around the jungle. No, it was not a fit battlefield for any men. But how many had died here! She thought of the general and Chung, and of all those others, and yet she had not the heart to reproach this tired and confused man who walked beside her. He was no more to blame than she was.

At last it was dark and they could walk no more. "Let's stop here where we are," the Englishman said. "I don't think we all ought to sleep. We three men will walk around the rest of you in regular beats and keep off the snakes at least."

"We will all take our turns," Mayli said.

"Nonsense, you women must sleep," he protested.

But Mayli said, "We Chinese women are used to doing as men do."

Thus they passed their first night in the jungle, between sleep and walking. The dawn came early and they went on their way again.

Now what more is there to tell of such a journey? The weariness numbed their brains and dulled the feeling in their flesh and bones. Fatigue passed into deeper fatigue and they grew drowsy while they walked, so that when leeches stuck to their ankles and legs, they did not even feel them. They were thirsty all day and faint, and did not speak to each other except for the few words that must be said, for talk took breath and strength. The Englishman held Mayli's compass and they pushed steadily westward. They could only press on, hoping that somewhere this jungle would end.

Late that evening they came upon a muddy winding river and downriver they saw a swinging bridge of bamboo. They crossed the bridge and followed a small beaten path until it came to a village near the river. On the other side of the village they could see that the jungle had been cut back to make small rice fields. They halted when they were in sight of the village, and talked together of what to do.

It was decided that Mayli and the tall Englishman would go forward and the others would stay behind. If they came back, all would be well; if they did not, then the others must go on. But when Pansiao was told this, she would not stay behind and so she went, too.

"Your sister?" the Englishman asked, glancing at the slender girl who put her hand in Mayli's.

Mayli was about to answer no, and then she thought of Sheng and said, "Yes—my sister."

It was late afternoon, and the villagers were in the rice fields, except for a few old ones and children. When these saw the strangers, they let out cries and the others came running from the fields. For a moment they all stood staring at the strangers and speaking in their own language. They were kindly looking, cheerful and childlike, and the more Mayli looked at their faces, the easier she felt.

"I believe these are only peasants," she said to the Englishman. She put on a hearty smile and opened her mouth and pointed into it to show she was hungry. Immediately the women climbed the ladders into their little houses set on posts and brought down cold rice and fish in large leaves. This they offered to the three, who were so hungry they took the food and ate it in a moment.

"We can stay here safely," Mayli said.

They went back to get the others and the villagers followed them at a little distance. When they saw them, great talk burst out, and they circled them as they all went back to the village, laughing and talking and staring very much at the guns of the three Englishmen.

Then the women brought out more food, and all ate and there was great friendliness. The children pressed near to stare and the women laughed and talked and the men handled the guns. Not one of these men had ever seen a gun before, and the short Englishman, wanting to amuse them, lifted his gun to his shoulder and shot a small bird that sat on a branch. At this the villagers screamed and ran back from the visitors.

"Oh," Mayli cried, "why did you have to do that?"

"It was only in fun," the short Englishman stammered. "I thought they'd like to see it."

"Not everybody is as ready to kill as you are," she retorted, and she said to the tall Englishman, "Quick—pretend you are angry—pretend to punish him!"

So the tall Englishman strode forward and slapped the other's cheeks. "Take this," he said. "Don't utter a word. I've got to do it—she's right." He jerked the man's gun away and offered it to the oldest man of the village. But this man would not have it and all the villagers backed away from the dreadful thing. So the Englishman took all three of the guns and set them in a row against a tree. When the villagers saw this, no one went near the tree, and so the danger was past.

They stayed at this village three days until they were rested and washed. Yet in less than three days Mayli began to be anxious to be gone from the village, for one of the white men could not contain himself and began to follow a pretty village girl. Mayli was frightened when she saw this and went to the tall one.

"You must tell this fellow to stay away from the girl," she warned him. "These people will not allow it."

"I'll tell him," he promised.

But of what use is a promise? She saw that, without meaning ill, these white men angered the villagers in a score of other small ways. So on the morning of the third day Mayli said to the tall Englishman, "It is time that we went on before trouble breaks out between them and us."

She went that day to the old man who was head of the

village and she made signs and asked him for the path, and he understood and made signs for a man to guide them to the roads out of the jungle. So they left the village that had treated them so kindly and went on their way again.

SHENG AND those with him had been traveling, too, but their journey had been made harder by a curious thing. For the Indian had begun to show a mighty hatred of the solitary Englishman, so much so that Sheng said to Charlie, "This man of India will do harm to the white man if he is left alone with him. Do you see how he has his hand always in his bosom where he keeps his knife?"

"I have seen his hatred when he looks at the white man," Charlie said.

"We must keep our eyes on him day and night," Sheng said. "Not for love," he added, "but for justice."

They did this, although their task was made harder because the Englishman was altogether ignorant of the Indian's hatred and treated him in small ways like a servant.

They pressed steadily north, and found a road that led toward the west. They halted there and tried to decide whether they should go east or west. Sheng would have gone eastward if he could, but the first village toward the east was full of the enemy, so they turned westward.

This was the same road to which the guide from the village had led Mayli and the others, but how could anyone know this? And because Sheng and the men with him went more quickly than Mayli and the women, Sheng came nearer each day to Mayli, so that the time must come when they would meet. This came about one day near noon at a small town.

Mayli and her women and the Englishmen came near the town and entered it a little too carelessly, without seeing whether the people were friendly or not. A young yellow-robed priest saw them first and ran secretly to his fellows to tell them that Englishmen had come into the town with Chinese women, and the most evil thoughts came up from his words until in less than an hour, while they paused at a streetside table to eat and drink, the whole town had turned against them. But they did not know it. They sat there on wooden benches on the main street, eating rice and curried vegetables and drinking tea. One moment all was peace and the next moment they looked into sullen, furious faces.

"Why—what the devil?" the tall Englishman muttered. He leaped to his feet with his gun, and so did the other two men. But Mayli put her hand on his arm and turned the bayonet point down.

"You and your guns," she murmured. "Put down your gun—tell the others to put theirs down. Sit down all of you and go on eating." Unwillingly the men obeyed. Then she held out her hands to the people and showed them empty and bare. She took up a gun, shook her head and put it down. She pointed up the roadway, and signified that they were going on. She took out money and paid the innkeeper for the food. Then she motioned to the others. "Come," she said, "show no fear. Let us go together as though nothing were wrong."

Whether it was because of her calm or because she spoke in a language they did not know, the people allowed them to pass, but then closed in behind them and pressed close as they walked.

While this was happening, Sheng and his men and the Englishman with them had entered the town and seen the great crowd and halted.

"Is this the enemy?" Sheng asked Charlie.

"Let us go down a side street," Charlie said, "and avoid whatever it is."

At that very moment they heard a voice shouting in English, "Let's run for it!"

"I'll be damned," the Englishman with Sheng said when he heard this voice, and they all stood still and stared ahead of them. In a moment they saw three Englishmen holding the hands of Chinese women and running toward them. Behind them came a yelling mob, ready for attack. Sheng and those with him fired their guns over the heads of the crowd. At the sound of these guns the crowd stopped, then turned and went back into their town.

It was only now that Sheng and Mayli saw each other, and for one full instant each stood staring at the other. Then Mayli ran toward him. "Sheng!" she cried. "It is you! And your arm—is it healed?"

But Sheng, as soon as he saw Mayli and the company she was in, was thrown into a turmoil of jealousy. Who were these white men with whom she traveled? And he remembered with sharp pain how easily she talked with white people and he felt the old wall of difference between him and Mayli. He looked very cold and put on a false smile and said, "I see you are with friends. As for my arm, it is healed enough to fight with."

At this Mayli stopped and stamped her foot in the dust of the rough road and shouted at Sheng, "What do you mean, you Sheng? What are you thinking? How can you speak to me so?"

But Pansiao went up to him and put her hand on his arm and said, "Brother, now that you are here, we can leave these strangers."

"I am not sure you wish to leave them," Sheng said with his great eyes full of anger still on Mayli.

Mayli suddenly felt weary enough to lie down in the road and die. Her lips began to tremble and Charlie saw it. He said to Sheng, "Elder Brother, ought you to be angry when she has just escaped so great a danger?" And as he spoke, his eyes went sidewise at Pansiao and she looked sidewise at him and he said to her, "Are you well?" and she said, "Yes," and with these few words each felt much was said.

All this time the Englishmen had looked on, much astonished and understanding not one word. The Englishman with Sheng stood silent with doubt because he had run away from his army. But now the tall Englishman went toward him with his hand outstretched as white men do when they see each other.

"I say, you're English," he said.

That other one put out his hand and smiled eagerly. "Rather," he said.

"We were taken prisoner by the Japs," the tall one said, "but we got away."

"I say," the other one answered, then he went on carefully, "I got lost myself. The retreat was frightful, wasn't it?"

"Frightful," the tall one agreed.

Then all the Englishmen came together, shaking hands and murmuring to one another in low voices, and in a moment the two kinds, English and Chinese, stood separate again. It was a strange moment. Around them was the brilliant green of the country that was foreign to them all. The sky above their heads was smooth and blue, but in the west thunderheads piled themselves slowly higher on the horizon. There was no one in sight and the air was silent and hot about them. They were for this moment cut off from the whole world, alone and yet apart. The Englishmen stood together, bearded and filthy and in diffident unease. The Chinese stood together in their faded and torn uniforms, barefoot, bareheaded, their eyes cool, and behind them was the Indian, but no one heeded him. Mayli looked at Sheng. Then she said, "Shall we go on?"

"Go on with them?" he asked, thrusting out his chin at the Englishmen. "No," he said, "I have had enough."

She turned to the Englishmen and said, "Where do you go?"

"Westward," the tall one said, "to India."

They turned their eyes westward and there were the thunderheads slowly rising. They were silver-edged against the sun, but on the horizon they massed black.

"There will be a storm," she said.

"I daresay," the Englishman said, "but it won't be the first we've had."

They hesitated a moment longer. Then the Englishman put his hand into his pocket and took out the compass she had let him carry through the jungle.

"I say, here's your compass—thanks awfully," he said.

She was moved for a moment to tell him to keep it, for how

could those Englishmen find their way unguided? But Chung had given her the compass and she did not wish to give it away, so she took it in silence. Then the Englishman shouldered his gun. His face was pale and tired but his eyes were resolute. "Well," he said abruptly, "we'd better be moving on."

He turned sharply as he spoke and strode off, and behind him the other Englishmen in their dirty, sweat-streaked uniforms fell in smartly. And so they marched away down the road toward India. The Chinese stood watching as the brave and tattered figures grew small against the thunderous sky and then were lost in the rising darkness.

But here was the strangest instant of this strange moment. That man from India who all through these days had followed silently and faithfully behind Sheng now darted after the Englishmen. This he did without a sound, with no cry or word of farewell. They saw his wild face for one instant, the whites of his great sad eyes and the flash of his white teeth. Then he was gone.

All were too amazed at first to speak, until Sheng said, looking at Charlie, "That man of India—has he still his knife?"

And Charlie said, "You know he lives with it in his hand and he sleeps with it under his pillow."

"Then the outlook is not good," Sheng said grimly.

As the Chinese stood, a deep wind began to come out of the clouds. It rose steadily with a distant roar, and hearing it, Mayli was troubled and turned to Sheng. "Where shall we go?" she asked. "I am afraid of that storm."

Sheng examined the clouds curling and boiling over the western sky. "Certainly we must escape it," he said soberly.

Now they looked toward the east and they saw the sky there was still clear and blue.

"Let us go home," Sheng said suddenly.

And Pansiao, hearing the word home, cried out, "Oh, I want to go home."

"Home—home," the weary women sighed.

But Mayli said sadly, "Between us and home there are

hundreds of miles of jungles and mountains and rivers. Can we go so far on foot?"

"I go," Sheng said.

He set off at once and Pansiao ran after him and Charlie went after her and one by one the women followed until only Mayli still stood, too weary, she told herself, to take up so long a march. Ahead of them the pure bright sky shone still more clearly. But could she walk toward it?

Sheng stopped and looked back at her. "Do you come with me?" he shouted.

Yet she hesitated. What if they never reached home? "Sheng!" she cried. "Will you promise me—"

He cut across her pleading voice. "I make no promises," he shouted. "I am not one of those men who make promises!"

She saw him standing tall and straight in the livid light. If she stayed here, or if she ran after those Englishmen, would not the storm overtake her? The sunlight still fell upon the land from the clear sky ahead. What could she do except go with Sheng? And promises were nothing but words, and words were bubbles of air, falling easily from men's lips, and then broken and gone as though they had never been. She bent her head. No, even though he would not promise—

"I am coming," she said, and so they began the march home.

FAR AWAY IN Ling Tan's house Jade sat watching her sons play on the threshing floor in front of the door. It was near noon and in a little while Lao Ta and Lao Er would come home to their noon meal. They were in the fields, cutting the ripe wheat. It was a heavy harvest and they had twice thinned it secretly so that the enemy inspectors, searching the fields, could not see how good a harvest it was. The secret grain they had threshed by night, and it was hidden in the bins in the cave under the kitchen.

Jade was sewing on a garment of Lao Er's, despising the stuff of which it was made as she stitched. Someday, she mused, she would weave once more the old fine strong blue cloth that lasted from father to son, someday when they were free again. Yes, they would be free again, she knew it. There was no promise for eye to see nor for ear to hear, and yet men and women, in the midst of present evil, had begun to hope out of their own unyielding hearts. Out of such musing she lifted her head from her sewing and saw the two men coming across the fields, their sickles in their hands. They walked side by side, sturdy and strong.

She rose to go into the house and put the meal on the table. Then she stopped, for she heard an uproar from her twin sons. They were quarreling, the larger one against the smaller, and she was about to defend the smaller one, for he was bawling and hard pressed. Then she did not. She only stood watching the two while this weeping went on, waiting to see how they fought this battle.

Suddenly she saw the small fellow stop weeping and she saw his face set itself in fury as he flew at the bigger one with all his strength, his anger bitter in his face and strong in his arm. And she laughed.

"Good, my son!" she called. "Fight for yourself—fight, fight!"

And she went into the house, content.

PAVILION
OF WOMEN

PAVILION OF WOMEN

A CONDENSATION OF THE BOOK BY

Pearl S. Buck

ILLUSTRATED BY SKIP LIEPKE

The elegant and beautiful
Madame Wu seemed to
possess everything a
Chinese woman of her time
could want—a kind, adoring
husband, three well-grown
sons and a renowned family
name. Yet something was
missing from her life;
something neither rank nor
riches could provide.
Thus, on her fortieth
birthday Madame Wu makes
the fateful decision to
seek in her own way for
that elusive thing that
will fulfill her life.
The moving story of her
search and of the man who
helps to guide her make
this a deeply personal
and richly textured novel.

I

Iᴛ ᴡᴀs her fortieth birthday. Madame Wu sat before the tilted mirror of her toilet case and looked at her own calm face, comparing it with the face she had seen in this same mirror when she was sixteen. On that day, she had risen from her marriage bed early, and putting on her new chamber robe, she had come into this same room and had sat quietly before the dressing table. "Can it be that I look the same today as yesterday?" she had asked herself on that first morning after her marriage. She had examined her face minutely—long eyes, delicate nose, small red mouth and the oval of cheeks and chin. Then Ying, her new maid, had hurried in.

"Oh, miss—madam," she had faltered. "I thought today you would not be so early!"

"I like to get up early," Madame Wu had replied in her gentle voice, the voice that in the night the husband—whom she had never seen before their wedding day—had told her was like the voice of a singing bird.

At this moment, twenty-four years later, as though she knew

what her mistress was remembering, Ying spoke, her hands busy with the coils of Madame Wu's shining, straight black hair. "My lady, you have changed not at all in these twenty-four years," she said.

"Are you thinking of that morning, too?" Madame Wu replied.

Ying laughed loudly. "I was more shy than you were that morning, my lady," she said. "*Ai ya*, how shy I was then—it's only natural, what goes on between men and women, but then it seemed some sort of magic!"

Madame Wu smiled. She allowed Ying complete freedom in all she said, but when she did not wish to carry on the conversation, she made her smile fleeting and kept silent after it. Ying fell silent, too. She put two jade pins into the coil, and wetting her hands with an oiled perfume, she smoothed Madame Wu's already sleek head.

"My jade earrings," Madame Wu then said.

"I knew you would want to wear them today!" Ying exclaimed. "I have them ready."

She opened a small box covered with flowered silk and took out the earrings and fastened them carefully. Twenty-four years ago young Mr. Wu had come into this room with this box. Since he was too well-mannered to speak to his bride before a servant, he had handed the box to Ying, saying, "Put these on your mistress."

He had stood watching while Ying put the flawless jade earrings on Madame Wu. Madame Wu had seen his face in this very mirror, the handsome face of a willful and proud young man.

"*Ai*," he had said, in a sigh of pleasure. Madame Wu's eyes met his in the mirror and each took measure of the other. "Go and fetch me hot tea," he had said abruptly to Ying, and the maid had scuttled away.

Then they were alone again, as they had been in the night. He had put his hands on her shoulders and stared beyond her into the face in the mirror. "If you had been ugly," he had said, "I would have killed you last night on the pillow."

She had smiled at this. "But why?" she had asked. "To have sent me home would have been enough."

At this moment twenty-four years later, Ying now said, "Jade is as beautiful as ever against your skin. It is no wonder that the master has never wanted another wife."

"Do not speak quite so loudly," Madame Wu said. "He is still asleep."

"He should wake early on your fortieth birthday, madam," Ying replied.

"I will have my breakfast," Madame Wu said to Ying. "After I have eaten, I will speak with my eldest son. And then you will dress me for the feast at noon."

Madame Wu rose from the chair. A woman's fortieth birthday in a rich and old-fashioned family was a day of dignity. She remembered very well when her husband's mother had passed such a day, twenty-two years ago. On that day the old lady had formally given over to her the management of the big house with its many members. For twenty-two years Madame Wu had held this management, skillfully maintaining its outward habits so that the old lady did not notice the changes. Thus when the overgrown peony bushes just outside these rooms died one winter, she called it to the old lady's attention. Hadn't something else better be planted there for a generation or two? "Narcissus?" Madame Wu, then eighteen, had suggested gently. "Orchids? Flowering shrubs?" She had put orchids—her preference—in the middle of the sentence so that the old lady would think she did not care for them.

"Orchids," the old lady said. She was fond of her daughter-in-law, but she liked to show her own authority.

Within five years Madame Wu had the finest orchid garden in the city. Now, in the early part of the sixth month of the year, the delicate silver-gray blossoms of the first orchids were beginning to bloom. She went into this garden and plucked two of the scentless gray flowers and took them back with her into her sitting room, where her breakfast was waiting. A maidservant came in, smiling. She carried a plate of long-life steamed rolls, very hot. They were made in the shape of peaches, the symbol of immortality, and each one was sprayed with red dye.

"Long life, long life, mistress!" the maidservant called in a hearty voice. "We servants bring these for good luck. The cook made them himself."

"Thank you," Madame Wu said mildly, "thank you all."

Out of courtesy she took one of the steaming rolls and broke it open. A dark sweet filling was inside, made of crushed beans and red sugar. "It is delicious," she said and began to eat.

The maidservant leaned forward. "I ought not to tell you," she said in a loud whisper, "but I do it because I think of the good of the house. That old head cook is charging three times the price he pays for fuel. He thinks he can do anything because he is married to Ying and Ying is your maid."

Madame Wu's clear black eyes took on a look of distance. "When he brings in the accounts, I will remember," she said. Her voice was cool.

The maidservant went away, and Madame Wu resumed her thoughts. She had no intention on this day of resigning her position to Meng, the wife of her eldest son. She had three sons, two of whom already had wives. The old lady had had only the one, and so there had been no question of jealousy between young wives. Madame Wu's eldest son, Liangmo, had been married in the old-fashioned way. She had chosen his wife for him, the daughter of her oldest friend, Madame Kang. It had not been her intention to marry Liangmo so quickly, since he was only nineteen; but her second son, Tsemo, who had gone to school in Shanghai, had fallen in love with Rulan, a girl two years older than he, and had insisted upon marriage at eighteen. This meant that Rulan was older than her sister-in-law, Meng, who was nevertheless her superior in the house. Out of this embarrassment, Madame Wu's only refuge had been to keep her own place for the next few years.

She had long looked forward to this birthday. Everyone else

in the family was still sleeping as she finished her breakfast. She was a little surprised, therefore, when she heard a commotion in the court just beyond her own. "It is not every day that my best friend is forty years old! Does it matter if I am too early?"

She recognized the voice of Madame Kang, the mother of Meng, the wife of her eldest son, and she made haste to the door of the court. "Come, please," she exclaimed and held out both her hands.

Madame Kang lumbered across the court toward her friend. She had grown fat over the years, while Madame Wu had remained slender. "Ailien," Madame Kang exclaimed, "am I the first to wish you long life and immortality?"

"The first," Madame Wu said, smiling.

"Then I am not too early," Madame Kang said and looked reproachfully at Ying, who had tried to delay her.

"I had rather see you than anyone," Madame Wu said. Their mothers had been friends, and while they had gambled all day and late into the night, their two little girls had come to be as close as sisters.

Madame Wu linked her slim fingers into her friend's plump ones and drew her into the orchid garden with her. Under a drooping willow tree two bamboo chairs stood, and toward these the ladies moved. A small oval pool lay at their feet. Blue water lilies floated on the surface, and minute goldfish darted in and out among the pads.

"How is your eldest son?" Madame Wu asked her friend. During the years when Madame Wu had borne her three living sons and three children who had died, Madame Kang had borne eleven children, six of whom were girls. There was none of the peace of this court to be found in Madame Kang's house. There, fat, good-natured Madame Kang was surrounded by a continuous uproar of children and bondmaids and servants.

"He is no better," Madame Kang said. Her round face was suddenly woeful.

"I will send Ying with a bowl of broth made after an old recipe for just such a cough as he has. I have used it often on my first and third sons."

"You are always kind," Madame Kang said gratefully. She looked lovingly at her friend. "Ailien, I did not know what to bring you for a birthday gift. So I brought this—" She reached into the bosom of her blue satin robe and brought out a little box.

Madame Wu recognized the box. "Ah, Meichen, do you really want to give me your pearls?"

"Yes, I do." Across her plain good face passed a flicker of pain.

"Why?" Madame Wu asked, perceiving it.

Madame Kang hesitated. "The last time I wore them, my sons' father said they looked like dewdrops on a melon." She smiled. Then tears came to her eyes and rolled slowly down her cheeks.

Madame Wu saw them without appearing to do so. She had often heard Madame Kang talk of her difficulties with Mr. Kang. Neither of them had ever talked of Mr. Wu. "I have been wanting for a long time to tell you something," she said after a moment. "At first, when I began thinking about it, I thought I would ask your advice. But—I have not. Now it is beyond advice. It has already become certainty."

"Whatever you want to tell me," Madame Kang said.

Madame Wu lifted her eyes. "Meichen, I have decided that today I shall ask my sons' father to take a concubine."

Madame Kang's round mouth dropped open. "Has he—has he, too—" she gasped.

"He has not," Madame Wu said. "No, it is nothing like that. No, it is only for his own sake—and mine."

"But how—for you?"

"I wish for it," Madame Wu said. She was gazing into the depths of the clear little pool.

"But will he consent?" Madame Kang asked gravely. "He has always loved you."

"He will not consent at first," Madame Wu said tranquilly.

Madame Kang was full of questions. "But will you choose the girl—or he? And, Ailien, if she has children, can you bear it? Oh, me, is there not always trouble in a house where two women are under one man's roof?"

"I cannot complain of it if he takes her at my wish," Madame Wu said.

Someone coughed, and both ladies looked up. Ying stood in the doorway and behind her was Liangmo, Madame Wu's eldest son.

"Mother, I should have come before to wish you long life," he said.

"Come in, my son," she said.

"Long life, Mother!" Liangmo said with affection. "And greetings to my son's other grandmother."

Madame Wu accepted his greeting with a graceful bow, but Madame Kang rose hastily. "Excuse me," she said. "I left my family affairs unsettled." She bowed and walked out of the court with heavy footsteps.

Madame Wu sat down again in one of the bamboo chairs and motioned Liangmo to the other. "How well you look, son," she said, examining his handsome young face. He was, if possible, more handsome than his father had been at the same age, for he had something of her own delicacy, too. This morning he wore a long robe of summer silk, the color of pale green water. His dark short hair was brushed back, his dark olive skin was smooth, and his eyes were quiet with content.

I have married him happily, Madame Wu thought. "And the little child, my grandson?" she asked aloud.

"I have not seen him this morning," Liangmo replied, "but had he been ill, I would have heard of it."

He could not keep from answering his mother's smile. There was great affection between them. He trusted her wisdom far more than he did his own. When she had asked him to marry before the marriage of his younger brother to avoid confusion in the family, he had said at once, "Choose someone

141

for me, Mother. You know me better than I know myself." He was completely satisfied with his pretty wife, Meng, and with the son she had given him within a year of their marriage.

"I have been saving some good news for this day, Mother," he said.

"It is a day for good news," Madame Wu replied.

"My son's mother is to have her second child," he announced proudly. "She told me three days ago, and I said we would wait until your birthday to tell it to the family."

"That is good news indeed," Madame Wu said warmly. "I shall send her a present."

At this moment her eyes fell on the little box of pearls. "I have the gift," she exclaimed. She took up the box and opened it. "Her own mother gave me these pearl earrings. But pearls are for young wives, I think, and it would be fitting for me to give them to her daughter. I will go to her with you. But first, my son, I have decided upon a thing, and I feel I should tell you what I am planning to do. I have decided to invite your father to take a concubine." She said these stupendous words in a calm voice.

Liangmo heard them without understanding them. Then they crowded his mind and deafened him like thunder. His handsome face paled. "Mother!" he gasped. "Mother, has he—has my father—"

"Certainly not," she said. "Your father is still so youthful and so handsome that it is no wonder that even you should put that question. No, he has been and is most faithful."

She paused, then went on, "No, I have my own reasons for the decision. But I should like to be assured that you, my eldest son, will accept her coming and help the family to accept it."

By now Liangmo had recovered himself. "Of course, the matter is between you and my father," he said. "But if you will let me step beyond my place, I beg you will not ask it of him if it is not his wish. We are a happy family. How do we know what a strange woman will bring into the house? Her children will be the same age as your grandchildren. Will this not be confusing the generations? If she is very young, will not your sons' wives be jealous of her position? I can foresee many sorrows."

"Perhaps you cannot understand, at your age, the relationship between men and women of my generation," Madame Wu replied. "But it is because I have always been happy with your father, and he with me, that I have decided upon the step. I require of you only to obey your mother in this as you have in all things. You have been the best of sons. What you say will influence your younger brothers."

Liangmo struggled against this in his own mind. But so deep was his habit of obedience to his mother that he obeyed her now. "I will, Mother, but I will not pretend that what you have told me does not sadden this day."

She smiled slightly. "I am really saving you greater sadness on other days," she said. So she rose and took up the box of pearls. "Come," she said. "We will go and see Meng, and I will give her my gift."

He stood beside her, young and strongly built as his father was, head and shoulders above her. She put out her little hand and rested it on his arm in a gesture of affection so rare that it startled him. She did not easily endure the touch of another human being, even her own child. "In you," she said distinctly, "I have built my house upon a rock."

MENG WAS PLAYING with her little boy in the courtyard of her own house within this great house. She was alone with him except for his wet nurse, who squatted on her heels, laughing and watching. Both young women, mother and nurse, poured out the love and attention the child demanded all day long.

Meng's breasts had been full of milk. But no one, not even she herself, had thought of allowing the baby to pull at them and spoil their firmness. Lien had been hired to provide milk. She was the young wife of one of the farmers on the Wu lands. Her own child, also a boy, was being fed flour and water and rice gruel by his grandmother instead of his mother's milk. For this reason he was now thin and small and yellow, while Lien's nursling was fat and rosy. Lien was allowed to go home once a month, and when she saw her child, she would weep and put him to her breast, but the child would turn away his head. He had never tasted his mother's milk, and he did not know how to suckle. By midafternoon Lien's breasts would be aching, and she would hasten back to the Wu house. There her nursling would be waiting for her, shouting with rage and hunger, and at the sight of him she would forget her own child.

Now Meng and Lien laughed together as the child grasped her breast like a cup and drank. To see the two women as they watched the child, it would have been hard to tell from the two faces which was the mother. The child smiled radiantly on both. He was learning to walk, and he took a few steps from one to the other, laughing and falling upon each in turn.

"A little godling," Lien said fondly.

Before Meng could do more than smile, they heard footsteps. The child ran to Lien, and from her arms stared at his grandmother and father. "Here you are, Meng," Madame Wu said. "Sit down, child. Rest yourself, please. Come here to me, son of my son."

Lien pushed the little boy forward and inched herself along on her heels so that he was always in the shelter of her arms. Thus he stood at Madame Wu's knee and stared at her with large black eyes. "A lovely boy," she murmured. She turned her eyes from the child's face and remembered why she had come. "Meng, Liangmo tells me you have added happiness," she said. "I have come to thank you and to bring you a gift."

Meng blushed and put out both hands to receive the gift. "My mother's pearls!" she breathed.

"She gave them to me, but I am too old for pearls," Madame Wu said. "Now everything happens for good in this house. You declared your happiness today and I had these pearls ready to give you."

"I have always craved these pearls," Meng said. She opened the box and gazed down at the jewels.

"Put them on," Liangmo commanded her.

Meng obeyed. "I used to put them on and beg my mother to let me keep them," she confessed.

"Now you have earned them," Madame Wu said. She turned to her son. "See how rosy the pearls have become against Meng's skin. They were silver gray."

"*Ai ya*," Lien cried. "She must not look too pretty or the baby will be a girl!"

They laughed, and Madame Wu said as she rose to depart, "I would welcome a girl. After all, there must be female in the world as well as male, is it not true, Meng?"

But Meng was too shy to answer such a question.

It was the hour of the birthday feast. Madame Wu had taken her place at the left of the old lady, who had been given the highest seat. Mr. Wu sat on his mother's right, and on the other side of him sat Liangmo. Tsemo, the second son, sat on Madame Wu's left, and on Tsemo's left sat Fengmo, the third son.

Madame Wu looked with pleasure on this great gathering of her family. At six other tables there were uncles and aunts and cousins and friends and their children, and at one table Madame Kang presided. All had sent gifts to Madame Wu before this day. These gifts were of many kinds—vases, cakes and sweets, scrolls of silk, each carrying a good wish in gold paper characters. As their gift, the family had ordered a painting, by the best artist in the city, of the goddess of long life. In the place of honor, the painted goddess held the immortal peach in her hand; by her side was a stag; red bats flew about her head in blessing. All the guests agreed as to its beauty when they came to offer their first greetings to Madame Wu.

To all their good wishes Liangmo responded for Madame Wu. Before they were seated, he and Meng, as the eldest son and daughter-in-law of the house, had gone to each table and thanked the guests.

Now and again Madame Wu rose from her seat and moved among the guests to make sure that all of them had been properly served. When she had done so twice, Mr. Wu said, "I beg you not to rise again, my sons' mother. I will take your place when the sweet is served."

When the sugared rice with its eight precious fruits was brought in, Mr. Wu went to every table and begged the guests to eat heartily of the delicacy. Madame Wu followed him with her eyes. Did she imagine that he lingered a moment beside Madame Kang's pretty third daughter? The child's hair was curled in the foreign fashion, for she had been to school for a year in Shanghai. Now she frequently made her mother and father wretched because she was discontented with life in this small provincial city.

Madame Wu watched her as the girl lifted her head and replied pertly to something Mr. Wu had said. When he returned, she looked at him with clear eyes. "Thank you, my sons' father," she said, and her voice was music.

The feast went on. Instead of rice the cook had made long fine noodles, a symbol of long life. Madame Wu wound them with graceful skill around her chopsticks, but the old lady had no such patience. She held the heaped bowl to her mouth with her left hand and pushed the noodles into it with her chopsticks like a child. "I shall be ill tonight," she said in her penetrating voice. "But it is worth it, daughter, on your fortieth birthday."

One by one, the guests rose with small wine bowls in their hands, and toasts were drunk. To these Madame Wu did not reply. She looked at Mr. Wu, who rose in her place and accepted the good wishes of all. Madame Kang, catching her friend's eye, silently lifted her bowl and as silently Madame Wu lifted hers and the two drank together in secret understanding. After this moment, Liangmo looked at her with pleading in his eyes, but she merely smiled a little and looked away.

By this time the old lady was full, and she staggered to her feet. "I am going to bed," she said. "I must prepare to be ill."

Madame Wu rose. "Do go, Mother," she said. She waited while two servants led the old lady out, and all the others stood. Then she looked at Mr. Wu. "Will you take your guests to the main hall?" she directed gently. "The ladies will come into my own sitting room." She moved away as she spoke and the women followed her.

In Madame Wu's sitting room, the talk ebbed and flowed. She herself spoke little, but her silence was not noticed because she was by habit a silent woman. A small troupe of actors had been hired for entertainment, and they performed their tricks. The women watched while they sipped hot tea of the finest leaves plucked before the summer rains. Madame Kang slept a little. Madame Wu said to Ying, "Go and see if the old lady is ill."

Ying went away and came back laughing. "She has cast up everything," she told Madame Wu. "But she still says it was worth it."

Everyone laughed, and at the sound of the laughter Madame Kang woke. "It is time we went home," she said to Madame Wu. "We must not weary you, Ailien, for you are to live a hundred years."

Madame Wu smiled and rose as one by one the guests came to her to say good-by. So at last she was alone again, and she allowed herself to be weary for one moment. Then she straightened her slender shoulders. It was too soon to be weary. The day had not yet ended.

AN HOUR LATER, after she had rested, Madame Wu arose and went to her dressing table. Ying came in and helped her undress. Then she let down Madame Wu's long hair and began to comb it in firm strokes with a fine-toothed sandalwood comb. In the mirror she saw how large and black Madame Wu's eyes looked. "Are you tired, my lady?" Ying asked.

"Not at all," Madame Wu replied.

But Ying went on, "You have had a long day. And, my lady,

now that you are forty years old, I think you ought not to work so hard."

"Perhaps you are right," Madame Wu replied. "I have been thinking of such things myself. Ying, I shall ask my sons' father to take a young wife."

She said this so calmly that for a moment she knew Ying had not comprehended. Then she felt the comb stop and Ying's hand tightened on the hair at the nape of her neck. "It is not necessary for you to speak," Madame Wu said. The comb began to move again too quickly. "You are pulling my hair," she added.

Ying threw the comb on the floor. "I will not take care of any lady but you!" she burst forth.

"It is not asked of you," Madame Wu replied.

But Ying went down on her knees on the tiled floor beside Madame Wu, and she wept and wiped her eyes with the corner of her new sateen jacket. "Oh, my mistress!" she sobbed. "Does he compel you, my precious? Has he forgotten all your goodness and your beauty? My lady, please tell me just one thing—"

"It is my own will," Madame Wu said firmly. "Ying, get up from your knees."

Ying rose and took up the comb from the floor and, sniffling in her tears, continued to comb Madame Wu's hair.

Madame Wu began to speak in a quiet, reasonable voice. "I tell you first, Ying, so that you know how to behave among the servants. When the young woman comes—"

"Who is she?" Ying asked.

"I have not decided," Madame Wu said. "But she is to be received as one honored in the house, a little lower than I am, a little higher than any of my sons' wives. Above all, there is not to be a word spoken against my sons' father, for it is I who will invite the young woman to come."

Ying could not bear this. "My lady, since we have been together so many years, is it all right for me to ask you why?"

"You may ask, but I will not tell you," Madame Wu said.

In silence Ying finished scenting and braiding Madame Wu's hair. Then she opened the door of the bedroom. It was still empty, for Mr. Wu never came in until Ying had gone away. "Shall I not draw the bed curtains?" Ying asked. "The moonlight is too bright."

"No," Madame Wu said, "let me see the moonlight."

So the curtains remained behind the big silver hooks, and Ying felt the teapot, and she saw that the matches were beside the candle.

"Until tomorrow," Madame Wu said.

"Until tomorrow, my lady," Ying said and went away.

Madame Wu lay very still and straight under the silken sheet and the soft summer quilt. The moonlight shone on the wall opposite her bed. She lay, not thinking, not remembering, but simply being all that she was. She was neither waiting nor expecting. If he did not come tonight, she would presently fall asleep and tell him at another time. Times were chosen and appointed. If one forced them, they were wrong. All the quiet strength of her decision would gather around the opportune moment, and then it would become actually right.

At this moment she heard the footsteps of Mr. Wu in the courtyard. He came through the outer room and into her sitting room. Her sensitive nostrils caught the smell of heated wine. But she was not disturbed, for he did not drink to excess at any time, and tonight of course he had been drinking with friends at the end of a feast day. He had his pipe in his hand, and he was about to put it on the table. Then he delayed for an instant. "Are you tired?" he asked abruptly.

"Not at all tired," she replied tranquilly.

He put the pipe down, and then got into bed. Since this was the last night that she would spend with him, she was careful to be almost exactly the median of what she had always been. That is, she was neither cold nor ardent. She was pleasant; she was tender. Fulfillment and not surfeit was her natural gift in all things.

"You were more beautiful today than you have ever been," he murmured. In the half-light of the candle on the floor by the bed, she saw his dark eyes flicker and burn with a flame certainly more intense than she had seen for a long time. She closed her eyes, and her heart began to quicken. Would she regret her decision? She lay for the next two hours, thinking about her decision, and at the end, she knew she would not regret it.

While he slept, she rose and went silently into her bathroom and bathed herself in cool water. She did not go back to bed but went instead to the window and stood watching the sky. Peace filled her being. She would never sleep in this room again. She had already chosen her place. Next to the old lady's court was an empty court where Mr. Wu's father had once lived. It was a beautiful court in the very center of the great house. She would live there, alone and at peace.

Mr. Wu suddenly yawned and woke. "I ought to go back to my own rooms," he said. "You have had a long day—you should sleep."

Whenever he said that, and he always said it, being a courteous man, she replied, "Do not move, I beg you. I can sleep very well." But tonight she answered, "Thank you, father of my sons. Perhaps you are right."

He was so astonished at this that he climbed out of the bed and fumbled for his slippers on the floor. She came quickly and knelt and found them, and still kneeling, she put them on his feet. He suddenly leaned his head on her shoulder and twined his arms about her body. "You are more fragrant than jasmine," he murmured. He drew her toward him again, and she grew alarmed.

"Please," she said, "may I help you to rise?" She rose, suddenly steel-strong, and pulled him upward with her.

"Have I offended you?" he asked.

"No," she said. "How can you offend me after twenty-four years? But—I have come to an end."

"Come to an end?" he repeated.

"Today I am forty years old," she said. She knew suddenly that this was the moment. She moved away from him, and then she lit one candle after another until the room was full of light. Then she sat down by the table and he sat on the bed.

"I have been preparing for this day for many years," she told him. In her white silken garments, in the moonlight, she summoned all the forces of her being. He leaned forward, staring at her.

"I have been a good wife to you," she began.

"Have I not been a good husband to you?" he asked.

"That, always," she replied. "As men and women go, there could not be better than we have had. But now half of my life is over."

"Only half," he said.

"Yet the same half of your life is far away," she went on. "Heaven has made this difference between men and women. You are a young man still. Your fires are burning and strong. But I have completed myself."

He straightened his lounging body, and his full handsome face grew stern. "Can it be that I understand what you mean?" he asked.

"I see that you do understand," she replied.

"I do not want another woman." His voice was rough. "I have never looked at another woman. You are still more beautiful than any woman I ever saw." He hesitated, and his eyes fell from her face to his hands. "I saw that young girl today—and when I saw her, I thought how much more beautiful you are than she!"

She knew at once what young girl he meant. "Ah, Linyi is pretty," she agreed.

He pursed his smooth lips. "What would my friends say? I have never been a man to go after women."

She laughed softly and was amazed as she laughed that she suffered a small pang in her breast. If he could begin to think of how it would seem to his friends, then he would be soon persuaded, sooner than she had thought.

He looked at her. "Have you ceased altogether to love me?" he asked.

She leaned forward toward him. "I love you as well as ever," she said. "I want nothing but your happiness."

"How can this be my happiness?" he asked sadly.

"You know that I have always held your happiness in my hands," she replied. She lifted her two hands as though they held a heart. "I have held it like this ever since I first saw your face on our wedding day. I shall hold it like this until I die."

"If you die before me, my happiness will be buried with you," he said.

"No, for I will put it into other hands, hands I will prepare for it," she said.

He sat motionless, his eyes on her hands.

"Trust me," she whispered.

"I have always trusted you," he said.

She let her hands fall.

He went on doggedly, "I do not promise, I cannot, so quickly—"

"You need not promise," she said. "I would not force you even if I could. We will put this aside now. Go back to bed and let me cover you. The night is cool—it is almost dawn."

He obeyed her unwillingly. "Remember I have promised you nothing," he kept saying.

"Nothing," she agreed, "nothing!" And tenderly she drew the covers over him.

But he held her hand fast. "Where will you sleep?" he demanded.

"Oh—I have my bed ready," she said half playfully. "To-morrow we will meet. Nothing will be changed in the house. We will be friends, I promise you."

He let her go, lulled by her soothing voice. She walked softly to the court next to the old lady's. A few days ago she had had fresh bedding put upon the mattress. Into this bed she now crept. It felt chilly, and she trembled for a moment with a sudden strange deathlike fatigue. Then she fell asleep.

II

MADAME WU woke with a new feeling of lightness. She lay in her new bed alone and delicately probed her heart. She knew it would have been ineffably comforting to her had Mr. Wu been ready to enter into the latter half of life with her, if out of his own fulfillment, he had reached the same point of life that she had. Why had Heaven not made women so that their beauty and fertility might last as long as man lived and fade only with the generation? Why should a man's need to plant his seed continue too long for fulfillment in one woman?

Women, she thought, are therefore more lonely than men, and so Heaven has prepared them. Heaven put the bearing of children above all else so that mankind would survive. Any woman who clung to a man beyond the time of her fertility was defying Heaven's decree.

Who was this young newcomer to be? Madame Wu decided that she would send for the old woman who had been the go-between for Meng. She had employed a go-between even with her friend, for fear that Madame Kang in her kindness would demand too little. Old Liu Ma must be called, Madame Wu thought, and I will tell her plainly just what I want.

Then she let her mind drift to these rooms in which she now would live. She would make very few changes here. She had always been fond of the old man who had been her father-in-law. Since he had never had a daughter, he had put aside the convention that forbade a man to speak to his son's wife. Many times he had even sent for her so that he might read to her something from the books in his library. It gave her pleasure to think that the library full of books was now hers. Today, after years of giving her body and mind to others, she felt she needed to drink deeply at old springs.

Someone knocked at the door. "Come in!" she called.

Ying came in, looking frightened. "I did not know where

you were," she stammered. "I went everywhere. I even went into your old room and woke up the master, and he was angry with me."

"You will find me here now every morning until I die," Madame Wu said calmly.

THE NEWS FILTERED through the household as the day went on. Son told wife, and one wife told another, and Ying told the cook, and the head cook told the undercook, and so by the end of the day there was not a soul in the house who did not know that Madame Wu had moved into the old gentleman's rooms. Madame Wu had purposely not told the old lady. She knew that the old lady would hear it from her maid, and this was good, for then the old lady's first temper would be spent on a servant. After this was over, the old lady would not know whether to quarrel first with her son or with her son's wife. If she went first to Madame Wu, it would mean she blamed her. If she went first to her son, it would mean she felt her son was at fault.

Toward noon, when Madame Wu was going over the month's accounts, she saw the old lady's maid leading her across the court. Madame Wu rose and went to her side. When she took her elbow, the old lady pushed her spitefully. "Don't touch me," she said peevishly. "I am very angry with you."

Madame Wu did not answer. She followed the old lady into the sitting room. "You didn't tell me your were moving in here," the old lady said in a harsh voice. "I am never told anything in this house." She sat down as she spoke.

"I should have told you," Madame Wu agreed. "It was very wrong of me. I must ask you to forgive me."

"Have you quarreled with my son?" the old lady asked severely.

"Not at all," Madame Wu replied. "We never quarrel."

"Do not make words for me," the old lady commanded. "I am able to hear the truth."

"I will not make words, Mother," Madame Wu replied.

"Yesterday I was forty years old. I had long made up my mind that when that day came, I would retire from my duties as a female and find someone for my lord who is young."

The old lady peered at her. "Does he love someone else?" she demanded.

"No, there is no other woman," Madame Wu replied. "Your son has been nothing but good to me. I am selfish enough to want to keep fresh between us the good love we have had. This cannot be if I am ridden with fear of a belated child, and surely it cannot be if my own fires slacken while his burn on."

"People will say he has played the fool and you have revenged yourself," the old lady said sternly. "Who will believe you have of your own will withdrawn yourself—unless indeed you have ceased to love him?"

"I have not ceased to love him," Madame Wu said.

"What is love between a man and woman if they don't go to bed together?" the old lady inquired.

Madame Wu paused for a long moment before she answered. "I do not know," she replied at last. "I have always wondered, and perhaps now I shall find out."

The old lady snorted. "I hope that we will not all suffer from this," she said loudly. "I hope that a new troublemaker will not come into this house!"

"That must be my responsibility," Madame Wu admitted. "I should blame myself entirely were such a thing to happen."

The old lady was still aggrieved, but she felt her anger melting against her will. It was true that no woman wanted to conceive after she was forty. She herself had had this misfortune, but luckily the child had died at birth. Yet she remembered as though it were yesterday her deep shame when she knew that she was pregnant at such an age. She had quarreled with her husband through all those months of discontented waiting. "Find yourself a whore," she had told the distressed man. "Go and find yourself some young girl who is always ready!"

The old gentleman had never come near her again, but

he had never loved her as much again, either. Even now as she remembered her anger against him she felt a vague sense of guilt. She groaned, "O Heaven, that has made man and woman of two different earths!"

Madame Wu smiled at this. "You may blame Heaven, and I will not deny it."

There seemed nothing to say after that. The old lady's memories saddened her. And whenever she was sad, she immediately felt hunger also. She turned to Madame Wu with a piteous look. "I am hungry," she said plaintively. "I haven't eaten anything for hours."

Madame Wu said to the maid, "Take her back to her own rooms and let her have anything she wants."

When the old lady had gone, she sat down again to her accounts. No one came near her. The family was unhappy and silent. She studied one book after another, first the house accounts, which the steward kept, then the clothing accounts, then the house repairs and replacements, always heavy in so large a family, and finally the land accounts. The ancestral lands of the Wu family were large and productive, and upon them and the shops the family depended. Madame Wu administered these lands as she did the house. It had been many years since Mr. Wu had done more than read over the accounts before the old year passed. But Madame Wu studied them twice monthly. This time, the accounts were accurate and satisfying. Less had been spent than had been taken in. The granaries were not yet empty and soon the new harvests would be reaped. Watermelons had ripened and were hanging in the deep wells to be cooled. "Nineteen watermelons, seven yellow-hearted, the rest red, hanging in the two north wells," the steward had written. She might have one drawn up tonight before she slept. Watermelons were good for the kidneys.

When the account books were closed, she sat for a moment, enjoying the silence. Then she heard approaching footsteps, clacking lightly on the tiles. She wondered for a moment— leather shoes? Who among the women wore leather shoes?

For it was a woman's footsteps. Rulan, who had come from Shanghai, the wife of Tsemo, her second son. She sighed, reluctant to yield her solitude. But she restrained herself. No one must think she had withdrawn from the house.

"Come here, Rulan," she called. When she looked up, the young woman stood in the doorway, tall and slender. Her face was wide at the eyes, narrow at the chin. Her mouth was square and sullen.

Madame Wu ignored the sullenness. "Come in and sit down, child," she said. "I have just finished our family accounts. We are fortunate—the land has been kind."

The girl was plain, and yet she had flashes of beauty, Madame Wu thought, watching her as she sat down squarely upon a chair. She had none of the polish and courtesy of the other young women in the house. Instead it seemed that Rulan took pleasure in being rude and abrupt.

"Did you come to speak to me about something?" Madame Wu inquired. It was the first time she had ever been alone with Rulan.

Rulan looked disturbed, yet she did not know how to begin.

"Yes, child?" Madame Wu asked mildly.

"Mother," Rulan began, "you have upset everybody."

"Have I?" Madame Wu asked, wondering.

"Yes, you have," Rulan repeated. "Tsemo said I wasn't to come and talk with you. He said that it was Liangmo's duty as the oldest son. But Liangmo won't. He said it would be no use. Meng does nothing but cry. I said someone must come and talk with you."

"And no one came except you." Madame Wu smiled.

Rulan did not smile in reply. "Mother, I have always felt you did not like me, and so I ought to be the last one to come to you."

"Child, you are wrong," Madame Wu said. "There is no one in the world whom I dislike."

Rulan flinched. "I am older than Tsemo, and you do not like me for that. And you never forgave me because we decided ourselves to marry instead of letting you arrange our affairs."

"Of course I did not like that," Madame Wu agreed. "But when I saw you, I knew that Tsemo was happy, and so I was pleased with you. That you are older than he, you cannot help."

"Mother, you must not let Father take another woman," Rulan said impetuously.

"It is not a matter of letting him," Madame Wu said, still mildly. "I have decided that it is the best thing for him."

The color washed out of Rulan's ruddy face. "Mother, do you know what you are doing? It is now actually against the law for a man to take a concubine, do you know that?"

"These new laws," Madame Wu said, "like the new constitution, are still entirely on paper."

She saw that Rulan was taken aback. She had not expected Madame Wu to know about the constitution.

Rulan stared at her in stubborn despair. This cool woman who was her husband's mother was beyond the reach of all anger, all reproach. Rulan knew long ago that against her she could never prevail with Tsemo. His mother's hold upon him was absolute. He was convinced that whatever his mother did was for his own good.

"My child," Madame Wu asked, "what would you do if one day Tsemo should want another wife, someone, say, less full of energy and wit than you are, someone soft and comfortable?"

"I would divorce him at once," Rulan said proudly. "I would not share him with any other woman. And Liangmo told us our father does not want another woman," she added doggedly.

Madame Wu thought, Ah, Liangmo has been talking to his father today! She felt a moment's pity for her husband, now at the mercy of his sons through no fault of his own. She sighed and suddenly wished this young woman would go away. And yet she liked her better than she ever had before. It took courage to come here alone, to speak these blunt words.

"Child," she said, leaning toward Rulan, "I think Heaven is

kind to women, after all. One could not keep bearing children forever. So when a woman is forty, Heaven in its mercy says, 'Now, poor soul, the rest of your life you shall have for yourself. You have divided yourself again and again. Now take what is left and make yourself whole again.' "

"Do you hate us all?" Rulan asked. Her eyes opened wide, and Madame Wu saw for the first time that they were very handsome eyes.

"I love you all more than ever," Madame Wu said.

"Our father, too?" the girl inquired.

"Him, too," Madame Wu said. "Or why would I so eagerly want his happiness?"

"I do not understand you," the girl said after a moment.

"Ah, you are so far from my age," Madame Wu replied. "Be patient with me, child, for knowing what I want."

Rulan rose. "I shall have to go back and tell them," she said. "But I do not think any one of them will understand either."

"Tell them all to be patient with me," Madame Wu said, smiling at her.

In Liangmo's court the two elder sons and their wives talked together until the water clock had passed the first half of the night. The two young husbands felt confused and shy for their father's sake. For their father, too, was a man as they were men now. When they were in their middle years, would it be so with themselves and their wives? They doubted themselves and hid their doubt.

Of the two young wives, Meng was the silent one. She was too happy in her own life to quarrel with anyone for anything. She thought Liangmo to be the handsomest and best of men, and she wondered continually why she had been so fortunate as to be given him for life. She found no fault in him. She was lost in him and content to be lost. To be his, to lie in his arms at night, to serve him by day, to listen to his every word—this was her joy and her mission. And above all, to bear him many children. She was his instrument for immortality.

Rulan was contemptuous of Meng for having no mind of her own. She, too, loved her young husband, and secretly she grieved because Tsemo was not the elder son. He was stronger than Liangmo, quicker and sharp-tongued. Even while she quarreled with Tsemo she loved him well. But quarrel with him she did very often, hating herself for it even while she did. Every quarrel ended with her stormy repentance, and this repentance came from her constant secret fear, hidden even from herself, because she was older and because she knew that she had loved him before he loved her. It was her secret shame that she had set her heart on him in school when they had met, and her heart had compelled her to seek him out with ill-concealed excuses. Hers had been the first offer of friendship, and hers the hand put out first to touch his. She knew that Tsemo had never known a woman and that he was hard-pressed by her love and had yielded to it, but not with his whole being. "You are afraid of your old-fashioned mother!" she had cried.

To this he had answered thoughtfully, "I am afraid of her because she is always right. Even when I wish her to be wrong, I know she is right. She is the wisest woman in the world."

He had said these words innocently, but with them he had thrust a dagger into Rulan's heart. She had come to the Wu house ready to hate Tsemo's mother and be jealous of her. But Madame Wu's cool kindness to everyone gave her no opportunity. If she felt Rulan's hatred, she did not show it, and the young woman soon saw that Madame Wu cared neither for love nor hate. In one of their quarrels she had flung back at Tsemo, "Why do you love your mother so much? She does not love you so."

To this Tsemo replied with his usual coolness, "I do not want to be loved too much."

"I suppose you think I love you too much!" she had cried.

But this he would not answer. "Leave me a little privacy," he said harshly then.

She cursed her nagging tongue. Yet there were times when he did love her with all the kindness she demanded. She raged against his cheerfulness and longed to be free of her own love because it made her dependent on him. But how could she be free of chains she had put upon herself?

In this tempest she kept her thoughts as secretly as she could, but she could not hide them all. Her temper was quick and her scorn hot. She was peevish often and thought everything in the house was inconvenient and old. But who heeded her? She was only one among the sixty-odd souls under the Wu roof, and she had not even borne a child yet.

When, therefore, she complained too long this night against his father, Tsemo yawned and stretched himself and burst out laughing. "Our poor father!" he said cheerfully. "After all, it is he whom we must pity. We will only see the woman in passing, but he must have her as his burden day and night. Come, Rulan, it is midnight. Go to bed and rest yourself—and give me rest."

He whistled to her as if she were his dog, and began to walk away. What could she do but follow him to their own court?

III

WHEN YING CAME in with the morning tea, Madame Wu said after greeting her, "As soon as I have eaten, I will talk with that go-between, old Liu Ma."

"Yes, my lady," Ying said sadly, and in silence she helped Madame Wu rise and dress.

Madame Wu had scarcely finished her breakfast when Liu Ma appeared. "You are early, my lady," she panted as she entered. She was a fat woman who in her girlhood had been in a flower house. But she became fat soon after and so had married a shopkeeper and taken up the profession of go-between.

"I like the early morning," Madame Wu replied gently.

She motioned the old woman kindly to a seat, and Ying poured tea for her and went away.

Liu Ma supped her tea loudly. "You are more beautiful than ever. Your lord is very lucky."

This she said in order to introduce the subject of concubines. For now, she thought, Madame Wu would sigh and say, alas, that her beauty stood her in no stead. But Madame Wu only thanked her.

"I thought that you might be wanting a fine young girl for your third son, and so I brought some pictures with me." Liu Ma had paid spies in every rich household, and thus she knew that a concubine was to be found for Mr. Wu. But she was too shrewd to let Madame Wu see that she had any such knowledge.

She had on her knees an oblong package tied up in a blue cotton kerchief. This she untied. Inside was an old foreign magazine with pictures of motion picture actresses. She opened this and took out some photographs. "I have now three young girls, all very good bargains," she said.

"Only three?" Madame Wu murmured, smiling. Liu Ma always roused her secret laughter. Her merchandise was the passion between men and women, and she bartered it as frankly as cabbage.

"I do not mean to say three is all I have," Liu Ma made haste to reply. "But these are my very best."

Madame Wu took the photographs without touching Liu Ma's dirty hand and looked at them, one by one. "But these three faces look alike," she objected.

"Do not all young girls look alike?" Liu Ma retorted. "Bright eyes, shining hair—and if you take off their clothes, what difference is there between one and another?" Her belly shook with laughter under her loose coat of shoddy silk. "But we must not tell the men that, my precious, or my business will be gone."

Madame Wu smiled slightly and put the photographs face down on the table. "Have you any girls whose families live at a distance?" she asked.

"Tell me exactly what you want," Liu Ma said.

"A young woman," Madame Wu began and then hesitated.

She knew nothing could be hidden from this hard old soul.

Liu Ma waited, her sharp small eyes fixed on Madame Wu's face. Madame Wu gazed into the court. "I seem to see the woman I want," she said. "A pretty woman, very pretty but not beautiful. A girl—about twenty-two years old, round-cheeked and young and soft as a child—someone who will not love any man too deeply—but who loves children, of course—and whose family is so far away that she will not be always crying to go home—"

"I have exactly what you want," Liu Ma said in triumph. Then her round face grew solemn. "Alas," she said, "no, the girl is an orphan. You would not want one of your sons to marry an orphan who does not know what her parents were. No, no, that would bring wild blood into the house."

Madame Wu shifted her gaze from the court and let it fall on Liu Ma's face. "I do not want the girl for my son Fengmo," she said calmly. "No, this girl is to be a young wife for my own lord."

Liu Ma pretended horror and surprise. "Alas," she muttered, "alas, even he!"

Madame Wu shook her head. "Do not misjudge him," she said. "It is entirely my own thought. He is very unwilling. It is I who insist."

"In that case," Liu Ma said briskly, "perhaps the orphan is the very thing."

"She must be healthy," Madame Wu insisted.

"That she is," Liu Ma replied. "In fact, also, she is pretty, and had she not been an orphan, I could have married her off months before this. The girl's one fault is that she is simple and ignorant. I had better tell you the worst. She cannot read, my lady. In the old days this would have been considered a virtue, but now it is fashionable for girls to read even as boys do. It is the foreign way that has crept into our country."

"I do not care if she cannot read," Madame Wu said.

Liu Ma's face broke into wrinkles of pleasure. She struck both her fat knees with her palms. "Then, my lady, it is done!"

she cried. "I will bring her whenever you say. She is with her foster mother on a farm."

"Who is this foster mother?" Madame Wu inquired.

"She is nothing," Liu Ma said eagerly. "I would not even tell you who she is. She found a child, my lady, one cold night, outside the city wall. Someone had left it there—a girl not wanted."

"Will she give the girl up altogether?" Madame Wu asked.

"She would be willing," Liu Ma said. "She is very poor, and after all, the girl is not her bone and flesh. She would only want heavy silver in her hand."

"One hundred dollars is not too little for a country girl," Madame Wu said calmly. "But I will pay more than that. I will pay two hundred."

"Add fifty, my lady," Liu Ma said coaxingly. "Then I can give the two hundred whole to the woman. She will let the girl go for that."

"Let it be then," Madame Wu said so suddenly that she saw a greedy sorrow shine in Liu Ma's eyes. "You need not grieve that you did not ask more," she said. "I know what is just."

"I know your wisdom, my lady," Liu Ma said eagerly. Now that the bargain was made she was almost crying with joy.

"Bring the girl this evening at twilight," Madame Wu said. "She is to come empty-handed, bringing only what she wears."

"I promise you—I promise you," Liu Ma babbled as she hurried away.

Almost immediately Ying came into the room with fresh tea. Madame Wu watched in silence while Ying wiped the table and the chair where the old woman had sat and gingerly took up the tea bowl she had used. When she was about to leave, Madame Wu spoke. "Tonight about twilight a young woman will come to the gate. Bring her straight to me," Madame Wu directed, "and put up a little bamboo cot for her here in this room."

"Yes, my lady." Ying's voice choked in her throat.

As THE DAY moved on toward night, Ying stood at the door. Her solid shadow was black against the gray of the twilight. In the court behind her was another shadow. "My lady," Ying said, "the girl is here."

Madame Wu's hands flew to her cheeks. "Light the candle," she commanded Ying.

Ying moved aside, and in the candlelight Madame Wu saw almost exactly the face she had imagined. A healthy, red-cheeked girl gazed back at her with round childlike eyes. Her black hair was long and sleek and fell over her forehead in a fringe, in the fashion of countrywomen. She held something behind her back.

"What do you have in your hands?" Madame Wu asked. "I told them you were to bring nothing."

"I brought you some eggs," the girl answered. "I thought you might like them, and I had nothing else. They are very fresh." She had a pleasant voice, hearty but a little shy.

"Come here. Let me see the eggs," Madame Wu said.

The girl came forward timidly, tiptoeing. Madame Wu looked down at her feet. "I see your feet have not been bound," she said.

The girl looked abashed. "There was no one to bind them," she replied. "Besides, I have always had to work in the fields."

Ying spoke. "Doubtless she has gone barefoot as country children do, and her feet have grown coarse."

The girl stood looking anxiously from Ying's face to Madame Wu's.

"Come, show me the eggs," Madame Wu commanded her again.

The girl put the bundle on the table carefully. Then she untied the kerchief and picked up each egg and examined it. "Not one is broken," she exclaimed.

She paused, and Madame Wu understood that she did not know what or how to address her. "You may call me Elder Sister," she said.

But the girl was too shy for this. Madame Wu could not keep from smiling at her. "Do you think you would like to stay here?" she asked. She felt a little pity for this young creature, bought like an animal from a farmer. She saw in her something delicate and good in spite of her sunburned cheeks and rough garments.

The girl sensed this kindness and into her dark, clear eyes there sprang a light of instant devotion. "Liu Ma told me you are good. She said you are not like other women. She told me to please you first above all, and that is what I will do." She had an eager, fresh voice.

"Then you must tell me about your life," Madame Wu replied. "If you are honest, I shall like you very much." She perceived the girl's devotion and felt, to her own surprise, a pang of something like guilt.

"I will tell you everything," the girl promised. "But first shall I not take the eggs to the kitchen?"

"No," Madame Wu said, hiding a smile. "Ying will take them. You must sit down there in that chair across from me, and we will talk."

The girl sat down on the edge of the, chair. She looked distressed.

"Are you hungry?" Madame Wu asked.

The girl laughed suddenly, a quick burst of rippling laughter. "I am," she said frankly, "but Liu Ma told me I must say 'No, thank you' if you asked me or I would seem too greedy at the first moment."

"Did you not eat your supper before you came?" Madame Wu inquired.

The girl flushed. "We do not have much food. My foster mother said—"

Madame Wu interrupted her. "Ying!" she commanded. "Bring food."

The girl sighed and her body relaxed.

"Liu Ma told me you were an orphan," Madame Wu said. "Do you know anything of your own family?"

The girl shook her head. "I was newborn when they left me. I know the place where they laid me down, for my foster mother has pointed it out to me many times. But she told me there was no sign on me of any kind, except that I was not wrapped in cotton, but in silk . . . ragged silk."

"Do you have that piece of silk?" Madame Wu asked now.

The girl nodded again. "How did you know?" she asked with naive surprise.

"I thought you would want to bring with you the only thing that was your own," Madame Wu said, smiling.

The girl put her hand in her bosom and brought out a folded piece of silk. It was washed and clean but faded from its first red to a rose color. Madame Wu took it and unfolded it. It was a woman's garment, a short coat, slender and long-sleeved. "If this was your mother's, she was tall," Madame Wu observed. She examined the garment. It had a band of embroidery around the collar, down the side opening and around the sleeves.

"It is delicate embroidery," Madame Wu said, "and it is done in a Peking stitch of small knots."

"You tell me more than I have ever known," the girl said under her breath.

"But that is all I can tell you," Madame Wu said. She folded the garment again and held it out to the girl.

"You keep it for me," the girl said. "I do not need it here."

"I will keep it if you like," Madame Wu said. "But if you find later that you want it again, I will return it to you."

"If you let me stay here," the girl replied with pleading in her voice, "I shall never want it again."

But Madame Wu was not ready yet to give her promise. "You have not even told me your name," she said.

The girl's face changed as plainly as a disappointed child's. "I have no real name," she said humbly. "My foster parents never gave me a name. They called me Little Orphan when I was small and Big Orphan when I was grown," the girl said.

"That, of course, is no name," Madame Wu agreed gently. "When I know you better, I will give you a name."

"I thank you," the girl said humbly.

At this moment Ying came in with two bowls of food and set them on the table. "Serve her," Madame Wu commanded.

Ying obeyed, her lips tight and silent. The girl accepted the bowl of rice with both hands, rising a little from her seat in country courtesy. Madame Wu soon saw that she was torn between hunger and the wish to be polite, and so she rose and made an excuse to leave the girl alone. "I shall return in a little while," she said. "Meanwhile, eat heartily."

She moved into her bedroom and walked slowly back and forth on the smooth tiles. "It is impossible to tell what this girl is," she murmured to herself. The girl seemed as open as a child. All her heart and nature lay revealed to anyone. Her eyes were quick with intelligence. Was she perhaps too intelligent? There was also the silk garment and the fine embroidery. Did she want to take into her house so unknown a being?

When Madame Wu went back to the library, the girl was sitting there alone, looking frightened in the big, shadow-filled room, with her hands clasped on her knees. As she saw Madame Wu she rose, and relief showed on her face. "What shall I do now, Elder Sister?" she asked. The name had come to her lips trustfully.

"What do you usually do at this hour?" she asked.

"I always go to bed as soon as I have eaten at night," the girl replied. "It wastes candlelight to sit up after it is dark."

Madame Wu laughed. "Then perhaps you had better go to bed," she said. She led the way into the room where the bamboo cot lay waiting. "There is your bed, and beyond that door is the room where you may make yourself ready."

"But I am ready," the girl replied. "I washed myself before I came here. I will take off my outer clothes and that is all."

"Then I will see you tomorrow," Madame Wu answered.

"Until tomorrow," the girl replied. "But I beg you, Elder Sister, if you want anything in the night, please call me."

"If I need you, I will call," Madame Wu said.

When Madame Wu awoke it was late. The sun was shining across the floor, and Ying stood waiting by the bed. Madame Wu rose quickly and the rite of dressing began. Ying did not mention the girl, and Madame Wu did not speak. The rooms were silent. This silence grew so deep that at last Madame Wu broke it. "Where is the girl?" she asked of Ying.

"She is out there in the court, sewing," Ying replied. "She had to have something to do, and I gave her some shoe soles for the children." From the slight scorn in Ying's voice Madame Wu understood that she did not think more highly of this girl for wanting to be busy, like a servant.

Madame Wu went out into the court. There the girl sat on a small three-legged stool in the shade of the bamboo. Her fingers were nimbly pushing the needle through the thick cloth sole. She rose when she saw Madame Wu and stood waiting.

"Please sit down," Madame Wu said. She herself sat down on one of the porcelain garden seats with her back to the round gate of the court.

The girl had no sooner taken her seat on the stool opposite when Madame Wu saw her glance up toward the gate and immediately the peach-colored flush on her cheeks deepened. Madame Wu turned, expecting to see a man, perhaps the cook. But it was not the cook. It was Fengmo, her third son, who stood there staring at the girl.

"Fengmo, what do you want?" Madame Wu asked. She was angry because he had come upon her unexpectedly. He was, she knew, the son whom she loved the least. He was willful and less amiable than Liangmo or Tsemo. When he was small, he had preferred the company of servants to the company of the family, and this she had thought was a sign of his inferiority. She had treated him outwardly exactly as she treated the others, but doubtless he had felt a difference, for he seldom came to her now unless she sent for him.

"Fengmo, why have you come?" she asked again when he did not answer but continued to stare at the girl.

"I came to see—to see how you are, Mother," Fengmo stammered.

"I am quite well," Madame Wu replied.

"There was something else, too," Fengmo said.

Madame Wu rose. "Then come into the library."

She led the way and he followed. Fengmo motioned toward the girl. "Mother," he said, "is that—the one?"

"Fengmo, why have you come here to ask me?" Madame Wu said severely. "It is not your affair."

"Mother, it is," he said passionately. "How do you think it is for me? My friends will laugh at me and tease me—"

"Is that what you came to tell me?" Madame Wu inquired.

"Yes," Fengmo cried. "It was bad before. But now I have seen her—she is so young and my father—he's so old."

"You will return at once to your own court," Madame Wu said coldly. "It was an intrusion for you to come here without sending a servant first. As for your father, the younger generation does not make decisions for the elder."

She saw his handsome face flush and quiver. Without a word he turned and left the room and the court.

But Madame Wu was deeply annoyed that these two had seen each other. In spite of the many old customs that she herself had broken—and she did not hesitate to break them when she chose—she had steadfastly followed the custom that separated male from female after the age of seven. Now Fengmo had seen this girl before she had taken her place in the house and the girl had seen him. Who could tell what fire would blaze out of this? There are moments in the tide of youth when any chance meeting may be as dangerous as a rendezvous. The matter must be decided at once. Madame Wu walked back and forth in the library. Each time she passed the open door she could see the girl's head bent industriously over the shoe sole. Her mind was suddenly made up. She went out into the court with a swifter step than usual and sat down again. "I have made up my mind," she began abruptly. "You shall stay in this house."

The girl looked up, holding the needle ready to pierce the cloth, but she did not move to take the stitch. She stood up in respect to Madame Wu. "You mean that I please you?" she asked in a low and breathless voice.

"Yes, if you do your duty," Madame Wu said. "You understand that you are here to serve my own lord—to take my place—in certain things."

"I understand," the girl said. Her eyes were fastened on Madame Wu's face.

"In that case," Madame Wu said abruptly, "there is no reason why the matter should not be concluded."

"But ought I not to have a name?" the girl asked anxiously.

Madame Wu found something pathetic and touching in this question. "Yes," she said, "and I will give it to you. I will name you Ch'iuming. It means bright autumn. With this name I make your duty clear. He is the autumn; you are the brightness."

"Ch'iuming," the girl repeated. She tried the name on her tongue. "I am Ch'iuming," she said.

IV

MR. WU DID not come near Madame Wu, and she let it be so. She knew what was going on in his mind. Had he been resolute against the girl, he would have come to tell Madame Wu so. That he had stayed away proved that he was not unwilling for the girl to come into his court and, she thought, that he was secretly ashamed because he was not unwilling.

Madame Wu had sent Ying to a cloth shop for flowered cotton cloth of good quality and silk of medium quality, and a clerk had brought bolts of these materials to her home for her selection. From these Madame Wu then chose enough to make Ch'iuming three separate changes of garments. She allowed the girl to point out her favorite colors and patterns, and she was pleased that Ch'iuming chose small patterns and mild colors. She was still more pleased when the girl set to work at once, making the garments herself.

Slowly and carefully Ch'iuming stitched while Ying looked on, examining each stitch for size and evenness. Watching them, Madame Wu felt again that pang of guilt, as though she were doing something wrong.

She made up her mind that she must go and tell Mr. Wu herself that Ch'iuming had been found and was ready. If Mr. Wu agreed, she would send Ch'iuming to him that night. She expected to find Mr. Wu in her old courts rather than in his, and so there she went. He was sitting inside the room in loose garments. Because of the heat he wore a pair of white silk trousers and a silk jacket unbuttoned over his smooth chest. He was fanning himself. The empty dishes of his breakfast were on the table. She discerned some sullenness on his well-fed, handsome face. She looked at him affectionately. "How are you this morning?" she asked.

"Well," he replied, "very well." But she sensed a certain impatience in him.

She smiled. "I have not forgotten you," she said.

"I feel as though you had," he grumbled. "I have been very lonely. I am a good husband, Ailien! Another man would not have stood for this separation for so long. All these days! Enough, I say!"

"I have not forgotten you for one moment, father of my sons," she said. "I have diligently searched, and the young woman is here."

A bright red sprang into Mr. Wu's face. "Ailien," he said, "do not speak of that again."

Madame Wu moved gracefully to a garden seat. "The young woman is truly suitable," she murmured. "Healthy, pretty, innocent—"

"Do you have no jealousy whatever?" he interrupted her.

"You are so handsome," she said, smiling, "that I might be jealous were she not a child, so simple—less than nothing between you and me."

"I cannot understand why you have grown so monstrously cold overnight," he complained.

She saw Fengmo pass the door. He looked in, saw his parents side by side, and went away quickly. "Fengmo!" she called. But the boy did not return.

"We must marry that third son of ours," she told Mr. Wu. "What would you say if I spoke to Madame Kang at once—perhaps tomorrow—and asked for Linyi?"

"Well enough," he said. She was pleased to see that there was no interest in his voice at the thought of Linyi.

"Unless you are unwilling, I will send the girl to you tonight," she said.

The red came back again to Mr. Wu's cheeks. He brought out a package of foreign cigarettes from the small pocket of his jacket, took one out and lit it. "I know you are so devilishly stubborn a woman that I could kill myself beating against your wish," he muttered between clouds of smoke.

"Have I ever made you less happy by my stubbornness?" she inquired. "Has it not always been stubbornness for your sake?"

"Do not talk to me about this matter," he said.

"There is no reason why we should talk about her," Madame Wu agreed. "I will send her to you tonight. Her name is Ch'iuming. She will brighten your autumn."

Mr. Wu heard this, opened his mouth, closed it, and walked out of the room.

He wanted to curse me, Madame Wu thought, but he was not able to bring himself to do it. She suddenly felt tired and longed to return to her own quiet rooms.

Returning to her court, she found Ch'iuming sitting on a stool, sewing on her new garments. She stopped and the girl began to rise. But Madame Wu pushed her down with a gentle hand on her shoulder. "You must prepare yourself for tonight."

The girl sank back and did not speak. Her young face was fixed and told nothing, but from under her hair, Madame Wu saw two fine streams of sweat pouring down.

"You must not be afraid," she said. "He is a very kind man."

The girl threw her a quick look from under lowered eyelids.

"You have only to obey him," Madame Wu said. She felt somehow cruel even as she said these words. Yet why should she feel cruel? The girl was no longer a child. Had she lived on in the house of her foster mother, what could she have hoped for except to marry some poor farmer? Surely this fate was better than that!

The girl put up her hand stealthily, wiped her cheeks and remained silent.

"You had better take her now," Madame Wu said abruptly to Ying, who stood waiting.

Ying stepped forward and took the girl's sleeve between her thumb and finger. "Come," she said.

Ch'iuming rose. Her full red mouth opened, and she began to pant softly. Her eyes grew wide and very black.

"Come," Ying said heartily. "For what else have you been brought into this house?"

The girl looked from Ying's face to Madame Wu's. Then, seeing nothing in either face to indicate the possibility of escape, she bent her head and followed Ying out of the room, out of the gate, and so out of the court.

V

MADAME WU SLEPT all that night without waking. When she awoke in the morning, she was completely rested. Fatigue had left her body. But there was something familiar in this feeling. Thus she had felt after each of her children had been born. Her first thought when she heard that sharp cry of the new child was always of reclaiming her own freedom. That joy of freedom was in her again. She smiled, and Ying came and caught her smiling.

"You, mistress, are too happy this morning!" Ying chided her. "You look like a mischievous child."

"Do not try to understand me, good soul," Madame Wu said gaily. "Dress me for visiting. I shall go to see Madame Kang as soon as I have eaten. I have a matter to talk about with her. What do you think of her Linyi for our Fengmo?"

"Two knots on the same rope," Ying replied musingly. "Well, mistress, better to repeat a good thing than a bad one. Our eldest young lord is happy enough with the eldest Kang daughter. But our second lord beat his wife last night."

"Tsemo beat Rulan?"

"I heard her sobbing," Ying said. "It must be she was being beaten."

Madame Wu sighed. "Will I never have peace under this roof?"

Two hours later she stepped out of the gate of the Wu house. Mr. Wu had some two years before bought a foreign-made car, but the streets were so narrow and crowded that Madame Wu would never willingly use it. She disliked seeing the common people flatten themselves against the walls of the houses while the big car passed. She liked the privacy of the old-fashioned sedan chair that had been part of her wedding furniture. One of its four bearers lifted the curtain and Madame Wu stepped in and sat down. From the small glass window behind this curtain she could see the streets and yet not be seen.

The distance between the house of Wu and the house of Kang was not short. It was almost an hour's walk across the entire city. But Madame Wu had no sense of haste. She enjoyed seeing the gay people, the sunshine in the streets, and the brightness of the sky. Ying had, of course, sent a manservant ahead to the Kang house to tell of Madame Wu's coming. The great red varnished gates swung open, and a servant was waiting.

Before Madame Wu had crossed the first court Madame Kang herself came to greet her friend. The two ladies clasped hands. "How good of you, Ailien!" Madame Kang cried eagerly. She searched her friend's lovely face. It was not in the least changed. The tranquil eyes, the exquisite mouth, the pale pearl skin—all were at their best.

"How beautiful you always are," Madame Kang said tenderly and was conscious of her own unbrushed hair.

"I rise early," Madame Wu said. "Now let us go inside and I will wait while your hair is brushed."

"Do not mind my hair," Madame Kang urged. "I get it combed in the afternoon."

Together the two friends reached Madame Kang's own court. There Madame Kang led Madame Wu into her own room and closed the door. "Now we are alone," she said, sitting down as soon as Madame Wu was seated. "Tell me everything."

Madame Wu looked at her friend. A certain blankness mingled with surprise appeared in her eyes. "It is a strange thing," she said after a second's pause, "but I feel I have nothing to tell."

"How can that be?" Madame Kang cried. "The girl—did you like her? Did he like her?"

"I like her," Madame Wu said. Now she knew, as her friend paused, that she had deliberately avoided thinking of Mr. Wu and Ch'iuming this morning. "I gave her a name—Ch'iuming. She is only an ordinary girl but a good one. I am sure he will like her. Everybody will like her, because there is nothing about her to dislike."

"Heaven!" Madame Kang exclaimed in wonder. "And you say all this as though you had hired a new nurse for a grandchild! When my father took a concubine, my mother tried to hang herself, and when he took a second concubine, the first one swallowed her earrings, and so it went until he had the five he ended with. They all hated one another." Madame Kang's hearty laughter rolled out. "They used to hunt for his shoes because he would leave his shoes in the room of the one he planned to visit that night. Then another one would steal them."

"They must have been silly women, those concubines," Madame Wu said calmly.

"At least tell me—could you sleep last night?"

"I slept very well."

"There never was a woman like you, Ailien." Madame Kang laughed.

"I do have a matter to talk about with you, Meichen," said Madame Wu seriously.

Madame Kang grew grave whenever she heard this tone in her friend's voice. "I will laugh no more. What is it?"

"You know my son Fengmo," Madame Wu said. "Do you think I should send him away to school?"

This question was put very skillfully. If Madame Kang declared it was not necessary, she would at once ask for Linyi.

"It is altogether a matter of what this boy will do with himself," Madame Kang answered.

"He has never shown what he wants," Madame Wu said. "He has until now merely been growing up. But after seventeen, a mother must watch a son."

"Of course," Madame Kang agreed.

"Come," Madame Wu said frankly, "why do I not speak the truth to you? I had thought of pouring our blood into the same stream again. Fengmo and Linyi—what do you say?"

Madame Kang clapped her hands twice together. "Good!" she cried. Then she let her plump hands drop. "But that Linyi—" she said mournfully. "It is one thing for me to say good, but how do I know what she will say?"

"You should never have let her go to a foreign school," Madame Wu said. "I told you that at the time."

"You were right," Madame Kang said sadly. "Nothing at home is good enough for her now. She complains about everything." Madame Kang looked doubtfully at her friend. "I would be glad for you to have her," she said. "She needs to be married, but I love you too well not to tell you her faults. Even if she is willing to marry Fengmo, she will think it shameful that he speaks no foreign language."

"But with whom would he speak it?" Madame Wu asked. "Would they sit together and talk in foreign tongues? It would be silly."

"Certainly it would," Madame Kang agreed. "But it is a matter of pride, you know, for these young women nowadays to chatter in a foreign tongue."

The two ladies looked thoughtfully at each other. Then Madame Wu said plainly, "Either Linyi must be satisfied with Fengmo as he is, or I shall have to let the matter drop. War is in the air, and I do not want my sons to go off to study in coastal cities. Here we are safe, for we are provinces away from the sea."

"Wait!" Madame Kang was suddenly cheered. "I have it," she said. "There is a foreign priest in the city who speaks several languages. Why do you not engage him as a tutor for Fengmo? Then when I speak to Linyi, I can tell her Fengmo is learning foreign languages."

Madame Wu considered the matter thoughtfully. "Well," she said at last, "it would be better than sending Fengmo away from us."

"So it would be," Madame Kang agreed.

"Then you will speak to Linyi and I will speak to Fengmo." The two ladies rose and walked hand in hand out of the room.

UPON HER RETURN, Madame Wu summoned Ying. "Go and tell Fengmo to come here," she said. "And when you have, invite the second lady to appear at the family meal tonight." If Fengmo agreed with what she had decided, she would eat tonight with the family instead of alone, as she had done during the last few days. It was time for her to come out and take her place among them again.

In a few minutes she heard Fengmo's step. She knew the step of each son. Liangmo's was slow and firm, Tsemo's quick and uneven, but Fengmo walked with a rhythm, three steps always quicker than the fourth. He appeared at the door of the library, wearing his school uniform of dark-blue cloth. On his head was a visored cap with a band giving the name of his school, the National Reconstruction Middle School.

Madame Wu smiled at her son and beckoned to him to come

in. "What is the meaning of this National Reconstruction?" she inquired half playfully.

"It is only a name, Mother," Fengmo replied.

"It means nothing to you?" Madame Wu inquired.

Fengmo laughed. "At present I am having difficulty with algebra," he replied. "Perhaps when I have overcome that, I will understand National Reconstruction better."

"Algebra," Madame Wu mused. "In India several such studies were first devised and then found their way to Europe."

Fengmo looked surprised. He never expected his mother to have any knowledge out of books, and Madame Wu knew this and enjoyed surprising him. She leaned forward, her hands clasped in her lap. "Fengmo," she said, "it is time we talked about your life."

"My life?"

"Yes," Madame Wu repeated, "your life. Your father and I have already discussed it."

"Mother, don't think I will consent to your choosing a wife for me," Fengmo said hotly.

"Of course I would not," Madame Wu said quickly. "All that I can do is to bring certain names to you. I have considered your taste, as well as the position of the family. I have put aside any thought of such a girl as the Chen family's daughter, who has been brought up in old-fashioned ways."

"I would never have such a girl," Fengmo declared.

"Of course not. But there is another difficulty," Madame Wu said calmly. "The girls are also demanding much today. They do not want a young man who cannot speak at least one foreign tongue."

"I study some English in school," Fengmo said haughtily.

"But you cannot speak it very well," Madame Wu replied. "I hear you stammer and halt when you make those sounds."

"What girl will not have me?" Fengmo asked angrily.

Madame Wu rode to her goal on his anger as a boat rides the surf to the shore. "Madame Kang's third daughter, Linyi," she said.

"That girl!" he muttered. "She looks too proud."

"She is really very handsome," Madame Wu retorted. "But I do not speak of her except as one of many."

"You could send me away to a foreign school," Fengmo said eagerly.

"I will not do that. There will be war over the whole world in a few years. At such a time all my sons must be at home."

The boy was silent, his eyes fixed on his mother's face. They were large and black like hers but had not their depth. He was still young.

"I have heard there is a foreign priest here in the city," she went on, "and he is a learned man. It is possible that he would teach you to speak other languages. Are you willing? Foreign languages may serve you well someday. And I am not thinking only of marriage."

"He would try to convert me to his religion," Fengmo said sullenly. "I do not believe in religion."

"Do you need to yield to conversion?" Madame Wu asked. "Are you so weak? Come, try this priest for a month, and if you wish then to stop his teaching, I will agree to it."

One of the secrets of her power in this house was that she never allowed her will to be felt as absolute. She gave time and the promise of an end, and then she used the time to shape events to her own purpose.

"A month then," he said. "Not more than a month if I do not like it."

"A month," Madame Wu agreed. She rose. "And now, my son, we will go to the night meal together. Your father will have begun without us."

In the Wu household men and women ate at separate tables. At the threshold of the great dining room Fengmo parted from his mother and went to one end, where his father and brothers and the male cousins were already seated, and Madame Wu walked to the tables where the women were seated. She saw at once that Ch'iuming had taken her place among them. The girl sat shyly apart from the others and held a small child on her knee. Madame Wu took her own place at the highest seat and picked up her chopsticks. Meng had been serving the others, and Madame Wu said, "Proceed for me, please, Meng. I have been busy all day with household matters, and I am a little weary."

She leaned back, smiling, and as usual she gave a word to each of her daughters-in-law. Then she spoke directly to Ch'iuming. "Second Lady," she said kindly, "you must eat what you like best. The fish is usually good."

Ch'iuming looked up and flushed a bright red. She rose and gave a little bow, the child still clutched in her arms. "Thank you, Elder Sister," she said in a faint voice.

By her kind address Madame Wu had told the whole house that Ch'iuming's place was set and that the life of the family must now include this one. They all had heard the few words, and a moment's silence followed them. Madame Wu accepted the food given her and began to eat slowly.

Her little grandson now clamored suddenly to come and sit on her knee. Meng reproved him tenderly. "You with your face and hands all dirty!"

Madame Wu looked up. "Is it me the child wants?" she asked.

"He is so dirty, Mother," Meng said.

"Certainly he is to come to me," Madame Wu said. She put out her hands and took the child and set him on her knee. With a pair of clean chopsticks she chose bits of meat from the serving bowls. "Son of my son," she murmured, putting meat into his small mouth.

The child sat as though in a dream of content, chewing each morsel with silent pleasure. And Madame Wu was content with her grandchild. In him her duty to the house was complete, and in him, too, her secret loneliness in this house was assuaged. She did not know then that she was lonely, and had anyone told her that she was, she would have denied it, amazed at such misperception.

When the child was fed, she gave him back to his mother.

Before the others had finished, she rose and walked slowly out of the room. As she passed Mr. Wu and her sons they greeted her, half rising from their seats. She smiled and inclined her head and went on her way.

To Ch'iuming the half hour of Madame Wu's presence was her marriage ceremony. The night before had left her confused. Had she pleased him or not? Mr. Wu had not spoken one word to her, and he had left her before dawn. No one had come near her except a woman servant. Then she had been bidden by Ying to join the family meal. One by one, the ladies who were now her relatives had greeted her shyly, and she had only bent her head a little in reply. She could not eat.

But after Madame Wu left the room, she suddenly felt ravenous, and she quickly ate two bowls of rice and meat.

When the meal was over, Meng in her gentle kindness stayed a moment to speak to her. "I will come to see you tomorrow, Second Lady," she said.

"I am not worthy," Ch'iuming replied faintly. She lifted her eyes, and Meng saw how timid and desolate she was.

"I will come and bring my child," she promised.

That night Mr. Wu came early to the court. Ch'iuming was still sewing when she heard his step. He sat down and cleared his throat and looked at her. "You must not be afraid of me," he began.

She could not answer.

"In this house," Mr. Wu began again, "there is everything to make you happy. My sons' mother is kind. There are young women, my sons' wives and our young cousins' wives, and many children. You look good-tempered, and certainly you are obliging. You will be very happy here."

Still she did not answer. Mr. Wu coughed and loosened his belt a little. "For me," he went on, "you have only a few duties. I like to sleep late. Do not wake me if I am here. In the night, I like tea if I am wakeful, but not red tea. These and other things you will learn, doubtless."

Ch'iuming looked up at him and forgot her shyness. "Then—I am wanted?"

"Certainly," he said. "Have I not been telling you so?" He smiled, and his smooth handsome face brightened from a sudden heat within him. She saw it and understood. But tonight she would not be afraid. It was a little price to pay for a home at last.

VI

SEVERAL DAYS later, Ying came running into Madame Wu's court. Her round eyes were glittering with surprise. "My lady, my lady!" she cried.

Madame Wu was walking among her transplanted orchids, and she stopped in displeasure. "Ying!" she said firmly. "Tell me what is the matter."

Ying began again more calmly. "The largest man I ever did see—a foreigner! He says you sent for him."

"I?" Madame Wu said blankly. Then she remembered. "Oh, yes, I did," she said.

"My lady, you said nothing to me," Ying reproached her. "I told the gateman by no means to let him in. We have never had a foreign man in this house."

"I do not tell you everything," Madame Wu replied. "Let him come in at once."

Ying retired, and Madame Wu resumed her walk in the orchid garden. She heard a deep, resonant voice from the round gate into the court. "Madame Wu!"

She looked up and saw a tall, wide-shouldered man in a long brown robe tied about the waist with a rope. It was the foreign priest. His right hand clasped a cross that lay on his breast. She knew that the cross was a Christian symbol, but what interested her was the size and the strength of the hand that held it.

"I do not know how to address you," she said lightly, "or I would return your greeting. Will you come in?"

The priest bent his great head and came through the gate into the court.

"Come into my library if you please," Madame Wu said. She stood aside at the entrance for the priest to enter ahead of her. But he made a slight gesture toward the door. "In my country," he said, smiling, "it is the lady who enters first."

"Is it so?" she murmured. She went in and sat down in her accustomed seat and motioned toward the other chair across the table.

The priest's huge body filled the big carved chair. Yet he was lean to the point of thinness. His complexion was olive and his large brown eyes were very clear. His hair was neither short nor long, and it curled slightly. He wore a beard, and the hair was black and fine.

"How am I to address you?" Madame Wu inquired.

"I have no name of my own," the priest replied. "But I have been given the name of André. Some call me Father André. I would prefer, madam, that you call me Brother André." Brother André gave Madame Wu a long look. There was no boldness in this look, and Madame Wu was not startled by it. It was as impersonal as a lamp that a man holds up to reveal an unknown path. "I was told you wanted to speak to me, madam," Brother André said.

"Ah, so I do," Madame Wu said. But she paused. She now perceived that Ying had scattered the news of a monster. She heard whisperings and flutterings at the door and saw glimpses of children. She called out in an amiable voice, "Come, children—come in and see him!" Immediately a little flock crowded about the door.

"They want to look at you," she explained to Brother André.

"Why not?" he replied and turned himself toward them. The children shrank back at this, but when he remained motionless and smiling, they came near again.

"Why are you so big?" a child asked breathlessly.

"God made me so," Brother André replied.

"What is your country?" a lad inquired.

"I have no country," Brother André said. "Wherever I am is my home."

"You speak our language perfectly," Madame Wu said.

"I speak many languages in order to be able to converse with many people," he replied.

By now the children were bold. "What is that on the chain around your neck?" one of them asked.

"That is my cross," Brother André said. He took up the heavy plain cross as he spoke and held it toward them.

"May I hold it?" the child asked.

"If you like," Brother André said.

"No," Madame Wu spoke sharply. "Do not touch it, child."

Brother André let the cross drop and kept silent.

Ying came in with tea, pushing a pathway among the children. "Your mothers are calling you," she said loudly. "All your mothers are calling!"

"Return to your mothers," Madame Wu said calmly, without raising her voice. Immediately the children turned and ran away.

Brother André looked at her with sudden appreciation. "They do not fear you, but they obey you," he said.

"They are good children," she said.

"You are also good," he said calmly. "But I am not sure you are happy."

These words struck Madame Wu as sharply as a hidden knife. She began at once to deny them. "I am, on the contrary, entirely happy. I have arranged my life exactly as I wish it."

He lifted his deep and penetrating eyes and listened attentively. It was the quality of this attention that made her falter. "That is," she went on, "I am entirely happy except that I feel the need of more knowledge of some sort. What sort I do not know myself."

"Perhaps it is not so much knowledge as more understanding of what you already know," he said.

How did it come about that she was speaking of herself to this stranger? "It was not for myself that I have invited you to come here," she said. "It is for my third son. I wish him to learn a foreign language."

"Which language?" he inquired.

"Which is the best?" she asked.

"French is the most beautiful," he answered, "and Italian is the most poetic, and Russian the most powerful, but more business is done in English."

"He had better study English then," Madame Wu said with decision. "What is your fee?"

"I take no fee," Brother André said quietly.

"But you put me in an awkward position if you compel me to take something for nothing," Madame Wu said. "Shall I not give money to your religion then—for good works?"

"No, religion is better without such gifts," Brother André replied. He considered a moment and then went on. "From time to time there will be things that ought to be done in your own city—perhaps a place for foundlings to be housed. I have taken care of some of these foundlings myself until I could find good parents for them. When there are such things to be done, I will come to you, madam, and your help will be my reward."

"But is there nothing I can do for you?" she asked.

"This is to do for me, madam," he replied.

"Will you come every evening?" she asked. "My son goes to the national school during the day."

"As often as I am wanted," he replied.

She saw Fengmo approaching through the gate opposite. "Fengmo!" she called.

Fengmo was there in an instant, very young and slight in comparison to the great priest. She was surprised to see how small he was, he whom she had always thought was tall.

"This is my third son, Fengmo," she said to Brother André.

"Fengmo," the priest repeated. "I am Brother André," he said. "Your mother has asked me to teach you the English language."

"And only the language," Madame Wu stipulated. Now that

the lessons were to begin, she asked herself if she had done wrong in giving the mind of her son to this man.

"Only the language," Brother André repeated. "You need not be afraid, madam. Your son's mind will be sacred to me."

He turned to Fengmo. "Tomorrow," he said, and after bowing to Madame Wu, he strode through the gate with long, unhurried steps.

ALL THROUGH THE great house the news of the big foreign priest went on wings, and Mr. Wu heard it, too.

It was midafternoon of the next day when Mr. Wu approached Madame Wu in the library. He sat down and took out his pipe and lit it. "I have heard that you have engaged a foreign tutor for Fengmo without telling me," he said.

"I should have told you, indeed," Madame Wu said gently. "It was a fault of mine. I felt it necessary for Fengmo to have his eyes turned toward Linyi."

"Why?" Mr. Wu inquired.

"Fengmo happened to see Ch'iuming the other day while she was here," she said. "I do not think anything passed between them, but Fengmo is at the moment in his youth when such a thing might happen with any woman young and pretty."

"I wish you would not imagine such things so easily," he said. "You have a low opinion of men. I feel you have made even me into an old goat."

She saw he was hurt, and she felt humiliated that she had been so clumsy. "I wish you could see the way you look today," she said with her charming smile. "You look years younger than you did a few days ago."

He broke into a laugh. "Do I, truthfully?" he asked. He leaned toward her across the table between them. "Ailien, there is still nobody like you," he exclaimed. "What I have done has been only because you insisted."

"I know that," she said, "and I thank you for it. All our life together you have done what I wished."

"I am always thinking of you. Even in the night," he muttered, not looking at her.

She was very grave at this. "You must not think of me in the night," she said. "It is not fair to Ch'iuming. After all, her life is now entirely in your hands. Is she not pleasant to you?"

"Oh, she is pleasant," he said grudgingly. "But you—you are so far away from me these days. Are we to spend the rest of our lives as separately as this? You have always lived in the core of my life—" His full underlip trembled.

Madame Wu was so moved that she rose involuntarily and went over to him. He seized her in his arms and pressed his face against her body. Something trembled inside her, and she grew alarmed. She drew herself very gently from his clasp until only her hands were in his. "You will be happier than you have ever been," she promised him.

"Will you come back to me?" he demanded.

"In new ways," she promised. The moment was over. She felt her body turn to a shaft of cool marble. She withdrew even her hands. "As for Fengmo," she continued, "do not trouble yourself. It seems Linyi wants him to speak English. She says he is too old-fashioned otherwise. He will be ready to marry her in a month. See if he is not!"

"You plotter," Mr. Wu said, laughing. "You planner and plotter of men's lives!" He was restored to good humor again, and shaking his head, he rose and went away.

"How DOES LINYI feel now that Fengmo is learning English?" Madame Wu asked Madame Kang when her friend had come to see her late one evening.

"I am surprised at my child," Madame Kang replied. "She says she will marry Fengmo if she likes him after she has spoken English with him several times. How shameless she is!"

Madame Wu laughed—a little ripple of mirth. "The hearts of the young are like fires ready to burn. Yet how can we arrange meetings between our two?"

The friends were sitting in the cool of the evening. On a

table near them Ying had put a split watermelon. The yellow heart, dotted with glistening black seeds, was dewy and sweet.

"Eat a little melon," Madame Wu said gently. "It will refresh you. You look tired tonight."

Madame Kang took out a flowered silk handkerchief and covered her face with it and began to sob.

"Now, Meichen," Madame Wu said in much astonishment, "tell me why you weep."

She pulled away the handkerchief. Madame Kang was now laughing and crying together. "I am so ashamed," she faltered, "I cannot tell you, Ailien. You must guess for yourself."

"You are not—" Madame Wu said severely.

"Yes, I am," Madame Kang said. Her merry eyes were now tragic.

"You, at your age, and already with so many children!"

"I am one of those women who conceive when my man puts even his shoes by my bed."

Madame Wu could not reply. She was too kind to tell her friend what she thought.

Madame Kang looked at her and said sadly, "Perhaps you are lucky, Ailien, because you do not love your husband."

Madame Wu was pierced by these words. She was not accustomed to sharpness from this old friend. "Perhaps the difference is not in love but in self-control," she replied. "Or," she added, "perhaps it is only that I have never liked to be laughed at."

"Don't quarrel with me," Madame Kang pleaded. She put her warm plump hand upon Madame Wu's cool narrow one. "We have the same trouble, Ailien. All women have it, I think. You solve it one way, I another."

"But is yours a solution?" Madame Wu asked. Love for her friend softened her heart as she spoke.

"I could not bear—to do what you have done," Madame Kang replied. "Perhaps you are wise, but I cannot be wise if it means somebody between—my husband and me."

Madame Wu's heart was wrenched by an inexplicable pain.

She was suddenly so lonely that she was terrified. She stood on top of a peak, surrounded by ice and cold, lost and solitary.

In the midst of this strange terror, Brother André's huge figure appeared, and her loneliness was dispelled in the necessity of speaking to him. "Brother André," she said gratefully, "come in. I will send for my son." She rose. "Meichen, this is Fengmo's teacher," she said. "Brother André, this is my friend, Madame Kang, who is as a sister to me."

Brother André bowed and went on into the library.

"What a giant!" Madame Kang exclaimed in a whisper. "Do you not fear him?"

"A good giant," Madame Wu replied.

"I must go home," Madame Kang said. "But before I go, shall Linyi speak with Fengmo or not?"

"I will ask him," Madame Wu said, "and if he wishes it, I will bring him to your house. Then one day you can come here and bring her. Twice should be enough."

"You are always right," Madame Kang said, pressing her friend's hands.

MADAME WU DELAYED Fengmo that night after his lesson. The two men had sat long over their books. Madame Wu had walked past the door of the library, unseen in the darkness, and had looked in. Something in Fengmo's attentive look, something in Brother André's deep gravity, frightened her. Fengmo's soul was at that moment of awakening when, if a woman did not bewitch it, a great priest might. Should she enter and break the spell she saw being woven? She, only the mother, was not strong enough. Fengmo would turn against her. No, she must have a young woman to help her.

When the lesson was over, she called out from the darkness, "Brother André, my thanks for teaching my son so well. Until tomorrow, my greetings!" She came forward.

Both men stopped as though shocked by her presence. Brother André bowed and went swiftly away. Fengmo was about to follow, but Madame Wu put her hand to his elbow and clung tightly to him. "My son," she said, "stay with me a little while. Come and sit down in this cool darkness."

"If you wish, Mother," Fengmo said. But she could feel him stiffen, longing to be free of her.

"Fengmo, I do not know how to tell you," she said. "You are so grown now—a man. Linyi wants to talk with you. Such a thing I would have said was impossible when Liangmo was your age. But Linyi is very different from Meng, and you are very different from Liangmo."

It was difficult for Fengmo to believe that this was his mother's voice, so young, so shy. "How do you know?" he asked brusquely.

"Today her mother told me," she replied. She felt an excitement, as though she were pitting herself against a force stronger perhaps than her own. But she would win.

"It is perhaps very wrong of me," she said plaintively now to Fengmo's silence. "My first feeling is to say that if Linyi is so bold, I do not want her in the house."

These were the right words. Fengmo answered hotly out of the darkness. "Mother, you don't understand! Many young men and women meet together these days," he declared. "It is not as it used to be when you were young."

"Perhaps you are right," she sighed. "I want you to be happy. I do not want you to see Linyi if you would rather not."

"Of course I will see her," Fengmo said in a lordly way. "Why should I object?"

"Fengmo," she pleaded, "there are many young women who would like to come into our house. Now that I think of it, I have always thought that Linyi was a little cross-eyed."

"If she is, I will see it clearly," Fengmo declared.

"Then shall I tell her mother that you and I will—"

"Why you, Mother?" he asked very clearly. "I shall see her alone. Must I be led by my mother like a small child?"

"What if I say you shall not go at all?" Madame Wu asked.

"Mother, do not say it. I do not want to disobey you."

Madame Wu rose. "You insist, then, on going to see Linyi?"

"I will go," Fengmo said doggedly.

"Go, then," Madame Wu said and swept past him and into her own room.

Ying was waiting for her. She had heard the loud voices. "My lady, what—" she began.

But Madame Wu put up her hand. "Wait!" she whispered. "Listen!" Her eyes were shining, and her face was lit with laughter. They heard Fengmo's angry footsteps stride from the court. Madame Wu hugged herself and laughed aloud.

"My lady," Ying began again, "what is the matter?"

"Oh, nothing," Madame Wu said gaily. "I wanted him to do something, and he is going to do it—that is all!"

Two days later Madame Kang came again. "Fengmo and Linyi have met," she said.

"How was the meeting?" Madame Wu asked, smiling.

"I sat far off, pretending not to be there," Madame Kang replied, smiling back. "They could not speak. They were miserable together, only gazing at each other. I went away for only a few minutes, and when I came back again, they were exactly as they had been. Neither had moved. They were still staring at each other. Then he rose, and they both said, 'Until we meet again.'"

"Only those common words?" Madame Wu asked.

"But how they said them!" Madame Kang replied. "When I saw those two young things—so much happiness and so much trouble ahead—one dares not tell the truth to the young!"

"Let the wedding be soon," Madame Wu said.

"The sooner the better," Madame Kang agreed. "It is wrong to light the fire under an empty pot."

VII

THUS ON A DAY in the ninth month of the year, Linyi came to the house, a bride. The season was a good one for marriages, for the harvest was ready to be cut and the rice was heavy in the ear. Summer had paused and autumn had not yet begun.

The two families came together in mutual joy for this second union between them. Meng, swelling with her child, looked beautiful and ripe with happiness as she welcomed her sister.

The two mothers had decided they would follow the children's wishes. Three days of feasting was too long for Fengmo and Linyi. They wanted the swift marriage of the new times. "There are some good things about these new ways," Madame Kang said at the end of the marriage day as the women sat in Madame Wu's court.

"Certainly we do not have the broken furniture and filthy floors we had after Liangmo's marriage," Madame Wu agreed.

She felt happy tonight. For a week Fengmo had taken no lessons and Brother André had not come. Madame Wu did not object. This was the hour of the flesh. She did not fear Brother André's power now. She had saved Fengmo for the family.

The court was lit with red-paper lanterns, and these drew moths out of the darkness. Now and again, among the small gray creatures, a great moth would flutter forth. The women cried out and could not rest until it was impaled on the door where all could exclaim at its beauty.

One such moth had just been caught when Ch'iuming came into the court. The girl looked thin and a little too pale, but somehow prettier than she had before, Madame Wu thought in unwilling self-reproach.

As they were all looking at the new moth, Ch'iuming, too, went to look at it. It was of a creamy yellow color, with long black antennae. As it felt itself impaled, its wide wings fluttered and dark spots on them showed green and gold. Then the moth was still. "How quickly they die!" Ch'iuming said suddenly.

They all turned at the sound of her voice, and she shrank back, smiling shyly. She stood waiting until they were all seated again. Then in silence she came to Madame Wu and felt her tea bowl. "Your tea is cold," she said. "I will warm it."

"Thank you," Madame Wu said. She looked into the girl's face. A look of humility was there.

"May I have some talk with you tonight, Elder Sister?" Ch'iuming asked in a low voice.

"Assuredly you may," Madame Wu replied. She could not refuse.

When the guests were gone, Ch'iuming waited alone, hesitating.

"You are with child," Madame Wu said abruptly. She used the common words of the common woman.

Ch'iuming looked up at her. "I have happiness in me," she acknowledged. She used the words that women in a great house use when an heir is expected.

"I suppose he is pleased," Madame Wu said sharply.

Ch'iuming looked at her. "He does not know," she said. "I have not told him."

"Strange," Madame Wu retorted. She was angry with Ch'iuming and amazed at her own anger. "Concubines usually hasten to tell the men. Why are you different?"

Ch'iuming's eyes filled with tears. "I wanted to tell you," she said in a low voice. "I thought you would be pleased, but you are only angry. Now I would like to destroy myself."

These desperate words brought Madame Wu to her right mind. It was common enough for concubines in great houses to kill themselves, but this always brought shame to the house. "You speak foolishly," she said. "Why should you destroy yourself when you have only done your duty?"

"I thought that if you were glad, then I would be glad, too," the girl continued in the same heartbroken voice.

Madame Wu began to be frightened. "What now?" she asked. "Are you not glad for your own sake? You will have a little toy to play with, someone to laugh at, a small thing of your own to tend. If it is a boy, you will rise in your place in this house. But I promise you that if it is a girl, you will suffer no reproaches from me. When my own daughter died before she could speak, I wept as though a son were gone."

The girl did not answer this. Instead she fixed her sad eyes on Madame Wu and listened.

"You must not talk of destroying yourself," Madame Wu went on briskly. "Go back now and tell him your good news." She spoke coldly to bring the girl back to her senses, but in her own heart she felt the chill of the mountain peak coming down on her again. She longed to be alone and she rose to leave.

Ch'iuming sprang forward and clutched the hem of her robe. "Let me stay here tonight," she begged. "Let me sleep here as I did when I first came. And you—you tell him for me. Beg him—beg him to leave me alone!"

Now Madame Wu was truly afraid. "You are losing your mind," she told Ch'iuming severely. "Remember who you are. Today you are second only to me in this family, the richest in the city. You are dressed in silk. Jade hangs from your ears. Go back at once to the court where you belong, and the duty for which you were purchased."

Ch'iuming let go of the hem of Madame Wu's robe. She lifted herself to her feet and fell back toward the gate. Madame Wu's hardness cracked at the sight of her desperate face. "Go back, child," she said in her usual kind voice. "Do not be afraid. Fall asleep early and do not wake if he comes in. He will let you sleep. He is good enough. And I will do this for you—tomorrow I will tell him. That much I will do."

Ch'iuming whispered her thanks and slipped out of the court. Madame Wu put out the lanterns one by one until the court was dark.

THE NIGHT was not a good one. Madame Wu slept and woke and slept again throughout the night, never wholly forgetful.

Ying came in at dawn when she saw her mistress awake. "The old lady is ill," she told Madame Wu. "She says she feels that she must have eaten a cockroach at the feast yesterday and it is crawling around in her belly. She says it is as big as a mouse and it's sitting on her liver, scratching her heart with its paws. Of course there can be no cockroach. My man, whatever his faults, would never be as careless a cook as that."

Madame Wu hastened into the next court where the old lady

lay high on her pillows. She turned dim eyes toward her daughter-in-law. "Do something for me quickly. I am about to die," she said in a weak voice.

Madame Wu was frightened. Yesterday the old lady had been as lively as a mischievous child, boasting because she had won at Mah-Jongg and eating anything at hand.

"Has she vomited?" Madame Wu asked the lady's maid.

The old lady piped up for herself, "I have vomited enough for three pregnancies. Fill me up again, daughter-in-law. I am all water inside—water and wind."

"Can you eat?" Madame Wu inquired.

"I must be filled somehow," the old lady declared in a faint but valiant voice.

Madame Wu directed that thin rice soup be brought, and she herself took up a spoon and fed it to the old lady.

"I am better," the old lady sighed at last.

"Sleep a little," Madame Wu said soothingly.

The old lady's eyes opened very sharply at this. "Why do you keep telling me to sleep?" she demanded. "I shall soon sleep forever."

Madame Wu was shocked to see tears well into the old lady's eyes. "Daughter, do you think there is any life after this one?" she muttered. She put out a claw of a hand and clutched Madame Wu's hand. The old lady's hand was hot and full of fever. "Do you believe that I shall be born again in another body as the priests tell us?"

Never before had the old lady talked of such things. Madame Wu searched for an honest answer. "I cannot tell, Mother," she said at last, "but I believe that life is never lost."

The old lady's eyelids, wrinkled as an old bird's, fell over her eyes, and she began to breathe deeply. Madame Wu went away, staying only to whisper to the servant, "Try to keep rich foods out of her sight so that she will not crave them."

"The old lady is willful," the servant murmured to defend herself, "and I do not like to make her angry."

"Obey me," Madame Wu said sternly.

But as she passed through Mr. Wu's court, she was pleased that the old lady's illness gave her a reason to go there beyond the real one. Mr. Wu came into the main room, buttoning his gray silk jacket.

"Your mother is very ill," she said abruptly.

"You don't mean—" he said.

"No, not this time," she said. "But her soul is beginning to wonder what is to come next, and she asked me if I believed in another life after this one. Such questions mean that the body is beginning to die."

"What did you tell her?" he asked. His face turned suddenly solemn.

"I told her I believe that life is never lost, but how can I know?" she answered.

He was inexplicably angry. "Now, how cruel you are!" he cried. "How could you show your doubt to an old soul?"

"What would you have said?" she asked him.

"I would have assured her that nothing but happiness waits for her at the Yellow Springs. I would have said—"

"Perhaps you had better go to her and say it," she said angrily.

They were silent for a moment, each struggling for calm again. Each wondered at being angry with the other, and neither knew why it was. She was the first to speak. "I have another matter to mention."

"Speak on," he said.

"Ch'iuming asked me to tell you that she is pregnant." She did not look at him but sat motionless.

He was silent for so long that at last she looked up. He was staring at her, a sheepish smile on his face. He laughed aloud. "Poison me," he said. "Put wolfsbane into my rice—or ground gold into my wine. I am too shameless. But, mother of my sons, I was only obedient to you."

Against her will laughter came creeping up out of her. "Don't pretend you are not pleased," she said. "You know you are proud of yourself."

"Alas, I am too potent," he said.

Across the bridge of laughter they met again. In that laughter she perceived something. She did not love him! Meichen had been right. She did not love him, had never loved him, and so now how could she hate him? It was as though the last chain fell from her soul. She was wholly free of him.

"Listen to me," she said when their laughter was over. "You must be kind to her."

"I am always kind to everybody," he insisted.

"Please," she said. "It is her first child. Do not plague her."

He wagged his head at her. "It may be that one concubine is not enough," he teased.

She only smiled. "Now," she said, "you can go to your mother. And better than talking about her soul, tell her that you are to have another son."

But Madame Wu had scarcely reached her own court when Ying came running to her. "The old lady is worse," she cried. "She is calling for you, mistress! Our lord is there and he begs you to come."

Madame Wu hastened to the old lady's bedside. "She has taken a turn for the worse!" Mr. Wu exclaimed when he saw her.

A light flickered in the old lady's glazed eyes, but she could not speak. Neither sound nor tears came as she gazed piteously at her daughter-in-law.

"Fetch some hot wine quickly," Madame Wu murmured to Ying. "We must warm her."

The old lady continued to look at Madame Wu, begging her for help, her face fixed in a piteous mask.

"Do not be afraid, Mother," Madame Wu said in a soothing voice. "There is nothing to fear. Everything is as usual around you. The children are playing outdoors in the sunshine. In the kitchens the cooks are making the evening meal. Life goes on as it always has. Life goes on eternally, Mother."

The old lady heard and slowly the lines of her face softened and changed and the mask of weeping faded.

Ying hurried in with the hot wine in a small jug with a long spout. Madame Wu held the spout to the old lady's parted lips and let the wine drip into her mouth. Once and twice and three times the old lady swallowed. A faint pleasure came into her eyes. "I can feel—" Then a look of surprise and anger sprang out of her eyes. Even as she felt the hot wine in her stomach, her heart stopped beating. She shuddered, the wine rushed up again and stained the quilt, and so the old lady died.

"Oh, my mother!" Mr. Wu moaned, aghast.

With a fine silk handkerchief Madame Wu wiped the old lady's lips, and she lifted the old lady's head. But the head was limp, and she laid it down again on the pillow.

"Her soul is gone," she said.

"Oh, my mother!" Mr. Wu moaned again. He began to weep openly and aloud, and she let him weep. There were certain things that must be done quickly for the dead. The old lady must be exorcised before the spirits of the flesh did harm in the house. Priests must be called. In her heart Madame Wu did not believe in priests nor in their gods. But she was surprised to find in herself the urgent wish to call Brother André and give him the task of exorcising evil from the house. But, for the sake of the family, she followed the old ways.

So now one generation was fulfilled and passed from the house. The old lady was not buried at once. When the geomancers were consulted, they declared that a day coming in midautumn was the first fortunate day for her burial. Therefore, when the rites were finished and the old lady slept within her sealed bed of cypress wood, her coffin was carried into the quiet family temple within the walls.

After the old lady's death, a stillness seemed to come over the family. With her passing, each remaining generation in the house became more aware that they were all nearer to the end. When Mr. Wu had taken off his garments of sackcloth, he was not quite what he had been. His face looked older and more grave. Now sometimes he came to Madame Wu's court, and together they talked over family matters. They would discuss crops and taxes and whether they should undertake an expense of one sort or another.

Madame Wu, alone, pondered on many things. Now more than ever her life was divided: that part which was lived in the house and that part which was lived within herself. When the household was at peace, she lived happily alone with her thoughts. When there was trouble of some sort, she mended it as she could.

About the middle of that autumn she became aware of trouble beginning in the house that could swell if she did not pinch it off, like an unruly bud on a young tree. Linyi and Fengmo began to quarrel. She saw their ill-temper one day by chance when she made her inspection of the house. For all her pert beauty, Linyi was slatternly in her own court. At first Madame Wu had not wanted to speak of this, because Linyi was her friend's daughter. But Meng was Madame Kang's daughter too, and rather than reproach Linyi, Madame Wu went to her elder sister.

She found Meng in the middle of the morning combing her long hair. "How many more days?" Madame Wu asked.

"Eleven, by the moon," Meng answered. "I hope, Mother, that you will give me your counsel. You know I suffered very much with the first one."

"You will not suffer as much with the second one," Madame Wu said to Meng.

"Linyi says she wants no children," Meng said suddenly. "Linyi says she wishes she had not married Fengmo."

Madame Wu looked up, startled. "Meng, be careful of your words," she exclaimed.

"It is true, Mother," Meng said.

"Meng, I came here to speak of your sister's being a slattern, but what you tell me is more grave than dust under a table. I should have inquired earlier into the marriage. But I have been busy with the old lady's death affairs. Say what Linyi told you," Madame Wu commanded.

"She says she hates a big house like this one," Meng said.

"She says Fengmo belongs to the family and not to her, and that she belongs to the house against her will, too, and not to him. She wants to go out and set up a house alone."

Madame Wu could not comprehend what she heard. "Alone? But how would they eat?"

"She says Fengmo could work and earn a salary if only he knew more English. Then he could get some money for the two of them to live alone."

Madame Wu felt outraged that under her roof there should be this dark spot of rebellion. "Is she a prostitute that she does not belong to this house?" she asked.

Meng kept silent, seeing that Madame Wu did not like what she heard. And Madame Wu pressed her no more. She rose and went back to her court with this new knowledge of fresh turmoil in the house. But a weariness overcame her that day. She was not strong enough to handle all these young men and women whose lives were dependent upon her. Her wisdom was too ancient for them; she knew only the unchanging human path from birth to death. She thought of Brother André. He had a wisdom that went far beyond these walls. She would call Fengmo and suggest to him that he begin again his studies. Then when Brother André came, she could share with him the troubles of those who leaned on her.

Fengmo came at once, having nothing to do and happening at that moment to be at home. He looked sullen and dissatisfied.

"Fengmo, my son," she said in a pleasant voice, "I have been too busy all these weeks since your grandmother left us to ask how things are going with you. Now, son, talk to your mother."

"There is nothing to talk about, Mother," Fengmo said carelessly.

"You and Linyi," she said, coaxing him.

"We are well enough," he said.

She looked at him in silence. He was a tall young man, spare in the waist, fine in the wrists and the ankles, lightly made but exceedingly strong. She smiled. "Sometimes when I look at you, it seems to me that you are just as you were when you were first put into my arms."

"Mother, why are we born?" Fengmo asked suddenly.

"Is it not the duty of each generation to bring the next into being?" she replied.

"But why?" he persisted. "Why should any of us exist? If I exist only to bring forth another like myself, and he but to bring forth still another, then of what use is this to me?" He did not look at her. "There is a me," he said slowly, "that has nothing to do with you, Mother, and nothing to do with the child to come from me."

She was frightened. Such questions and such feelings she herself had, but she had not dreamed to find them in a son. "Alas," she cried. "Your father never had such thoughts. It is I who have poured some poison into you."

"But I have always had these thoughts," he said. "I thought they would pass from me. Yet I continue to think them."

She grew very grave. "I hope it does not mean that you and Linyi do not go well together," she said.

He frowned. "I do not know what Linyi wants. She is restless."

"You are with her too much," she declared. "It is not good for a husband and wife to be continually together."

"Perhaps," he agreed.

She continued to look at him anxiously. "Fengmo, let us invite Brother André here again. While you were with him, it seemed to me you were happy."

"I might not be now," he replied listlessly.

"Come," she said firmly. She had learned long ago that listlessness must be met with firmness. "I will invite him."

He did not answer.

"Fengmo," she began again, "I desire the happiness of my sons. You are right to ask why you should only be a link in the chain of the generations. I have other sons. If you and Linyi wish to leave this house, tell me so."

"I do not know what I want," he said.

"Do you hate Linyi?" she asked. "How long have you been married to her? Only three short months. She is not pregnant and you are listless. What does this mean, Fengmo?"

"Mother, you cannot measure us by such things," he declared.

But she was too shrewd. "If man and woman are not well mated in body, there is no other mating. If the body is mated, then other mating will come. The body is the foundation of the house. Soul and mind, and whatever else, are the roof and whatever one adds to a fine house. But all this fails without the foundation."

Fengmo looked at her. "Well, let Brother André come," he said at last. He thought again awhile, and then he said, "He will be my only teacher. I shall stop going to the school."

"Let it be so, my son," she said.

VIII

IN THIS WAY Brother André came again into the house of Wu. He made no mention of the time since he had been here last. But when he was passing through the court after Fengmo's lesson, Madame Wu called to him gently. Brother André stopped. "Did you call me, madam?" he asked.

"Yes." She rose as she spoke. "If you have some time, please spare it to me to talk for a little while about this third son of mine. I am not pleased with him."

Brother André inclined his great head. She motioned him to a chair and he sat down and waited. His deep eyes were fixed on her face.

"Why is Fengmo unhappy?" she asked him directly.

"He is too idle," Brother André replied simply.

"Idle?" Madame Wu repeated. "But he has his duties. He is learning about the grain shops where we market our grains in the city. He is busy at this for several hours every day."

"Still he is idle. Fengmo has an unusual mind and a searching spirit," Brother André said. "He learns quickly. You bade me teach him English. But while he learns the language, he takes in something more. I found today he had forgotten nothing. The knowledge I gave him months ago has rooted in him and has sent up tendrils like a vine, searching for something on which to climb. Fengmo will always be unhappy until he has found something to fulfill his mind and his spirit."

Madame Wu listened to this. "You are trying to persuade me to let you teach him your religion," she said shrewdly.

"You do not know what my religion is," Brother André answered.

"Explain it to me," she commanded him.

"I will not explain it, for I cannot," he said. "I have no set ways of prayer."

"Then where is your religion?" she demanded.

"In bread and in water," he replied, "in sleeping and in waking, in cleaning my house and in making my garden, in feeding the lost children I find and take under my roof, in teaching your son, in sitting by those who are ill, and in helping those who must die so that they may die in peace."

"When my husband's mother died," Madame Wu said suddenly, "I had a strange wish to call you. But I was afraid the family would still want the temple priests."

"I would not have kept your priests away," Brother André said. "I never forbid anyone who can bring comfort anywhere. We all need comfort."

"Do you also?" she asked curiously.

"Certainly I also," he said.

"But you are so solitary," she exclaimed. "You have no one of your blood."

"Everyone is of my blood," Brother André said. "There is no difference between one blood and another."

"Why are you a priest?" she asked. This she knew to be rude. "You must forgive me. I am too curious."

"Do not ask my pardon," Brother André replied. "Indeed, I scarcely know how I became a priest, unless it was because I was first an astronomer."

"You know the stars?" she asked in great surprise.

"Madam, no one knows the stars," he replied. "But I study their coming and their going across the heavens."

"Do you still do this?" she inquired. She was ashamed of her curiosity concerning him. Yet his manner was so frank, so calm, that it piqued her.

"Unless the night is cloudy, I do so," he replied.

"You are very lonely," she said abruptly. "All day you work among the poor and at night among the stars."

"It is true," he agreed calmly.

"Have you never wanted a home and wife?" she asked.

"I once did love a woman," he replied, "and we were to be married. Then I entered into loneliness, and I no longer loved her, nor did I need her."

"This was very unjust to her, I think," Madame Wu said.

"Yes, it was," he agreed, "and I felt it so, but I could only tell her the truth. Then I became a priest in order to follow my loneliness."

"Is there no god in your faith?" she inquired.

"There is," he said. "But I have not seen His face."

"Then how can you believe in Him?" she asked.

"He is also in everything around me," Brother André replied.

"But your foundlings," she urged. "If you love your loneliness, then why have you taken in these unfortunate children?"

He looked down at his huge workworn hands. "These hands, too, must live and be happy," he said as though they were separate creatures and did not belong to him.

"Are there other men like you?" she asked.

"No man is quite like any other one," Brother André said. His sun-browned face took on a warm, almost smiling look. "But your son, young Fengmo, I think he could become like me. Perhaps he will become like me."

"I forbid it!" Madame Wu said imperiously.

"Ah!" Brother André said, and now he smiled. His eyes glowed for an instant, and then he said good-by. And she sat gazing up into the handful of stars above her court.

MADAME WU AWOKE the next morning when Ying came running in. "The wife of your eldest son is beginning labor," she cried.

"Ah," Madame Wu said, "send for her own mother. Meanwhile, I will go to her at once."

It was the day of women, as all days of birth are. The main room of Liangmo's court was full of excited maidservants and female relatives. "How are matters?" Madame Wu inquired of the midwife who had come out of the bedroom.

"All is well," the woman replied. "It is surely a boy." Her broad face beamed. "She carried him high."

But suddenly Meng screamed, and the midwife ran back into the bedroom.

In less than half an hour Madame Kang came hurrying in. She herself was already shapeless under her loose robes. Silence fell as she crossed the threshold. Curiosity and pity made the silence. She felt it and covered her shame with words. "Sisters!" she exclaimed. "Here you all are. How good you are to care for my child!"

"I have waited for your coming," Madame Wu said. "Let us go in together."

They went into the room where Meng lay upon a narrow couch. Sweat poured down her cheeks and wet her long hair. The two ladies, one on either side, held her hands.

"Mother," Meng gasped, "it's worse than last time."

"Truly it is not," Madame Kang comforted her. "It will be much quicker."

"Do not talk!" Madame Wu commanded them both. "Now is the time for effort."

To Madame Wu's cool thin hand, to Madame Kang's plump warm one, Meng clung. She shuddered and screamed and twisted the two hands she held. She flung herself straight and her body arched in pain. She opened her mouth wide and groaned and that groan rose into a final scream. Madame Kang pushed the midwife aside, put out both hands and caught the child.

"Another boy," she said reverently. The child, who had drawn in his breath, now let it out with a yell.

Madame Wu smiled down into the small wrinkled, furious face. "Are you angry that you are born?" she asked the child tenderly. "Hear him, Meng, he is blaming us all." But Meng did not answer. Released from pain, she lay like a flower beaten down to the earth by the rain.

THAT NIGHT Madame Wu and Madame Kang sat together. All was well in the house. The child was sound. The young mother slept. The two friends now sat in mutual contentment. Madame Wu had not spoken all day of Madame Kang's own shamefully swelling body. While they talked of family matters and many small things, a long shadow fell across the open door. It was Brother André coming to give Fengmo his lesson.

"The foreign priest?" Madame Kang asked.

"He comes here still to teach Fengmo," Madame Wu said.

Both ladies watched his shadow move away.

"Linyi—" They both began and stopped, each waiting for the other.

"Go on," Madame Kang said.

"Well, then," Madame Wu said after an instant, "I will proceed. Fengmo is not happy with your daughter, Meichen."

"Fengmo!" Madame Kang exclaimed. "Fengmo not happy!" she repeated with some scorn. "Ailien, let me tell you, it is Linyi who is not happy!"

"Meichen," Madame Wu said, "recall yourself."

"Yes," Madame Kang declared, "in a marriage there must be two. Can there be hand-clapping with only one hand? You have not taught Fengmo his part in marriage."

"I?" Madame Wu said sharply.

"Yes," Madame Kang said. "Liangmo is like his father, and so Meng is happy with him. But Fengmo is like you."

"That is to say, he demands something a little above the common," Madame Wu said bitterly.

"Then let him find it outside," Madame Kang said. "Let him

find work to soak up his discontent. It has nothing to do with Linyi."

"Meichen, you affront me!" Madame Wu exclaimed.

"Linyi had better come home for a while," Madame Kang replied.

Madame Wu saw their dear friendship tremble and crack. "Meichen, do we quarrel?" she exclaimed.

Madame Kang replied with passion, "I have never judged you even though I saw you thinking thoughts above a woman. But I have always known that you were too wise, too clever, for happiness." Madame Kang rose as she spoke and gathered her loose robes about her and deliberately walked away.

Late that night when Madame Wu was in bed, Ying said, "Do you know that Madame Kang took your third son's wife home with her tonight, my lady?"

"I know," Madame Wu said. She closed her eyes as though for sleep. But she did not sleep. She had not believed that Madame Kang would take back her daughter, as though Linyi still belonged to her. Fengmo must go and bring her back.

The next morning she called for Fengmo. He came in looking pale but calm.

"Son," she said, "I have sent for you to confess my own fault. Linyi's mother and I quarreled. Like stupid women, each of us declared for her own child. It was not Linyi's fault. Now we must invite her to come back to us."

To her horror Fengmo shook his head. "I will not invite her, Mother," he declared. "Linyi and I are not suited."

"How can you say that?" Madame Wu asked. "Any man and any woman, with intelligence, can suit each other. Marriage is a family matter." She leaned forward in her chair. "Fengmo," she said, "tell me what happened between you and Linyi."

"Nothing," Fengmo said doggedly.

"Nothing," she repeated, aghast. "You mean you two went into the same bed and nothing happened?"

"Oh, Mother," Fengmo groaned. "Why do you think that is the only thing that happens between men and women?"

"It is the first thing," Madame Wu insisted.

Fengmo set his lips together. "Very well, Mother," he said. "It was the first thing. Then I expected something more." He flung out his hands. "Some kind of talk, some kind of under-standing, companionship—"

Madame Wu began to see that she had not understood Fengmo. This so astonished her that for some time she sat looking at her son. "I feel I cannot command you to do anything," she said at last in a low voice. "I see now that I have violated your being."

He looked up and she saw tears in his eyes. "I should like to go away," he said.

These words wrenched her heart. But she only asked, "Where would you like to go?"

"Brother André said he would help me to cross the sea," Fengmo said.

"If Brother André had never come into this house," she said, "would you have thought of this?"

"I would have thought of it," he replied, "but I would not have known how. Brother André showed me the way."

She sat mute and thoughtful. "Very well, my son," she said at last. "Go free."

IX

In less than a month Fengmo went away. The entire household stood at the gate to see him go. The street that went past the gate ended at the river, and the menfolk, and with them Madame Wu, walked with him to the water's edge, where the riverboat would take him to the ocean and the great ship that lay waiting. The boat pushed off, and a score of farewells followed Fengmo. Madame Wu did not call after him. She stood, a small straight figure, and watched this son of hers cast off from the shores of his home. She was frightened and sad, but she comforted herself by these words, "He is free."

Fengmo's marriage had been patched together before he left. Madame Wu had gone to the Kang house and told Linyi that Fengmo was going away and invited her to return in order that he might leave her with child.

"I do this not only for the sake of our house," Madame Wu said to Linyi, "but also for your own sake."

Madame Kang had heartily agreed to Linyi's return. She had repented her anger at her friend. Linyi had aided her in this. For, when the girl had come back to her home, Madame Kang had realized after some days that her daughter was a willful young woman. Perhaps Fengmo had had something to complain about. She, too, was eager for Linyi to return to Fengmo.

"How can I make that naughty girl become a woman and a wife?" Madame Wu now asked herself. Brother André came into her mind again. But could he teach a young girl?

Clearly enough Linyi felt the change in her own mother. Silently she went back into Fengmo's court. He had been busy preparing for his journey.

"I have come back," she had said to him.

He did not say he was glad. She did not ask if he was. She helped him with new docility to fold his garments, and she dusted his books. At night they slept together. He took her and she yielded, partly for duty's sake, partly because they were young and hungry. In the morning they parted.

"Heaven give you safe journeying," she said and stood leaning against the door to watch him as he left. Then she yawned widely, and returned to the big bed and rolled herself into the quilts and slept.

Madame Wu awakened her as soon as Fengmo was gone. "Come, Linyi," she said, "you have slept long enough. Now you must wake and begin your education."

"My education?" Linyi faltered.

"You will learn cooking and embroidery in the morning," Madame Wu said. "In the afternoon Brother André will teach you foreign languages so that you will know something of what Fengmo knows when he returns."

Linyi's big eyes became startled. "Now?" she asked her. "At once," Madame Wu said firmly.

Because she did not trust Linyi, she stayed by her that afternoon when Brother André came. Then, too, for the sake of honor she herself should supervise the hours this foreign priest was with her daughter-in-law.

In this way she listened to everything Brother André taught Linyi. While the girl plodded unwillingly along, Madame Wu's mind flew ahead and wandered into a hundred bypaths. Each night after André left, she meditated on the meaning of what she had learned. She thought of scores of questions to which she wanted answers.

André's manner of answering was exceedingly simple, but this was because he was so learned. He put into a handful of words the essence of truth. And Madame Wu's mind was so eager, so bladelike and piercing, that she took his words and from them comprehended all. Young Linyi sat between the two, her eyes wide, as these few words were said. It was all far above her and beyond her.

But Brother André marveled at Madame Wu. "You have lived behind these walls all your life," he said one day, "and yet when I speak as I have spoken only to one or two of my few brother scholars, you know what I mean."

One afternoon when Brother André was putting his books together, she asked humbly, "Dare I ask you to take me, too, as your pupil?"

"I am honored by the wish," he replied in his grave way.

"Then for an hour, perhaps, after you have taught Linyi?"

He inclined his head. Thereafter each evening for an hour he answered Madame Wu's questions. Scrupulously, she bade Ying sit on the seat nearest the door during the lesson.

"Madam, I must ask you a question. If it makes you angry, I beg you to send me away," Ying said one morning.

"Why should I be angry now when for years you have spoken as you liked?" Madame Wu asked. She put down her book.

"I cannot please you with what I am about to say," Ying began. "But while you have been wandering around the earth with this big priest, this household has been at sixes and sevens. At night there is quarreling in your second son's court. And the second lady and our master—well, I say it is wrong for a lady to withdraw into books as you do."

Madame Wu listened. "Thank you, good soul," she said.

She rose and went into her bedroom. The morning was cool, and she put on a fur coat before she went out. In the court the orchids were dying with frost, but the sprays of berries on the Indian bamboo were turning scarlet. It occurred to Madame Wu as she went through the old lady's empty court that it would be well if Liangmo brought his family here to live, near her, so that she could watch over the children. Then she could move Tsemo and Rulan into Liangmo's present court, and the larger space might contribute to their peace.

The day was fair. She moved through the clear sunshine in a state of well-being that she herself did not understand. These four walls around this piece of earth were full of human troubles, but she felt able to meet them because she was no longer a part of them. Thus she stepped into Tsemo's court to minister and not to share.

At this hour Tsemo should have been supervising their produce markets. But he was still at home.

"I am making my rounds," Madame Wu said. "I stopped to say that I shall give Liangmo's court to you because I gave him the old lady's rooms in order that my grandsons can be near me."

"I will tell Rulan," Tsemo said.

As he said her name she detected a slight coldness in his tone. She spoke straightforwardly to him as was her habit. "I am told that Rulan cries in the night."

"Who told you?" he asked shortly.

"The servants," she replied.

"You were right, Mother," he said. "I should not have married this woman."

"Has love ended between you already?"

He walked about the tiny court. "We have nothing to say to each other without quarreling," he replied at last.

"How is it that she is not with child?" Madame Wu asked. "Quarreling always comes between men and women when there is no child."

"How can I tell?" he replied and shrugged his shoulders.

"You must be patient with her until she conceives. Once that happens, you will find her a new woman."

"Am I nothing to Rulan?" he asked arrogantly.

"She loves you too well," Madame Wu replied. "She has no defense from you, no refuge. She has no place to hide from you and be herself."

She could see he was deeply hurt by what she said. "You must take a journey somewhere," she went on. "Then when you come back, be gentle with her, not arrogant. Go away and leave her with me."

Now Rulan came out of the house. She could no longer pretend she did not hear all that was being said outside her window. In courtesy Madame Wu carried on the pretense. "I was telling Tsemo that if you please, my daughter, you may move into Liangmo's larger court since I will move them into the court next to mine."

"We thank you, Mother," Rulan said. But no thanks showed in her voice or in the expression on her face. She was carelessly dressed in an ugly robe of gray and green.

"I hate that robe," Tsemo said violently.

"Buy me another," Rulan said insolently, tossing back her head.

Madame Wu rose. She would not sit and watch the two of them quarrel. "Tsemo is going away for a while," she told Rulan, her voice revealing her displeasure. "I have given my permission. Be peaceful for these few days until he goes. Tomorrow busy yourself with moving into your new court."

"If Tsemo goes, I go," Rulan said. She stood very straight in the ugly robe, her hands clenched at her side.

"You do not go," Madame Wu said distinctly. "You will stay here with me. You have much to learn, and I will teach you."

After Madame Wu left, Rulan looked at her young husband with suffering eyes. "Tsemo, do you really hate me?" she whispered. She came nearer to him, and he looked down into her face.

"Why do you tear at me and wound me and give me no peace?" he said between clenched teeth.

"Peace so you can forget me!" she said passionately.

"I know that is why you want me angry at you," he retorted. He laughed sourly. "You make me angry so that you can force my mind toward you for that, at least."

He had plucked truth out of her, truth she hid even from herself. She saw him turn his head away from her, and the sight was dreadful to her. I must save myself from him, Rulan thought. I must rid myself somehow of love.

It was strange that at this moment when she longed to be free of him she thought of his mother. Impulsively, she ran past him and through the courts, and she did not stop until she found Madame Wu sitting in her library.

"Mother," she cried, "let me go free, too!"

Madame Wu did not reveal her consternation. She gazed at her tall daughter-in-law. "Calm yourself," she said.

"I want to go out of this house, away from Tsemo," Rulan said.

"I told you Tsemo is going away," Madame Wu said. "Of him you will be free."

"I want to be free of him forever," Rulan cried. "I hate what I feel for him. I am a slave to it." And then she added in a whisper, "Tell me how to free myself."

Madame Wu felt a great welling pity for her. Now that she saw how much Rulan loved Tsemo, she pitied the girl and forgave her everything. "If you had a child," she said, "you might be free of him. At least you would divide your love. Or it might be that you could undertake study, or painting, or some such thing. You must divide yourself, my child. You have allowed all your love to flow in one deep narrow river. Now you must dig yourself canals to drain off your love here and there."

"Forced labor," Rulan said bitterly.

"If need be," Madame Wu said gently. "But it is your only way to peace."

The two women looked steadily into each other's eyes. Madame Wu discerned the young hot soul, trembling with distress, and some loyalty deeper than that to the Wu family reached out and poured its balm upon her. "You are free when you gain back yourself," Madame Wu said. "You can be as free within these walls as you could be in the whole world. And unless you are free, however far you wander, you will still carry inside yourself the constant thought of him."

"I cannot live without love from him," Rulan faltered.

"Then hang yourself tonight," Madame Wu said calmly, "for I promise you he will not love you unless you let him first go free. Love only lives in freedom."

"I would be his slave if he loved me," Rulan said.

"You are not his slave," Madame Wu exclaimed. "You are striving to master him through your love. He feels it, he will not have it so. O foolish woman, how can I make you see how to be happy?"

Then Rulan fell at her knees. "I do see," she sobbed. "I know what you mean, but I am afraid to do it!"

But Madame Wu would not let her weep. "Get up, get up," she said, and she stood and lifted Rulan to her feet. "If you are afraid," she said sternly, "then I am finished with you. Never come back to me. I have no time for you."

Looking down at this exquisite, indomitable slender creature, Rulan felt her restless, bitter heart grow still. Madame Wu appeared now to be the only happy woman she had ever known. "I will obey you, Mother," she said humbly.

When she had gone, Madame Wu reflected with quiet astonishment at herself that she had sent two sons out of her house because of two young women, neither of whom she loved, and that upon herself she had taken their burden. "I, who myself crave my freedom!" she exclaimed.

"I CANNOT EXPLAIN myself," Madame Wu said to Brother André the next day. She had told him of Tsemo's going.

"Is an explanation necessary?" Brother André asked with a smile that began in the thicket of his eyebrows. The immensity of his head, his bulk and hairiness would once have terrified her. Now she was used to it.

"You often say we are all kin on this earth," she told him, "and yet how can you explain your own appearance?"

"What do you find strange in me?" he asked.

"You are too big," she said calmly, "and too hairy."

She saw glimmers of white teeth in the darkness of his beard and points of laughter in his dark eyes. "I have read that foreigners are hairy because they are nearer the animals," she observed.

"Perhaps," he replied. He opened his great mouth and let out a roar of laughter. . . . In the depths of the night, when Brother André lay alone on his bamboo pallet, he had thanked God that he had not met Madame Wu when she was a young girl. "I would not have answered for my soul, O God," he said grimly in the darkness.

In spite of her troubles in the house, Madame Wu met each day with relish and joy. Her only impatience was with the tasks of the house, though she did each task with firm self-discipline. Yet here in the library, Madame Wu forgot her own house. Brother André told her the history of the world, the rise of peoples and their fall. He told her of the discovery of electricity and of radium; he explained to her how waves of air could carry man's words and his music around the world.

"Have you the instrument for catching these words and this music?" she inquired.

"I have," he said. "I made such an instrument myself."

"Will you bring it to me?" she asked eagerly.

He hesitated. "Alas, it is fixed with many wires into the walls. Would you like to come to my poor house and see it?" he asked in return.

She felt suddenly shy. "Perhaps," she said, turning away.

"Do not be disturbed," he said. "There is nothing in me to disturb you. The man in me is dead. God killed him."

With these strange words he went away, and she was comforted as she always was after he had gone. He put much into her mind. She sat thinking, half smiling, her mind wandering over the world of which he had told her.

I wonder if I shall ever go beyond this city, she mused in her heart. I wonder if I shall ever sail on those ships and fly on those wings.

For the first time she felt sorrowful at the shortness of life. Forty years only, at the most, could be left to her. What could she do in forty years? She had spent forty years already and had not stirred from her own doors.

What do I know even about my own city? she mused. And here is our nation, set in the midst of these seas and mountains. Thus the enchantment of the world took hold of Madame Wu.

DAY UPON DAY Madame Wu came and went among her family, smiling and unseeing. They gathered at meals, and she sat in her accustomed place among them and saw none of them while she looked at them all.

Ying broached this subject rudely one day when she was cleaning her mistress's jewels. It was midwinter, and Madame Wu had set some lilies into a dish on the table. At that moment the sunlight chanced to break through the latticed windows.

"See how alike they are in the light, the pearls, the emeralds, the topaz, and the white and green and yellow of these flowers," Madame Wu exclaimed.

Ying looked up from the bracelet she held in her hands. "My lady, you are so quick to see such things, it is strange you do not see what is happening in your own house," she said.

"What do I not see?" Madame Wu asked, thinking of her two daughters-in-law.

"Our lord," Ying said.

"What of him?" Madame Wu asked quickly.

"Flower houses," Ying said shortly.

"He would not!" Madame Wu said.

"He does," Ying insisted.

Madame Wu thought deeply for a moment. "Ask our second lady to come here," she said.

Ying went away and Madame Wu took up her jewels and began to look at them. Every piece except the bracelets that her mother had given her at her wedding had come from Mr. Wu. Two moth hairpins made of silver filigree and pale jade made her remember Fengmo's wedding night when the women had caught moths and impaled them on the door. The antennae were fine silver wires tipped with pinpoints of jade, and they trembled as though alive.

At this moment Ch'iuming came in. She was heavy with child now.

Madame Wu held out the moth pins. "I will give these to you," she said. "I use them no more."

Ch'iuming put out her hand and took the pins and examined them silently. "They are too fine for me," she said. "I would not know how to wear them."

"Nevertheless, keep them," Madame Wu said. She turned over the jewels in the box with her forefinger. She had the wish to give Ch'iuming everything that Mr. Wu had given her, but this she knew she must not do. "I suppose he gives you jewels?" she asked.

"No," Ch'iuming said slowly. "But I do not want jewels."

"Does he go to flower houses?"

Ch'iuming's face flushed red. "I hear that he does," she said simply, "but he does not tell me."

"Can you not see for yourself?" Madame Wu inquired. "What is the measure of his feeling for you?"

Ch'iuming looked down. "It is too much for me, whatever it is," she said, "because I cannot love him."

These words she said sadly but firmly. Madame Wu heard them, and then to her amazement she felt pity for Mr. Wu. "Between you and me," she said, "we have dealt him evil—I with my age, you with your youth. Have you tried to love him?"

Ch'iuming lifted her dark, honest eyes. "Oh, yes, I have," she said. Then she added with humble sadness, "I obey him in everything. That at least I do."

"Does he know you do not love him?" Madame Wu asked.

"Yes, for he asked me and I told him," Ch'iuming said.

"Ah, alas, you should not have done that!" Madame Wu exclaimed. She sighed. "Well, there is no end to trouble between man and woman. When is the child to be born?"

"Next month," Ch'iuming said.

"Go back," she said. "I will speak to him and see where his heart is."

Ch'iuming rose, bowed and went out. In a moment she came back again and held out her hand. The jewels shone on her palm. "I forgot to thank you for these," she said.

"Wear them and that will be my thanks," Madame Wu replied.

That day Madame Wu sent her excuses to Brother André, and asked Ying to announce her impending arrival to Mr. Wu. He received this message and instead came to her court at once. "Let me come to you, mother of my sons," he said courteously.

She was surprised to see that he was thinner and less ruddy than he had been. His eyes were dull, and his full lips were pale.

"You look ill," she said. "Are you ill?"

"Not at all," he replied.

"The second lady?" she inquired.

He put up his hand. "She does her best for me."

"But she is not good enough for you." She decided to seize the truth. "I hear you visit flower houses," she said.

He shrugged. "Yes," he admitted. "You see, it is easier simply to buy women without expecting them to love. There is no pretense. I never pretended with you, Ailien, I did so love you. Now with this second one—I cannot either love or not love—it is better simply to go to a flower house."

"But next month your child is to be born," she reminded him.

"Yes, well." He rubbed his head in a puzzled fashion. "The strange thing is, I do not feel it is mine. After all, you and I, we have the three boys."

"It seems to me then that this Ch'iuming is of no use in the house," she said after a little time.

"Well, no, perhaps she is not," he agreed.

"I think you have not treated her well," she said severely.

He looked apologetic. "I am very kind to her."

"You have given her no gifts," she declared.

He looked surprised. "That is true, I have forgotten. I forget her continually."

"What happens at the flower houses?" Madame Wu asked.

"Nothing much," he said. "We usually have something to eat and drink. We gamble while the girls play lutes."

"How many girls are there?"

"Five or six—whoever is free," he said. "Kang and I are kindhearted, and they . . . " His voice trailed off.

"And then?" she inquired.

"Well, then, you see, the evening goes very quickly. The girls are full of stories and tricks." He was unconsciously smiling.

"And do you stay all night?" she inquired.

"Not usually," he said evasively.

She studied his bland face. The youthfulness that she had thought permanent was fading.

"Tell me, would you like to bring one of these flower girls into the house?" Madame Wu asked abruptly.

He looked surprised. "Why should I?" he asked.

"You really go there just to play," she declared.

"Perhaps," he agreed.

"How childish you are!"

"I am not as clever as you, Ailien," he said with humility. "And there is not much I need to do. Even with Tsemo and Fengmo gone, Liangmo manages everything." He sat there, handsome and kind and willing and childlike, and she had no heart to reproach him.

When they parted, she saw with sadness that he was cheerful again because they had talked together. She knew that as long as she lived she could not be free from him. It was not enough that she had never loved him. Love had nothing to do with responsibility.

X

MR. Wu entered the gaily decorated flower house with the air of a familiar and was greeted on all sides. The proprietor called to his assistant, "Tell Jasmine that Mr. Wu is here."

Mr. Wu proceeded amiably to an inner room and was at once served with tea and then with wine and a bowl of small dumplings. He ate these, and before he was through, Jasmine came into the room. She had been perfuming her long black hair. Since she was named Jasmine, she had usually one or two of those flowers tucked into the coils of her hair. Her face was powdered almost a pure white, and her lips were red and her eyes round and very dark. She was plump and her lips were always smiling. She came running in on her little feet and perched on the arm of Mr. Wu's chair.

He pretended not to notice her, and she pouted. "I am hungry," she whimpered. He dipped his porcelain spoon into the dumpling soup and fed it to her gravely, and she leaned forward like a child to receive it. Between them in silence they finished the food. He pushed his chair from the table and she slipped to his knee.

He remembered Madame Wu's question. Did he want to bring Jasmine into the house? Certainly it would be a pleasure, but he could not persuade himself to add to the house of his ancestors a flower girl.

As though she knew his thoughts, Jasmine slipped her arm about his neck. "I wish I could come and live with you," she said. "I would not trouble any of the great ladies. I would stay by myself all the time until you came."

"No, no," he said hastily. "I don't want you there. I like to visit you here. If you were to come to the house, I would have nowhere to go for my own pleasure."

"Couldn't you buy a little house for me, Mr. Wu?" she asked. "I would wait for you all day and all night."

Mr. Wu had already considered this possibility. "You see, my small flower," he said tenderly, "my sons' mother is a wonderful woman. She keeps the accounts. What would I tell her if I wanted to take a house for you?"

"Couldn't you sell a piece of your land and not tell her?" Jasmine asked. She had a childish little voice that went straight to his heart.

"I have never deceived her," Mr. Wu said, troubled.

"Does she know about me?" Jasmine asked.

"She knows," Mr. Wu replied.

Jasmine hid her face on his shoulder. "I am afraid I have happiness in me," she whispered. "That is why I want the house. I can't have a child here."

Mr. Wu was alarmed. He took her from his knee and set her on her feet. "Now," he said sternly, "there were others before me."

She took her hands from her face. The powder was undisturbed. "But there have been none since you came, and this is within the last three months. You came before that."

She wiped her eyes with the edge of her sleeves. "Never mind." Her childish voice was sad. "It is my fate. Girls like me—sometimes it happens in spite of ourselves. Especially when we really love a man. That is my mistake."

"Now," he said kindly, "whether it is my fault or not, you know there are ways of purging yourself. Here is something to help you."

He put his hand in his purse, but she would not take the money he held out to her and pushed his hand away. "No, please," she said. "I will bear the child. I want to bear him."

They were interrupted at this moment by loud cries from the outer room. "Mr. Wu, Mr. Wu!" the proprietor was shouting. The door burst open.

"Master, master!" Mr. Wu saw his own servant, Peng Er.

"You are wanted at home. The second lady has hanged herself from the old pomegranate tree!"

Mr. Wu leaped to his feet and strode away, leaving Jasmine in the middle of the floor frowning with anger.

The commotion of his own house rose over the walls of the compound and met him on the street. Priests had been called, and they were beating their gongs and crying for the lost soul of Ch'iuming. He ran through the open gate and hastened into his court. There the whole household had gathered to wail and to weep and to call Ch'iuming's name. She lay in the midst of them on the flagstones of the court. Madame Wu knelt beside her. Ch'iuming's pale face hung over Madame Wu's arm, wholly lifeless.

"Is she dead?" Mr. Wu shouted.

"We can find no life in her," Madame Wu replied. "I have sent for the foreign priest. If we have all these priests, why not him?"

At this very moment Brother André appeared, and the crowd divided before him. The other priests were silent in jealousy. In the center of this silence, Brother André fell to his knees and thrust a needle into Ch'iuming's arm.

"I do not ask what you do," Madame Wu said to him. "I know whatever it is, it is wise."

"A stimulant," Brother André said. "But it may be too late."

Ch'iuming's lips quivered; her eyelids fluttered. Madame Wu sighed. "Ah, she is alive. Then the child is alive."

"But why did she try to hang herself?" Mr. Wu exclaimed.

"Let us not ask until she can tell us," Madame Wu replied. "Announce to the priests that her soul has returned. Pay them well, father of my sons. Let them think they were successful so that they will go away and we can have peace."

As Ch'iuming came to, it became clear that her child was to be born early. She must be carried to her bed and the midwife sent for. These things were done, and Brother André was about to go away when Ch'iuming spoke. "Tell him to come here—only for a moment," she begged.

Madame Wu was surprised. She did not know that Ch'iuming knew Brother André. She stayed him as he was about to leave. "She asks for you," she said.

So Brother André turned and went into the room where Ch'iuming lay in the huge bed. When Ch'iuming spoke in so faint a voice he could not hear her, he leaned closer over her, and she said, "If a girl is born, I give it to you when I die. It is only a foundling."

"How can a foundling be born in this house?" he inquired gently.

"I am only a foundling," she said, "and this is the child of a foundling."

With that she closed her eyes and gave herself up to pain. He went away with a grave face and told no one what she had said.

Late that night a girl was born to Ch'iuming, a creature so small that Madame Wu took her and wrapped her in cotton fleece and put her into her bosom to keep her alive. Then she went quickly into her own courts, leaving Ch'iuming to the midwife and to Ying. In her own room she put the child into her bed to keep her warmed. A woman servant came in to see what was needed.

"Heat bricks and bring them here," Madame Wu said. "This child is a bud that must be carefully opened."

"Oh, mistress," the woman said, "why not let her die? A girl—what can she grow into but a sickly thing to make trouble in the house?"

"Obey me," Madame Wu said.

Two days later Brother André told Madame Wu of Ch'iuming's strange request.

"Certainly the child is not a foundling," Madame Wu said with dignity to Brother André. "She has been born into our house."

"I knew you would say that," he replied. "But why does this young mother say she is a foundling?"

"She was, until she came here," Madame Wu replied. She hesitated, and then to her own surprise she found herself telling Brother André how she had brought Ch'iuming into this house.

Brother André listened, his eyes downcast.

"I suppose since you are a priest, you cannot understand either man or woman," she said when the whole story was told.

"Being a priest, I can understand both man and woman," he said.

"Then tell me what I have done that is wrong."

He answered, "You have not considered that man is not entirely flesh, and you have treated your husband with contempt."

"I?" she exclaimed. "But I have thought of nothing but his welfare."

"You have considered only the filling of his stomach and the softness of his bed," Brother André said plainly. "And even worse, you have bought a young woman as you would buy a pound of pork. You have been guilty of three sins."

"Guilty?" she repeated.

"You have despised your husband, you have held in contempt a sister woman, and you have considered yourself unique and above all women. These sins have disturbed your house. Without knowing why, your sons are restless and their wives unhappy, and in spite of your plans no one is happy. What has been your purpose, madam?"

Confronted by his clear calm eyes, she trembled. "Only to be free," she faltered. "I thought if I did my duty to everyone, I could be free."

"What do you mean by freedom?" he inquired.

"Very little," she said humbly. "Simply to be mistress of my own person and my own time."

"You ask a great deal," he replied. "You ask for everything."

She felt nearer to tears than she had felt in many years. He had shattered the calm core of her being, her sense of rightness in herself.

"What shall I do?" she asked in a small voice.

"Forget your own self," he said.

"But all these years," she urged, "I have so carefully fulfilled my duty."

"Always with the thought of your own freedom," he said.

She could not deny it.

"Instead of your own freedom, think how you can free others," he said gently.

She lifted her head.

"From yourself," he said still more gently.

He rose to his great height, smiled down at her, and went away without farewell. This, which in another would have seemed rudeness, simply gave to Madame Wu the feeling that there was no break between this time they had spent together and the next time, whenever that would be. Nothing, she reflected, was as easy as she had thought. Freedom was not a matter of arrangement. She had seen freedom hanging like a peach upon a tree. She had nurtured the tree, and when it bore, she had seized upon the fruit and found it green.

She heard Ch'iuming's little child cry in the next room, and she went to her and took her into her arms. Some comfort came into the child, and she ceased crying and lay looking up into Madame Wu's face. I do not love this child, Madame Wu thought. Perhaps I have never loved any child. Perhaps that is my trouble, that I have never been able to love anyone.

When Ying came in, she said to her, "I will take her to her mother. She will live, this small woman, and she will hold her mother to life."

She carried the child into the room where Ch'iuming was. Ch'iuming lay with her eyes closed. She was very pale.

"Here is your child," Madame Wu said gently. "She is strong enough to come and lie on your arm."

When Ch'iuming did not move, Madame Wu lifted her arm and put the child into its circle and covered her with the quilt. Ch'iuming's arm tightened. She opened her eyes. "Forgive me that I did not repay you with a son," she said humbly.

"Do I not know that sons and daughters alike come from Heaven?" Madame Wu replied.

Then she remembered what Brother André said, and she went on quickly, "You must not feel that you have a duty to me. You have none."

Ch'iuming looked surprised at this. "But why else am I here?" she asked.

Madame Wu sat down on the edge of the bed. "It has been shown me that I did you a great wrong, my sister. It is true that I brought you here as I might have bought a pound of pork. How could I dare so to behave toward a human being? What can I do to make amends?"

Ch'iuming's face grew frightened. "But where shall I go?" she stammered.

Madame Wu saw that Ch'iuming had altogether failed to understand her and thought that she was useless and not wanted.

"I do not want you to go anywhere," Madame Wu said. "I am only saying that I have done wrong to you. Why did you ask the foreign priest to take your child if you died?" Madame Wu asked.

"I did not want to trouble you with a girl," Ch'iuming said.

"Why did you try to die before your destiny day?" Madame Wu asked.

"Because Ying told me she saw from my shape that I would give birth to a girl, and so I said, in my heart, we will both go together and be no trouble to anyone."

Madame Wu rose, feeling for the moment entirely helpless. "Give up these thoughts," she exclaimed. "Should you die, it would be a great trouble to bring up this child, and you know that I have never been one of those who think a female child can be allowed to die."

Ch'iuming closed her eyes again. The tears crept out from under her eyelids. But Madame Wu saw also that Ch'iuming's arm now held the child tightly, and so she took it for a good sign and went away.

When she was crossing the courtyard she met Mr. Wu coming in from the street.

"Mother of my sons!" he exclaimed.

"I have just been in to see our second lady," she said amiably. "She tried to die because she feared the child would be a girl and that the two of them would be a burden in the house. I have need of your wisdom. I will turn back with you."

They went back together and came into the large square room where they had spent so many hours of their common life.

"What shall we do with her, and the one she has brought?" Madame Wu said. "I see that she is not close to your heart. Yet here she is. I must apologize to you."

"I feel ashamed after your thoughtfulness—" he began.

"I was very selfish." She did not look at him. Instead she gazed at the shadows on the floor. She thought of Brother André, and suddenly she understood what he had meant. She could never be free until she had offered herself up utterly. "I see my wrong," she said. "We will send Ch'iuming away if you like. And I will return. We will forget, you and I, these last months."

She waited for his assent, but the silence went on too long. She looked up and saw his face was streaming with sweat. He laughed with misery and snatched open his collar, and then pulled out his silk handkerchief and wiped his face. "Had I known," he gasped, "had I dreamed—"

An ice-cold pressure crept into her heart. He did not want her. He had found someone else.

"Tell me about her," she said gently.

With embarrassed laughter, he told her that Jasmine was young, she was childish. "I do not want to add to your cares under this roof," he said.

She opened her lovely eyes. "Can it add to my cares if you are happy?" she asked tenderly. "Let her come and live under your own roof."

He rose and went over to her and took her hand. "You are a good woman," he said solemnly. "It is not given to every man to have what he wants and at the same time to live in peace under his own roof."

Long after they had parted she was amazed at her wounded pride. For her to choose a woman to take her place was one thing. To know that his love had ceased and have him choose a woman was quite another. Brother André had been right. She had thought herself free of him because she thought always and only of herself.

"How shall I forget myself?" she asked Brother André.

"Think only of others," he replied.

"Does that mean I am always to yield to others?" she asked. "My sons' father wants to bring another woman into the house."

"Is it not better to have her under this roof with your consent than under another without?" he replied.

She opened her book without further talk, and under his direction she studied the poetry of the Hebrew Psalms. She was deeply moved as the hour went by. Here the human heart cried out for that which it could worship. And what was worship except trust and hope that life and death had meaning because they were created and planned by Heaven?

"Is our Chinese Heaven your God, and is your God our Heaven?" she inquired of Brother André.

"They are one and the same," he replied.

"Then anywhere upon the round earth, by whatever seas, those who believe in any God believe in the one?" she asked.

"And so are brothers," he said, agreeing.

"And if I do not believe in any?" she inquired willfully.

"God is patient," he said. "God waits. Is there not eternity?"

She felt a strange warm current pass through him and through her. But it did not begin in him, and it did not end in her. They seemed only to transmit it, from the ends of the earth to the ends of the earth.

"Heaven is patient," she repeated. "Heaven waits."

Upon these words they parted. Brother André tied his books

and put them under his arm. She stood at the door of the library watching him as he walked across the court. His great form was beginning to stoop, she told herself, or perhaps it was because he walked with his eyes fixed upon the path just ahead of him. Seldom did he lift his head to see what lay at the end of the road.

She turned and went back into the library as was her habit when the lessons were over. She sat sometimes for as much as an hour to fix in her mind the words Brother André had spoken. But this day she had scarcely sat an hour when she heard loud voices shouting in the outer courtyard. She saw Ying come running into her court, wailing and crying.

Madame Wu rose at once. Something very evil had come about. She thought of Liangmo, but this morning he had left the house as usual. She thought of Mr. Wu. Then Ying was on the threshold, crying out, "Alas—the foreign priest!"

"What of him?" Madame Wu asked sharply. "He left here but a few moments ago."

"He has been struck down in the street," Ying cried. "His skull is cracked open!"

"Struck down?"

"It is those young men," Ying sobbed. "The Green Band— the evil ones! They were robbing the moneylender's shop, and the priest tried to save the moneylender and the young men beat him over the head, too."

Madame Wu knew the Green Band—young ruffians who roamed the country roads and city streets. The land steward had always on his bills an item, "For fee to the Green Band."

"Where is Brother André?"

"They have carried him into his house and he lies on his bed. The gatekeeper is here and says he asks for you," Ying said.

"I must go," Madame Wu said. "Help me with my robe. I will take a ricksha at the gate."

Behind the ricksha runner's back Madame Wu said, "I will pay you double if you double your speed."

"Triple me and I will triple my speed," he cried.

MADAME WU STEPPED out of the ricksha in front of a plain unpainted wooden gate set in the midst of a brick wall and went within. An old woman waited, weeping.

"Where is our elder brother?" Madame Wu asked.

The old woman turned and led her across a court filled with crowding, sobbing children, into a low brick house. There Brother André lay on a narrow bamboo bed. Ragged men and women were standing about him. They parted to let Madame Wu come to his bedside, and as though he felt her presence, he opened his eyes. His head was rudely bandaged in a coarse white towel. Blood was running from under it down his cheek, soaking the pillow under his head.

"I am here," she said. "Tell me what I must do."

For a long moment he could not speak. Then she saw his will gather in the depths of his dark eyes. His lips parted, and his breast rose in a great breath as he gazed at her. "Feed my lambs," he said distinctly.

Death came. His eyelids flickered, his will withdrew. His great body shuddered, and he flung out his hands so that they struck upon the cold brick floor.

Madame Wu stooped and picked up his right hand, and a ragged man stepped forward and took up his left. She stared across the body into the man's eyes. He was nothing, nobody, a beggar. He looked at her timidly and put down Brother André's hand gently on the stilled breast, and she laid the right one over it.

The children came running into the room and swarmed about the bed crying and calling, "Father—Father!" She saw that they were all girls, the eldest not more than fifteen, and the older ones were carrying the little ones who could not walk. They leaned on Brother André and felt him with their hands and stroked his beard. With their sleeves they wiped the blood from his face.

"Who are you?" she asked the girls in a strange quiet voice.

"We are his lambs," they cried in a disorderly chorus.

"Strays," the ragged man said. "He picked the little ones up from outside the city wall where they are thrown. The big ones are runaway slaves. He took in anybody."

She wanted to weep alone and for herself, but the children were flinging themselves upon him, wrapping their arms around him. "Oh, he's cold," one little girl sobbed. The tears were shining on her cheeks. She held his hand to her wet cheek. "His hand is so cold."

Madame Wu stood immobile in the midst of this strange family. Then it occurred to her that she did not yet know all that had happened.

"Who brought him to his bed?" she asked in a low voice.

The ragged man beat his breast. "It was I. I saw him fall. Everyone on the street was frightened. Others hid. But I am only a beggar, and what have I to fear? This foreign priest often gave me a little money. And sometimes he brought me home into this house at night and I slept here until morning, and he gave me food."

"You carried him here!" she said.

"These brother beggars and I," he said. She saw half a dozen ragged men. "He is too big for one or two to carry." She looked down on Brother André's peaceful face. She had come, hoping for a few words for herself. Instead he had said, "Feed my lambs." She looked at the children and they looked back at her, transferring their hopefulness from Brother André's silent figure to her.

"What shall I do with you?" she said uncertainly.

"My lady, what did our father tell you to do?" a thin little girl asked anxiously. She held a fat, cheerful baby in her arms.

"He said I was to feed you," she said.

The children looked at one another. The thin little girl shifted the baby to the other arm. "Have you enough food for us all?" she asked gravely.

"Yes," Madame Wu said.

"There are twenty of us," the little girl said. "I am fifteen years old—at sixteen he provides for us."

"Provides for you?" Madame Wu repeated.

The old woman had come in now. "At sixteen he finds them homes and good husbands," she said.

They were speaking as if Brother André were still alive. Madame Wu looked at Brother André. "Go away from this room," she said abruptly. "All of you! Leave him in peace."

They went out obediently, beggars and children and the old woman, and only she was left.

Madame Wu closed the door. The foreign priest was neither foreign nor a priest to her now. She had never thought of him as a man when he was alive, but now that he was dead she saw him as a man lying dead. In his youth he must have been extremely handsome. The great body lying outstretched before her was of heroic proportions. His skin was pale and now in death was becoming translucent. Suddenly she recognized him. "You whom I love!" she murmured in profound astonishment.

In the instant she accepted this recognition she felt her whole being change. Her body tingled, her blood raced, and her brain was clear. She felt free and whole. Looking down upon his body she knew that he had escaped from it. Not in years had she entered a temple, and she did not now believe in an unseen God, but she knew certainly that this man continued. "André." She said his name to him in a low clear voice. Never again would she call him Brother André. "You live in me. I will do my utmost to preserve your life."

The moment she had said these words peace welled up in her being. Standing motionless in the bare room before his shell, she felt happy. This happiness was an energy that began to work in her mind and body. She would continue to do whatever he had been doing.

She went tranquilly into the other room where the old woman, the beggars and the children were waiting. She sat down on one of the wooden chairs. "Now as to his funeral," she said. "Did he leave any directions?"

The old woman sobbed and wiped her eyes with her apron. "Certainly he never thought of dying," she exclaimed, "nor did we think of such a thing as his death."

"Does he have relatives anywhere?" Madame Wu asked. "If so, we should send his body to them."

No one knew of relatives. He had simply come here and had never gone away again. Madame Wu considered this. André belonged wholly to her. There was no one else. She would buy a plain black coffin and bury him in her own land. She thought of a place upon a certain hillside above the rice fields. There a gingko tree grew, very old, and she always rested in its shade when she went out to watch the spring planting.

She rose. "I will see that the grave is dug."

The children and the old woman looked at her anxiously as she rose, and she understood their anxiety. What, they were all thinking, was to become of them? "This house," she said, looking about the bare rooms, "does it belong to him?"

The old woman shook her head. "It is a rented house," she said, "and we got it very cheaply because it is haunted. But evil spirits feared him and here we have lived safely."

"He owns nothing?"

"Nothing except two changes of garments, a few books and his cross."

Madame Wu was looking about the room as the old woman talked. "What is in that black box?" she asked and pointed.

"That is a magic voice box," the old woman said. "He used to listen to the voices in the night."

Madame Wu remembered that he had told her of it. She approached the box and put her ear against it and heard nothing.

"It speaks for no one else," the old woman explained.

"Ah, then we will bury it with him," Madame Wu said.

"There is one more thing he possesses, and it is magic, too," the old woman said hesitatingly. She then crawled under the bed and drew out a long wooden box. She opened it, and there lay an instrument, a pipe of some sort. "He held it to his right eye whenever the night was clear, and he looked into Heaven," she said.

Madame Wu knew at once that this was his means of gazing

239

at stars. "I will take that with me," she decided. "And now bring his books to me," she said, "and let his garments and the cross be buried with him."

All the children listened in breathless silence and fear. Their home was gone. They had nothing left. Madame Wu smiled down on them. She understood with a tenderness wholly new to her what they were thinking. "As for you, all of you, and you too, Old Sister, you are to come to my own house and live."

A great sigh went over the children. With the ease and confidence of childhood they accepted their new safety.

"When? When?" they began to clamor.

"I think you should stay here with him until tomorrow," she said. "Then we will all go to the grave together. And you will come home with me."

"Good heart," the old woman sobbed, "such a kind good heart!"

"Have you rice enough for their meals today?" Madame Wu asked.

"He always kept a day's food in the house," the old woman said.

Madame Wu let the children press against her for a moment, knowing that they were accustomed to cluster about André, and so they needed the same bodily reassurance from her. Then she said gently, "Until tomorrow, my little ones," and left the house where his body lay and went back to her own house.

She sat awake and alone for hours that night, searching out the whole of her new knowledge. She loved a dead stranger, a man who had never once put out his hand to touch hers, whose touch would have been unthinkable. Had he lived, they would have accepted renunciation.

She sat motionless. She would have to discover herself. I am a stranger now to myself, she thought with astonishment. I shall no longer live out of duty but out of love.

Again she felt the strange enrichment flow through her whole being, followed by serene content.

The funeral was like none that had ever taken place before in this city. Madame Wu could not let it be like a family burial. But she gave it honor as the funeral of her son's tutor. The children were dressed in white cloth, unhemmed.

After some thought, she had asked whether the other foreigners in the city should not be told of the death. She sent a message by a manservant to the few foreigners there were, and the man came back saying that he was told that Brother André was a stranger to them, not being of their religion, and they would not come.

The funeral took place not the next day as she had first thought, because no coffin was found big enough and one had to be made. Working night and day, the coffin maker finished it in two nights and the day between; and then early in the morning before the city was astir, Madame Wu in her sedan chair headed the procession, which came on foot behind her and André in his coffin. She herself had seen to the lifting of his great body into the coffin, and she did not delay by sign or word the fitting of the heavy lid. Then the lid went down and she saw him no more.

Neither did she weep. She heard the nails pounded into the wood and saw the ropes tied to great poles. Twenty men were hired to lift the mighty casket, and they carried it out into the streets and through the city gate to the western hill, and now she led the way and others followed, and under the gingko tree the hill was ready to receive him.

None spoke while the coffin was lowered into the cave made for it. The children cried and the old woman wailed, but Madame Wu stood motionless and silent, and the earth was filled into the cave and the mound made.

In her heart for a moment was a hard dry knot of pain that she would see him no more except as he lived forever in her memory.

When all was done, Madame Wu led the procession home again, and she led the children into her own gates, and from that day they were homeless no more.

XI

THE NEXT MORNING instead of waking to weariness and a longing not to begin the day, she was aware of fresh energy in herself. What she felt now for André warmed and strengthened her. Love permeated her brain as well as her body. André was not dead. He was living, and he was with her because she loved him.

At this moment Ying came into the room, looking very discontented. "Do you not get up this morning, my lady?" she asked. Her voice was querulous.

"It is a rainy day," Madame Wu said, smiling. "I can tell by your voice, and there are clouds on your face."

"I never thought I should have to see a flower-house girl in our house," Ying retorted sourly, "and the front court is full of beggar children."

"So the girl Jasmine has come?" Madame Wu said.

"She is in the back court waiting," Ying replied. Her underlip thrust itself out. "She says she's expected."

After her bath and breakfast Madame Wu rose to go to the girl Jasmine. "Shall I not bring her here, my lady?" Ying inquired. "It will give her big thoughts if you go to her."

"No," Madame Wu said calmly, "I will go to her." She wished as few persons as possible now to enter her own court. Here let the spirit of André dwell undisturbed. Then on the threshold of the moon gate, a new thought came into her mind. André never held himself back from anyone. He would have met this girl freely to discern what he could do for her. His spirit here will help me, she thought.

She turned to Ying. "You may bring her to me after all," she said.

In a few moments Ying returned, marching ahead of a rosy plump young girl. This was the sort of woman Madame Wu naturally most disliked, a robust and earthy creature, coarse and passionate. She averted her eyes scornfully but felt any protest cut off, stilled by André. "Tell me why you want to come here to this house to live," she asked of the girl.

Jasmine looked down at her feet. "I want to settle myself before the child is born," she said.

"Is there to be a child?" Madame Wu asked.

Jasmine lifted her head for one quick look. "Yes!" she said loudly.

"There is no child," Madame Wu replied.

Jasmine lifted her head again, opened her lips to respond, and stared into Madame Wu's eyes. She burst into tears.

"So there is no child," Madame Wu repeated. She motioned the girl to sit down on a porcelain garden seat. Jasmine sat down, rubbing her eyes with her knuckles and drawing her sobs back into her throat. Madame Wu began to speak. "You know," she said to Jasmine, "it is a very grave thing to enter a large and honorable family such as ours. You can come into it and ruin all our happiness here. Or you can come in and add happiness by your presence. If you come for rice and shelter, I beg you to tell me. I will promise you these. You may have them freely without having to buy them here with your body."

Jasmine looked shrewdly at Madame Wu. "Who gives a woman something for nothing?" she asked.

Madame Wu marveled at herself. Had this happened a month ago, she would have despised the girl's coarseness. Now she understood it. "But you are here for something more," Madame Wu persisted.

Jasmine's face was suddenly scarlet under its powder. "I like the old head—" she muttered in the jargon of the street.

Madame Wu knew she spoke of Mr. Wu, but she did not reprove her. Truth was stealing out of the girl's heart.

"He is much older than you, child," Madame Wu said.

"I like old men," the girl said. "He is so patient. When I don't feel well, he notices it. Young men don't care. They take what they want. But this old one always asks me how I feel."

"Does he indeed," Madame Wu replied. This was not the Mr. Wu she had known. "The important thing is, will you add happiness to this house or take it away?"

Jasmine lifted her head eagerly. "I will bring happiness, I promise you, my lady—"

"What position do you want?" Madame Wu asked sharply.

"I ought to be the third wife," Jasmine said.

"Why not?" Madame Wu said amiably.

"You mean I can live here—in this great house—and be called the third lady, and when my child—"

"I would not want any child of our house to be illegitimate," Madame Wu said. "That would be unworthy of our name. You will be honored."

Jasmine stared at her with rounding black eyes, and then she began to sob. "I thought you would hate me," she gasped. "I was ready for your anger. Now I don't know what to do."

"There is nothing you need to do," Madame Wu said calmly. "I will have a maid lead you to your rooms. They are small, you know, only two, and they are to the left of my lord's court. His second lady lives to the right. You need not meet. I will myself go and tell my lord you are coming."

When she was gone, Madame Wu thought in some wonder, I did well. If Jasmine really loved Mr. Wu, that love, too, must be allowed. All the unhappiness in homes came because there was not love.

When Ying came in, Madame Wu asked, "Have the children in the court been fed?"

"Certainly not, my lady," Ying said sternly. "No orders have been given."

"Then I give orders now," Madame Wu said gently. "Let rice be cooked at once, and bread brought and tea made for their noon meal."

She was amazed to see Ying run sobbing out of the room. "You are changed!" she cried. But at noon Ying had great buckets of rice set in the court, and when Madame Wu went there it was to see the little girls eating happily and feeding the younger ones. The old woman who had been their caretaker rose and cried out to the children that they must greet Madame Wu as their mother.

"Now that your father has gone, I am your mother," Madame Wu said, smiling. The children looked at her with love, and suddenly for the first time in her life Madame Wu felt the true pangs of birth. These orphans were André's and hers.

"You all are my children," she said, wondering that the words could be hers. At the sound of her voice the children rushed to her to embrace her, to lean against her. "Your father did the best he could for you," she said, smiling, "but you need a mother, too." She touched a sore red scar on a child's cheek. "Does it hurt?" she asked.

"A little," the child replied.

"And how did you come by it?" Madame Wu asked.

The child hung her head. "My mistress held the end of her cigarette against me there—"

"Oh, why?" Madame Wu asked.

"I was her slave, and I couldn't move fast enough," the child replied. She put her hand into Madame Wu's. "Will you please give me a name?" she begged. "Our father was going to give me a name and then he died too soon. All the others have names."

"They shall tell me their names, and then I shall know what to name you," Madame Wu replied.

One by one, they repeated their names, and each was a word spoken from André. Pity, Faith, Humility, Grace, Truth, Mercy, Light, Song, Star, Moonbeam, Sunbeam, Dawn, Joy, Clarity—such were the names he had given the older ones. The younger ones he had called playful names. Kitten and Snowbird, Rosepetal and Acorn, Silver and Gold. "Because he said silver and gold had he none," Gold proclaimed, "until we came." They all laughed at such nonsense. "He did make us laugh every day," Gold said.

The nameless child pressed close. "And my name?" she asked.

Madame Wu looked down. The child was exquisite, full of beauty to come. The name rose in Madame Wu's mind. "I will call you Love," she said.

"I am Love," the child repeated.

By now the court was fringed with silent onlookers. The servants had made one excuse and another to pass this way, but the children of the household and distant relatives made no pretense of errands. Old cousins and poor nephews stood gaping at Madame Wu. She turned to them. "Where shall we house my children?" she asked gaily.

"Sister," an old widow answered, "if you are doing good deeds, let them be housed in the family temple."

Madame Wu accepted the widow's words at once. "How wise you are," she said gratefully. "No home could be better. There are courts to play in, and the pool and the fountain. The family gods will have something to do now."

In the back of the Wu courts was the old temple, built by an ancestor two hundred years before. Madame Wu led the way, and the children ran after her in the sunlight. Holding by the hand the child she had named Love, she stepped over the high wooden doorstep and into the temple, assigning rooms where until now only gods had stood silently gazing.

The child Love clung to her. "Let me come with you," she begged Madame Wu. "I will wash your clothes and serve your food."

Madame Wu's heart turned into warm flame. But she knew that André would not have showed favor to one child above another. "You must stay and help the others," she said. "That is what your father would have wished."

To announce Jasmine's coming to Mr. Wu, she entered his court through the moon gate.

"Are you well, father of my sons?" she asked courteously.

"Very well, mother of my sons," he replied.

"I have just spoken to the girl Jasmine," she said to him calmly. She seated herself to the left of the table against the wall, and he took his usual seat at the right.

He busied himself with his pipe and she saw now that he was afraid of her. She was sad to see the furtive turning of his eyes and the slight tremble of his plump hands. Where there was fear, no love could be. She understood, with a strange pang that held no pain, that Mr. Wu had never really loved her, or he would not now be afraid of her.

"Tell me how you feel toward this girl," she said to Mr. Wu.

A soft smile crept about his lips. "Jasmine is so little, so ignorant, so weak," he said. "No one has ever taken proper care of her. No one has ever truly understood her. She seems simple and ordinary, but there are good qualities in her heart. She is not, you understand, a creature of high intelligence. But she has deep emotions."

Madame Wu listened to this with amazement. "You really love her!" she exclaimed.

There was admiration in her voice, and Mr. Wu responded to it proudly and modestly. "If what I have told you is love, then I do love her," he replied.

This perception filled her with astonishment. It was not a wonder that a man like André should have awakened love in her. But that this common, rosy little street girl should have roused in Mr. Wu something of the same energy was a miracle.

"You do not mind?" Mr. Wu said. His face, turned toward her, was tender and pleading.

"I rejoice," she said quickly. "I ask only one thing," she added. "That Ch'iuming be allowed to leave."

"Indeed, I am quite willing for her to remain," Mr. Wu said kindly. "Where would she now go if you send her away?"

"I shall not send her away," Madame Wu replied. "For the present, let her move into my own court."

XII

The house of Kang was all in turmoil. In the main room of the inner court Mr. Kang sat weeping. He rose when he saw Madame Wu. "The child refuses to be born," he said.

"I know," Madame Wu said, looking away from him. Again she would have marveled that her friend could love this man, except now she knew how strange love could be. She moved quickly to the satin curtains that hung between this room and the bedroom. "I will go in at once, if you will allow me," she said.

"Go in, go in—save her life," he blubbered.

The smell of wasted blood was hot in the air of Madame Kang's bedroom. A lighted oil lamp flickered in the cavern of the great bed where she lay. Madame Wu looked down into the face of her friend.

"Meichen," she said softly.

Slowly Madame Kang opened her eyes. "You," she whispered, "you've come. I'm dying—"

Madame Wu had her friend's wrist between her fingers. The pulse was very faint indeed. "Meichen, do you hear me?" she asked clearly. Madame Kang did not speak, but Madame Wu saw consciousness in the depths of her eyes. She went on, "You will lie here quietly while I go and fetch some broth. You will drink it and you will rest. Then you will feel strong again and I will help you give birth to the child. Between us it will be easy."

The faintest of smiles touched Madame Kang's lips. Madame Wu covered her warmly and went into the other room.

"I need your help," she told Mr. Kang.

"Will she live?" he cried at her.

"If you help me," she replied.

"Anything, anything!"

She commanded a servant, "Bring me a bowl of the best broth you have ready, and put into it two spoonfuls of red sugar. Have it hot."

She turned again to Mr. Kang.

"You are to bring it in, not one of the maids."

"But I—" he sputtered. "I assure you I am clumsy."

"You will bring it in," she repeated.

She went back again into the shadowy bedroom. Soon she heard Mr. Kang's heavy footsteps. In his hands he held the jar of hot broth.

"We will put the broth into the teapot," she decided. Then she turned to the bed. "Meichen," she said, "you have only to swallow." She tested the heat of the soup in her own mouth and then put the spout of the teapot to Madame Kang's lips. Madame Kang swallowed again and again.

Madame Wu set the teapot on the table and turned back her satin sleeves and tied around her waist a towel that was hanging on a chair. Mr. Kang watched her, his eyes staring in horror. "I ought not to be present," he whispered. But she motioned to him to come nearer, and he obeyed her. He had begotten many children, but never had he seen what his begetting did.

Madame Wu turned back the covers and leaned over her friend. "Meichen," she said clearly, "allow your body to rest. I will work for you." But the moment she touched the sore flesh, Madame Kang groaned. Mr. Kang clapped his hands to his mouth and turned his head away.

"Hold her hands," Madame Wu said to him. "Give her your strength."

Her great eyes were fixed on him with stern power. He stepped forward and took his wife's hands. And this, this alone, made Madame Kang open her eyes. "You," she gasped, "you—the father of my sons!"

At this moment Madame Wu slipped her strong hands around the child, and Madame Kang screamed.

Mr. Kang burst into sweat. He groaned and clenched his hands around his wife's. "Heart of my heart," he cried. "Don't die, don't die—"

"I won't die," Madame Kang gasped.

At this moment Madame Wu moved the child out of the woman's body. Blood flowed, but Madame Wu stanched it with handfuls of cotton that the midwife had put by the bed.

Mr. Kang still clutched his wife's hands. "Is it over?" he mumbled.

"All over," Madame Wu said.

"The child?" Madame Kang whispered.

Madame Wu held the small body gently and wrapped it in the towel she took from her waist. "The child is dead," she said to them both, "but you two do not need this child."

"Certainly not," Mr. Kang babbled. "Meichen, I promise you, no more children. Never, never, I promise you—"

"Hush," Madame Wu said sternly. She felt the teapot and it was still hot. She put the spout to her friend's lips. "Drink," she said. "You have promised to live."

Madame Kang drank. Her eyes were closed again, but the pulse in her wrist, when Madame Wu felt it, was a little stronger. She motioned to Mr. Kang to loose his wife's hands. "She must sleep," she directed. "I will sit here beside her. Take the child away for burial."

On the morning of the second day, when Madame Wu was certain that her friend was recovering, she left the room at last. Outside the door Mr. Kang still sat waiting alone. He had not washed himself, nor had he eaten or slept, and all pretense and falsity had left him. He was tired and frightened. Madame Wu took pity on him and sat down in another chair.

"I owe her life to you," Mr. Kang said, hanging his head.

"Her life must not be put into this danger again," Madame Wu said gently.

"I promise—" Mr. Kang began.

Madame Wu put up her hand. "Can you keep that promise when she is well again?" she asked. "It is unfortunate that she loves you so much, unless you also love her."

"I do love her," Mr. Kang protested.

"Enough to make her life good?" Madame Wu pressed him.

His look faltered. "I didn't know—" he began. "I never knew about life. How hard it comes—it costs too much."

"Birth for any woman is always near to death," she replied. "Now for her it has become either birth or death. You can no longer have both."

He put his hand over his eyes. "I choose her life," he said.

She rose silently and went out of the room. She would never perhaps see him again. In their life men and women remained apart from each other, and she would once again merely bow to him across a room.

So Madame Wu went home, very tired and not a little sickened by all she had seen and done. Had she not known love in her own heart, she could not by any means have saved Meichen's life. The horror of the flesh would have overwhelmed her, the smell of blood, the ugliness of Mr. Kang's fat weeping face.

Ying came in, scolding. "My lady, my lady—look at your coat! Why, there's blood on it, and you're so pale—"

Madame Wu looked down and saw blood on her satin garment. She who was so fastidious now only murmured, "I forgot myself."

MADAME WU did not understand fully the change that had taken place in her being. Indeed, she did not know from one moment to the next where her path lay. But she felt that she was walking along a path of light. And the light that lit this path was her love for André. When she needed to know what step should be taken next, she had only to think of him.

Thus the next day when Ying brought her the little girl to whom Ch'iuming had given birth, she felt a great tenderness for the child. Whereas before she had felt this child a new burden, and the whole matter of Ch'iuming perplexing, now she felt that there was no burden and she must deal with both mother and child as André would have her do.

"Where is Ch'iuming?" she asked Ying.

"She busies herself about the kitchen and the gardens," Ying said.

"Is she happy?" Madame Wu asked.

"That one cannot be happy," Ying replied. "We ought to send her away. It is bad luck to have her sad face everywhere."

"Let Ch'iuming come here to me," Madame Wu said.

Near her in a basket bed the little girl lay playing with her hands. She lost them every now and again, and each time she saw them a look of surprise came over her tiny face. Watching this play, Madame Wu laughed gently.

Ch'iuming came slipping between the great doors that were closed against the coldness. Madame Wu looked up. The girl seemed part of the morning mist, all gray and still and cold.

"Look at this child of yours," Madame Wu said. "She is making me laugh because she loses her hands and finds them and loses them again."

Ch'iuming came and stood beside the cradle and looked down. Madame Wu saw that the child was alien to her. "Can it be you do not love your own child?"

"I cannot feel that she is mine," Ch'iuming answered.

"Yet you gave birth to her," Madame Wu said.

"It was against my will," Ch'iuming said.

The two women were silent, and each watched the unknowing child. "Whom do you love?" she asked Ch'iuming suddenly.

She was not surprised to see the young woman's face flush a bright red.

"I love no one," she said, lying so plainly that Madame Wu laughed.

"Now how can I believe you?" she said. "Your face tells the truth. Are you afraid to let your lips speak it, too? You do not love this child—that means you do not love the father. Well, let that be. Love comes from Heaven, unasked and unsought. Shall I blame you for that? I know the wrong that I did. But when I brought you here, I myself did not understand love. I thought men and women could be mated like male and female beasts. Now I know that we can unite ourselves without a touch of the hands. We can love even when the flesh is dead. It is not the flesh that binds us together."

This was such strange talk from Madame Wu that Ch'iuming could only look at her as though she were a ghost.

"Come," Madame Wu said, "tell me the name in your heart."

"I die of shame," Ch'iuming said. She folded the edge of her coat between her thumb and finger.

"I will not let you die of shame," Madame Wu said kindly. With much hesitating, Ch'iuming spoke a few words at a time. "You gave me as a concubine to the old one, but—" Here she stopped.

"But there is someone else to whom you would rather have been given." Madame Wu helped her so far, and Ch'iuming nodded. "Is he in this house?" Madame Wu asked.

This time Ch'iuming looked up at her and began to weep.

"It is Fengmo," Madame Wu said. Ch'iuming went on weeping.

"Do not weep anymore," she said to Ch'iuming. "This is all my sin, and I must make amends somehow."

At this Ch'iuming fell on her knees and put her head on her hands on the floor. "I should die of shame," she murmured. "Let me die. There is no use for a creature like me."

"There is use for every creature," Madame Wu replied and lifted Ch'iuming up. "Now I beg you, wait patiently in this house. Light will be given me, and I shall know what I ought to do for you. In the meantime, help me to care for the foundlings that I have taken. It will be of great use to me."

Ch'iuming wiped her eyes. "I will tend the foundlings, my lady," she said. "Why not? They are sisters of mine." She stooped and lifted her child out of the cradle. "I will take this child with me, for she is a foundling, too."

Madame Wu did not answer. Where happiness could be found for Ch'iuming she did not know. Only time would reveal it.

As THE DAYS passed into weeks and months, Madame Wu considered the family. Alone in the library where nowadays she always sat because she felt André's presence there, she pondered upon the differences between men and women.

Once, when André had sat in the chair across from her, she had said to him, "Is man all man and is woman all woman?"

André had answered, "God gave us each a core of our own; that is, a part simply human, neither male nor female. It is called the soul. It is unchanging and unchangeable."

"And what is the soul?" she had asked.

"It is that part of us that we do not inherit from any other creature," he had said. "It is that part that gives me my own self and makes me a little different from all those who came before me, however like them I am."

Was it not possible that there could be love and friendship between souls?

"It is possible," she murmured now.

It had been many months since Tsemo and Fengmo had left home. Their letters came regularly. From these letters Madame Wu had discerned clearly that her two sons were growing in opposite ways. Fengmo had gone abroad to study. His letters bore a strange postmark and stamp from America. Fengmo pursued the studies that André had begun. Madame Wu was relieved to learn that they had nothing to do with priesthood. Tsemo had not crossed the sea. Instead, he had gone to the capital, and there he had found a good position. He wrote that if the war that threatened should come, the government would retreat inland, and there it would depend very much on its highest families. In their province the Wu family was the greatest. Therefore Tsemo was given a good deal of preference, and he had to endure the envy and malice of those who were not. But he was young and a hard worker, and he made his own way for himself in spite of the circumstances.

Their concern for Tsemo was heightened by the sudden news of an attack by the East Ocean people that year on the coast. So other attacks had been made in many previous centuries, and the nation had always stood. It would stand now, and Madame Wu was not troubled. But the government was moved inland, and Tsemo came with it. He wrote one day in the early autumn that he would come home for ten or twelve days.

Tsemo's letter reminded Madame Wu that within this house—her world—there remained two disordered beings, Rulan and Linyi. Without haste, she decided to speak with them, first with Rulan, the elder.

In all these months she had seen Rulan often. At mealtimes,

at the usual festivals of spring and winter, Rulan was there, always quiet and sober in her dress. There were also times when Madame Wu had wished some writing done for the family records and she had called upon Rulan for this. But at no time had she drawn the girl out of her place in the family. Now, with Tsemo's letter, she knew the time had come.

Rulan walked quietly through the courts. She no longer wore the hard leather shoes that she had brought with her from Shanghai. Instead she wore velvet ones, cloth-soled. Madame Wu did not hear her footsteps, and when her tall shadow fell across the floor, she looked up in surprise. "Daughter, how softly you walk," she exclaimed.

"I put aside my leather shoes, Mother," Rulan replied.

Madame Wu said courteously, "It has been in my thoughts to ask about your family in Shanghai. When the enemy attacked, did they escape?"

"My father took the household to Hong Kong," Rulan replied.

"Ah, a long way," Madame Wu said kindly.

"But not long enough," Rulan said with some energy.

"You believe that the enemy will dare to attack so far?" Madame Wu inquired.

"It will be a long war," Rulan replied, "for it has been long in preparation."

"Where did you get this knowledge?" Madame Wu asked.

"Tsemo writes to me every week," Rulan said.

Encouraged, Madame Wu asked, "Are you and Tsemo good friends again?"

"We agree wonderfully when we are not together. As soon as he comes home we will quarrel again—I know it."

"But if you know it," Madame Wu said, laughing, "can you not guard against it? Which of you begins it—you or he?"

"Neither of us knows," Rulan said. "We have sworn to each other in our letters that whoever begins, the other will speak to stop it. But I have no faith in our ability. I know Tsemo's temper, and when he is angry, I am angry. There is something in me that he hates. When we are parted, he does not feel it. When we come together, it is there."

"This need not be true," Madame Wu told her. "Between men and women there is no duty. There is only love—or no love. Neither of you owes anything to the other."

Rulan interrupted her with surprise. "Mother, this is the strangest thing I ever heard said from a mother-in-law to her son's wife."

"I have learned it only recently," Madame Wu said. She smiled with secret mischief. "Credit me, child, that I am still learning!"

Rulan had come prepared for her mother-in-law's anger. Now hope stirred within her. It was not anger that she was to receive, but wisdom. She leaned forward to listen.

"Trouble between men and women always arises from the belief that there is some duty between them," Madame Wu went on. "But once having given up that belief, the way becomes clear. Each has a duty only to himself. And how to himself? Only to fulfill himself. If one is wholly fulfilled, the other is fulfilled also. You and Tsemo departed from the usual tradition. You chose each other because you loved each other. You thought only of yourselves as two beings separate from all others. But you are not separate, except in a small part of yourselves. Now you are trying to force all your lives into that small part. It will not contain that much. You are choking each other at your sources. You are too close. You will hate each other because that part of you which is you—your soul—has no space left to breathe and grow."

Madame Wu was suddenly intensely lonely for André. The knowledge that never again would she look upon his living face pierced her with an agony she had not yet felt. She closed her eyes and endured the pain. Then after a while she felt Rulan take her hand and press it to her cheek. Still she did not open her eyes. "And in secret the woman has to lead," she said. "The woman always has to lead, and she must, because life rests upon her, and upon her alone."

That night as she was being undressed for bed Madame Wu spoke to Ying. "In less than a month my second son will come home."

"I know that, mistress. We all know it."

"This is the task. Every night when you have finished with me, you are to go to my second son's wife and do for her what you used to do for me."

Ying smiled into the mirror, but Madame Wu did not return the smile. "You are to forget nothing that I used to do—the fragrant bath, the smoothing with oil, the perfume in the hair."

"What if she forbids me?" Ying asked. "That one cares nothing for her beauty."

"She will not forbid you," Madame Wu said. "She needs help, poor child, as all women need it. And she knows it now."

XIII

Tsemo came home on the fifth day of the ninth month of the year. The news of his coming was brought by electric letter to the city and by foot messenger to the house of Wu. Everything was prepared. On the very day of his return Madame Wu summoned Rulan.

Rulan had put on a new robe of dark red, and this color suited her. Madame Wu approved its close cut, its length, and did not mention the shortness of the sleeves, since Rulan had beautiful arms and hands. She bade Ying open her jewel box and from it she selected a thick gold ring set with rubies. This ring she put on the middle finger of Rulan's right hand, and Rulan lifted her hand to admire it.

"It suits you," Madame Wu said, "and what suits a woman makes her beautiful."

Rulan had just washed her hair, and it lay on her shoulders as soft as unwound silk. Ying had cut it even and smooth. It was a new fashion for young women to let their hair go unbound, and Madame Wu did not like it. But she saw that the softness set off Rulan's face, and she did not speak against it.

Tsemo was expected within four or five hours, but who could know that he was approaching through the sky? When his superior in the capital had heard of his return home, the importance of the Wu family was such that he had sent him with a government plane and pilot. Instead of coming to the land by the river, the plane carrying Tsemo came down and touched earth just outside the low wall on the south side of town.

The pilot took off again into the sky, and Tsemo walked calmly homeward, everybody greeting him as he went and asking him how he came, and goggling when he said, "I came through the empty air."

Children ran ahead to tell the house of Wu that the second lord was coming, but Tsemo walked in such long steps that he was very close behind. Thus Madame Wu and Rulan had barely heard the gateman's wife when Tsemo himself was at her heels. By rights he should have gone first to his father, but Liangmo had written him of Jasmine and he had no mind to see a strange woman before he saw his mother. Therefore he went first to Madame Wu and was confounded to see with her Rulan, his own wife.

It was an awkward moment, for by tradition he should not greet his wife before his mother. To his surprise Rulan fell back gracefully.

"My son, you have come at last," Madame Wu greeted him. She put out her hands and felt his arms and his shoulders. "You are thinner than you were," she said. "But hardier and healthier," she added, looking at his ruddy face.

"I am well," he said, "but very busy—indeed, busy half to death. And you, Mother, look well—better than when I went away."

This and more passed between them, and still Rulan stood waiting, and Tsemo wondered very much at this patience. To his further surprise, his mother now stepped back and put out her hand and took Rulan's and drew her forward. "She has been very good," Madame Wu said. "She has been obedient, and she has tried hard and done well."

Nothing could have pleased Tsemo so much as this commendation of his wife by his mother. She had never praised Rulan before, and it had been one of the causes of his anger against Rulan. Madame Wu saw the pleasure in his handsome face, in his brightening eyes. Tsemo spoke a few words to Rulan, cool words as words should be in the presence of the older generation. "Ah, you are well?"

"Thank you, I am well, and you?"

These were the few words they spoke with their lips, but their eyes said more. For Rulan lifted her eyes to his, and he saw her more beautiful than he had ever seen her.

He turned to his mother, stammering and blushing. "Mother, thank you very much for taking time to teach her, for taking time to—"

Madame Wu understood and answered him. "My son, at last I can say, 'You have chosen well.'"

She saw tears come into Rulan's eyes, and a tenderness she had never known before filled her being. How helpless were the young, and in spite of all their bravery, how they needed the old to approve them! Madame Wu felt an immeasurable longing to make these two happy in her house. She took Rulan's hand and Tsemo's hand and clasped them together. "Your duty to me is done, my son," she said. "Take her to your own courts and spend your next half hour with her alone. It will be time enough then to go and greet your father."

She watched them go away, still hand in hand.

FOR THE NEXT ten days the house was a turmoil of feasting. Every relative near and far wished to see Tsemo and talk with him and ask his opinions concerning the new war and the moving of the seat of government inland. No one thought of defeat by the enemy. The only question was whether there should be the open resistance of arms or the secret resistance of time. Tsemo, being young, was for open resistance.

Madame Wu, sitting among the family, listening, kept silent. Tsemo talked briskly of regiments and tanks and planes. All these things for her held no meaning. She believed that only by the secret resistance of time could they overcome this enemy as they had overcome all others. At last she forgot herself and yawned so loudly that everyone turned to look at her, and she laughed. "You must forgive me," she said. "I am getting old." She rose, and Ying hastened to her side, and nodding and smiling her farewells, she returned to her own courts.

On the eleventh day Tsemo went away. The airplane returned for him, and this time a great conclave of people from the house and the town gathered to see him depart. Madame Wu and Rulan were not among them. Instead, Madame Wu sat in her court, and there Rulan came to her. She knelt and put her head on Madame Wu's knees. Madame Wu felt a warm wetness seep through the satin of her robe.

"What are these, tears?" she asked gently.

"We were happy," Rulan whispered.

"Then they are good tears," Madame Wu said. She stroked the girl's head softly, and after a while Rulan wiped her eyes and smiled.

IF LIFE WERE known one moment ahead, how could it be endured? The house, which had only recently been filled with feasting and pleasure, was plunged in the next hour into the blackest mourning. Soon after Tsemo's plane had climbed toward the rising sun on that day, the steward came running in through the gates and behind him followed all the tenants and farmers of the Wu lands, wailing. Madame Wu had just gone into her library when she heard sobbing and people shouting her name. Instantly she knew what had happened.

She met them at the gate of her court. Mr. Wu was first, the tears streaming down his cheeks. The orphan children and the old woman and every servant and follower and neighbor from the streets were crowding in through the open gates.

"Our son—" Mr. Wu began and could not go on.

The steward took up his words. "We saw fire come whirling down out of the sky above the farthest field," he told Madame

Wu. "We ran to see what it was. Alas, madam, a few wires, a foreign engine, some broken pieces of what we do not know—that is all. No body remains."

"There is nothing left even to bury," Mr. Wu muttered. He looked at her, bewildered. "How can our son, alive only an hour ago, now be nothing?"

She grieved for him, but first she thought of Rulan. "It is of his young wife we must think now," she reminded Mr. Wu.

Mr. Wu dried his tears. "Go to her," he said to Madame Wu. "Comfort her."

So Madame Wu went alone to the court were Tsemo had so lately lived with his young wife.

IN THE COURT where she had been so happy, Rulan sat crouched on the floor beside Madame Wu, her forehead pressed against Madame Wu's hand. Both were silent, bonded together in love and sorrow. Madame Wu longed to tell Rulan of herself, and how she had felt when André died. But she could not tell it, now or ever. Rulan's sorrow was worse than hers. She had buried André's body, but of Tsemo there was nothing left. The winds had taken his fresh ashes and scattered them over the land. She, Tsemo's mother, had the memory of his babyhood, his boyhood, his young manhood. What had been between her and the son was altogether of the flesh, and it was no more except in her memory.

For Rulan, what was left? Had they, in these past ten days, gone beyond the flesh? Did the young wife now hold fast what the mother had not?

It was Rulan who first moved, who stood, who wiped her face and ceased weeping. "I shall thank you forever, Mother," she said, "for those ten days."

"Are you able now to be alone?" Madame Wu asked. She felt her love for Rulan grow exceedingly strong.

"I am able," Rulan said. "When I have been alone awhile, Mother, I will come and tell you what I must ask for myself."

"Night and day, my doors are always open for you," Madame

Wu replied. She rose, accepting the help of Rulan's hand. It was hot but strong, and the fingers did not quiver.

"I shall not forget," Rulan said.

Madame Wu, walking away, heard the door of Tsemo's court close behind her. She halted. The girl was not going to shut herself up in order to do some damage? No, she decided, this would not be Rulan's way. She would sit alone and lie alone, sleepless on her bed, and alone she would return to life again, somehow.

EVEN THOUGH THERE was no dead body, a coffin was brought and prepared, and into it were put the possessions that Tsemo had loved best. The day of the funeral was decided upon by the soothsayers of the town, and on that day Tsemo's coffin was buried in the family graveyard on the ancestral lands, and his tablet was set up in the ancestral hall.

In her mourning Madame Wu accepted the help of her friend Madame Kang. For many months there had been little going to and fro between the houses. Madame Wu's own inner concern, her constant remembering of André, had weaned her away from her friend. Moreover, she still thought of that birth night with repulsion.

But the loss of a son is too grave for any breach, and the two ladies came together again. Nevertheless Madame Wu knew that this friendship had passed. She had entered too deeply into the private life of her friend. Madame Kang could never quite forgive her for this, in spite of her gratitude.

"Had you not come that night, my sister, I would have died. My life is yours."

But there was shyness in her look even when she spoke, and Madame Wu knew that while she was thankful to be living, she was not thankful that her friend had been there at the hour of her greatest weakness. Madame Wu did not blame her friend, but inwardly she withdrew from her. I cannot love her the same anymore, she thought.

This thought reminded her of André and of a passage between them. He had been reading some words from his holy book. "Love thy neighbor as thyself."

"Love!" she had exclaimed. "The word is too strong."

She had always been critical of his holy book, jealous, perhaps, because he read it so much and depended upon it for wisdom. But he had agreed with her. "You are right," he had said. "Love is not the word. No one can love his neighbor. Say, rather, 'Know thy neighbor as thyself.' That is, understand his hardships, deal with his faults as gently as you deal with your own. This is the meaning of the word *love*."

The morning after Tsemo's funeral, Madame Wu woke up restless. Yesterday the countryside had been so beautiful in the midst of her sorrow that she longed to reach beyond this house of mourning. When Ying came in, Madame Wu said to her, "It will be well for me to go and see the land. Then my heart will rest."

She ordered her sedan and spent the day in the village listening to those who came to call upon her. Some came with thanks and some with complaints, and she received them all. Her spirits were refreshed by the calm countryside and by the simplicity of the people. They were honest and shrewd and did not hide their thoughts. Mothers brought their children to see her, and she praised their health and good looks. She inspected the lands near the village and looked at the seed set aside for various crops.

Before the sun sank too far she did what she had long wanted to do. She said to the bearers of her sedan, "Take me to the grave of the foreign priest who was teacher to my son. I will pay my respects to him, since he is here with no one to mourn him."

They carried her there without wonder, for they admired this courtesy, and she stepped from her sedan some distance from the grave so that she might be alone. Alone she climbed the low hill and came into the shade of the gingko tree. In the evening wind its small fanlike leaves dappled the shadows of the setting sun on the grass. She knelt before his grave and bowed her head to the earth three times while at a distance the bearers watched. Then she sat down on the mound of earth encircling the grave and closed her eyes and let him come to her mind. He came in with all his old swiftness, his robes flying about his feet, the wind blowing his beard. His eyes were living and alight.

"That beard," she murmured half playfully. "It hid your face from me. I never saw your chin and your mouth for myself. And those feet of yours!" she went on, smiling. "How the children laughed at them!"

It was true. Sometimes when she went to visit the foundlings in the evening, they would tell her how huge the soles had to be made for his shoes. They measured off space with their little hands. "Like this and like this!" they told her, laughing.

When she went home again, her heart was filled with thankfulness. In her lifetime it had been given to her to know one wholly good man.

XIV

IN THE next year there came an electric letter across the sea from Fengmo. Madame Wu read it in all possible ways and still she could not understand it. Fengmo announced his coming, and that was all. He would be home within the month at soonest and within two months at the latest. "Clearly something has happened," she said to herself. "He planned to be away five years."

Madame Wu now put aside everything else to get ready for the return of Fengmo. Her first duty was to prepare Linyi for her husband. She did not deceive herself that she was doing this purely for her son's sake. She wanted herself to hear from Linyi what André had taught her. She wanted to hear his words as well as to know how they had taken root in this young woman's heart.

When Linyi came in, dressed and painted and powdered,

and the ends of her hair curled, Madame Wu welcomed her with her usual smile. With a gesture of her hand she invited Linyi to sit down and be at ease. The young woman was very pretty, and she knew it and did not fear Madame Wu's gaze. Madame Wu smiled at her bold and innocent eyes, eyes that could also be careless and gay. "I smile when I think of how times change," Madame Wu said. "When I was a young girl, I would have wept to see the ends of my hair curled. Straight and smooth and black—that was what we considered beautiful hair then. But now curls are beautiful, are they?"

Linyi laughed. "I think Fengmo will be used to curly hair," she said. "All foreign women have curly hair."

"Ah," Madame Wu said. She looked suddenly grave. "Tell me why you have always been so fond of what is foreign."

"Not of everything foreign," Linyi said, pouting. "I was never fond of that hairy old priest."

"But he was not old," Madame Wu said in a low voice.

"To me he was old," Linyi said, "and hairy—ah, how I hate hairy men!"

Madame Wu felt this talk was unbecoming to them both. She considered how to begin otherwise. "But he taught you very well," she suggested. "I believe what he taught you was full of goodness, and I should like you to recall it for me, if you please."

When she said the words "if you please," it was in such a tone of voice that Linyi knew she must obey. "He was always saying that Fengmo was born to do something great and that my part in it was to make him as happy as I could so that he could work better."

"How are you to make him happy?" Madame Wu inquired.

"He said I must find out the stream of Fengmo's life," Linyi said unwillingly, "and he told me I must clear away the sticks and things that hinder the flow and I must do all I can to let the water rise to its level. He said I mustn't be like a rock thrown into a clear stream, dividing it. I must not divide Fengmo's life."

Yes, Madame Wu thought, these could be André's words. "Go on, my child," she said gently. "These are good words."

Linyi went on. Her eyes were pensive as she talked. "And he said Fengmo would be lonely all his life if I did not follow closely behind him. Fengmo needs me, he said." She returned her eyes to Madame Wu's face. "But I am not sure if Fengmo knows he needs me."

Madame Wu met the childlike gaze. "Do you love him?" she asked.

Tears filled Linyi's eyes. "I could love him," she whispered, "if he loved me."

"Does he not love you?" Madame Wu asked.

Linyi shook her head so hard that the tears fell onto the pale-blue satin of her robe.

"No," she whispered, "Fengmo does not love me."

With these words she bent her head on her two hands and wept. Madame Wu waited. She knew that nothing was so good for a woman's troubles as tears.

She waited until Linyi's sobs grew softer and then silent before she spoke. "Ah," she said, "Fengmo does not love anybody. That is his lack. We must heal it. I will help you, my child."

Linyi took away her hands from her face and smiled. "Thank you, Mother," she said.

FENGMO RETURNED on a day in the last heat of autumn. He looked about the house as though he could not believe it so. "Nothing is changed!" he exclaimed.

"Why should anything be changed?" Madame Wu replied. And yet she knew she did not speak the truth. There was the great change in herself, the inner change that daily found expression in all she said and did. "You are changed, my son," she said instead.

Later she sat in the library, dressed in her robe of silver-gray brocaded satin. She had made up her mind that they should sit here in the great room where they had so often sat with André.

After the festivities at the gate were over, she had sent word to Fengmo that she waited for him.

He had changed his foreign garments and had put on his own robes. No one had spoken to him of Tsemo, for it is not lucky to speak of the dead to one just returned. But Fengmo spoke now himself of his brother. "I miss my second brother," he said.

Madame Wu wiped her eyes delicately. While Tsemo was alive she had not missed him much, but now she missed him very much and thought of him often. She knew that what she missed was not what she had known, but what she had never known. She reproached herself very much that she had allowed a son to grow up in her house and had never really become acquainted with his being.

"How is my second sister-in-law?" Fengmo asked next.

"Rulan is silent," Madame Wu said. "When I have time, I shall discover a way for her to live. She is too young to become like a nun. Meantime, she and Ch'iuming have become close friends."

"She will not marry again, surely?" Fengmo asked.

"If she will, I will help her," Madame Wu said.

This astonished Fengmo a good deal. He would not have imagined that his mother could put a woman above the tradition.

Seeing his surprise, Madame Wu continued in her soft way, "I have learned as I have grown older," she said. "There is a debt due to every soul, and that is the right to its own true happiness."

"That is what Brother André used to say," Fengmo said suddenly. Mother and son felt themselves drawn together, as though by some power or presence they did not see.

"Mother, do you remember Brother André?" Fengmo asked her.

Madame Wu hesitated. How much should she tell? Her old diffidence fell on her. No, the silence between the generations must not be wholly broken. Life itself had created the difference, and it was not for her to change the eternal.

"I do remember Brother André."

"Mother, he changed me very much," he said in a low voice. He gazed at André's empty chair. "He made me understand true happiness. He showed me my own soul. And that is why I have come home."

She did not speak. She heard a quiver in her son's voice and waited, inviting him by her readiness to listen.

"No one will understand why I came home suddenly," he began. "They will ask and I cannot tell them. I do not know how to tell them. But I want to tell you, Mother. It was you who brought Brother André into this house."

She had such a profound feeling of André's presence that she dared not speak.

Fengmo lifted his head. "I came home because I learned to love a foreign woman over there, and she loved me and . . . we parted from each other."

Had Madame Wu been her old self, she would have cried out her indignation. Now she said gently, "What sorrow, my son!"

"You understand!" Fengmo exclaimed with amazement.

He had grown very much. He was taller by inches, thin and straight as the old gentleman had been, Madame Wu now saw. Indeed, she perceived what she had never seen before, that Fengmo was not at all like his father, but he was very like his grandfather. The same sternness showed in his features, the same gravity shone in his eyes.

"I learn as I grow older," Madame Wu said.

"Ah, Mother," Fengmo breathed in a sigh. "I wondered if there would be anyone in this house who could understand." The story poured out of him. "She was one of the students, like me. She sought me out, not boldly, you know, Mother, but because she said she had never seen anyone like me. She asked me hundreds of questions about our country and our home, and I found myself telling her about everything, even about myself. And she told me of her life. We knew each other so well—and so quickly."

"And at last you had to tell her about Linyi," Madame Wu said gently.

His shoulders drooped. He turned his face away. "I had to tell her," he said simply, "and then I had to come home."

"To put the sea between you," Madame Wu said in the same voice.

"To put everything between us," he agreed.

She sat in the calm stillness so usual for her. André had nurtured her son's soul and had made it exceedingly good. She longed for him to be happy, and yet this son was not like other men. He could not find happiness in women or in his own body. When she had asked André to be his teacher, she had asked blindly. She had only touched the lock, half turned the key, but a wide gate had opened and her son had gone through to a new world.

"And now," she said, "and now, my son, what will you do?"

"I have come home," he said. "I shall never go away again. I shall make my life here somehow."

They sat in silence, the long silence of two who understand each other.

"You must help Linyi, my son," she said.

"I know that," he said. "I have thought about her. I owe her much."

And so they sat and would have continued, so comforting were they, mother and son, to each other, except that at this moment Ch'iuming chose to come and make a request of Madame Wu that had long been in her mind to make.

All these months Ch'iuming had listened to Rulan's sorrowful talk about her love for Tsemo. And the more she listened, the more Ch'iuming found her thoughts turning to Fengmo, and the more she knew that she must leave the house and take her child and go away. Yet where could she go?

One night, when they had talked for a long time about the things deep in women's hearts, Ch'iuming broke her own vow of silence and told Rulan of her love for Fengmo. "I am wicked," she said. "I allow myself to think of him."

Rulan had listened to her with complete attention. "Oh, I wish you and I could get out of this house," she cried. "Here we are all locked behind these high walls. We love where we should not and we hate where we should not. We are all too near to one another."

"Are we not safe behind these walls?" Ch'iuming asked. She was always a little timid before Rulan, admiring her but fearing her boldness.

"We are not safe from one another," Rulan had retorted.

It was at this moment that the same thought had come to them both. They stared into each other's eyes.

"Why should we stay?" Rulan had asked.

"How dare we go?" Ch'iuming had asked.

And then they had begun to plot. Ch'iuming would ask first to be allowed to live in the ancestral village nearby. If Madame Wu demurred, saying that a young woman should not live alone in a farmer's village, she would ask for Rulan to come with her. And when Rulan had to speak for herself, she would say that now that she was widowed she wanted to begin a school for young children in the village. Rulan wanted to go immediately and speak out for herself. But Ch'iuming pointed out the discourtesy of this, for how could they put Madame Wu in the awkward position of refusing her daughter-in-law's request? It was better for Ch'iuming to take the brunt of refusal if it must come. Then there need be no words between Madame Wu and her daughter-in-law. And so it was settled.

Now Ch'iuming knew well enough where Fengmo was, but she had decided in her own mind that although she would approach Madame Wu in his presence, never would she speak to him otherwise.

Thus Madame Wu looked to the door and saw Ch'iuming. It was late afternoon. The sun had left the court, but it was filled with mellow light, and in this light Ch'iuming stood. And Madame Wu saw to her dismay that she looked almost beautiful. Ch'iuming's love, secret and unrequited though it was, had made her soft and alive.

"Ah, you have come home," Ch'iuming said to Fengmo.

He answered as simply, "Yes, yes. Are you well?"

"I am well," Ch'iuming replied.

She looked at him once and then did not look at him again. Instead she said to Madame Wu, "Elder Sister, may I ask a favor even now and not be held too rude for disturbing you?"

Madame Wu knew that Ch'iuming must have a purpose in coming at this time, and so she nodded. "Sit down," she said.

So Ch'iuming, blushing very much, did as she was told. She asked to be allowed to move to the village.

Madame Wu understood at once the purpose that Ch'iuming had in coming here at this time. She wished to make clear to Madame Wu that she wanted to retire from this house, now that Fengmo had come home, so as to keep peace in the family. Madame Wu was grateful.

When permission was given, Ch'iuming then asked for Rulan also. "Since the family mourning is over and since her own mourning can never cease, she wishes to ease her sorrow by good works," Ch'iuming said. "She wishes to make a school for the children of the farmers."

At this, Fengmo, who had been staring down at the floor, looked up in astonishment. "That," he declared, "is what I have come home to do."

Ch'iuming was aghast. Madame Wu was confounded. "But you said nothing of this, my son," she exclaimed sharply.

"I had not reached the point," Fengmo declared.

Madame Wu held up one narrow hand. "Wait," she commanded him. She turned to Ch'iuming. "Have you any other requests?" she asked kindly.

"None," Ch'iuming replied.

"Then you have my permission to go, you and Rulan as well," Madame Wu said. "I will call the steward in a few days and bid him find suitable houses for living and for the school, and you shall go when you like after that. Decide what you need, and I will tell Ying to prepare it. You will need two maids with you and a cook."

In the room that Ch'iuming had left, Madame Wu spoke to her son. "Explain your heart to me," she commanded him.

He rose and walked restlessly to the open door and stood looking out. "It is necessary for me to devote myself," he said. "Brother André taught me so much. After I left here I cast about for devotion. Religion is not for me, Mother. I am no priest." He sat down again. "The way was shown me entirely by accident. There was in the city where I lived in America a laundryman of our own race," he told her. "I took my clothes to him every few days to be washed."

Madame Wu looked surprised. "Did he wash clothes for others? Even for foreigners?" she inquired with some indignation.

Fengmo laughed. "Somebody has to wash clothes," he said and went on, "One day when I went to fetch my clothes—"

"You fetched your own clothes!" Madame Wu repeated. "Had you no servant?"

"No, Mother, over there none of us had servants."

She restrained her curiosity. "I see it is a very strange country. You must tell me more. Go on, my son," she urged.

"I went to fetch my clothes, and the man brought me a letter from his home," Fengmo went on. "Mother, he had been away from his home for twenty years, and he could not read the letters that came to him. Nor could he write. So I read and wrote his letters for him. He told me that in his village no one could read or write, and they had to go to the city to find a scholar. I had never understood the pity of this until I came to know him. He was very intelligent, but the poor old man could not read. Then I remembered that this is true in our villages, too. None of our own people can read and write either."

"Why should they?" Madame Wu inquired. "They do not come and go. They only till the fields."

"But, Mother," Fengmo exclaimed, "to know how to read is to light a lamp in the mind, to release the soul from prison, to open a gate to the universe."

The words fell upon Madame Wu's ears and lashed her heart. "Ah," she said, "those are the words of Brother André."

"I have not forgotten them," Fengmo said.

How could she forbid Fengmo after this?

"Rulan will be just the one to help me," he said eagerly. "I had not thought of her before. And Linyi shall help me too— we will forget ourselves." He was on his feet again. "You know, Mother, if I succeed here, in our own villages, schools might spread everywhere. How great that would be—"

She saw his thin young face light with something of the light that had burned eternally in André's eyes. She would not put it out. "My son, do what seems right to you," she said.

"Now MY English books," Fengmo commanded.

Linyi ran to fetch them out of the box. There were two armfuls of them. "How many you have!" she exclaimed.

"Only my best ones," he said carelessly. "I have boxes yet to come." He knelt by the bookshelves against the wall and fitted onto the shelves the books as she brought them. Outwardly calm, inwardly he was deep in turmoil and pain. He was feverish to settle his things, to put all his possessions into their places, to put his traveling bags out of sight.

"Must you put everything away tonight?" Linyi asked.

"I must," he replied. "I want to know that I have come home to stay."

She was happy to have these words said, and too young to dream why it was he said them without looking at her. Indeed, when he said them, he saw a face very different from hers. He saw Margaret's face—blue eyes, brown hair, and skin so white and smooth that he would never forget the touch of it. Would he ever be sorry that he had done what he did that day in the forest across the sea? For he had forced himself to let her go almost as soon as he had taken her in his arms.

"I can't go on," he had said.

She had not spoken. She had stood, her blue eyes fixed on him. There was something strange and wonderful about blue eyes. They could not hide what was behind them. Black eyes were curtains drawn down, but blue eyes were open windows.

"I am married," he had told her bluntly. "My wife waits for me at home."

She knew something about Chinese marriages. "Was she your own choice or did your family arrange it?"

He had waited a long time to answer. They sat down under the pine tree. He had hugged his knees in his arms and hid his forehead on his knees, feeling for the truth. It would have been easy, and partly true, to say, "I did not choose her." But when he prepared to say these words, Brother André came into his mind.

"To lie is a sin," Brother André had taught him simply, "but it is not a sin against God so much as a sin against yourself."

"I was not forced to marry," Fengmo said to Margaret. "Let us say—I chose."

She had sat motionless after that while he tried to explain to her what marriage meant in his family.

"With us marriage is a duty not to love or to ourselves, but to our place in the generations."

"I want to marry for love," Margaret said.

Had he been free, he would have said to her, "Then let us marry each other. I will send Linyi away."

But he was not free. The hands of his ancestors were fastened on him, as would be the hands of his sons and grandsons not yet born.

"In America we always marry for love," Margaret had insisted.

"No, you do not," Fengmo had answered. "You marry as we do, to preserve your species, but you deceive yourselves and call it love. You worship the idea of love, but we are the truthful ones. We believe that all should marry, men and women alike. That is our common duty to life. If love comes, it is added grace from Heaven. But love is not necessary for life."

He was speaking from the depths of his being. And how long had the silence been that fell between them then! He did not break it. He had allowed it to grow and swell, an ocean in depth and distance.

She broke it by putting out her hand. "Then it's good-by for us, isn't it?"

He had held her hand for a long moment and put his other hand over hers. "It is good-by," he had agreed.

The last book was put away, the last garment folded. He took the bags and set them into the passageway where a servant would find them in the morning. Then he went back into their bedroom. Linyi stood in the middle of the floor, uncertain and waiting. He went to her without hesitation and gripped her shoulders in his hands. "You are going to help me," he said. "I have work to do here, and I need you. You must promise to help me with all you have in you."

"I will help you," she whispered.

FENGMO WAS like a fire in the house. Everything was fanned to feed the flames. He rose before dawn and ate by candlelight, and in the early morning he rode his horse across the fields to the village he had chosen for his first school. Even some of the old farmers wanted to learn when they saw how the younger ones profited by it, and Fengmo lost no chance to make it widely known when a young farmer gained by his ability to read a bill or check an account. Other villages asked for schools, and Fengmo was so busy that months went by without Madame Wu's knowing how he did.

Ch'iuming and Rulan moved into the village to live. This made Madame Wu uneasy, for Fengmo pressed them both into the service of his schools. How could Ch'iuming hide her love from Fengmo? Madame Wu wondered.

Fengmo came in one night to see her. She received him immediately, for she knew by now that Fengmo had no time for anything except what he held important. He sat down squarely on his chair, put his hands over his eyes and began at once. "Mother," he said, "I do not know how to tell you what I must, but not knowing, I will begin."

"Is it about Ch'iuming?" Madame Wu inquired.

"How do you know everything?" he asked, surprised.

"I have my ways," she said. "Now, what have you to say?"

"You know, Mother, that no woman can ever move me."

She smiled and something in his serious young face touched her at the very center of her heart. Ah, perhaps the old ways of love and marriage were wrong—who knew? "What shall we do?" she asked.

He had already a plan. "I ask your permission to take Linyi with me, and we will live in the country, too."

Madame Wu was sad to think of another empty court under the roof, but she was pleased that he thought of Linyi as a safety for himself.

"I will agree to this," she said, "with one condition, and it is that when she gives birth to your children, you return here for the time of the birth. The grandchildren should be born under our own roofs."

To this Fengmo agreed, and a few days after that Fengmo and Linyi moved into an earthen-walled house in the village.

XV

THE NEXT YEAR when Linyi was about to give birth to her first child, a strange thing happened. It was the year of the great retreat, when the enemy from the East Ocean islands drove many from their lands and their homes. Through the city and the countryside these wanderers now passed, and since the town where the Wu family lived was in that region, many passed by there.

Among those who came was an elderly woman, a widow, who was staying at the inn with her son and his wife and children. This son was now her only child, and he told the innkeeper why they had come.

"My mother lost a daughter here many years ago," he said. "Is there any way of finding lost children?"

"Was the child alive?" the innkeeper asked. The guests were well-to-do, and he was courteous in what he said.

"She was alive, but cast away by my grandmother, who had a fierce temper and was angry because my mother gave birth to three girls, one after the other," the man replied.

"Why did you come here that year?" the innkeeper asked.

"It was an evil year in our region near the northern capital," the man said. "The harvests failed, and we moved to these parts where food was plentiful. Here my mother gave birth."

The innkeeper mused over this. "It must have been in this very inn then," he said, "because it is the only one in our town."

"It was at this inn, my mother says, and that is why we have come. My two sisters are dead, and my mother still yearns for her lost child."

"I will go and tell this to our gentry," the innkeeper said. "If anyone knows, Madame Wu knows it."

So the innkeeper sent word to Madame Wu that he had a question to ask her if she would receive him. She replied that she would, for the innkeeper's family had been old servants of the Wu family. An hour later he stood before her in the main hall and told his tale. She listened, and said, "Let the mother come to visit me."

"The very best thing, my lady," the innkeeper agreed and went back with his message.

The next day Madame Wu received the mother in her court. Now, Madame Wu had expected to meet a woman of common origin, but as her visitor came in, leaning upon a maidservant's arm, she saw this was no common woman, but a lady. She gave her greeting and asked the widow to be seated in the place of honor.

After all the courteous words had been said, the lady told of the casting away of her child. "I know my child did not die. She was so healthy—healthier than any of my others. And the child's father was not willing to have her killed, even at his mother's demand. He was a good man with an evil mother.

Alas, he died before she did." She paused to weep. "How we were punished! One child after another died—only my youngest son is left. Now I seek the child I lost, and that is why I have come so far."

"You know the child was not killed?" Madame Wu asked.

"I know that," the lady answered, "for even while I lay in bed after the birth I heard my husband pleading with his mother, and she agreed at last that the child should not be killed, but only cast away over the city wall."

"Was the child wrapped in a red silk coat?" Madame Wu asked.

The lady stared at her. "In my red coat," she gasped. "I thought if she were wrapped in it, she might be seen by someone."

Madame Wu rose and went to the chest. There folded among her own garments was the one Ch'iuming had long ago given her to keep. "Here is the coat," she said.

The lady's face turned the color of lead. "It is the coat!" she whispered. She clutched it in her hands. "But the child?"

"Living," Madame Wu said.

And then she told the story of Ch'iuming and how the girl had come into this house, and the lady listened, grateful and yet reproachful. At last Madame Wu said, "Let us go to the village to see for ourselves. You will see that your child has been well cared for."

So without more delay she called for sedans, and the two ladies went at once to the village.

As they reached the village Madame Wu was amazed at the changes she saw. It was clean and prosperous as it had never been. The children were clean and their hair brushed. Proudly the villagers pointed at the new earthen building that was the school.

Beside the school was Fengmo's own house, and since a messenger had run ahead to tell of their coming, they were ready for them. Linyi was with child, but Madame Wu was not prepared for her healthy looks. Her cheeks were red, and she had put on flesh with motherhood. But Madame Wu was even more pleased by the change in Linyi's manners. The girl was respectful and prompt, and her lazy ways were gone.

So they went into Fengmo's house and sat down, and Fengmo was sent for, and when he arrived, the whole story was told again, and Ch'iuming and her child were sent for and Rulan came with her.

The moment that Ch'iuming came in mother and daughter looked at each other and knew who they were. No two women could have faces so alike if one were not made of the other. They all burst into laughter at so magical an ending. Madame Wu was the most silent, yet she was the most pleased.

"My mother!" Ch'iuming cried.

"This is my child," the lady said.

The two wept, and the lady embraced her grandchild. Of course the lady wanted Ch'iuming and the child to join her own family. And for this Ch'iuming politely asked permission of Madame Wu. "May I go, Elder Sister?"

Now, Madame Wu saw that Ch'iuming did not look well. In spite of the clean village air and the country food, Ch'iuming was pale and her eyes were hollow as though she spent sleepless nights. It would be well for Ch'iuming to leave the house of Wu.

"If it were any person other than your mother," Madame Wu said, "I could not let you go, but Heaven has brought mother and daughter together, and how dare I keep them apart? You shall go, but not before I have new clothes made for you and the child and have provided the things you will need on your journey. You must not go empty-handed from our house."

So Ch'iuming left the house of Wu a few weeks later with her mother. Madame Wu was glad that Ch'iuming did not come to bid her any private farewell. She knew the young woman's tender heart well enough to know that this was not because she was ungrateful. No, Ch'iuming did not come because she wished to spare her pain.

MADAME WU never saw Ch'iuming again. Once a year a letter came, written by a letter writer and signed by Ch'iuming. In these letters Ch'iuming told her that she was well, that the child grew, and at last when the war was over, that she was married again to a widower, a small merchant in Peking. He had two young sons whom Ch'iuming soon learned to love. Her mother died at last, and Ch'iuming had a son of her own and then twin sons. These letters Madame Wu answered carefully with admonition and wisdom. And in each, from the kindness of her heart, she put news of Fengmo and his family.

Fengmo's family grew also. Whatever his inner life, his body was fruitful, and Linyi had children—a son, a daughter, and two more sons. For each birth she returned to the house of Wu, but when the child was a month old, she went back to Fengmo. Madame Wu knew that Fengmo had other fires. He burned with zeal for the people. He was hungry for schools and more schools, and then he was not satisfied until he began to dream of hospitals. He had put aside all his silken robes and wore plain garments cut like a uniform.

Fengmo could never find enough teachers for his schools, and seeing Meng, his sister-in-law, idle and fattening, he asked her one day why she did not help Linyi and Rulan with the older women who struggled to learn their letters and to sew more cleverly. Meng opened her round eyes at him.

"I?" she exclaimed. "But I never leave our gates except to visit my mother."

"But you should, sister-in-law," Fengmo told her. "It is your duty. Your children are cared for by nurses, and your household is tended by servants. You should come for an hour or two each day and help us."

Meng grew very agitated. "I cannot," she exclaimed. "Liangmo would not allow it."

"No one in our country who has learning ought to keep it for himself," Fengmo insisted.

"I will ask Liangmo," Meng faltered at last, and Fengmo went away satisfied that he had stirred her heart.

But Liangmo was only made angry when Meng told him, weeping, how Fengmo had spoken. "He made me feel wicked," she sobbed.

Liangmo took off his spectacles and folded them up and put them in his pocket. Then he slapped the table with his hand. "Fengmo is really too troublesome," he exclaimed. "Meng, I forbid you to have any more talk with my brother. I will talk with him myself."

This Liangmo did, and there was a great quarrel between the two brothers and the quarrel was worse because Liangmo was outraged by Linyi's appearance. She dressed like any common schoolteacher and looked older, he declared, than Meng. Hearing this, Linyi was inclined to pity herself, but Rulan plunged into the quarrel on the side of Fengmo and the people. And Liangmo was the less pleased because he saw that Rulan was healed of her sorrow, for all her ardor was fulfilled in the work she did in the villages. Both parted in anger, and Liangmo complained to Madame Wu.

Now, Madame Wu in these days never left her own court except to visit the children in the temple. As each girl became sixteen, she betrothed her to a suitable young man, and such was the fame of these girls that there were always lists of young men who wanted wives from among them. Madame Wu did not only tell the girls the name and the age and the qualities of the young men, but she showed them pictures also.

"Shall only men see pictures?" she answered when anyone inquired why she did this. "Shall it not be just for a woman to also see the face of the man?"

It became a matter of rivalry and honor that young men sent their pictures to her. When the girl had chosen, she sent her picture to the young man, and such was the fame of the temple girls that never had one been rejected by the man she chose. They were all good wives, and Madame Wu became famous in that whole region for these girls.

When Liangmo came in with his lips pursed to complain concerning his brother Fengmo, she saw him as a prosperous man of affairs, the coming head of a great family, a merchant and a maker of money.

After greeting her, Liangmo came straight to the heart of the matter that concerned him. "My younger brother is becoming a fanatic," he complained. "He wishes Meng to go out and teach. This is impossible. Linyi looks like a common laborer. Her hair is cut off, and it has turned brown with the sun. It is all hateful to me. Is this suitable for our family?"

Madame Wu smiled. "Did you not find the villages very clean?" she asked.

But Liangmo would not see any good. "I think first of our family, not of strangers and common folk," he said stubbornly. "The responsibility of the family rests upon me, Mother, after you and my father are gone."

Seldom did his sons speak of Mr. Wu. They all knew that whatever had been his place, it was all but empty now. He was drowsy and content and asked nothing more than to be left alone with Jasmine. It is true that he was the beloved of his grandchildren. They went clamoring into his court, and he fed them sweetmeats and laughed at them and napped while they played, and Jasmine, who was barren, enticed them often and treated them as her own so that the old man who protected her would feel no lack of their companionship.

Liangmo waited for his mother to speak.

"You are well pleased in your own courts, my son?" she said at last.

"Certainly I am," Liangmo said. He put down his tea bowl. "I am obeyed there. My children are healthy and intelligent."

"And in the city, is all well?"

"Well enough," Liangmo said. "The markets are somewhat poor, perhaps. Some foreign goods come in, now that the war is ended. The foreign hospital is raising a new building, and I hear new foreigners are coming."

"Is this a good thing?" Madame Wu inquired. "I remember I cured a grandson in the Kang house with our grandmother's herb brew," she murmured. "I suppose he is a great lad now—"

The year before this Madame Kang had died. At this moment Madame Wu thought of her as she remembered seeing her in her coffin, dressed in her satin robes, her plump hands by her sides. After she was dead, Madame Wu thought of her sometimes and their friendship seemed as it was in its early days. Mr. Kang had soon married a second wife, a young woman whose willfulness stirred the great unwieldly household continually like a ladle in a pot of stew.

Madame Wu pushed back her thoughts and smiled at Liangmo. "Well, my son," she said. "The soul of every creature must take its own shape, and no one can compel another without hurting himself. Live in your house, my son, and let Fengmo live in his."

"Teach Fengmo one thing, if you please, Mother," Liangmo said in anger. "Bid him keep his long arm out of my house."

"I will," Madame Wu promised.

THE YEARS passed over Madame Wu. Now she never left her own gates. She was famed for her patient listening and her wisdom, and many came to her for help.

After the end of the war, the whole countryside was in confusion and many men came from overseas to mend and to meddle in this confusion. It did not touch the house of the Wu family. Their city remained remote as ever, but foreigners continued passing through for one reason or another, and one of the reasons was that Fengmo invited them. Whenever he heard the name of a man from the West, he invited him to come and advise him about the work he did, and the men came, for the work was becoming known everywhere with not a little praise for Fengmo.

Madame Wu did not receive these foreigners, for she did not know their language. But one day Fengmo sent her word that a man from across the ocean had come, whom he wished to bring to see her. She gave her consent, and a few hours afterward Fengmo came with a tall foreign man, young and dark. Indeed, she looked at him and then turned to Fengmo.

"He is foreign," Fengmo said. "His ancestors, indeed his parents, came from Italy, the birthplace, Mother, of Brother André."

How Madame Wu's heart stirred! She forgot that she could speak no language but her own, and she leaned forward, her hands on the silver head of her cane, and she asked the young man, "Did you know the foreign priest?"

Fengmo stepped in quickly to translate, and then Madame Wu and the young man spoke through him.

"I did not know him," the young man said, "but my father and mother have told me of him, madam. He was my uncle."

"Your uncle!" Madame Wu repeated. She gazed at the dark young man and found one resemblance and then another. Yes, here were the dark eyes of André, but they were not as wide. Yes, here was the shape of André's skull, and his hands. She looked again at the young man's hands, more slender perhaps than André's but with the shape she knew so well. But the look in his eyes was not at all André's. His soul was not the same.

She sighed and drew back. No, this man's soul was not the same. "You came here to find your uncle?" she inquired.

"I did," the young man answered. "My parents knew where he was, although he never wrote to any of us in his later years. When I passed near here, I said to myself that I would come and see if he still lived, and write the news home to my father."

"He is buried in our land," Madame Wu said.

They sat for a moment in silence. "I suppose you know, madam, why he lived so far away from all of us and why he never wrote any letters?"

Fengmo answered for her. "We never knew."

"He was a heretic," the young man said solemnly. "The church cast him out as a renegade—homeless, without support. We never heard from him afterward. He refused to come home."

"But he did no evil," Fengmo exclaimed in horror.

"It was not what he did," the young man declared. "It was what he thought. He thought it was men and women who were the divine. It seems hard to think this a sin, in our generation. But it was a great sin in his day. He felt compelled to write a letter to his cardinal and tell him. In the last letter he wrote my father he told us the whole story."

Fengmo translated for Madame Wu, and she listened and said not a word. They had rejected him—his own people!

They went away after saying farewell, and Madame Wu was glad. She needed to be alone to comprehend the new knowledge she now had of André. All those years he had lived here, solitary!

But not solitary, she thought. There were the children he had found and the beggars he had fed.

And she herself—how had she opened the gates to let him in? She would never know. He had been led to her, and she had opened the gates to him and he had come in, and with him he had brought her eternal life.

Yes, she now believed that when her body died, her soul would go on. Gods she did not worship, and faith she had none, but love she had forever. Love alone had awakened her sleeping soul and had made it deathless.

She knew she was immortal.

A BRIDGE
FOR PASSING

A BRIDGE FOR PASSING

A CONDENSATION OF THE BOOK BY

Pearl S. Buck

ILLUSTRATED BY JOHN SUCHY

When her husband, whom she
deeply loved, died suddenly,
Pearl Buck discovered there
was a bridge that she was
less prepared to cross than
she believed—the bridge
that separated marriage
from widowhood.

The news came while she
was in Japan during the
filming of one of her
novels. What follows in
A Bridge for Passing
is a diary of those weeks
and months; an amalgam of her
thoughts, emotions and ex-
periences as she lived them
—and lived through them—
to shape a new life for
herself.

I

I REMEMBER the day when I decided to make the picture in Japan, an April day a year ago, a day like this one on which I begin the story of my return to Asia. I had always known that the return was inevitable, not a permanent return, for I am too happy in my own country to live elsewhere, but a return, nevertheless. One does not live half a life in Asia without wishing to return. When it would be, I did not know, nor even where it would be, or for what cause. The friendly country of China, the home of my childhood and youth, was for the time being forbidden.

China is not the whole of Asia, however, in spite of being most of it. There were other countries to which I could have returned—Japan, India, Korea and all the rest. Japan, I suppose, was the one I knew best after China. Logically, the return would be there, but when? I do not enjoy visiting a country merely to see the sights. Nor do I enjoy visiting as a special person. When I return, I told myself, it will be for a project, a piece of work, something that will explain why I

cannot accept all the dinner invitations, weekends and entertainment that hospitable people offer to friends.

Then quite unexpectedly one day in 1960 it was proposed to
me that I go to Japan to work on the filming of my book *The
Big Wave*. The work would be something new and therefore
exciting. *The Big Wave* is a book of adventure. It involves a
remote fishing village, a tidal wave, a volcano—none of which
I had seen for decades.

But there was my family to consider, a large family—some
old, some very young. Could I, should I, leave them all at this
time? The family doctor assured me that there was no reason
to delay going. The children, grown and half-grown, were
hearty and healthy. And—my husband? He was as he would
always be now. If I waited for the final possibility, it might be
years. Six months before I could not have left him. But what had
happened in the interval made for me the difference between
day and night: he had slipped into a world of his own.

"Go," the doctor said. "You must have a change. You have a
long road ahead."

"Go," my responsible daughter said. "I will look after
everything."

Thus I was encouraged; the contracts were signed and the
tickets bought.

The book, of course, had to be put into a new form. *The Big
Wave* is a simple story, but its subject is complex. It deals with
life and death and life again through a handful of human
beings in a remote fishing village on the southern tip of the
lovely island of Kyushu in the south of Japan. The book had
always had a vigorous life of its own. It had been translated
into many languages but never into the strange and wonderful
language of the motion picture. I hoped that we could make a
picture true to the people of whom I had written.

Japan had been a near neighbor all during my years in
China. When I was a child, if we sailed from Vancouver or San
Francisco, Japan was the last stop before Shanghai, the gate-
way to my Chinese home. If we sailed from Shanghai, then

Japan was the first stop on the way to my American home. It had been, too, a country of refuge when revolutionary wars drove us out of China. I once spent many months in a small Japanese house in the mountains of Kyushu, near Unzen. I had taken a motor trip around the island and had stopped briefly in Obama to bathe in the hot springs there. In my mind I now saw my fishing village somewhere in that region with its glorious seacoast, green mountains and smoking volcano.

"I shall recognize it the moment I see it," I told my family. "It will be a little village hugging a rocky shore, a sandy cove between the mountains, a few houses of stone behind a high sea wall. I see it as though I remember it, although I do not know its name."

ON A MORNING in May I boarded a jet in New York, two hours or so away from my stone farmhouse, and we were airborne in a matter of minutes. I reflected upon the incredible changes I had witnessed during the span of my life. Though, God willing, I have decades more to live upon this beautiful globe, yet in life experience, I began in the Middle Ages. As a small child I traveled by wheelbarrow, sedan chair, mule cart, or in a boat pulled along a lazy canal by men walking the towpath. I was twelve years old before I saw a train in China and fifteen before I rode on one. Ships I knew, for there were ships on the Yangtze River to take us to Shanghai and from there across the Pacific. I did not see or ride in an automobile until I attended college in the United States. Then I became a modern woman and traveled by air as a matter of course. Anything slower than a jet makes me impatient now—I who began my life at a speed no greater than four miles an hour by sedan chair!

Soon after the jet lifted us from the earth to the sky that May morning, we floated over a sea of silvery clouds, and I settled back in my chair to work on the script of my picture.

The Hawaiian Islands are stepping-stones between Asia and the United States. I remember them as islands of hope when I was a child and traveled on ships. Ten days from San

Francisco to Honolulu or eight days from Yokohama to Honolulu was the expectation. But eastward or westward, I was
always eager to reach the islands of eternal green, where
coconuts could be had for the picking and garlands of fragrant
flowers were everyday greetings.

The jet came down smartly and sharply in Honolulu, not
a moment late. It was night and the moon shone on the white
surf and the dark sea. I was driven immediately to my hotel, and as I crossed the immense lobby to claim my room,
men and women were still coming and going, people of a
variety of races and costumes. None of them seemed strange to
me except the women tourists dressed in Mother Hubbards,
those garments devised by missionaries in the early days
when, like Adam and Eve in their Eden, the Hawaiians did
not know they were naked. I have sometimes wondered
whether it was the early missionary men who commanded that
the lovely naked women be covered, or whether it was the
missionary women in their long skirts and high collars who
knew they could never compete with the smooth brown bodies
of the Hawaiian women wearing nothing except flowers in their
hair. Only God knows, and He keeps such secrets to Himself—
with a smile, perhaps! Today the girls of Hawaii wear smart
Western clothes and the tourists wear the flowing Mother Hubbards, and again the Hawaiian women have the best of it.

The air of Hawaii is divine, no less. I lay in my comfortable
bed and slept and woke to breathe in the soft, pure atmosphere blown in by a gentle wind from the sea. I rose then and
breakfasted alone on the small terrace outside my room. I
enjoyed my terrace and the view of the sea and mountains,
and I let the day slip past me until it was time for luncheon
with friends and a drive in an open Jeep around the island. It
is only when one leaves Waikiki that one sees the other
beaches, sheltered in coves, where people gather to play and
picnic. We stopped often as we drove to watch the heavy surf
crash against the black rocks of ancient lava.

We went back to the hotel to find that the evening newspaper carried headlines of a vast earthquake in Chile. I remembered that just off the western coast of Chile there is a long deep trench—a compensation for the Andes—produced probably by a creeping river of cold material flowing out from the center of the ocean and pushing its way under the rocky continental mass. A strange silent underworld, this ocean bed, a violent world when catastrophe takes place in the conflict between fire and water, heat and cold.

But Chile seemed far away from the pleasant islands of Hawaii. We went to a nightclub across the street to enjoy Hawaiian food and music and dances. The master of ceremonies prefaced each event with a pleasant introduction, and several times he mentioned a tidal wave. He said, tossing it off as a joke, that perhaps all of us would enjoy the excitement of a tidal wave, and therefore he had ordered one as an added attraction for the evening. Suddenly I heard sharply and clearly—he was not announcing a tidal wave but warning us of its approach.

I returned to the hotel at once. There all was confusion. Guests were being sent to the upper floors, and the streets facing the sea were barricaded. What a to-do! The jet was scheduled to fly at an hour after midnight. It was now just short of eleven o'clock. I rushed to my room, packed my bag and took the last available taxicab to the airport.

The airport in Honolulu is on a narrow peninsula just above sea level. When I arrived, it was alarmingly empty. A few employees stood staring at the horizon and the taxi driver was in haste to be paid off. In a few minutes my fellow passengers and I were escorted by a gloomy attendant to a comfortable club room on an upper floor. We sat down and listened to the blaring jazz coming from the loudspeaker above our heads. Every moment or two the music broke off and an inexorable voice announced that the tidal wave had reached another Pacific island. In a few minutes it would strike the Hawaiian island of Hilo at an estimated height of over sixty feet. We also learned that the wave was a result of the earthquake in Chile.

We considered our fate, and conversation ceased. The air-craft had been removed from the field, the voice told us, and all flights were canceled. There was nothing to do but wait.

Suddenly at one o'clock sharp the door opened. A breathless young man shouted to us to come at once. Our jet would take off in the next few minutes. The luggage was all on. We tore after him. We were pushed aboard, and faster than I have ever seen a jet rise into the sky, we rose. At exactly the moment we left the earth the radio announced the arrival of the tidal wave.

Yet before we could arrive on earth again, the tidal wave, traveling more swiftly than our jet, had struck with cruel force on the northeastern shores of Japan. The people were warned by their government but could not believe what they heard. In their experience, earthquakes and tidal waves came to Japan as companions. They could not comprehend that an earthquake in Chile might mean a tidal wave on their shores. What a strange and sad coincidence that we were to arrive in Japan at this very moment to make a picture called *The Big Wave.*

I HAD EXPECTED a quiet arrival. The hour was between two and three after midnight, Tokyo time, and I could not imagine that anyone would be at the airport to meet me.

A man in a white uniform stepped forward. "Are you Pearl Buck?"

"Yes, I am," I said.

"Welcome to Japan," he said. "I am with Japan Airlines. This way, please . . . Just a moment . . . "

Cameras snapped. Reporters crowded around with questions. "How did you manage the tidal wave?" they asked jokingly. "Who is your publicity man?"

"Thank you," the man in the white uniform said to them when I showed signs of exhaustion. Then: "Your friends are waiting for you."

Friends waiting? Then smiling faces, warm voices, some-times eyes brimming with tears—these claimed me for their own. Men and women I had known when young were there, looking as changed as I did, and with them were children and grandchildren like mine, the boys in Western clothes, the girls in formal kimonos.

"My daughters rose at one o'clock so that they could wear kimonos to welcome you," a friend said proudly.

I knew how long it took to put on a kimono properly and make the suitable coiffure. The girls were beautiful, and I was glad they wore kimonos to make me feel at home when I arrived. When I lived in Japan before the war, all my women friends wore kimonos. Now Japanese women wore Western dress except for the few formal occasions of life. There were exceptions, of course. Old women wore kimonos and certain distinguished women, even in business, wore kimonos always. One special friend of mine, a film executive, wore a kimono because it was becoming to her. She had reached the position and the age when she could wear what she liked.

Behind the friendly crowd that night I was aware of Tokyo itself. I knew how severely it had been bombed in the war, and now it had been rebuilt, new and prosperous, a Japan that was strange to me. Yet even the people who came to greet me seemed changed for the better, I thought. The old stiff formality was gone. I heard ready laughter, spontaneous and real, not the old polite laughter. Everyone talked freely. That was new. The sweet courtesy remained, but life and good spirits bubbled through, as though an ancient restraint had been removed. This was my first impression that night, and later I found that it was expressed everywhere and in many ways.

Embanked in flowers and encircled by friends, we moved into waiting cars, and I was at last driven at breakneck speed to the Imperial Hotel. I do not know why it is that I have never been terrified by Japanese drivers. They dash through unmarked streets and packed crowds, shouting and warning, and yet I have not seen accidents. It all seemed natural enough, reminding me of other days, years ago, when I was driven in just such fashion along the edges of cliffs, up and down mountains or above the sea and roaring surf. Perhaps my lack of fear was simply because in Asia I relax into a state of oriental acceptance and realize there is practically nothing I can do about anything. I arrived finally and alive at the Imperial Hotel, that haven where Japan meets the world with her own grace and style.

For a long time I could not sleep. Pictures passed through my mind. The first was the vivid face of my mother—dark skin, brown hair, brown eyes. We were on the wide veranda of our house in China. I was perhaps seven, a barefoot child with long yellow hair, sitting on the floor before her, hugging my knees and listening. She was telling me the story of my sister, who died before I was born.

"On the Yellow Sea," my mother said, "between Japan and China. We had gone to Japan for the summer, to the mountains behind Nagasaki. It was so hot in the Yangtze Valley that I was afraid for the children. We had a lovely summer in Japan—the air was cool and healthy up on those mountains. We came back on a Japanese steamship—the *Hiroshima Maru*—when the baby fell ill. I don't know what it was—a high fever and dysentery. She was only six months old and not strong. And I am always so seasick—I couldn't even hold her. Your father tried to take care of me. And so old Dr. Martin walked up and down the deck with the baby in his arms. I'll never forget how he looked—so tall and straight and the little baby in his arms."

Here her eyes always filled with tears and I always wept because she did. I crept to her side. She held out her hand to me and I clasped it in both mine. "Then what?" I begged.

"Well, you know, dear. She died in his arms. I was lying in a steamer chair so sick! It was a breathlessly hot night, and there was an old moon, sinking into the sea. And suddenly I saw him stop and look down into the baby's face. And I—knew."

I felt her hand against my cheek, and I longed to comfort her and did comfort her, I suppose, in my childish way. For the story usually ended by her wiping her eyes and saying briskly, "Now let's have a little music before we go to bed."

From my mother's lips, then, I first heard the names of Japanese cities and saw in my mind's eye scenes of the mountains and seashore. The name of Hiroshima remained for me the name of the Japanese ship on which my baby sister died until years later, decades later, when it became the city of the dead, after the bomb fell. And my little sister was buried in the Christian cemetery in Shanghai. I saw her name there with the names of the three other children in our family later to be born in China and to die there. This happened before I myself was born in my grandfather's colonial home in West Virginia.

THE LOBBY OF the Imperial Hotel is a place where anyone can meet anyone from anywhere in the world. The instant I descended there the next morning my hands were caught in a warm grasp, and before me was an old friend from India. "Fancy seeing you here," he shouted. "Why aren't you in New Delhi? Our guest room there is waiting for you."

After we had sat down and exchanged news for a few

minutes, Sumiko, my Japanese secretary, was at my elbow. She bowed and smiled placatingly. "Please, now it is time for the press conference. Everybody is waiting."

Press conference! I have been at many press conferences, but there was a peculiar excitement about this one. The big room where we sat at a long table in carefully arranged protocol was crowded with reporters and photographers from more than seventy papers and magazines. As usual in Japan, the press conference began with speeches from selected persons. As an introduction I said simply that I was happy to be in Japan again, grateful to them for their kindness on my last visit, and ready to report progress on our project, *The Big Wave*, a story of Japan. I said that we were pleased that one of their own companies was coproducing with us and that I had asked the head of that company to make the formal announcement.

This film executive was well known and highly respected. He was a man on the young side of middle age, with a calm disposition and complete assurance. His speech went on at some length. When it was translated to me afterward, I was quite moved. The film executive had said that once he himself had thought of making *The Big Wave* into a picture, for he read it at a time of deep depression when for the first time in history Japan stood before the world a defeated nation. He did not know how to recover his own spirits. Then one day he found this little book and read it. He felt the author wished to convey hope to the Japanese people, a belief that as they had lived through centuries with the possibility of tidal waves and earthquakes, and indeed had often suffered tragically from such catastrophes only to survive with renewed courage and strength, so again they would survive even defeat. Now, through a peculiar coincidence, he had the honor to take part, on behalf of his company, in the making of the film version of the story.

I listened with gratitude. It is the highest reward when a writer hears that a book written in doubt and solitude has reached a human heart with a deeper meaning than even the writer had been aware of. It is the something extra, the unexpected return. Many questions from reporters followed the speech. We were not ready yet to announce the actors, for we had many candidates to hear and to see. Suddenly, as we were about to disperse, word came in that the negotiations had been successfully concluded in regard to one star. We could announce that the well-known Japanese actor Sessue Hayakawa would take the role of the Old Gentleman in *The Big Wave*.

The press departed, and I was alone again. This was the changeless pattern of my days since my husband had ceased to be himself—a crowd of people, and then no one. I missed him now especially. He had presided over many press conferences for me, in many parts of the world. The first one was when I came from China, determined in my secret mind that whatever lay ahead, I would not allow my life to be changed. It was changed, of course, the moment he met me in Montreal. Although I knew him somewhat through his letters—he wrote the most charming and articulate letters I had ever read—I saw him for the first time, sun-browned and with eyes of a startling blue. I was speechless with my habitual shyness, but he was completely at ease, as he always was, everywhere and with anyone. The next day I faced the formidable press in New York. He knew the reporters, however, and set us all at ease. I found myself answering their questions frankly. Too frankly, he told me afterward with amusement, for when I was asked my age it did not occur to me not to tell it, since in China every year was considered an added honor.

As a child my first Japanese friend was the wife of an Englishman who lived in a big house on the mountainside near our home in China. I saw her only as she passed by in her sedan chair, borne by four uniformed bearers. She wore a kimono always, and her hair was brushed in the high lacquered coiffure of the ladies of ancient Japan. Her face was powdered white, and her onyx eyes gazed blankly ahead until she saw me standing in the dust of the road. In summer she held a small parasol, white silk painted with cherry blossoms, and in winter she wore a brocaded coat over her kimono. We exchanged looks, hers sad and incurious until she smiled at me, and mine wide with wonder and admiration because she was so beautiful. I remembered her, because of the smile, as somehow my friend.

In later years I knew more intimately as friend an occasional Japanese woman. She seemed always remote, somewhat sad, overburdened with duty, whether she was the wife of a farmer or the wife of a man of wealth and position. Her voice soft and gentle, her demeanor modest and considerate of others, she wore silence as a garment, and unless addressed directly, she seemed to merge herself with the background.

None of this was true now. The old-fashioned woman had simply disappeared from Japan. The men had changed very little either in appearance or behavior. But the women? Let me approach the extraordinary differences I found through the individual women I came to know while we made the picture.

Sumiko, my secretary, and I had no sooner stepped into the offices of the motion picture company than I was astounded by what I saw. In other years I would have been greeted by a young man and the office would have been staffed by young men. Now, however, it was staffed by young women, all in smart Western clothes, and several of them were speaking good English. I had the impression, too, that all of them were efficient and pretty. Modern looks are nothing, however, compared to modern behavior. Gone was the modest downcast gaze, gone the delicate reserve, gone the indirect approach to men. Instead bold looks and frank speech were the rule of the day.

One of these young women led us to the inner office. I confess that it was reassuring to see my special friend sitting behind a very modern desk, to be sure, but dressed in a silver-gray silk kimono and a pale-pink obi. She rose to meet us, bowing deeply with old-fashioned grace. Her English was perfect, and I knew she spoke French and German and Italian as well, for part of her work involved travel in European countries for Japanese films. There was really nothing old-fashioned about her except her dress. She had a full partnership with her husband and two other associates, both men. They deferred to her wisdom and efficiency and judgment.

We sipped green tea and made small talk. She invited me to come and spend a weekend at her country home in Kamakura and I accepted. On this office visit we did not stay long, for it is never good manners in Japan to stay too long on a first call. In fifteen minutes or so, a pretty young woman directed us to the office of the head of the company.

While the men talked, I examined the room, sparely but excellently furnished with modern furniture, calm in atmosphere. On the wall near us hung three impressive oil portraits—the deceased founders of the company, I was told. On the opposite wall there hung a large calendar, whereon was printed in poster style the lively form of a bathing beauty in full color, an engaging object on which the eyes of the three solemn gentlemen seemed to be fixed. I wondered, laughing inwardly, if one of the pretty office girls had hung her counterpart there with humorous intent.

Meanwhile the conversation was proceeding briskly. It was obvious that our host understood English perfectly, but his secretary, another pretty young woman, interpreted for him just the same. He obviously relied on her good sense as well as on her competence. She appeared to be extremely useful as well as ornamental and, above all, she seemed to be happy.

In an amazingly short time the details of our cooperation were fixed. The amenities finally over, the head of the great company invited me to meet the production manager. I had reached the ultimate, the practical, the man with whom I must deal again and again. To meet him, however, would not be possible until after the weekend. It was the ideal time to accept the invitation from my special friend to visit her country home.

NOT FAR FROM the huge city of Tokyo, new and busy and not beautiful, is the quiet town of Kamakura, famous now because it is the home of some of Japan's best-known writers. My friend's husband was in Europe. She herself came for me in her comfortable and chauffeured car. It was a sunny afternoon, but we did not know it was sunny until we got out of the city because of the smog, which in Tokyo can be thick.

I greatly enjoyed the drive, nevertheless, not only because it gave me the opportunity to see the general outlines of the amazing new Tokyo, at least in one direction, but also because I found that I could really talk with the equally amazing new Japanese woman at my side. She remained beautifully Japanese in her gray silk kimono, her hair smooth, her face amiable and composed, but her mind was cosmopolitan and sophisticated in the true sense of the word. She could and did remain herself anywhere in the world, at ease in any capital. I am accustomed to cosmopolitan and sophisticated women in many countries, but my friend has an unusual and individual quality. One could never mistake her for any but a Japanese, and yet this national saturation of birth and education is only the medium through which she communicates a universal experience with wisdom and charm. A rose is a rose anywhere in the world, and yet in a Japanese room, arranged in a Japanese vase in a Japanese tokonoma, the rose becomes somehow Japanese. That is my friend.

I asked hundreds of questions, I fear, and was delighted by her frank replies. Two hours slipped past like minutes.

"I have invited some of our writers to meet you," she told me at last. "We will have dinner at a famous inn."

The sun had already set, and we went directly to the inn. To reach it we walked along a narrow footpath, far from the main street of Kamakura. At the end of the path we entered a wooden gate, and there stepping-stones led us across a garden to a wide lawn, lit by stone lanterns. The low roofs of the buildings nestled beneath great trees that climbed the abrupt slopes of a mountain behind the inn.

The guests were waiting for us, a few of Japan's best-loved writers, sitting outdoors on a long stone bench, sipping tea. I was introduced to them, one by one, and we sat for an hour, admiring the moon and enjoying cool fruit juice. The conversation was in English or in Japanese translated into English for my benefit. Then we were summoned, and we sauntered into the restaurant, took off our shoes at the entrance and walked into a large room, open on two sides to the garden.

It was the season of sea trout, the first good season in a long time, I was told. The fish were served individually roasted on hot stones instead of on plates, each placed as though it were swimming on the ocean bed. A line of salt symbolized the beach, a bit of cedar twig the seaweed. It was almost too exquisite to eat, but we ate and found it delicious. Next came a length of green bamboo, split, and steamed inside was the tender flesh of young quail. But let me not go into this matter

of delicacies, for there is no end to the ingenuity and imagination of the Japanese in culinary matters. The evening passed, and too soon the hour of separation arrived. We said our farewells and went our way.

My friend's house was a large one, a combination of ancient and modern Japanese architecture, set in a huge garden and surrounded by a stone wall. I was taken to an upstairs room where a mattress and a spotless sheet and pillow were laid on tatami on the floor. She showed me the private bath, felt a thermos teapot to make sure it was hot, and bade me a kind good night.

When we had parted, I slid back the shoji screen and found beyond it a wide veranda overlooking a beautiful garden, just now drenched in golden light from the moon. The scene was one of ineffable and eternal peace, the moon riding high over the treetops as it had for unnumbered years. I turned away from the moon and went to bed. The ancient lanterns burned in the gardens all night and crickets sang while I slept.

IN THE MORNING my friend declared that I must see the famous Kamakura shrine. We left the house after a late breakfast. It was Sunday and a crowd of sightseers was already at the shrine. Young Japan sauntered about, boy and girl, hand in hand—to my astonishment—or side by side, with lunch baskets. Country folk had come into town and the elders walked sedately, the women still a few paces behind the men.

When we approached the great entrance pavilion, however, we found a commotion. A television film was in the process of being made. Men dressed in the ancient garb of shogun and daimyo times were fencing and fighting in a historical play. We joined the watching crowd. Just as the director, a harried young man wearing dark glasses in the best Hollywood style, shouted "Action!" action stopped. Into the medieval scene a youth on a bicycle came wheeling down the hill from the shrine. There were loud yells from the director as he warned

the young cyclist to take to the woods. The boy obeyed in
alarm, and the warriors took their places again and plunged
into battle. Alas, at this moment a horde of schoolchildren
burst into view. Yells again, the children were sent into the
woods, and once more we returned to the past. There was
something symbolic about it, old and new—one saw the combination everywhere in Japan.

The day was spent in pleasant peace, in conversation in the
garden and library. I rode back to Tokyo alone in the evening
and reflected upon the weekend. As I did, one small incident
stayed above all others in my mind. In that house there was a
younger sister, gentle and unobtrusive and no longer young. It
was none of my business why she was there. But my insatiable
novelist's curiosity got the better of me just before I left. I
began with an apology. "I am ashamed to ask so many questions," I told my friend. "Yet how else shall I know?"

"Ask whatever you like," she told me kindly.

I asked, "Please, has your younger sister never married? It
is so unusual."

There was an instant's hesitation on the older sister's face.
Then she answered. "She did marry once, twenty years ago.
He was a good man—an old friend. . . . Four days after the
wedding she came home."

I waited, then another question came rushing to my lips.
"Why did she come home?"

The elder sister answered quite simply. "We don't know.
We have never liked to ask."

Twenty years and they did not like to ask! The answer
revealed the exquisite reticence of an entire people. . . . No,
not new wine in old bottles. Reverse the metaphor—old wine
in new bottles. The difference is subtle but profound.

THE NEXT MORNING I met the production manager. The
production manager is an important figure in any film opera-
tion, but in that Japanese company he held the position of
prime minister. Everything was referred to him, miracles

were expected, and all yeas and nays from the top came through him.

Ushered into his office, I beheld a huge man in shirtsleeves, with wild hair, wild eyes, heavy jowls, a pursed mouth, a loud voice. He was bellowing into one telephone while at three other telephones in various parts of the room three pretty girls spoke from his dictation but in soft voices. He rolled his huge fiery eyes at me and with an imperious wave of his enormous hand bade me to be seated. A pretty girl served tea. He broke off the conversation at last and came to greet me, all cordiality and kindness and impatience and a certain air of desperation, which I later learned was his habitual mood.

He put aside formalities and spoke with apparent frankness—certainly frankness of the moment. I make this qualification, for I have learned that the charming and disarming frankness of the permanent citizens of the theater world does not necessarily convey what is commonly called truth. Truth in the theater may be strictly momentary and confined within the limits of hope, expectation, or even possibly, intention. The production manager belonged strictly to the theater world. He spoke in Japanese; his interpreter, educated in the United States, softened what he said without destroying its force. That day he merely said, looking harassed, that he would do everything he could to help us, asking of his American partners only one favor: we were to allow him to arrange financial matters with the cast. Americans paid absurd salaries, and this made the actors discontented and unruly afterward. We promised, and took our leave.

Programming was the next task. In making a motion picture, all the necessary ingredients must be provided, and in such order that the proper result is assured. We had to think of finding locations for the filming as well as choosing the actors and the composer and the cameraman and all the other things that go into the vast complexity of a film. Now that our picture is finished, I find that I have a great deal more respect for all motion pictures, even the bad ones, than I had before.

Immense pain and effort, many disappointments and much agony go into their making, not to mention the weariness of mind and body.

While the production manager was helping us to find our cast, we set to work on locations. A seacoast, a fisherman's house, a farmhouse, a gentleman's home, and a live volcano were the settings we needed. There was also to be the tidal wave—but more about that later.

First, the volcano. The strange black island of Oshima is not far away from Tokyo—only a few hours by coastal steamer. We hoped that as we sailed along the indented shores we might discover a fishing village to which we could return. Privately I had no such hope, for in my memory I saw a little village set in a wide cove beside the sea, the terraced hillside of a farm above it, and somewhere near it the Old Gentleman's house. Such a landscape was not, I was certain, to be found near Tokyo.

The ocean was likely to be rough, we were told, and the ship was small. It was a clean little ship, however, and when we went aboard, it was already filled with touring schoolchildren and their teachers. Children are the darlings of Japan, as anyone can see. From the smallest village and the most ancient, at eight o'clock in the morning bevies of smartly dressed little boys and girls, all spotlessly clean in Western clothes, each with a knapsack and a thermos, wend their way to school. On holidays or special days they proceed in the same spotless state to various famous places, always in order and apparently very happy.

The day was fine and the sea bright with whitecaps. We skirted the superbly beautiful coastline all morning without seeing a village that looked possible, drew up at last at a wide dock on Oshima and went at once to the hotel where we were to spend the night. We then engaged a car and were driven around the island.

Oshima is black. The entire island is the overflow of the volcano, and this means that the soil is lava, crushed by time and weather. There are no farms, but the valleys and lower hillsides are green with wild camellias. When they are in bloom in early spring the island is transformed into a bower, famous in all Japan. The livelihood of the people depends upon the oil extracted from their seed pods. Camellia oil—how luxurious it sounds! Actually it is a thin, scentless liquid, used for everything from cookery to hair oil.

The coastline is wild, and I stopped the car often so that I might enjoy the fearful beauty of the high white surf crashing against the ebony black cliffs. The roads were very rough, and we were glad to give up our search for a fishing village at last and go to the volcano itself. All day I had seen it smoking and steaming above us, rolling out its clouds of sulphur-yellow gas. When we reached its base we were really appalled. Smoke and gas and steam had killed everything for many square miles and the gaunt mountains encircling the volcano raised black crests against the sky, smooth and completely devoid of grass or even of camellias.

It was not necessary for us to climb the volcano to know that we had found what we were looking for. I stood for a long time at the foot and saw the setting sun redden the swirling white steam until it looked like flames of living fire. Here we would come later with our actors and cameraman and crew, climb to the top of the crater and take the scene of our little hero, Yukio, the farmer's son, as he stands looking down into the center of our earth.

We were driving on a hillside road in the middle of the afternoon and the sky was turbulent with clouds when we saw unexpectedly the snowy cone of Mount Fuji, rising above the clouds, its perfect crest white against the sudden blue sky. Visitors in Japan may stay for months and not see Fuji. It is entirely by chance that the sacred mountain appears before human eyes. A few, a very few, famous sights are better than the rumor of their beauty. The Taj Mahal is one of these and Fuji is another. We stopped to gaze in delight and awe. Then clouds hid again the majestic shape.

I OPENED MY eyes in Tokyo the next morning at five o'clock, wide awake, totally aware. I had been summoned in some way. I did not hear a voice. I was simply conscious somehow of having been summoned. The room was neither dark nor light. Night had ended, but dawn had not yet come. I lay motionless in my bed, listening, waiting, convinced that there was something to come. I must be ready for it.

At quarter to six the telephone rang. I knew immediately what the message would be. "Overseas call, please," a voice said. "From the United States, please, are you ready?"

"I am waiting for it," I said.

My daughter's voice came to me over the thousands of miles of land and sea between us. "Mother?"

"Yes, darling."

"I have to tell you something."

"Yes, darling."

"Mother." The clear, brave young voice faltered and went on resolutely. "Mother, Dad left us this morning in his sleep."

"I thought that was what you had to tell me."

"How did you know?"

"I just—knew."

"Will you come home?"

"Today—on the first jet."

"We'll meet you in New York."

"I'll cable as soon as I know the flight."

"Everybody has come home. We're all here. We'll take care of everything until you come."

"I know."

We exchanged a few private words, heart spoke to heart, and I hung up. For a moment there was the longing: oh, that I had never left; oh, that I could have been there when he went. I put it aside. I had discussed this very moment thoroughly with our family physician. Years ago he had said, "It may be many years away, it may be tomorrow. You must continue to live exactly as you have. His heart is strong, I think he will live a long time. But remember, whenever it comes, however it comes, you can do nothing to prevent it. Even I could not, though I might be sitting at his side."

He had hesitated, then continued. "The brain is severely damaged. Of course you must expect a total change in personality. We don't know—"

That brilliant brain, responding so quickly to my every thought—yes, there had been a change in personality in him. The man I knew so well, the wise companion, became someone else, a trusting child, a gentle, helpless infant, whom no one could help loving. We were fortunate, even so. For he continued to be what he had always been—lovable, patient, unwilling to cause trouble, except that slowly there ceased to be any communication. Language was lost, eyesight failed, the brain ceased to live except in sleep. The long, slow preparation of the past seven years was now complete. The day I had dreaded had come. The final loneliness was here.

There was no concealing the news. Within an hour the telephone was ringing and friends were at my door. None of it seemed near or real. I heard their voices asking. I heard my own replies. Yes, it is true and I must get the first jet home. No seats were available, but someone gave up his place for me when he heard. The jet was to leave at midnight. I had the whole day to live through somehow. The kindness, the rising sympathy, became too much to bear. I knew that I must get out of the city, into the country, away from telephones.

At that moment a friend, Miki, said, "Come to my house for the day."

Miki lives about two hours from Tokyo. We drove to the foot of a steep hill, and the gate opened to admit us. "From here up you will have to walk," Miki said briskly.

There was comfort in that confident, practical voice, and relief in knowing that Miki would conduct herself exactly as though I had merely come to spend an ordinary day. I had never seen her home. I knew about her work for the half-American children born in Japan. She is unique among Japanese women. Why do I say Japanese? She is simply unique. She is modern to the last cell of her brain, but her blood is ancient and highborn Japanese. Her husband has held honored posts. She has lived in Europe, and she visits the United States once or twice a year. She wears Western dress because she can move more freely in it, but anywhere in the world she could only be Japanese. She is handsome, her eyes are lively and her air is that of a person accustomed to being listened to. Her story as she tells it herself is something like this:

One day, during the most rigorous period of the war, she entered a train to go to the country and hunt for food. The train was crowded, and she took the last seat. As she sat down a bundle loosely wrapped in newspaper fell into her lap from the baggage rack above her head. There before her horrified eyes was a little newborn baby boy. He was dead. At that moment the military police came into the car to search for black marketeers. They immediately arrested her for trying to dispose of a dead child. She had a bad few minutes until an old farmer spoke up for her. "It is not her child. A young woman came in and put that bundle up on the rack and went away again."

The police were finally convinced and she was saved. But she never forgot. "I feel the weight of that dead baby on my knees forever," she always says.

Days later, as she was walking in her beautiful garden in the early morning, she noticed something moving under a big bush. She stooped and discovered a tiny baby. Some desperate young mother had left him there. She took him into the house and cared for him. From then on she devoted herself to the half-American children born in Japan. What began with a small dead baby grew into a great living work for thousands of children, born of Japanese mothers and fathered by American men, black and white. She organized an adoption agency and placed more than a thousand half-American orphans in the United States. But many of them continue in her home until they are grown and able to take care of themselves.

On that day as I climbed the hill I heard their voices from above, shouting, laughing, screaming in play. The path wound among great trees. The day was beautifully mild, and the sunshine fell between the tree trunks on the moss-covered earth. I walked slowly, my usually strong energies sapped from within. My mind and heart were numb. I realized suddenly that Miki was talking and I did not know what she had said. "How many children have you here, Miki?" I asked, merely to have something to say.

"One hundred and forty-eight," she told me.

One hundred and forty-eight! They were scattered everywhere in the fine old Japanese buildings and gardens of Miki's ancestral home. She had built some utilitarian modern houses, too, for the school and dormitories. Most orphanages are sad places, but somehow Miki had made her huge establishment a home instead of an orphanage.

Miki's great delight was the school, and she had been engaged in a neck-and-neck race for ten years to build a senior high school, keeping just ahead of her children. She continued to lead the way through the kitchens and the dining rooms. Everywhere children were helping, chattering and laughing as they worked. She made a few suggestions to them, and the children listened with attention but without fear. I thought I observed a secret fondness for what she called "my naughty boy" or "my naughty girl." She explained that she herself had been "a naughty girl" when she was small. She herself slept, I discovered, in a room with the naughtiest and the newest. "Sometimes a boy wants to run away," she told me. "He is used to wild freedom on the streets. If I think he will try to run away, I tie a strong string around his ankle that he cannot untie, and the other string to my own ankle. If he runs in the night, I wake and catch him."

Her greatest pride was her beautiful little theater. "After luncheon," she said, "my children will sing and dance for you."

The morning that had loomed ahead of me had already passed. I had not once forgotten that I was alone in the world, but somehow the eternal knowledge had not penetrated deeply enough to me. All day Miki had made me walk from one center of life to another. And now, before we went to luncheon, she had one more gift of life for me. "We will look at the babies," she said.

We walked to the end of the garden and there, in a sunny house built for babies, we saw them, tiny ones newly born, little ones learning to sit up and to walk. Kind women were caring for them, and the babies clung to them. It comforted me to see how the babies turned away from me, a stranger, to those who cared for them. Too often I have visited orphanages where the children ran to strangers and clung to them when they left.

"The babies will all go for adoption," Miki said, "except this little one who is mentally retarded. I shall have to think of something for him. . . . I am taking them myself—eleven babies to their new American parents."

I looked at each little one closely. They are always beautiful children, those who carry the East and the West in their veins. Kipling forgot about them when he said there could be no meeting of East and West. They have always met, as true hearts must meet, in love, if not in politics. It is love only that brings human beings together, many kinds of love. I left the little children with reluctance, for they brought me deep comfort.

We walked back through the gardens and came to an enormous Japanese house, built of aged wood, open along one full side to what had once been a fine Japanese garden but was now a dusty baseball field. A group of boys had eaten their food in a hurry and were back on the field with bats and balls. We entered Miki's big beautiful living room. At the far end of the room was a long, low dining table and two polished antique cabinets.

I wish I could convey the exquisite tact of my hostess and of my fellow guests during the delicious meal. Each of them knew what had happened to me, and yet no one spoke of it. They did not, on the other hand, pretend to a false cheerfulness. Rather they talked with quiet interest about various subjects, skillfully rousing my attention if I sank too long into silence, urging me to try one delicacy after another, not out of appetite, of which they knew I had none, but as a courtesy to the cook. Once I heard a telephone ring, but the message was postponed apparently, until the meal was over. I listened and smiled and made what I think were suitable replies and was upheld by that strong atmosphere of complete understanding never put into words.

A vigorous baseball game went on while we ate, and I heard again and again the sharp click of bat against ball, the sounds of running feet, screams and clapping hands. Miki kept a lively eye on the game, and every now and again she shouted instructions or approval.

When the meal was over, Miki told me a call had come for me from overseas. She went with me then into a small room and closed the door and handed me the receiver. Across the thousands of miles of earth and sea I heard my daughter's voice again as clearly as though she were in the next room. "Mother, we have planned everything, but we want to know if you approve. The service will be the day after tomorrow and our own minister, of course, will take charge. We thought it would be best to have it in the library because he loved that room, you know. And nobody there except the people from the farm and the house—and the nurses who took care of him— and all of us. Then we'll take him to the family cemetery—no flowers, we thought, but we'll ask people to give the money to Welcome House."

The children had planned everything as I would have done. I said yes, yes, yes, over and over again. Then when I had hung up the receiver, it was suddenly all too much. For the first time I let myself acknowledge that it had all been too much from that day, seven years ago, in the sunny park in Sheridan, Wyoming, when the first blow had fallen. Such a little blow it had seemed at the time—no more than mild heat exhaustion, we thought.

We had planned for several years to take a family summer trip to Yellowstone National Park and then into Oregon and Washington. It had been a comfortable and happy time. "I think the trip will be good for him," our family doctor had said, "if he does not do the driving." So it had seemed, until that sunny day. We stayed another day in a pleasant ranch house, still thinking it was nothing, but that we had better go home to be near our own doctor. Later we knew it was not heat exhaustion. But he seemed as well as ever, as vigorous, still carrying on his busy life in the New York offices and in the country office at home.

I hid my face with my hands. And Miki, with that delicacy so natural to Asia, ancient and accustomed to human sorrow, sat beside me in silence, knowing that all comfort was vain, except the comfort of a friend sitting quietly beside me. I struggled through and wiped my eyes, and Miki rose. "The children are waiting for us," she said.

Those were her words, but what she really said was that I must begin now to live. Death must not interrupt life. There were others waiting for us.

The afternoon came to an end. It was time to go back to Tokyo and time to go home. Miki refused to leave me until the last moment.

THE JET TOOK off at midnight. There was a certain comfort in being at last among strangers, to whom I needed to make no response. It was the first moment that I had been totally alone since the moment that morning when the world had changed. Long ago, when I knew my child was to be permanently retarded, I learned that there are two kinds of sorrow—one that can be assuaged and one that cannot. This one was different, yet alike in that it, too, was not to be assuaged.

Nevertheless, years ago I had learned the technique of acceptance. The first step is simply to yield oneself to the situation. It is a process of the spirit, but it begins with the body. There, belted into my seat, I consciously yielded my body, muscle by muscle, bone by bone. As the body yielded itself to the will, the spirit found it easier also to yield to the same command. At last I slept.

Time was meaningless in this swift flight. When I woke, the sky was already light. I had left Tokyo the night before, Sunday, but I would reach New York on Monday morning, after another day and night of living, if not of time. We were flying into the sunrise, into a fountain of light, glorious and majestic, rising over the curved edge of the globe. People woke and stirred. There was the fragrance of coffee in the air; a hostess was alert and ready with fruit juice. The first full day of my new and solitary life had begun. It did not matter how many people surrounded me; within myself would be, from now on, a permanent solitude. What would this mean? It remained to be discovered. I must not insist upon knowing everything at once. Long ago I had learned that if one is to be patient with others, one must also be patient with oneself.

I did not learn this lesson all at once. I was often impatient with myself until I realized, I think through the practice of music, that learning is a day-by-day process. One can work fourteen hours solidly on memorizing a Beethoven sonata for a single performance, but this learning is not permanent. To hold the music forever in one's mental grasp, it must become a part of one's being over a period of time and through continuing practice. What I had to discover about solitude, what I had to learn about its meaning, was only to be acquired through daily life and new experience.

There is a comfort at once superficial and organic in the necessities of washing and clothing the body, in eating and drinking. It seemed to me when I looked into the mirror that never again would I care about how I looked, since I would never again hear his words of appreciation and praise.

Was this same face the one I had been compelled to look at for so many years? I was another person, so the face must belong to someone else.

Nevertheless, I made it up as usual and took care with my long hair. That hair! Even as a little girl it was my bane, always long and tangled. Without caring in the least, my hands did their habitual task, and I could not believe when I looked in the mirror that I looked the same after all, but I did.

When I returned to my seat, the stewardess gave me breakfast—coffee and bacon and toast. Though the spirit was remote and took no part in any of this, the body performed as usual. Everyone in the jet was awake now, and I knew no one and no one knew me, for which I was grateful. The stewardess took the breakfast tray away at last, half finished, and I tried to read a novel and then put it away. I did not want a story of human beings. I opened my dressing case and took from it a thin book, *Science and Human Values,* by Jacob Bronowski. This book I read all morning, my mind working sharply apart from my individual life.

> Whether our work is art or science or the daily work of society, it is only the form in which we explore our experience which is different; the irresistible need to explore remains the same. . . . For this is the lesson of science, that the concept is more profound than its laws, and the act of judging more critical than the judgment. In a book that I wrote about poetry I said:
> "Poetry does not move us to be just or unjust, in itself. It moves us to thoughts in whose light justice and injustice are seen in fearful sharpness of outline."
> What is true of poetry is true of all creative thought. . . . The values by which we are to survive are not rules for just and unjust conduct, but are those deeper illuminations in whose light justice and injustice, good and evil, means and ends, are seen in fearful sharpness of outline.

A strange peace flowed through me. I leaned back against the seat and closed my eyes. It was as though we had communication, my husband and I, through silence instead of words.

It was night again. We had run through a whole day in a short space of time, and the voice over our heads announced that we had arrived in Honolulu.

The usual bustle of disembarking and lining up for customs inspection took place. While I waited, a customs official came to me and asked me to step aside. Leaning across the counter, he spoke in a low voice. "I don't want to hold you up, but there's something I want to talk about, confidentially."

I was surprised. I had never seen this man before, a big burly fellow, a kind round face, very American.

"You see," he said quietly, "I have a retarded daughter."

Ah, now I knew why he had drawn me aside! I am accustomed to having people take me aside and tell me this, everywhere in the world.

"Tell me about her," I said.

I listened while he talked, and I was filled with inner wonder. How could it be that at this very moment when I needed desperately to want to live, this man should be here, recalling me to life? For much of my life has been spent in working with and for retarded children and their parents. This has been my destiny. Yet since my daughter's voice had come to me over the telephone in Tokyo, I had not once remembered this part of my life. Now here it was, claiming me again.

"You see," the man was saying, "my wife and I are having an argument. She says that Americans always put their retarded children into institutions because it's better for them there. That we ought to be doing what Americans do now that Hawaii is a state. And I say that our girl is no trouble—she's gentle and quiet and she'd be lonesome in an institution."

"Would your wife be happier if she were there?" I asked.

"No, she cries when she talks about it, but she says it would be better for the girl."

"Do you want her there?"

"Me? It would break my heart."

I considered. "What if both of you happened to die? Who would take care of your daughter?"

"My wife's Hawaiian. She's got one of these big Hawaiian families. They'd all take care of our girl. Matter of fact, they get mad when we talk about an institution. It's just that my wife—"

"Tell your wife she is wrong and the rest of you are right," I said. "Your daughter is lucky. She has a family who wants to keep her. I am sure that American parents in your circumstances would wish they were as lucky."

His honest face cleared. "Thanks," he said.

He led me back to the luggage station. "Anything to declare?"

"Nothing," I said. I had nothing.

"Okay," he said and marked my bags with chalk and smiled at me. "So long," he said. "I'll never forget you. This is my lucky day. Wait till I tell my wife. She won't believe me. It's a miracle."

It was a miracle for me, too. No one could take my husband's place, but strangers would come when I needed them, and I could learn from them.

WHEN NEXT DAWN came, it poured its golden light on the landscape of America. The voice on the loudspeaker announced that we would now begin the descent, over the city of Allentown in Pennsylvania, only a few miles from my farm home. We came swiftly down and down, and I saw the gleaming towers of New York.

Now family had to be faced again, and for a moment I dreaded it. It had been easier in the plane, where I did not have to meet the strain of sympathy.

Sunshine poured through the mists as I walked across the airfield. Inside the airport my dear and only sister and two of my daughters waited, and with them the faithful Pennsylvania Dutchman who has driven my cars for many years. I looked into each face and whatever I had dreaded melted away. It was good to be with those who knew me and loved me and whom I loved.

I am rich in having three sons and six daughters. Of the

Right, Pearl Buck in her later years. Below, with her husband, Richard J. Walsh.

six daughters, the eldest is the child who never grew, to whom I owe so much, and the five others range from my competent, professional, occupational-therapist daughter to the gentle half-American child of eleven who came to me from Japan. The two youngest daughters are half-Japanese; their fathers were American soldiers. The next, lively and an organizer, is half-German; her father was an American, too. The little middle one, married, with three perfect babies, is the one who lives across the brook from me, the one with dark hair, big violet eyes and a fiery temper, softened by a quick sense of humor. Each son has his individual strength, each daughter her peculiar grace, each an indispensable place in my life. Today the middle and older daughters were here to meet me with my sister—three strong and understanding women.

We were closer than we had ever been. His death quickened every bond between us. Nor did I overlook the quiet understanding of our driver. He took my baggage checks and led us to the car. In a few minutes we were on our way home through the streets of New York to the Lincoln tunnel. It was a journey I had made hundreds of times through the years, always with him until the last five years.

What fun it had been from the very beginning, how satisfying the years together! We had begun in New York, where his life had been for thirty years before we met. The first winter we lived in a cosmopolitan hotel, in a suite of pleasant rooms. The next year, when we adopted our first two babies, we moved to a terraced apartment and began our life as parents. He had always wanted a big family, and how we enjoyed its gradual accumulation! Two years slipped by, and they held nothing but joy and content, and we took two more babies. Then his next dream, to live in the country, became a necessity. Four small children can scarcely be contained successfully in any apartment. We moved to our farm home, and he devoted himself, as he had always hoped he could, to editorial work. He was a reluctant businessman, and had his brilliance been only a little more channeled, he might have been a writer of many books. As it was, he wrote a few as varied as he was himself: clever rhymes for children; a humorous mystery novel; a fine nonfiction work on Marco Polo, simplified for young people; and a critical study of Buffalo Bill, a character in whom he took much skeptical interest.

As the years passed, the farmhouse developed into a rambling, comfortable home for an increasing family. He taught the children tennis and baseball and golf, and they learned early to swim and to ride. Our life was organized casually around work and children. Our pleasures were in music and people and books and the world of woods and mountains and sea.

I do not know whether it is easier to have the end come suddenly or gradually over the years. I think if I had been given the choice, I would have preferred a sudden end, shock and all. Then memory would not be entangled with the slow, agonizing fading of perception and speech, and at last the loss of recognition even of those loved and dear.

Slowly, slowly, the change came. When his eyes failed and he could no longer read, we sent for records from the Library of Books for the Blind. They provided a continuing stream of records coming into the house, free of charge, and his brain was kept alive and stimulated. But the day came when words ceased to have meaning for him, and even music faded, and he was content merely to exist. He would have suffered had he known, and I thank a kind intelligence, wherever it is, that he never knew. The body lived on, relieved of any strain of mind or spirit, and assumed a strange durability of its own.

The end had come quite unexpectedly. I listened as my middle daughter talked while we drove homeward through the green countryside of late spring. She had come across the brook with her three little children after breakfast on her morning visit. She found him awake and ready for the day. The children climbed on his bed and kissed him and stroked his cheeks. Since they were born, he had always been there in bed, so they had no memories of his being different. They all went away, and when my daughter returned a little later, he was gone. It was so simple a story that I could bear to hear it told. For a long time he had not known he was living, and then he did not know when he died.

"There was nothing anyone could have done," my daughter told me.

"I know," I said. "I have known that for a long time."

I could feel nothing for the moment but finality, an immense weariness of mind and body, now that I knew all there was to know. I sat in silence, my hands in my daughter's warm young grasp until the car drove up the familiar driveway at last.

All our children were at home, gathered from everywhere. They had done everything. His room, which for so long had been a sickroom, was already a guest room. The hospital bed was gone; the carpets were fresh and clean; crisp white curtains hung at the windows. My room was immaculate and cheerful with roses. I saw everything and felt nothing. I was walking in my sleep. After luncheon, I lay on the couch in the living room, I who am never exhausted, and while the children planned, I slept. It was not like any sleep I have ever known. I simply fell into unconsciousness.

THE NEXT TWO days centered upon three events. We went, all of us, to tell him our last good-by. Of course, it was only his body we saw. He was not there.

But the body is precious. Through the body we express our love and with the body we live. I remembered my mother one day when I was a small child, not more than seven. I was desperately ill with diphtheria in a Chinese city. My younger brother had just died of the same disease, and they were burying him that day, and my mother was sobbing. A friend reproached her. "It is only his body," she told my mother. "His soul is in Heaven with Our Lord."

My mother flew into anger, sobs and all. "But his body is

precious," she cried. "I gave it birth. I tended it and loved it. Wherever his soul is, it is out of my reach. Now they are taking his body away, and it is all I have."

These words came back to me as I stood by his beloved body. He was wearing his tweed suit, the one he liked, a blue-gray, and the dark blue tie I had given him last Christmas. His beautiful hair, only partly white, was brushed as he always wore it, back from his forehead. His face was young again, the lines gone, the lips tranquil. I kissed his cheek. I touched his hand that had always been warm and quick to respond.

The next day we had the simple service that the children had planned. When I came downstairs, our household people and those on the farm, the children and their families, as well as the nurses who had cared for him were waiting for me in the library. His coffin was set before the chimneypiece, the lid closed. As our family minister spoke a few words of friendship, I sat thinking of the many hours we had spent in this room. It had first been the children's playroom. Then, when they grew bigger, we made the barn into their play place and this room into the family library, lined with bookshelves. Above the chimneypiece he hung an evocative and poetic painting, an illustration of a story by John Galsworthy, which he had published in *Collier's* when he was editor of that magazine. The story was the first by Galsworthy ever published in America, I believe.

I went upstairs to my own room again as they carried him away, and this somehow was the worst moment. He was leaving our house and our home forever. And then came the long drive to his family cemetery in New York. In the midst of that sorrowful ride, I chanced to see from the rear window the long slow procession of black cars. At the very end were two station wagons, and they were fire-engine red. I recognized them immediately. One belonged to my second son and one to my equally youthful son-in-law. I had winced when they brought them to show me proudly before I went to Japan, and heroically I had admired them. Now here they were, bright and alive in the morning sun. My heart dissolved again in tears and laughter. What a shame, what a pity, that he could not see those two shining red station wagons doing him honor upon this occasion—how he would have laughed!

When we arrived in the quiet place, birds were singing and flowers were blooming. It did not take long to perform the last ceremony of giving his body back to the earth. Our minister spoke the final words of peace and acceptance. My sons and my stepson stood beside me, strong young men, the stepson to carry on his father's publishing firm. My daughters walked with me back to the car, and we drove away. . . . But oh, that silent last moment when he must be left behind, and the arrival at the house, now empty! Of these I cannot speak.

To other women in like circumstances who may read these pages I can only say there is no escape from such moments when they come. They must be lived through, not once but many times in memory. I have been told that they grow easier. I do not find it so. Now whenever I leave my home, I come back to it as to a haven, but it is not the same, and it will never be the same. I know that now. Since there is no escape from the fact, there can only be acceptance. And acceptance comes at last, but not at once—oh, never at once.

I SHOULD NOT, I suppose, have gone to Vermont. But we have always gone there when the summer gets too hot in Pennsylvania. Perhaps I felt that I could escape, somehow, from his continuing absence. It took me long to learn how impossible that is, wherever I go in the world. In the house in Vermont, I set myself to writing, and I practiced my piano and spent hours on the high terrace facing Stratton Mountain. I do not know why I imagined that anything would be easier here. For one thing, I could not write. My mind, lost in thought and memory and question, simply would not busy itself with the creation of other people's lives. I needed work that I had to do, work with others, compelling me daily to rise early and go to an appointed place.

I made up my mind. I would go back to Japan and resume my work on the picture. My coworkers there had found loca- tions—a fishing village that they thought ideal for our picture, a terraced farm, an empty beach, a fisherman's house, a gentle- man's house. The volcano we had. They were ready for me to return to the job. When was I coming?

Immediately, I said. It was nearing the end of August. The girls would go back to school soon, and they could live with their elder sister. There was no family reason to hold me at home and I welcomed the thought of work and Japan.

II

THE ATMOSPHERE INTO which I descended from the jet near Tokyo was one of welcome and unspoken sympathy. The deeper the feelings, the Japanese believe, the less should be spoken. We Americans find it necessary to speak, to send letters and cards of condolence. Hundreds of letters had poured into my office from all over the world. And people, friends or strangers, had stopped me on streets and country roads to tell me, "I am so sorry to hear—"

In Tokyo nothing was said, yet everything was conveyed. Consideration was delicate but complete. My room in the hotel was bright with flowers and baskets of fruit. The little maids were ever present and solicitous. I understood, for in Japan even love is not to be expressed in words. There are no such words as "I love you" in the Japanese language.

"How do you tell your husband that you love him?" I once asked a Japanese friend.

She looked slightly shocked. "An emotion as deep as love between husband and wife cannot be put into words. It must be expressed in attitude and act."

Nor are there Japanese equivalents of our love words— sweetheart, darling, dear, and all the rest. Certain young Japanese are beginning to use the English words, not seri- ously, perhaps. But perhaps no one uses these words seriously anymore. I hear American directors scattering them carelessly and casually upon the loved and the unloved alike, in the fashion of Hollywood and Broadway, and I always remonstrate. To a writer all words are significant and valuable, each to be used only in its fitting place, like jewels. The English language is peculiarly rich in the words of love, their roots deep in ancient Anglo-Saxon soil. To hear a man call a girl whose name he does not remember by the precious words of love always make me—well, angry! It is a desecration of true feeling, the deepest in the human heart. Any woman who has heard the man she loves call her his sweetheart, his darling, his love, can only be profoundly angered when these words are destroyed.

Our locations were set, although I had not yet seen them except on film; the next task was to find our cast. Since the story of *The Big Wave* is altogether Japanese, the cast was to be Japanese. For the first time an American film company was making a picture in Japan, coproduced by a Japanese film company, with a Japanese crew and cameraman. It was an experiment, a profoundly interesting one.

I had seen motion pictures made of my books before, but none had been made with my help. I did not intend to interfere with the directing or in any of the professional aspects, for I know my areas of ignorance, but I was to have the privilege of being anywhere I liked, and of speaking whenever I wished. On the whole, I believed my fellow workers had confidence in my ability to be silent. I am, in fact, a quiet woman by nature, unless oppressed by what I consider injustice. Then I become, I am told, excruciatingly articulate.

We were given office space in the handsome building owned by our coproducers. Each day of casting I went early and stayed late, looking, listening, judging, disapproving or approving, while those in command gave auditions to actors and actresses, adults and children. Two boys and two girls were to begin the story.

I have seen many stage children, and they can be sad and

tense. These Japanese stage children, however, were like all other Japanese children, healthy and happy and much loved. They came in, one after the other, each mother unobtrusively following her particular star, and they bowed with the grace bestowed by that extra hinge that seems to have developed in the Japanese back.

Days passed and the actors narrowed down to the impossibles and the possibles, the latter by far the smaller group. Japan has many excellent actors, but we were looking for excellent actors who also spoke English. At first we hoped, unrealistically, that their English would be perfect. Later we merely hoped their English could be understood well enough to give American audiences the illusion they were hearing Japanese.

That illusion reminds me of an incident of my own life in China. I had stopped to rest one day at a wayside inn in a remote province. An old woman came to pour tea into my bowl. I thanked her in Chinese and asked her how she did. She stared at me in terror and dropped the teapot. "The gods save me," she gasped. "What is the matter with me? I can understand English!"

Something like this we hoped to achieve.

IN SUCH DIVERTING work the day passed until evening fell, and the trouble with every day was that at the end of it there was always night. For the first time in my life I was sad when evening came. The others went to their husbands and wives, but I came back alone to my hotel room. The windows looked over the roofs of new Tokyo—as I have said, not beautiful, for there had not been time enough to create beauty. The city was hastily rebuilt after the war when people were desperate to begin living again and the government was all but bankrupt. Houses went up helter-skelter.

Evenings in lonely hotel rooms are impossible, at least for me. I had invitations in plenty, but these did not fill my need. One had always to maintain a front, and this could be done during the day when the mind was engaged. It was different when one had to respond individually to others. In despair and loneliness I took to wandering the streets at night, unknown and free. Tokyo is filled with theaters and motion picture houses, and usually I stopped by in one or the other. Though I did not understand the dialogue, the drift of the story was easy to catch, and I could be mildly amused, superficially at least, by what I saw. The houses were always packed, the audiences grave and intense until a comic moment brought loud, staccato laughter, stopped instantaneously by intent gravity again.

I had a warmly comfortable feeling when I was alone in a Japanese crowd. They accepted me because they had become used to Americans as part of the world landscape. Tokyo has, of course, its darker aspects. There were streets in which I did not enjoy walking alone any more than I do in certain parts of New York and Philadelphia. Cities are cities and hooligans are found in all.

Those were the days of the student riots in Tokyo, about which we North Americans had so much misinformation. I can only say that I was there, that I saw the crowds of young men and women, earnest, determined, informed. They were not anti-American, but Japanese who liked their constitution, although it had been engineered by Americans. They liked especially the part in which Japan as a nation promises never again to wage war. Now they, the Japanese, were being asked by Americans, in the event of war, to take sides with the West, although they were oriented toward Asia, and in the future must be a neutral people. With American bases on their soil, they felt themselves forced to be partisan. It amounted to a situation that to them was unendurable in its confusion. The Japanese are a well-organized people. Whatever their attitude, however short-lived, it is that one and no other. Therefore they rioted to proclaim their confusion, but they did not hate anybody.

Students have always been an exciting and interesting part of my life. I do not mean the relatively placid students of North America. I mean the students of China and India, Korea and Japan. In China the new age—whatever it was—was always announced by an uprising of students. The people respected these young men and women because they were presumably better informed than the average citizen. Books, the Asian peoples believe, are treasure houses of human wisdom, and since students alone had access to books, the position of a student in Asia carried—and still carries—a prestige far out of proportion to age and class. During the Nationalist regime in China I had seen many students killed because they were suspected of being communists. Doubtless some were, but most were simply dedicated young patriots, desperately desiring to better the conditions under which their people lived. If one wants to know what is about to happen in an Asian country, watch the students.

FOR THE PICTURE, we needed a tidal wave and an earthquake. The earthquake, of course, had to come first. The earthquake in Chile had sent a tidal wave rushing across the sea to northwest Japan, but more often earthquakes occur in Japan itself, or under the sea nearby. Earthquake—I cannot even say the word to myself as I sit here upon the solid earth of Pennsylvania without a touch of that bottomless sickness of heart and body that overcomes a human being when the earth quakes beneath his feet. It is as if the very earth were dissolving into space.

The second day after I came back to Tokyo, as I was writing at the desk in my hotel room after midnight, I felt that deep troubled tremor of the earth and once more the old sickness rose in me. For that instant my hand went out of control, and the desk shook. Most of the people slept through it, but the morning newspaper reported a sharp tremor. Such tremors come often in Japan—hundreds, thousands of them in a year, on the average of four times a day—and each time it is a reminder to a courageous people that they live on dangerous islands. The effect on them of this eternal tension is obvious. They have extremes of temperament—an exaggerated gaiety, a profound and sometimes frenzied melancholy. A disciplined and studied surface, smiles and calm and casualness, is underlaid, without exception, I might say, by a dark sadness, born of the knowledge in child and adult that catastrophe is endemic in spite of the beauty of the mountains and the sea and the kindliness of life. This universal knowledge begets in them a consideration, a tender courtesy, as though to say that since the world may end at any moment, let us be kind to one another. When this inherent kindness has to be unlearned, as in times of war when men must be taught to be brutal, they may be cruel beyond imagination. . . . But I was speaking of earthquakes—and tidal waves.

We needed a tidal wave then. The earthquake we could reproduce by camera, but the tidal wave was beyond us. Here we had good fortune. Our Japanese coproducers had the finest special-effects studio in the country for the reproduction in miniature of scenes in nature. The Japanese are supremely talented in such work, and of all the Japanese, Tsuburaya is the most talented. We met him by appointment.

Dressed in work clothes, he greeted us with a charmingly natural courtesy. He had already made sketches to show us. They were startlingly accurate watercolors of the rising horizon, the onrushing wave, and the towering crash of the crest. A tidal wave does not appear at first as a wave. Instead the horizon lifts, the sea mounts toward the sky in a smooth brimming line, then it runs toward the land, a wall of water that may be two hundred feet high. A powerful suction gathers the sea into the wave, so that the bottom of the ocean beyond the beach is laid bare. Then the gigantic wave curls over its own base and overwhelms the land, houses and people.

I watched Tsuburaya's beautiful face as he described the sequences he had painted. It was as sensitive as a child's, a genius child, but not in the least childish. It was wise and gentle, yet fresh and strong and humorous, the face of an artist purified by the satisfaction of fulfillment through his art. He intended to come to the fishing village with his cameraman and photograph everything. Then he would build sets in the studio and recreate the scenes and adapt them to the film.

ALWAYS AT THE end of the day, every day, there came the return to no one. After the problems, solved and unsolved, after the coming and going of many people, the excitement of discovery, the shared laughter, the growing confidence in the work, each day had the same end. I went back to my hotel rooms and locked the door. Flowers were fresh, letters heaped on the table. But the one letter I longed for could never be written because he was gone. I did not open the others. Let them wait until my Japanese secretary came and I was forced to work in order that she could work. The invitations were many, but I had no enjoyment in accepting them. I fell then into the habit of having dinner sent to my rooms and of eating alone. When night came, life was suddenly meaningless.

Had he been with me, it would have been the best part of the day. Much of our life together had been spent in separation during the day, for each of us had a profession, a work. But how eagerly we looked forward to the evening, and to what lengths we went in order to spend it together! We went together wherever we had to go, I yielding to his necessity, he to mine. And in the twenty-five years of our married life we did not spend a night apart until he ceased to know whether I was there or not. And when he ceased to know, everything was different, except memory.

I had discarded that time of not knowing. When I thought of him, I thought of him as I knew him, vivid, alive, with infinite variety in thought and word, dominant, invincibly prejudiced in some matters, as I used to say impetuously when we disagreed, and he smiled and accepted the accusation with amusement and no intention of changing himself. But he knew I did not want him changed. Whatever he was, he was himself, and I liked that.

For example, he could not drive a nail without pounding his thumb and therefore he wisely refused to drive nails. He took no part in household matters, however busy I was. He refused to have any part in disciplining our big family. I am no disciplinarian myself, being given to laughter over naughtiness unless I am angry, and neither mirth nor anger is the right atmosphere for discipline. Teachers of our nine children were unanimous in one simple comment: "Your children are spoiled." I agreed helplessly. Looking at these same children now, I can only say that so far as I know, they have turned out well.

Am I being quite fair to him as a disciplinarian? Perhaps not, for there was one offense that he would not tolerate from any child, and this was an act or word that he considered a sign of lack of respect for me. His response was instant, invariable and thunderous. "Don't you know your mother is the greatest person in the world?"

The absurdity of this remark wilted me at once into a state of embarrassment, which the children understood and suffered with me, especially as they never intended disrespect. I enjoyed free argument and spirited disagreement, and his outburst killed communication. If we were at the table, our appetites failed and we sat in silence. What he thought of this silence I do not know, for he allowed no protest or discussion on the subject of respect for me, even from me myself!

As for me, I obeyed him far too literally, and this for two reasons. In China I had been taught that woman should obey man, if possible. Second, I was disgracefully ignorant about my own country. My parents had lived decades in China before I appeared in their life. They were young when they left home, my father twenty-eight and my mother only twenty-three, and both of them were idealists and intellectuals. They grew to maturity in Chinese culture and society and not in their own. When I came to live finally in my own country, he said that among other enjoyments it was fun to be married to me because he could tell me all the old American jokes and they were new to me. This was true; at any moment he might tell me something that sent me into laughter.

Into such half-smiling, half-tearful reminiscence I relapsed too easily, and it was necessary to take myself in hand. So, when dinner was over, I sauntered again into the streets of Tokyo. I went often to the Ginza—market, bazaar and amusement place—always diverted by the variety of people who came to enjoy the gaudy scene. Flags, balloons and paper flowers of every color tied to the eaves of the roofs floated above the streets and shops. American cars, a proof of wealth, stood waiting by the curbs, the chauffeurs zealously polishing the chromium while their employers explored toys or silks or jewelry. Bicycles dashed madly through the swarming crowds and women clattered along, their babies strapped to their backs.

Most significant of all were the young men and women who walked hand in hand in a state of dazed happiness, window-shopping, or just wandering. It takes getting used to, this hand-in-hand business in modern Japan. In old Japan lovers met in secret and climbed volcanoes and threw themselves into the fiery craters to signify the depth of their hopeless love. Nowadays they walk hand in hand in the Ginza or go on picnics to the famous spots where once they committed suicide together.

In the strange floating existence of those days and nights, I went one evening to the Kabuki Theater by invitation of the star actor. The play was called *The White Snake*. I knew the story well, for it is an ancient Chinese tale of a woman who assumes the form of a serpent for purposes of her own.

The night was clear and the streets of Tokyo were unusually crowded. When we arrived at the theater entrance, someone was waiting to meet me. The star had declared that he would not begin the show until he had met me and we had been photographed. I was led backstage, and there he stood, made up as a woman, the White Snake. It was perfect makeup, sinister and graceful. Even his lips were white, though lined at the inner edge with scarlet. The eyes were a snake's eyes, black and glittering, their glance darting here and there. When he saw me, he put out his hand, and I took it. It was as cold and smooth as a snake's skin, but it clung to mine, and thus, hand in hand, we were photographed. He talked for a few minutes, his stiff white lips scarcely moving, and then the gong struck and it was time for him to go on stage.

I went to my seat and spent a few hours of pure pleasure. The stage was enormous, larger than any stage I had ever seen, and the spectacle superb. There is no art in the world, in my opinion, which surpasses Kabuki in imaginative power. When the play was over, we walked out in a dream of silence.

THE MOST MODERN theater, by way of contrast to Kabuki, was more of a shock than even I could take. It came about in this manner. We went one day to the production manager's office with a list of our tentative cast. He pointed immediately to two doubtful names. He said that he was merely suggesting, not directing, that we make better choices for the two leading men. We reminded him that the man we wanted most

337

had not been released to us by his firm. Hearing this, he got up, walked around, rubbed his head and groaned loudly several times. He sat behind his desk and twisted his hair in both hands and groaned again. Then he knocked himself on the head with clenched fists and turned to us, beaming. He had an idea. A performance of Japanese rock 'n' roll singers and musicians was taking place at that very instant in his own rock 'n' roll theater. He suggested that he accompany us there, and then we could see all the best young men in rock 'n' roll and take our choice. He would command any whom we chose to be our actors. They would listen to him. "I am a big producer," he said loudly.

We agreed with alacrity. The theater was a huge place, and when I was led to a seat in a box—reserved, of course, for the production manager himself—I was stunned by what I saw. All the teenagers in Japan were assembled there, or so it seemed; certainly there were many thousands of them.

This was indeed a Japan new to me: rock 'n' roll, dancing girls and singing boys, American songs, Western songs sung in English, and only a very few Japanese songs. The girls screamed just as they do in the United States, and they sounded just as silly. Very young girls in skirts and blouses ran out from the audience to hang wreaths of paper flowers on their male favorites. Only one girl sang, a handsome girl of eighteen with an excellent voice.

Our business, however, was to find actors. After the grand finale we went downstairs into a small hot room and interviewed three or four young men who sang in English so well that we hoped they might speak English. Such was not the case. One bright exception was a boy who spoke beautiful English. His mother was half English and he had learned at home. We asked him to come the next morning for an audition.

While all this was going on, I observed a change in the production manager. He was softening. He saw our problem with the English and he was concerned. He invited us to have dinner with him and asked if we wanted to go where he always went, or to some more elaborate place. We accepted with grateful surprise, saying that we wanted to go where he went. It was a fascinating place, small but clean as only the Japanese know cleanliness, the rough wooden tables and counters made of thick unpainted log slabs scrubbed to snow-whiteness. The production manager gave orders in the manner of one always obeyed, and assigned our seats. Mine faced him, so I had full opportunity to observe this extraordinary man as we ate.

For now a new man appeared. He even announced that he was not the same man we had seen heretofore and proceeded to explain himself and his life. He was not married, he told us, and he insisted that he was the loneliest man in Tokyo. He lived with his mother, a wonderful woman whom he adored, but he was fifty years old. He did not look that age. He looked a somewhat battered thirty-nine. All day long he went from one conference to another, preparing the weekly film he was compelled to produce. He woke early every morning in spite of late nights, and in the cold chill of dawn he read.

"What do you read?" I inquired with interest. Perhaps he read poetry or Zen Buddhism.

He answered between clenched teeth. "I read screenplays only—hundreds pouring on me every day. . . . Always I am depressed afterward. So every night I am here, drinking."

The more he drank, the better he could speak English. It was never perfect, but it was expressive—and explosive. He did not cease also to speak Japanese. Indeed, he carried on an extraordinary bilingual monologue.

Suddenly the production manager struck his own head with clenched fists. He had an idea again, a glorious idea! "Drinking, I am a fountainhead for ideas," he declared, enraptured with himself.

His idea concerned my special friend's son-in-law, a young actor of promise. His wife was proficient in English and could be very useful to everybody. If we would place them in our cast . . .

We replied that of course we would like to see the two young people, but the picture must be considered before feelings. He was already on the telephone, however, and after an outburst in Japanese returned to us, all good cheer. "Now," he exclaimed, "we must be happy. Bar or geisha house?"

We asked him to decide for us. "Bar, of course," he declared. "Geishas are too old-fashioned. Top-class bar. I go there every night,"

We took cabs and rocked through crowded streets. The bar, as we entered, seemed to be a number of small, comfortable rooms crowded with businessmen and pretty girls. The production manager began relaxing immediately by loosening his belt and taking off his tie. I was introduced to a slender handsome woman of young middle age, whom the production manager declared was the best madam in Tokyo. She looked competent and modest, and upon hearing my name, she fell into a state of emotion, declaring that she had read all my books. I was touched but slightly embarrassed. She introduced her girls to me after we were seated on a circular bench against the bar itself; these girls sat by me, one by one, and through one of them who spoke English, I became somewhat acquainted with them. Most of them were married and had children. No, they did not enjoy bar work, they said, but their husbands had poor jobs, or no jobs, and this was easy work.

"Why such work?" I had inquired.

"At night the children are asleep and safe." "It is better than leaving them all day," and so forth.

Our talk was now interrupted by the production manager. "My best friend," he announced and presented a very small girl.

Her face was a cameo of sadness. I had already noticed her, sitting beside a fatuous businessman, serving him liquor. Once, with my accursed, noticing novelist's eye, I saw him put his arm around her too closely, and she shrank away with a look in her eyes that I will not describe. She sat beside me now, saying nothing, just looking at me with such deep quiet that I felt communication.

The night wore on. I rose to leave. Alone in the car I pondered upon this phenomenon of Japanese life, the night-life of men apart from their families. It is a force destructive to family life, a relic of feudalism. Old-fashioned Japanese women accepted the bars and the geisha houses as they accepted everything men did, but modern Japanese women longed for real companionship with the men they loved. Yet men continued to stay away from home. "I have learned," my Japanese secretary said one day with a cold calm, "to nag him no more. I have even learned how to greet him with a happy smile at two o'clock in the morning."

Yes, she could do it. The Japanese woman has always been stronger than the Japanese man, for, like the Chinese woman, she has been given no favors. She has never heard of chivalry or knights in golden armor. She was born a female—that is to say, an inferior person, a bearer of burdens, an obedient slave. In centuries of such existence, while she compelled herself to devotion and duty, she accumulated an inner strength that cannot be surpassed. She gave birth to man, tended him and cared for him, shielded and defended him without question. Why should she question when there was no one to answer? She was betrayed by another kind of woman, the woman who did not marry, the woman who was not bowed down with household cares and children, the woman taught and groomed to amuse men. She was betrayed by the geisha. All that a man could not find in his uneducated, houseworn wife, he sought and found in the geisha, whose only duty was to please him, to attract his eye, to entice him with music, to win his mind by her education. The best geisha is a brilliant and intelligent woman.

Her modern counterpart, the bar girl, is in every way her inferior. Any woman, it seems, can be a bar girl. If her face is pretty, she is lucky, but if not, she has other wares to sell. She is nearly always a prostitute. Geisha can be prostitutes but are not compelled to be. They may keep their hold on men in other ways, if they so desire.

I WENT TO my hotel full of such thoughts. How rare an experience of marriage mine had been. I am not an easy-to-marry woman, or so I imagine. I am divided to the bottom of my being, part of me being woman, the other part artist and having nothing to do with woman. As an artist I am capable of cruelty, for artists are ruthless and must be. My husband understood an artist. I doubt that he understood women or cared to understand them. He began life early, graduating from Harvard as an honors man when he was only twenty and marrying at once. He was attractive to women and knew it, with black hair and dark skin. He had a wonderful smile, beginning in his eyes—eyes wasted on a man, for they were pure violet with long black lashes. His manners were charming, deceptively so sometimes when he was talking with a woman. Yet he could make me happily furious sometimes. For example, he liked to say that I was unlike any other woman he had ever known because, he said, I had the brain of a man in the body of a woman. I flew out at him, invariably, at such a notion. Why should a woman, I demanded, be said to have the brain of a man merely because she had a good mind? Did nature give the supreme gift only to men?

"I apologize," he said, his eyes twinkling, but of course he never apologized for what he believed.

What was precious beyond diamonds to me was the fact, indisputable, that he enjoyed my mind. He liked profound conversation on abstruse subjects. He enjoyed repartee. And far beyond diamonds, he understood I had to be alone when I was writing. He never asked what I was writing or even what the book was about. When a novel was finished and typed and ready to be given to the publisher, I took it to his office next to mine and presented it formally, Chinese fashion, with both hands. He rose when I came in with the finished work and received it gravely.

"This is a big day," he always said.

He put aside everything else and sat down to the task he loved, he told me, above all others, the reading of a manuscript I had written. He edited carefully but sparely. I do not remember that he ever made a change involving anything more serious than a misplaced preposition or a time confusion. I have no sense of time. I pay no heed to what year it is, what month, or what day. He, on the other hand, had the disconcerting habit of perfect time recall. At any time during the day, he could look at his watch and ask, "Do you remember what we were doing ten [or twenty, etc.] years ago at this moment?"

I would say boldly that I did not remember.

Then he would tell me. "It was the first time I kissed you [or proposed to you—or you said you wouldn't have me—or I took you by surprise in Yokohama, etc.]."

The chase had indeed been a long one. We were past our first youth when we met, each resigned, we thought, to unsatisfactory marriages, and each well known in our own fields. I had firmly refused him in New York, Stockholm, London, Paris and Venice, and then I had sailed by way of India for home in Nanking, China.

In six months he cabled me to meet him in Shanghai, in order to hear "no" again and this time forever. I went alone after that to Peking for some months of research necessary for the completion of my translation of *All Men Are Brothers*. I had been there less than a week when he appeared unexpectedly in the midst of a violent dust storm out of the Gobi desert. We parted again eternally, and he went to Manchuria and I home again to Nanking to pack my bags for a summer visit to the United States to see that all was well there with my retarded child. I was in a resigned state of mind when I left, so far as he was concerned. I had, I thought, made the wise decision. I did not want turmoil in my life.

It was a fine July morning, I remember, and we were docking at the pier in Yokohama. I had planned not to go ashore, for I had been in the city many times. Instead I would work on my translation. I had no sooner settled myself to my lonely task when I heard the voice that was now the one I knew best in all the world. "I've turned up again—I shall keep on turning up, you know, everywhere in the world. You can't escape me."

There he was, lean and handsome, and smoking his old brier pipe. . . . In spite of that, I said no every day on board ship and again in Vancouver and all winter in New York. But spring in that magic city was my undoing, and we were married on the eleventh of June and lived happily ever after, together as man and wife, separately in our professional work.

He was a great editor. I have seen him take a muddle of a manuscript and make it a unified whole. He was a genius in coaxing books out of writers who did not know they were writers. A short manuscript came to him one day from an Englishwoman in Siam. He was then the editor and owner of *Asia* magazine. The article was entitled "The King's English," and the king was the king of Siam. He saw in the article more than a light little essay, and he invited the woman to write more about this king. At last, after his encouragement, a book-length manuscript arrived. He set to work to create a book out of the material he found there and to demand what was not there. The result eventually was the fascinating *Anna and the King of Siam*, the book that later became a fabulous Rodgers and Hammerstein musical, *The King and I.*

The list is distinguished: through his efforts works by Jawaharlal Nehru, the young Sukarno of Indonesia and Lin Yutang were brought to Americans.

And of myself, what shall I say? It was he who saw something in my first small book, a tentative effort rejected by all other publishers. He perceived the possibility that its author might one day write a better book. His staff was equally divided for and against the book, and it fell to him as the president of the company to cast the deciding vote. He voted for it, and on that narrow chance my life began.

Ah me, it does not do to dream too long. A new moon was swinging above the clouds when I walked outside to breathe the cooled night air. The new moon? I had been in Tokyo for three weeks. For two months I had been alone.

ONE DAY AT at the office hundreds of costumes were heaped on the floor, and several persons—men, boys and a girl or two—were pawing them over to a running accompaniment of Japanese. They were looking for garments demanded for various parts in the picture. The wardrobe man was of vague age but certainly not young. He stood something under five feet, and if he weighed ninety pounds, it would surprise me. His face was wrinkled, lively, full of fun and mischief—the face of an old faun. His hair surrounded a large bald spot and stood straight out from his skull, as though the old faun were undergoing electric shock. He was certainly full of some sort of electricity, for he was issuing orders without letup, as he modeled a fisherman's outfit made for a man four times his size. He was a good model, nevertheless. He gathered the trousers in at his waist, gave a twist to the belt, arranged the coat and became a fisherman. Everybody laughed and I sat down to watch.

He knew all the characters in *The Big Wave*, it appeared, and he modeled them all. When he modeled a man, he faced us. When he modeled a woman, he turned his back. I recognized each character, even the young girl, Setsu. How an old man could pose so that he suggested a gay young girl is something I cannot explain. I wished for the millionth time that I understood Japanese, for whatever the old faun was saying, the audience was convulsed. Every now and again he was dissatisfied and threw off a costume and pawed among the confusion of garments with all the fierce intensity of a monkey looking for fleas.

At this moment someone had an inspiration. "He's what we've been looking for—a wonderful attendant for the Old Gentleman. Does he speak English?"

The old faun smiled with all his teeth, none of them in good repair, and shook his head to the English.

The next day, modeling more costumes, he brightened as I entered the room. A stream of Japanese flowed from him. He would join the cast, but only if we promised not to cut his hair.

I regarded the circle of electrified black wire surrounding the bony, bald skull. "Tell him," I said, "that I would not think of cutting that hair."

"*Hai,*" the cheerful faun said with a smile that reached across the room.

We cut his lines to two essential words: "yes," and "no." These he says in the picture, impressively and with pride. He had, he said, waited his whole life to become an actor, but the nearest he had come had been to work with costumes. I shall never forget his beatific face when he knew he was to have the part. So far as he was concerned, he was a star. He gave us a great smile, and the faun became monkey again, pawing among the clothes, but now he was searching feverishly for his own costume.

That night for the first time since he left, I felt a release, slight though it was, from the dull oppression of a burden from which I could not escape. I laugh easily, but I had not laughed often in the past months. That afternoon I had laughed with all my heart and for an hour was healed. The fact marked a beginning.

THE ABALONE diving girls—I must speak of them, for they were a unique, tightly knit little group in our all-Japanese cast. Abalone is a delicacy in the Japanese cuisine. They cling with a powerful muscle to rocks far down where the sea is dark and the water icy cold. Japanese fishermen prudently refuse to dive for them and allot the task to young women, who are more able to endure the cold and the danger. Men row the boats to the abalone beds and wait patiently while the women plunge into the sea, clad only in shorts and belts into which they thrust the long, heavy iron knives necessary for hacking the abalone from the rocks.

To my amazement, their costume, so natural to them and so sensible, became a matter of controversy with our American producers. American audiences, it seemed, could not tolerate the sight of bare breasts.

"What can we do?" I inquired. "A woman is a woman, and she cannot properly be anything else."

"Bras," the American delegate said laconically. He relented slightly when he saw my amazement. "We'll take two shots of them, one with and one without."

That is what we did, and I was amused to see how embarrassed the women were when compelled to wear pink brassieres over their round brown breasts. They felt really naked, as Eve did in the garden, doubtless, when she was told to wear a fig leaf.

A PECULIAR satisfaction in translating my story from printed page to film was that the characters came alive in flesh and blood. I shall never forget the moment of pure angelic pleasure when, looking at a young woman, I recognized Setsu. The production manager told us she was a young star of his own company. More important to me was her lovely little face and large melting eyes of soft brown. She was under five feet. When she stood by our six-foot grown-up Toru in the film, it was exactly right as he looked down upon her, laughed and said, "I like you because you are so small and funny."

The president of another Japanese film company had been kind enough to lend to us one of his young stars to be our grown-up Toru. Our cast was complete at last. All the contracts were signed. Sessue Hayakawa, the Japanese star best known in the Western world, was playing the Old Gentleman. All the others were stars in Japan, except grown-up Haruko, a new actress chosen especially for the abalone diving girl who falls in love with Toru and fights for him against gentle Setsu.

When we were ready to leave Tokyo at last, Sessue Hayakawa invited us to a party at a geisha house and called for us in state in his own car. I had grown used by now to evenings spent in quiet inns with Japanese friends, secluded spots where low roofs spread over rooms open to gardens and small pools. The evening at the geisha house was not like the quiet evenings among congenial friends. We entered a huge room where the longest low table I had ever seen was already surrounded by guests, all of whom, our host assured us, were the highest of their class. Thus we were introduced to an aged prince, then to a minister of the present cabinet, then to a young giant seven feet tall and three feet wide who was the champion wrestler in Japan, and so on and on. Each male guest had several geisha surrounding him, and even I was given two to attend me, right and left. We were entertained by the traditional dancing and singing of trained geisha and two young girl magicians, among the best I have ever seen in any country. In contrast to the geisha, they were in Western dress, their arms bare to their shoulders. There was no nonsense therefore of hiding rabbits and fowl and pots of water up their sleeves. They simply did marvelous tricks, and I have no idea how.

The next day we obeyed Japanese custom by giving a party of our own for cast and crew before we set out on our great adventure. The big room we had rented from the hotel was crowded. All our actors were there, our cameraman, the makeup artist—the best in Japan, we were told—and many others.

Our child actors were in their best party clothes; Little Setsu, Little Toru and Little Yukio. Our entire cast, in fact, made me swell with pride. They were handsome, they suited their parts, and they were enthusiastic. Our coproducers were pleased, too, even the production manager. He made a speech in Japanese that was doubtless excellent, since there was loud applause. Hayakawa also spoke, the reporters took notes, cameras flashed again and again, and the party was on. There was plenty of food and drink and everybody soon knew everybody.

It was a lovely party. And we were slow to part. May all tomorrows shine as brightly as the one ahead shone, I told myself.

I did not wander forth alone that night but opened the window and sent my secret message into space, with love. Wherever he is, he heard, or so I dreamed, for a new comfort descended upon my heart and brought to me my first intimation of eventual peace. It was his blessing.

WE ARRIVED AT the delightful town of Obama on the island of Kyushu after a seven-hour journey by plane, train and car. It was midnight when we reached our hotel, and our beds, made Japanese fashion on the tatami on the floor, provided the exact combination of hard and soft for the most restful sleep. It was a real Japanese hotel—food, plumbing and all, a big hotel, and comfortable to the point of some luxury.

I woke early, eager to see the locations chosen for the filming of the picture. The wide windows of the small veranda upon which my room opened faced a curved bay, the bay surrounded by green mountains. Beneath my windows was a large pool of steaming hot water, for Obama is a famous spa, with natural hot springs.

As soon as I stirred, the paper-covered shoji slid back and a pleasant little Japanese maid in a gay *yukata*, or cotton kimono, came in, knelt and bowed, and chattered in Japanese while she put away the bed. In a few minutes my bedroom was a sitting room, a low polished table in the center, cushions to sit upon, a backrest to lean against. The toko-noma alcove held a landscape scroll and a graceful vase of fresh flowers. I went to my private bathroom and had a Japanese bath. The water in the little pool was natural hot water and very refresh-ing. Breakfast was an egg, some fruit, salt fish and rice. The min-eral bath had made me

hungry. After breakfast we set forth in a car for the village of Kitsu, chosen to represent the village where our boy Toru lived.

In Japan most roads are narrow. Not a few are only wide enough for one vehicle. When two cars meet face to face on such a road, both stop. The drivers take stock of each other. Sooner or later one of them makes up his mind that he is the weaker, and prudently he backs up until he finds a corner where he can wait and let the other pass. A bus or a truck driver does not take stock. He simply waits for the car to get out of the way, with an air of doing a favor. There seems always to be at least one cliff on the side of every road in Japan, very often without guardrails. Where nearly every road runs at the top of a cliff above the sea, there is no use in dreaming about guardrails. People must learn to take care of themselves. The result is that remarkably few accidents occur, at least in proportion to the hazards!

We drove for an hour through fantastically beautiful country and all my memories came alive. How well I remembered these sharply pointed mountains, sudden mists of rain, the indented shores and waterworn rocks, these villages sheltering in coves, the farmhouses with steep roofs thatched three feet deep, and the terraced fields, climbing step by step nearly to the top of mountains! Nothing was changed.

I cannot deny that my heart beat faster as we approached the village of Kitsu. Two hundred years ago Kitsu was washed away by a tidal wave. It was easy to see how it happened, for this small fishing village lies like a saddle between two mountains. I must have been thinking of Kitsu when I wrote *The Big Wave*, so perfectly did it fit the story. After the tidal wave the people rebuilt again in the same place, these stubborn, brave Japanese people. Sooner or later their village would again be caught by a monstrous wave. It is just as vulnerable today as it was two centuries ago, the houses set in just the same way, on the beach but with no windows to the sea.

I recognized it, every step, as we climbed down the narrow winding path from the road. Here were the narrow streets not three feet across, scarcely wide enough for two human beings. Down the worn stone steps we went to the sea, followed by twenty-nine children, exactly. When we stopped at Toru's house, it was, too, just as I had seen it in my book, and even Grandfather was there, with a cheerful ancient face, peering at us over the wall. He was past his fishing days and his sons and grandsons now carried on. His wife was dead, he told us, and his daughter-in-law and granddaughter tended the house and dried the fish and carried the water up from the well on the beach.

We sauntered about the village with deep content because it was so exactly right—the fishing nets drying on the shore, the houses nestled between the terraced hills, an old small cemetery. There was even a flight of stone steps that we could use as the entrance to the Old Gentleman's house on the mountain above.

The hours had passed and it was time for luncheon. We ate at a restaurant famous for eel. There we climbed two flights of stairs to a big airy room where we ate broiled eel on rice and drank green tea and congratulated ourselves on our location for the film.

I feared to see our next location, I confessed. It was to be the mansion of the Old Gentleman, a scholar and a landlord. Could we find a family living in such a house who would be willing to lend it to us? There must be space and beauty and elegance, set in lovely gardens. I toyed with various make-shifts while we drove along a country road.

The impossible became the possible, however, as it does so often in Japan. The moment I saw the house from the road I knew it was the Old Gentleman's house, no matter who lived in it. I entered the gate and found myself in a lovely garden. There were no flowers, for Japanese gardens are seldom flower gardens. A path made of wide, irregularly shaped stones led to the main entrance, and on both sides evergreens, low shrubbery, ferns and orchids not in bloom made a landscape. At the door a lady wearing a handsome dark kimono bowed low. We bowed in return, and I asked if I might see the rest of the garden. There was a pool, not large, but so designed that it presented the aspects of a lake. There was a bridge leading into a narrow path and a pavilion set among the trees. I saw everything from the point of view of the Old Gentleman. It was exactly the sort of garden he would have.

The handsome lady welcomed us into the house and led us from one spacious room to another. The Old Gentleman was a man of wealth and taste. These were his chosen pieces of furniture and art objects.

After I had made my speech of appreciation, the lady said that she considered it an honor to have their house used in my picture. Then she served tea in bowls so small that I knew it was precious before I tasted it. It was the rare delicious tea made from the first tender leaves of the tea plant in spring. I am sure my hostess did not serve it often, even to Japanese guests. That she did so for us meant that she gave a gift. I received it as such.

And as we talked, I in English, she in Japanese, through an interpreter, she asked if she could record the conversation for her son, who was studying English. I said of course, and I was amused to see a very modern tape recorder concealed until now behind a couch.

We said good-by at last, with many bows, promising to return soon—promising also to be careful and break nothing in the house and spoil nothing in the garden. The lady was very gracious and begged me to leave the hotel and live with her, but I said I must stay with the company, thanking her all the same.

Now there remained the farmhouse and the empty beach to be seen. The beach could wait, for the day was darkening, but the farmhouse we must see today. It stood among terraces, and was itself built on a wide terrace. The road in front of it was twenty feet above the rice paddy below. A wall of ancient brick ran across the front, but the wide wooden gate stood open.

Now I walked into the world of my story. Yes, this was the house, simple but spacious, wooden walls, rooms divided by shoji, a thatched roof so old that grass and flowers grew on it. Chickens, two goats, a little vegetable garden, some ornamental shrubbery, a few decorative rocks, a fine old-fashioned kitchen, a narrow veranda, a small pool for washing rice and vegetables— it was exactly right. And, best of all, the farm family was friendly and eager to be helpful. The farmer himself was a cheerful widower with a married daughter looking after him. When were we coming? Tomorrow? Good—good—the house was ours. Yes, they had electricity and a pump in the kitchen— a modern farm, the old man said proudly. And he would be

glad to have Americans see how he managed everything. Tea, please, before we left! It was night before he would let us go, and work was to begin at seven o'clock the next day. Every hour of light is precious when a film is made on location. The chickens, I noticed as we left, were of the most articulate variety. Only the darkness silenced them.

By the time we reached our hotel that night, rain was falling. Rain is always the hazard of filming on location, especially in the climate of southern Japan, where the sea and mountains are close neighbors. If the wind blows from the sea, the sky will clear; if from the land, it will rain. This I remembered from days long past, and while I lay in my Japanese bed listening to the rain and waiting for sleep, I pondered on the strange divisions of my life.

How incredible, above all, that for the whole first half of my life, I did not know he existed! When I was here in Japan before, where was he? And now when I am here again, where is he?

Did he know I was here in Japan? Was he still hovering about the house at home, the essence of himself, and were I there, would I perceive his presence? Lying there on my Japanese bed, the sound of the rising sea mingling with the rain on the tiled roof, I fought off the mighty yearning to go in search of him, wherever he was. For surely he was looking for me, too. We were ill at ease, always, when apart. But what are the pathways?

I thought of what my fourteen-year-old daughter told me the day after the funeral. She had wanted his room after it was empty because it was next to mine. She slept there quite peacefully the first night.

The next morning she said entirely naturally at breakfast, "Daddy came in last night. He looked wonderful—all well again and so cheerful. He just came back to see that everything was all right."

I restrained incredulity. "Did he speak to you?"

"No, just smiled."

"And what was he wearing?" I asked.

"I think it was his red velvet smoking jacket," she said.

But the red smoking jacket, though his favorite, had been laid away five years ago.

There in the darkness of the night by the Japanese sea, I besought him to let me know by some true sign that he lived somewhere. He made no sign. Yet silence is not finality. It may be only definition. He is there, I am here. We do not have the same wavelength yet. Is that faith? I dare not call it so. But I believe that all things are possible until they are proved impossible, and even the impossible may only be so as of now.

In this way my life continued to be lived on two separate levels, one by day, the other by night; one upon Earth, the other in search of a habitation that is in no way tangible.

RAIN CONTINUED to pour down for three days without letting up. The mountains were hidden in rain and the sea roared against the rocks. We looked at one another in alarm. What if this went on and on?

We decided to work on the script, planning each day's schedule, scene by scene and shot by shot. We sat around a long low table, together with our cameraman and our sound man and the assistant to the director. We sat on the floor, of course, and the cameraman was so unwise as to choose one end of the low table. I say unwise because he has long legs, very long, and he could not stretch his legs out when he was tired of sitting on them, because I had already grown tired and my legs were already stretched out, crosswise, under the table. I learned that one shoots all the scenes needed for each location at one time, regardless of where these belong in the time sequence of the narrative. Thus for the first four days we would stay at the farmhouse, shooting everything that had to do with its family of four—Father, Mother, Yukio and Setsu. This seemed confusing to me, but I could see its logic.

Now let me speak of the cameraman. First I must say that he was charming, kind, temperamental and, in his field, an artist.

He spoke little English, but he understood much more than we thought he did. He was obviously devoted to his work, and wanted us to know that he had a special devotion to *The Big Wave*. He was famous and could easily have earned as much on an easier job. But I was enchanted with him for other reasons. He was the most spectacular-looking human being that I had ever seen, very tall and very narrow in the feet, legs, body, arms, hands, neck and especially the face. He had a long, low-slung jaw. There was so much in that long face of his that I looked at him again and again. It was a sad face, I thought, and then again I thought it was not, so I kept looking at it.

Our Japanese assistant was such a contrast, a very modern young woman in shirt and slacks. As the production manager had told us, she spoke foreign languages and had studied ballet in Europe and was newly married to our leading young actor, the grown-up Toru. His other motion picture commitments prevented his being with us until later, and so this was their first separation. She was teased a good deal by other members of the cast, and they forced her to write hourly postcards to her bridegroom, addressing them for her, and so on. She lent herself good-humoredly to their fun, a calm young woman, intelligent and efficient and, incidentally but importantly, very much in love.

Alas, on the very day when it stopped raining and we had spent twelve hours filming our first scenes at the farmhouse, our cameraman fell into a rice paddy. This was not as mild an event as it sounds. The rice paddy was at the foot of a stone wall, and he fell not into soft mud and high rice, but upon rocks. His frame could best be defined at any time as a collection of very long, thin bones connected loosely by withered brown skin, and lying on a bench in the hall of the hospital he looked eight feet long.

He refused to share our alarm and was carried into the X-ray room against his will. In half an hour the doctor reported that there were no broken bones, only bruises. The cameraman himself came out, looking as gay as possible with his sort of face. He had permitted the doctor to put his right arm into a sling, but only until he got out of the hospital, for he insisted upon returning to the job. We rode back to the hotel with him and gave him numerous orders, through our interpreter, that he was to have an attendant who would carry his chair everywhere, together with a fan, an umbrella, a cool drink and fruit.

HERE I MUST consult my notes, scratched on the pages of my script, and written everywhere and anywhere in the farmhouse.

The first note says, "Feather—" Feather?

Ah yes, that is the scene where Toru lay in the long stupor after the tidal wave had struck, and mischievous little Setsu stole into the room and tickled him with a feather to wake him up. It was a pretty scene, interrupted by Mother, who came in with eggs in a small basket, followed by our latest addition to the cast, a small, very intelligent dog. Some geese and ducks that wandered about the farmyard were to be the very last addition.

While this scene was taken, I saw Father in another corner rehearsing his big scene with Yukio. Father is a good farmer, his face an honest brown. Our makeup man was dabbing at Father's face and delicately wiping away the sweat of concentration. Mother's personal attendant was doing the same to her in another corner. The attendant provided us with laughter. She was so very efficient, rushing in at the last moment before the camera began to call them, in order to set straight a hair on Mother's head and to add a touch of makeup to the corner of her eye.

"When work is over," my notes tell me, "it is a sight to see Mother in her elegant gray silk kimono wending her dignified way along the dirt road at the top of the wall above the paddy field. She is an actress of some distinction in Japan, Father acted in *The Teahouse of the August Moon*, and Toru and Yukio are both child stars. I am proud of our *Big Wave* family."

That was the day, I remember, when the postman brought me a letter from a Japanese friend in Tokyo, a fellow writer, who had taken the trouble to go to the public library and collect some data on tidal waves. He wrote me that before a tidal wave rolls in there is a dreadful hollow booming from the sea. The Japanese call it the "ocean gun." And one sign of an approaching wave is that the wells go dry, or rise, and the water is muddy. And the fish, especially the catfish, swim toward land.

While I read the fascinating pages I heard the assistant director call the new scene. *"Yoi!"* "Starto!" "Backo!" The actors took their places and the cameraman was alert. Then came the director's final command. "Action!"

"Schis-kani" was said again and again during the scenes. I did not know what it meant until an electrician echoed it by roaring in semi-English. "Silento!" The result was profound silence.

I was amazed by how effects were achieved with strangely simple means. The microphone was something tied up in a cotton bag and suspended at the end of a bamboo pole. The end of the pole was always sticking into someone, as my own ribs could testify, but it worked well enough. When I listened to the sound track played back, I was surprised to hear how clear it was. The camera was wrapped up as tenderly as a baby in a snowstorm. I could not think why, for the weather was steaming hot, and surely the camera was not cold. Upon inquiry I learned that the blankets were to silence the noise of

the camera itself so that the microphone would not pick it up.

We drove every morning from Obama to our location for the day, passing hundreds of gaily dressed schoolchildren. The children looked healthy and happy all day long. Once we turned an unexpected corner and came upon a robust and irate mother spanking her son for some wrongdoing. She finished the job, in spite of our appearance, the boy howling as loudly as possible, then she dusted her hands, smiled at us cheerfully while the boy retired to a corner of the wall to finish off his sobs, and went back to her housework.

Should one spank children? It was a question never settled in our family. He said he believed in spanking children at certain ages because they were not open to reason and functioned on instinct and emotion. I said I hated all physical punishment and believed it did no good. The difference between us was that when a child provoked me to anger, which in fairness to myself I must say was not often, I could and did find myself administering a swift and well-placed spanking. He, in spite of his belief in the principle, never had the heart to spank any child—except on one occasion.

"The boys should be spanked," he told me one day, his face very grave.

I do not remember what they had done, but they had got into some devilishness together. They stood before us one fine summer's day, the three of them so near of an age, all handsome and healthy and unrepentant.

"I can't do it," I said.

"Then I will have to," he said firmly.

To our astonishment, mine and the boys', he spanked each of them in turn. They still roar with laughter, grown men that they are now, when they talk of it together. They too do not recall what naughtiness they committed, but him they remember with love and amusement.

"We knew we ought to cry," the second son says, he with the gay sense of humor. "Just for his sake we should have cried, so that he'd have the satisfaction of knowing he was doing a good job, but it was so funny—we had to laugh."

I remember some sort of muffled noise and a pretense of rubbing their eyes with their knuckles and I was not fooled for one second. I knew they were laughing, bless them, and trying not to, because they did not want to hurt his feelings.

I suspected the Japanese boy of somewhat the same pretense. She was not hitting him very hard, and he was making a noise out of all proportion. Let my mother enjoy herself, he was thinking, let her believe she is doing me good.

That evening, at my solitary dinner—it was a great scarlet crab—I found myself laughing aloud as I remembered. It was the first time I had laughed spontaneously alone since we used to laugh together, and it was another milestone toward my new life.

THIS WAS the pattern of our day: By seven o'clock we all gathered at the front door of the hotel to exchange our slippers for our shoes. Then we filled several cars, after bowing to the assembled company of maids. The streets were clean, as everything is in Japan, the cobblestones gleaming. The mountains pressing closely upon the sea were brightly green and the sea sparkled blue under the morning sun, if the day was fair. There are times when I think Japan is the most beautiful country in the world. Yet it is the enchantment of Asia that every one of its countries is beautiful in its own way.

At the farmhouse, we found everything ready for us each morning. The family had already departed for the day. From time to time some of them would come and watch us filming, but courtesy forbade comment, whatever they thought. The surrounding villagers, however, frankly came to stare and they came in relays.

The first crowd, the early one, always consisted of children stopping on their way to school. They were mannerly and silent, their eyes unblinking. Precisely at a quarter past eight they left us in a body to begin school at half past. Next came mothers, who by this time had put their houses in order. They arrived with babies strapped to their backs and were not quite so mannerly. They could not refrain from whispered exclamations and laughter smothered behind their hands. They left, also promptly, at half past eleven in order to see that their working husbands were fed. About three o'clock grandparents and village elders arrived, after food and naps, to spend the remainder of the afternoon with us. They were joined at five by the working fathers, whose day was done. These stayed with us faithfully until we left about seven.

We began filming as soon as the cameras were set up, moving from room to room as the story required. The makeup man and his assistant kept a zealous watch on the actors, for fear that the heat would cause the cream and rouge to run in rivulets down their faces and spot their costumes—a true artist and a charming man, our makeup man, with his secret formulas and brushes made by his own hands.

Sound effects, throughout the day, were our bane. The ox lowed at the wrong time, the goat baa-ed too often, though merely to be friendly. As for the chickens, we gave up on them. Nothing could restrain them, and consequently they cackle happily throughout the farmhouse scenes whenever the film is shown.

The day's work went on until luncheon arrived from the hotel and we broke for an hour. The heat was frightening and we sat on stones and stumps under the big persimmon tree in the front yard. Each lunch was self-contained in a handsome lacquered box, the top layer holding fish and bits of browned meat, vegetable and pickle, and the bottom layer steamed white rice. Great pots of tea, with handles wrapped in thin strips of bamboo, completed our more than adequate meal. We ate with Japanese chopsticks, bamboo, sealed in waxed paper and thrown away after use, surely the most sanitary eating utensils in the world.

In twenty minutes the meal was over and for the rest of the noon hour the farmhouse was quiet. The crew and actors were stretched out on the tatami, like sardines, asleep. I found a quiet ledge behind a little table, close by the back room, and lay looking out at the mountains lifted against the sky. White clouds floated against the blue and cast their floating shadows. It seemed a dream that I was here, that I was seeing my little book come to life.

THAT HEAT! How restless the wild creatures were! Across the human voices the loud and ardent screech of a cicada shocked our sound man again and again. For me, it was a cry that summoned nostalgic memories of the hot summers of my childhood on the banks of the Yangtze River. The sound man, however, was furious with the cicada in the farmhouse yard. He shouted and half a dozen of the crew leaped at the big persimmon tree and knocked its branches with bamboo poles. For five minutes the lusty insect was quiet, and then we heard its screech begin to saw the air. This time the men climbed up into the persimmon tree and shook it until leaves began to fall and the green fruit trembled. For at least half an hour the cicada was prudent, and then it began all over again its endless song.

One day we had a bit of luck. As our little Setsu came flying out of the farmhouse gate, the oldest woman in the world chanced to come by, bent under a load of sticks. She had a beautiful old face, wrinkled and brown, but her eyes were as young as life itself. We invited her to be in our picture. The woman accepted graciously and posed, straightening herself for the occasion and clinging to her tall staff while her gay old face assumed nobility. Our assistant makeup man in mistaken zeal rushed to arrange the folds of her kimono, which had fallen open to show a glimpse of ancient breasts, but we shouted at him to put it as it was before, and so we have her picture. She is walking along the road, bent under her load while the child Setsu runs past. We wanted to pay her but were assured that it would hurt her feelings. The most that could be done with dignity was to give her some packages of cigarettes, which we did, and she went her way.

Rain and sun alternated through the days. Our actors worked well and became a working group. We lived in the story. I remember one day that ended with the bringing home of Toru after the tidal wave, when the young lad waked from his stupor and inquired where his father was and where his mother. A sudden comprehending emotion swept the actors. They knew, they understood all too well. Tears fell from the actress mother's eyes, and I felt a catch in my own throat, for suddenly they had portrayed a moment of utter reality.

The last scene of that burning day was outside in the barnyard. It was nearly twilight, the crowd was now several hundred people of all ages, quiet and respectful. The set was complete with cart, ox, produce and farm family. This time our family included Setsu's pet duck and her dog. The duck was huge, the great-grandfather of all living ducks, and when Setsu struggled to hold him under her arms, I was reminded of the flamingo and the duchess in *Alice in Wonderland*. The dog, a gay fox terrier type, would not gambol about harmlessly as it was supposed to do, but insisted upon chasing chickens madly, thereby upsetting a mother hen with a large family of chicks, not to mention an unknown number of white pullets. The duck was carried offstage by Setsu and the dog was controlled and chastened, and the scene proceeded.

At this moment I heard human cackles behind me as Father unloaded the cart. Two dirt farmers in the crowd were overcome with amusement at Father's unrealistic handling of the pole and two baskets. They obviously did not believe in him as a farmer.

The scene was over at last when suddenly I heard loud barks, as though from an immense and aged dog. I could not imagine what it was. There was no dog indigenous to the farm. I advanced to the stable to investigate and I smelled a pig. It could not be a pig because it barked like dog. But it was a pig, an enormous tough-looking old pig, male gender. I inquired through an interpreter why the pig barked like a dog when he was not a dog. The answer was simple: "We do not know why the pig barks like a dog." The pig continued to bark, the darkness fell. We could not finish the next scene because the light on the mountain had faded. We gathered ourselves and left. Tomorrow was a Sunday, although we had been warned that we were not to expect more Sundays off. From now on it was seven days a week, twelve hours a day.

THE SCHEDULE called for outdoor work, a picnic scene in a gray old cemetery with little Setsu and then a harvest scene, but it was raining again. The sky looked as though it would continue to empty itself for forty days. We decided to go to the farmhouse and shoot a rain scene, appropriately, and a kitchen interior. The assistant director was to go to Kitsu, our fishing village, and get ready for the scene when the boats put out in the rain.

The rain continued in a deluge. The farmyard became a lake of mud and the thatched eaves dripped dismally. Inside the farmhouse the crew worked without enthusiasm. The cameraman put off beginning work. The director grew impatient. Again and again the first scene was set, and again and again the camera made some monstrous mistake. It was twelve o'clock by the time we were ready to shoot the rain scene, and then the sun came out, weakly but enough to make it necessary to fake rain. So on a rainy day the men climbed on the farmhouse roof and rigged up the best rainmaking machine in the world, namely, a hollow bamboo pierced with holes, with a rubber hose attached to one end. A beautiful flow of fake rain dripped over the eaves. Finally we got a take, and lunch hour arrived. The day was so dismal it was not even a good lunch.

The kitchen scene and the rainy beach scene were among our best. The kitchen scene was the earthquake. Our farm mother, in a daze, hurried about, trying to save her dishes. She was so distraught that she forgot to put down a basket of eggs and they broke and increased the confusion. There is, in fact, nothing more confusing than a basket of broken eggs, especially when a woman forgets to put them down and sees in addition that the oil lamp is burning and may set the house on fire. In her reality of acting she cut her foot twice on broken glass and the trained nurse, whom we were required to have with us at all times, at last had a chance to save someone's life. She came forward with an air of importance and put some adhesive tape on Mother's foot.

The scene finished, the sun withdrew and again rain fell in a deluge. The farmhouse actors were dismissed for the day and the fisherman's family summoned for the beach scenes. It became apparent now that the American director had every intention of dismissing me, too, on the grounds of the storm, rain, lashing waves and so forth. When I declined to be dismissed, he put forth vague suggestions that I might break a leg or something on the steep and narrow path down to Kitsu, and he had had enough of falls. I refused this ridiculous reasoning, for in the mountains of Vermont I walk prodigiously everywhere and climb like a goat. So I went to Kitsu.

I shall never cease to be grateful that I did, for the experience gave me—well, here it is:

I walked down the narrow winding cliff path without mishap and descended to the beach. It was raining gloriously, a rough downpour, which I love. I was protected thoroughly by my raincoat and hat, and also by various umbrellas held over my head by kind villagers. With my back to the high wall in front of Toru's house, I gazed out at the gray sea and gray sky. Toru's father was a fisherman, and at the signal our actor began to blow the great conch shell for the boats.

"Cut!" the director yelled.

All the village was out under huge umbrellas to watch what was going on and some unwary boy had dashed across the scene to a better place on the other side. The village headman, who was our paid ally, had forbidden noise or movement, and at this he went into a fine paroxysm of fury. I do not understand Japanese, but I could see that he was calling his fellow villagers a lot of damned blockheads. Did they want to show the world what idiots they were, not knowing that when you cross a camera you ruin the picture being made by Americans here in the village of Kitsu for the first time in history? They all grinned sheepishly and fell back six inches or so. Suddenly another boy who had not been listening dashed between the frightfully bowed legs of the headman himself, not remembering to fold his umbrella first. The results were disastrous; the umbrella was ruined.

I remember that headman fondly. He had a round, shaven head, a rugged, beaming face, legs as crooked as a crab's, an iron will, and a heart fit for a king. He was a dictator, of course, and he ruled his people absolutely. Every night he told them what they could do the next day and what they must not do. His enthusiasm for the picture was touching, for he was convinced that the story was about him. Like Toru, his entire family had been swept away by a tidal wave when he was only a little boy.

Standing there, my back against the wet sea wall, I watched the cameraman get a lovely shot of fishermen carrying their nets down to the sea and putting off in their fishing boats through the waves and rain. The camera then raced to the big breakwater, which made an ideal platform from which to film the boats moving out into the open sea. The villagers rushed after the camera and I was swallowed among the crowd, all but pushed off the breakwater into the sea. I was fortunately saved by a strong villager who told me that he had seen me on Tokyo television, and then asked if he might hold his umbrella over my head and why wasn't someone looking after me? I said that no one ever looked after me when pictures were being made, and thanks, I didn't need the umbrella because I had a rain hat, and so I escaped him to go and sit upon a stone pier.

Sitting there in the rain, that slanting rain that Hokusai loved so well to portray in his prints, surrounded by the green and terraced hills and the higher mountains swathed in clouds, I watched for the boats to return and saw them as they rounded the end of the breakwater. How beautiful they were, how superb in shape and speed and grace! Three men sat in each boat, all rowing, not the choppy rowing of Western boats, but smooth . . . as a fish swims. These rowers never lifted their oars from the water. I studied the rhythm of those oars. It was in contrapuntal thirds, no oar moving at exactly the same instant as the other, and yet all movement flowing. Suddenly I recognized the rhythm—it was that of the fins of a fish. The boats moved through the sea as a fish moves by its fins. I felt the deep satisfaction of reaching the right conclusion. I was slow not to know it until this late date in my life, although I had been watching such boats since I was a child spending my summers in Japan.

The boats put out to sea again in a long row. They turned to the left as the bay turns until they were hidden by a rocky point, upon which stood by accident the figure of a man, solitary and unknown, looking toward the horizon. What beauty! It is enough for this day. I thank God, and may I see beauty all my life as clearly as this!

In the evening I sat by my window, I remember, dressed in a cool *yukata*. I had that day been steeped in beauty, and now it was unbearable because I could not tell him about it. Perhaps he knew, but if he could not communicate his awareness to me, how was I to be comforted? I had, I thought, been doing so well and suddenly I knew I had not. Beauty had undone me, had made me weak with longing. Strangers must again be my refuge. I took off the *yukata*, slipped into my own dress and went out to wander the streets again, alone.

THE DAY WE changed location to the mansion that was to be the Old Gentleman's house was one of the perfect days. The heavy heat of the land wind was changed suddenly by a west wind from the sea. The air was crisp and clean. The mountains were free of mists, the sun was shining, the world was new. We drove along the cliffs to the Old Gentleman's house. Far below us, fishing boats were drawing in the nets, a circle of white dots pulling closer and closer.

The tiled roofs of the mansion were shining with dew under the morning sun. The house was surrounded by a wall, and the entrance gate was imposing, two great wooden doors fastened with iron hasps and hinges, and to the right a small wicket gate barely wide enough to admit one person. The master of the house was at home today, a sturdy man in a dark kimono, who greeted us kindly and warmly. I wondered if the family knew what it was in for. Our amazingly efficient crew had simply moved in, carpenters and electricians and whatnot, and in a moment what had been a peaceful, old-fashioned, elegant home had become a sort of factory, in spite of the care the men took to do no damage. Sheets of matting were laid over the fine tatami, and under the clasps that fixed the klieg lights to the ceilings the crew put a protective layer of soft paper.

The ceilings of the house were beautiful, a copper-colored wood with a satin-soft finish. But everything was beautiful. Between the rooms and along the verandas fine bamboo curtains bound with satin provided decoration as well as a screen. In each room the tokonoma alcove had its special scroll and flower arrangement. The table and utensils for the tea ceremony stood in a special room, and panels in the wall opened to reveal a Buddhist shrine, shining in gold leaf. The gardens outside were not large, but each of them was well landscaped, and the big flat stones of the walks were arranged with skill and artistry. Our men were busily putting seaweed moss along the edges and in the cracks of the front walk.

Our Old Gentleman, Sessue Hayakawa, had dined with us the night before and, in Western dress, had looked like a young man of fifty. He told us he practiced yoga and expected to live to be a hundred. Whether yoga has anything to do with it I do not know, but he told us that everyone in his family does live to be over a hundred—they feel cheated if they die before they complete a century.

Now Sessue also looked stunningly handsome in the garb of an old-fashioned conservative Japanese gentleman. We examined his makeup, and pointed out to the makeup man that a hair was out of place in his beard and that the edge of his mustache had come slightly unglued. A secretary-maid fanned him all the while, lighted his cigar, gave him tea, and generally consoled him. She was young and efficient and took care of him as though he were a baby.

We were without our two boys that day, I remember—Yukio and Toru. They had gone to Nagasaki the day before, had drunk Japanese beer and eaten Chinese food, and had been ill during the night. Our star complained that he could not act without them, and for a moment the day looked bleak. Then he relented and said that if he had a young girl from the cast to inspire him, he could act. So we lent him our little Setsu until the boys arrived, and she sat at the foot of the camera and looked appealing and pretty and he proceeded with relish and gusto.

I remember that entire day as pure joy. We were all in a state of euphoria, I think, sharing the pleasure of the beautiful surroundings and the smooth grace with which the work went on. It was a joy to observe Hayakawa at work. It was like watching a great artist paint a portrait. Yes, I see the spacious Japanese room, the shoji open to the lovely garden. The Old Gentleman in his white silken robes, scholar and aristocrat, poet and prophet, is sitting upon a cushion before a low table. He is writing a poem on a wide sheet of paper. Before him kneel the two children. He reads the poem aloud and asks them what it means. They do not know, and he explains slowly and with grave dignity.

The dialogue is in English and his English is not perfect, but he is able to convey the meaning and the spirit of his own soul. The children respond to the illusion of reality. I go smiling all day after that. The evening approaches and I am filled with content and expectation. The high point in the story now has arrived, the hour when the Old Gentleman knows that the tidal wave is near. He orders the big bell to be rung and the torches outside the gate to be lit, the final warning to the people to come up the mountain to his house so that they may be saved. He fears—he all but knows—that they will not heed his warning, but it may be that a few will come.

It is dark when we assemble for this scene. A great crowd has gathered from the villages and countryside to watch the filming. The company manager, a burly fellow with a trumpeting voice, comes out and adjures the crowd to make no noise. It is the big scene, he tells them. There must not be a cough or a cry. The crowd shouts back promises and continues to wait. Endless time passes somehow while the last touches are made. The makeup man is frantic—the Old Gentleman has to wear a high ancient hat, his beard must be fast so the wind cannot blow away a hair. The servant—the old faun—must be made up with care.

I sit in quiet excitement. The assistant shouts his "Get ready—get set—" and the director says, "Action!"

We begin. I can scarcely breathe. I remember when I wrote the scene that I was exhausted when it was finished. Will the Old Gentleman be able to play it with the power and majesty that were revealed to me?

The crowd stands silent and absorbed. The crew is busy with lights and camera. Suddenly the strong glare falls upon the old servant coming out to light the torches. The leaping flames flare in the darkness to reveal the Old Gentleman, that proud old man, standing at the top of the stone steps, gazing out to sea. He is desperate, a prophet unheeded, yet yearning.

He sees all too well what will happen to his people, his ignorant, stubborn and beloved people. Yes, yes—he is the character I created. I see him clear and whole, perfect in conception and detail, and am surprised to feel tears running down my face—I who never weep!

Such realization comes seldom to an artist—a few times perhaps in a lifetime of creation. I am overcome with the need to share the moment with someone—someone! Hundreds of people are crowding around me, kind people but at this moment strangers. Among them there is no one. I turn and walk through the darkness to the waiting car and am driven away into the night.

In that moment I realized what before I had only known. He was dead. There was to be no communication.

The hotel room became intolerable again. The moon was full—somehow a month had passed—and by its light I left the town and walked out into the country. Silence, silence everywhere and only silence. I walked beside the sea, so calm that there were no waves, only the long swell of the deep tides. I remember how beautiful the landscape was by night, the mountains rising above silver mists in the valleys. I saw everything and felt nothing. It was as though I were floating and far away, in a strange country in which I had no life. I might have been dead myself, so profound was the silence within.

I turned inland then and was walking along a narrow path between rice fields. Suddenly a wind rose, and I stopped to feel the freshness on my face. At that same moment I heard a child cry, a baby. I looked about me. Yes, a farmhouse across the field was bright with lights. Was the child ill? I have heard so many babies cry that I know their language. No, this was not agony—surprise, perhaps, fear, even anger. It was the cry of a newborn child.

I sank down on the grassy bank, listening. The crying stopped, and I heard voices and laughter. The child was a boy, then! The child was another life. I lay back on the grass as though upon a bed and for a long time gazed up into the sky. A desperate weariness was creeping into my bones, the weariness of acceptance, the acceptance of the unchangeable. I must never again expect to share the great moments of my life, those moments of beauty, of excitement and exhilaration; above all, moments of achievement. In such moments he and I had turned to each other as instinctively as we breathed. That was no more to be . . .

The night was over. In the east beneath the horizon the sun was shining. It was time to go back to my room, time to prepare for the day's work.

THE FARMHOUSE location had been delightful, and I had made friends with all the family there, even with the cock and his hens and the goat. Only with the barking pig did I maintain a certain distance, feeling a mutual lack of interest, a result, doubtless, of our having nothing in common.

With the Old Gentleman's household I had much in common. I enjoyed to the full their cultivated minds, their delicate courtesy, their friendliness at once frank and restrained. Yet the end must come there, too. The Old Gentleman had performed his part with dignity and grace. His servant had led young Yukio, the farm boy, and Toru, the fisherman's son, into the stately house and had led them to the gate again after Toru had made his fateful choice to leave. The old faun had his great moment at that gate, for here it was that he had his momentous dialogue, his yes and his no.

We said our farewells, bowed and gave thanks, and I signed hundreds, I am sure, of the big autograph cards that are used for this purpose in Japan. Regretfully we gathered ourselves together and were conveyed by truck and car to our next location, the village of Kitsu. Our vehicles dislodged us on the top of a cliff and from there the approach was on foot and by a narrow path clinging to the rocky hillside. We walked down and down, until we came to the village itself, a cluster of stone cottages separated by narrow cobbled streets. I knew as I walked those streets that already I loved Kitsu the best of all our locations. A glorious bright day it was, but alas, this time the script called for rain. Therefore again we must make rain. We made rain all day and all night, it seemed, until we pumped the village well dry.

Now came the filming of the scenes in which the Old Gentleman came down the steps to warn the fisherman's family that the big wave was sure to come. Grandfather cackled that there would be no tidal waves, only rain. The village elders, very proud of their new careers as extras, assembled on the narrow veranda of Toru's house and agreed with him.

Those elders! I did not imagine that one village could have provided such a collection of snaggle-toothed, cheerful, wise-cracking, withered old men, but there they were. At first they were preternaturally grave and well-behaved, especially one eagle-faced old bird of a man who blinked his hooded eyes occasionally but otherwise gave no sign of life until the director

requested laughter at an appropriate moment. The old bird then shouted out a string of words that when translated went thus: "Put on your hat, American! That'll make me laugh!"

Everyone roared, for this hat had become a joke. It was a small bright yellow straw, with a vivid variegated band. It was useful in locating the director.

EVERY MORNING at Kitsu each person proceeded to his individual preparation for the day's scene. For an hour there was no need for me, and I walked along the beach past the stone breakwater to the foot of a steep hill. Stone steps led up this hill, and at the top was a little empty stone temple, once a Shinto shrine. A low wall surrounded it, and the view was the sea and mountains and sky.

I found my own niche behind the shrine. At the edge of the high cliff there was a hollow in the rocks that exactly fitted my body. There I went every morning and, held in this hollow as though in his arms, I lay at rest. It was the rest of the mind emptied, the spirit freed. He and I had never been here together. I cannot pretend that I heard his voice or even was aware of his presence. What did take place gradually was a profound insurge of peace. I became part of the whole. The warm rock bed in which I lay, the wind rising cool from the sea, the sky intensely blue and the drifting white clouds—of these I was a part, and beyond these, of the whole world. I ceased to be, at least for a time, a lonely creature with an aching heart. I was aware of healing pouring into me. At the end of the hour, I arose refreshed to join my fellow workers.

It became a habit. I woke eager for the hour and savored it with new zest each day. Then I discovered that something of each day's peace was left over for the night. I did not use it all up, there was an accumulation. I became stronger. I was able to miss a day, then two days, then more. Gradually I needed no more to climb to that high, lonely place and wait to receive. I was able to manufacture peace within myself merely by remembering the sweep of sea and mountain and sky and myself curled into the hollow rock. I had the peace inside me then, and the place became a shrine in my memory.

APPROXIMATELY one fourth of the way through the making of the film we arrived at the desert that seems to lie in the middle half of every creative project. How well I know the bleak prospect! I face it in every book I write. The first quarter of it goes like a breeze from the sea. The work is pure joy. Then I enter upon the middle half and joy departs. The characters refuse to move or speak or laugh or cry. They stand like pillars of salt. Why, oh, why was the book begun? Too much work has been done to cast it aside, yet the end is as far off as the end of a rainbow. There is nothing to do but plod ahead, push the characters this way and that, use every means of artificial respiration. Somewhere, someday, they do begin to breathe. What relief! The desert is past, the last quarter of the book breezes again.

On a morning in the middle of the desert period our star, Sessue Hayakawa, was waiting with grim patience to be called to the set. The scene had to be repeated because a fly had cunningly concealed himself on the microphone and buzzed enough to drown out everything else. As our star waited under his heavy robes, his secretary-maid fanned him.

On the set the director struggled with our grandfather, who, though actually old, had too young a voice. The director illustrated how an old man's voice should sound. I held my peace. I know that old men's voices are high and shrill, not low and husky, but I had learned to hold my peace.

When Sessue reached the last day of his contract with us and was finishing his scenes as the Old Gentleman, we were still in the middle desert. Everything continued to go wrong. The rushes had been delayed, film we had shot that we hoped to see a week ago. We had seen very few rushes, so that we were at least three days behind schedule. We drew apart and pondered dark thoughts. Could anybody understand the English our actors spoke? We were trying the impossible— Japanese actors playing in English! How would it sound even when our star spoke to an American audience?

In the midst of the desert we had a letter from our business manager in Tokyo. The rushes of the Old Gentleman were superb, she said, including the dialogue. They made her cry. Our hopes soared. Perhaps we were almost out of the desert.

In rejuvenated spirits we gave a dinner for Sessue in honor

of his leaving us. He was in a fine mood and drank a mixture of cold beer and sake, which he sustained admirably. Fifty years in the theater made a lifetime of stories worth telling. We were sorry to see him go, and I think he was sorry to leave us, but there is nothing permanent in theater life. We work together closely for a few days or weeks or months, growing fond of one another, and then we part and forget.

We filmed the last glimpse, the final close-up, of the Old Gentleman's servant. He was, of course, the little ancient wardrobe man—the old faun. He stood with calm and dignity while the cameraman took the close-ups we needed. When they were finished, we bowed and shook hands. We thanked him and he bowed in return. He told us that this was the greatest year of his life. He had become an actor, he had played a part with Sessue Hayakawa, and next month he was to marry off his daughter.

So the day ended.

"Otsukaresama!"

It means, "You are tired," a gentle Japanese way of saying, "You may quit for the day." It was true. We were tired.

We were now well past the desert. There was one big scene left for Kitsu. All this time our special-effects man had been creating the tidal wave in the studio in Tokyo. Twice he had come to take hundreds of pictures of Kitsu and the empty beach. We knew that the tidal wave would be perfect. Ours was the task of creating the approach to the wave, and the recovery from it.

An air of dread crept into the village as we prepared for the scene. This was cutting near the bone. Every man, woman and child feared above all else in their precarious lives the ungovernable tidal wave. Even to imagine the horror was almost more than they could bear as they set themselves doggedly to the task of acting out the dread reality. They played their parts well, however, when the torches flamed before the Old Gentleman's house and the panic-stricken Kitsu families fled from their ancestral homes to safety at the top of the cliff. This scene was to bring the boy Toru to the moment when he sees the village swept away, and we see it in his face. The tidal wave was to be inserted here, and after it, we took over again when Toru, in agony, clung to the cliff and was saved only by a strong hand put out to seize him. He acted the part superbly, but I remember especially the frightened people swarming up the hillside, taking the path their ancestors had used so often before them, but in reality.

That night we gained a new understanding of the incomparable courage of the Kitsu folk, their unswerving devotion to the sea and to their way of life. We said good-by with tender regret. I have memories of a crowd of kind faces in the lantern light, of the headman proudly receiving our praise and thanks, saying the only reward he wished was to know when the picture would be shown in Japan. "We will put on our best clothes and go even to Tokyo," he told us.

At last on the mountain the flames of the torches at the Old Gentleman's gate died into final darkness.

It was over. The picture was made. There remained only the volcano scene at Oshima to be shot.

OSHIMA HAD LOOKED hellish enough on our scouting trip in May, but now it was October and the volcano had been active and rebellious in the months between. We had chartered a plane to take us from Tokyo across the channel, but the morning dawned somber and gray and the pilot refused to fly. We were working against time now and to avoid delay we took passage on the night boat. A typhoon was in the offing.

In the driving rain and the howling wind we drove to the quay that night and boarded a top-heavy old-fashioned steamer. Fortunately, it was dark and we could not see how many people were embarking. We got ourselves on board, camera, crew, actors and all, and went at once to our cabins.

I shudder as I remember that fearful night. The sea was vicious, the wind and rain contending enemies, but worst of all, the ship was carrying four times its proper load of passengers, including hundreds of schoolchildren, who were off on an excursion to Oshima. They were seasick, the poor little things, and the lavatories and corridors became unusable and impassable. The real danger, however, was in the ship itself. The superstructure was far too high. I am a seasoned sailor and have crossed oceans again and again since the age of three months, yet never have I been in fear as I was that whole night. Sometime before dawn, a friend who was traveling with us came in to see how his wife, my cabinmate, was faring. His good face was green with terror. "We're breaking all the laws of mathematics," he groaned. "The ship is rolling at an impossible degree. We should by rights be flat on our side and floundering."

How is it that a mild-mannered, peaceable woman with no inclination for adventure manages somehow to be always in the midst of some daring expedition and loathing it? I have always particularly hated the thought of drowning at sea. Yet I cannot count the seas I have traveled upon, how many times the Pacific, scarcely less often the Atlantic, the Mediterranean, the Red Sea, and all the seas curling in and around the complex shores of Asia. Now apparently I was to meet my fate between Tokyo and Oshima. The Big Wave, indeed!

Dawn came at last, the pale sun fringed with mists, and the ocean still growling and snarling. The dim outlines of Oshima appeared from nowhere. In fifteen minutes we were due to dock. Fifteen minutes became an hour and then two hours while we continued to roll. We could not dock because the sea was too rough. We were compelled to go to the other side of the island where there was an inferior dock. A long procession of pale but determined schoolchildren disembarked, and then we got off and went in the rain to the hotel.

We had breakfast and set out by car to the foot of the volcano. There horses waited for those who wanted to ride. Experience had taught me to distrust the Asian horse, mule or pony. They lead a hard life, for the Asian is not sentimental about animals. The philosophy of the transmigration of souls leads him to believe that the human being who has been a criminal in life will in his next phase be an animal with the soul of a criminal. Judging by the behavior of horses I have known in Asia, it seems possible that they are indeed animated by some evil force. On foot, therefore, I climbed the volcano, ascending the dark and barren landscape, horrifyingly beautiful.

Under a stormy gray sky, streamers of white steam flew from every crack and cranny of the volcano. The crater of the volcano is very large, and had in the last few days become larger, for under the torrential rains the walls had crumbled at various places. Again and again I stopped on my way to look at the spectacle. I have seen some of the most magnificent scenery in the world, but for splendor and terror, I put first the volcano on Oshima island that day.

Two days we spent there. Only a short time before the volcano had erupted, throwing great rocks into the air and gnawing at the mountain. Guards stood everywhere now to forbid us passage, but we pushed our way to the very edge of the crater in spite of them, the camera perched precariously anywhere it could stand or be held. The drop into the crater was at two levels, the one an encircling terrace, the other without bottom and hidden in clouds of gas and steam.

The wind blew bitterly cold and work went on without the usual laughter and good cheer. Swiftly and with concentration each did his part. I confess my heart lost too many beats as I watched the crew walking about inside the crater, leaping across great cracks, sinking into soft ashy soil, standing at the very edge of the abyss. I recalled it all again when the rushes were shown in the theater in New York. I saw the boy Yukio standing there on the screen, his eyes wide with fear, the white steam curling upward from the crater and enclosing him. No wonder he cries out to his father, "We are unlucky, we people of Japan!"

"Why do you say that?" his father asks.

"Sea and the mountain," the boy says, "they work to destroy us."

We were glad when the two days were ended, the work finished. Five days later the volcano went into eruption and the lava-black soil upon which we had stood fell into the abyss.

ON MY LAST day in Tokyo I went to the special-effects studio. In a space as vast as Madison Square Garden in New York, the famous special-effects artist had reconstructed Kitsu, the mountains and the sea. The houses were three feet high, each in perfect miniature, and everything else was in proportion. A river ran outside the studio and the rushing water for the tidal wave would be released into the studio by great sluices along one side. I looked into the houses, I climbed the little mountain, I marveled at the exactitude of the beach, even to the rocks where in reality I had so often taken shelter. The set was not yet ready for the tidal wave. That I was to see later on the screen in all its power and terror.

My hotel room had become a sort of home, and I felt loath to leave it. It had been a pleasant place, and I had lived there in deepening peace. Now the old dread of facing another life without him and of returning alone to those places where we had always been together was with me again. It had to be done, however.

"Come back soon to Japan," my dear friends said, and I promised that I would and, tearing myself away, I went alone to the plane that was to carry me back again to New York.

I say New York, although of course New York is only on the way to my farmhouse home in Pennsylvania. But I have a stopping place in New York. He and I always kept an apartment there. He needed it for his work and for his spirit, and I have continued our tradition. It is not the same place we shared for so many years. That building was to be torn down.

And here I tell a story that has nothing to do with *The Big Wave*, except that it provides a closing scene. When I was looking for a new apartment, a daughter helped me by sorting out the impossibles and bringing me at last to see the two or three possibles. It was night, I remember, when I looked at these places. I was in haste and it did not seem to matter much where I lived. We entered bare, unpainted rooms. I saw a wide window and, through the darkness, a building. A school, my daughter said. There would be no high building to cut off the view. I decided upon impulse. "I'll take it."

The choice was haphazard, I would have said. But I am beginning to believe that there is no such thing as pure chance. For here is the preliminary to this closing story:

When I was a child and often reluctant to do my duty, my father used to say to me firmly but gently, "If you will not do it because it is right, then do it for the greater glory of God."

For the greater glory of God then, and for my father's sake, though still reluctant, I did do what had to be done, at least as often as possible.

Now to return to the apartment: I did not see it while it was being decorated. When it was finished, I opened the door and went straight to the big window. It was a bright day, I remember, the air was fresh and the sky blue. And facing me, under the eaves of the school building, I saw these words carved in huge stone letters: AD MAJOREM DEI GLORIAM.

They face me now as I write. To the greater glory of God! What does it mean, this voice from the grave, my father's grave? He lies buried on a mountaintop in the very heart of a China lost to me. I am alive and in New York, thousands of miles away. Are we in communication, my father and I? It is not possible.

How dare I say it is not?

Someday we shall know, perhaps, when saints and scientists unite to make a total search for truth. It is the saints, the believers, who should urge the scientists to discover whether the spirit continues its life when the mass we call the body ceases to be the container. Faith supplies the hypothesis, but only science can provide the verification.

There are no miracles, of that I am sure. If one walks on water and raises the dead to life again, it is not a matter of magic, but a matter of knowing how to do it. There is no supernatural; there is only the supremely natural, the purely scientific. Science and religion, religion and science, put it as I may, they are two sides of the same glass, through which we see darkly until these two, focusing together, reveal the truth.

On the day when the message comes through from over the far horizon where dwells "that great majority," the dead, then the proof will reach us, not as a host of angels in the sky, but as a wavelength recorded in a laboratory, a wavelength as indisputable and personal as the fingerprint belonging to someone whose body is dust. Then the scientist, recognizing the wavelength, will exclaim, "But that's someone I know! I took his wavelength before he died." And he will compare his record with the wavelength just recorded and will know that at last a device, a machine, is able to receive a message dreamed of for centuries, the message of our continuing individual existence, which we call the immortality of the soul.

Or perhaps it will not be a scientist who receives, but a woman, waiting at a window open to the sky.

THE THREE DAUGHTERS
OF MADAME LIANG

THE THREE DAUGHTERS
OF MADAME LIANG

A CONDENSATION OF THE BOOK BY
Pearl S. Buck

ILLUSTRATED BY WILLIAM HOFMANN

"Your eldest daughter is to return from America at once," the government minister informed her. Fear gripped Madame Liang, yet she maintained her outward calm. The words should not have come as a surprise. The old China into which she had been born was gone, replaced by the spying eyes of the New Order. And how soon before her other two daughters would receive the same official "invitation"?

Here is a dramatic novel of China's stormy recent past and the enduring strength and spirit of her people.

I

It was past midnight. Madame Liang put down her brush
pen and closed her account book. Her house was quiet. Downstairs in the restaurant the guests were gone. She rose from the
carved blackwood chair, which matched the huge Chinese
desk, and went to the window. The long red satin curtains
were drawn, and she did not pull them back. Though she was
secure in her favored position as the owner of the most fashionable restaurant in modern Shanghai, it would not have
been safe for her to be outlined against the window. One never
knew where the enemy hid. Many were jealous of the famous
Madame Liang who, seemingly unperturbed by political distur-
bances, managed to keep open a fine gourmet restaurant whose
patrons were the highest officials, the most successful merchants
and the top officers of the army.

She slipped behind the curtain and in its shadow she slid
open the window. The air was mild with coming summer and a
scent of jasmine floated upward from the gardens. Her house
had once belonged to a wealthy American businessman

named Brandon. He and his family had been her friends. In pre-Communist days Madame Liang had made many friends among the Americans, and she had sent her three daughters to America to be educated. Now, of course, there were no Americans left in China, and a whole generation of young Chinese was growing up without ever having seen an American face or heard an American voice. They heard only words of hate against a people who in her opinion had been the least hateful among the Westerners. Americans alone had seized no land from the Chinese and had imposed no cruelties.

She sighed, remembering the gay and impulsive Brandon family. How well they had loved China. When suddenly Mr. Brandon's banking business had been confiscated and they had been compelled to leave, Mrs. Brandon had sobbed on her shoulder, "Oh, Madame Liang, will they ever let us come back?"

She had put her arms about the American woman, but how could she say, "You will never come back"? So she had said nothing and the years had slipped past, each more difficult than the last. But she had sent her daughters to the Brandons, and sometimes—

Her thoughts were interrupted by Chou Ma, her old and faithful woman servant. "Lady, why will you stand by the window? The curtains cannot hide your shadow!"

"No one knows the shadow is mine," Madame Liang replied. But she came out from behind the curtain and allowed herself to be undressed by Chou Ma in preparation for her bath.

"Everyone knows you," Chou Ma retorted, "and who has a shape like yours? Certainly they know it is not my shape, and who else is here on this floor except us? They know everything, these accursed new people!"

"Take heed how you speak," Madame Liang commanded. "Remember they are my customers. I have no others now."

Chou Ma removed the last silken garment from the slim cream-pale body of her mistress, admiring in silence the fine-boned frame, the small round breasts, the exquisite delicacy of the nape of the neck. Then Madame Liang walked across the room into the bathroom. She was one of the few who still had the comforts of the past, and for this she must be grateful to her husband, Liang Cheng, whom she had left years ago when he had taken a concubine upon her failure to produce a son. He had been a friend and follower of Sun Yat-sen, the archrevolutionist, and in the eyes of these new people she was still respected as his wife—as in fact she was, since she had never troubled to get a legal divorce.

Yet she owed her well-being also to herself. The new rulers were Chinese and therefore gourmets. In these harsh times it was not easy to find the traditional delicacies: the specially fed Peking duck, the millet soup of the north and the steamed breads stuffed with spiced pork or dark sugar. Fortunately her chef had stayed with her through wars and governments.

The Soochow tub was brimming with hot water and she sank shoulder deep into the pleasant warmth. She had no sense of guilt in enjoyments. While she listened in docile silence to endless talk of self-sacrifice and equality, she preferred to believe with her Confucian parents that life was meant to be enjoyed.

"Lady," Chou Ma called, "I hear footsteps!"

Madame Liang turned her head to listen. "I hear nothing," she replied. "Are the doors locked?"

"Do I ever leave the doors unlocked?" Chou Ma's voice was reproachful.

"Go and listen," Madame Liang commanded. She stepped out of the tub and, after drying herself thoroughly, scented her body with gardenia oil—a fragrance her flesh had absorbed over the years until now she moved in its atmosphere. Long ago, in a faraway province, she had thus scented herself for her wedding night. She and Liang Cheng had been students together at the Sorbonne in Paris, and together they had become followers of Sun Yat-sen. Together they had returned to Peking to join the revolution.

"You are the wife I would have chosen for him," Sun had said when they announced their decision to marry. "You are strong and he is—well, too warmhearted! He is fire and you are earth."

On that day she had felt her first fear of Sun's death. His skin was clinging to his bones and his black eyes were sunken, for already he was ridden with liver cancer. Perhaps he, too, had known, for he had clasped her hands into Liang Cheng's. "Carry on the revolution," he had commanded them. He was dead by their wedding day three months later.

Chou Ma entered the room. "I looked through the keyhole and saw a bold black eye, which saw my eye and went away again."

"All eyes are bold nowadays," Madame Liang retorted and went into her bedroom and put on her white silk night-robe. Then she sat before her toilet table and Chou Ma brushed and braided her long hair, still black in spite of her fifty-four years.

"Bring me the cashbox and count the day's money," Madame Liang directed. The box was of polished wood with strong brass locks. It was so heavy that Chou Ma pulled it across the floor on the blue-and-white rug woven long ago in Peking.

Chou Ma finished counting the money and announced the amount.

"It was the minister's feast today that made us rich," Madame Liang declared. "Now lock the box and put it under the bed as you always do. Tomorrow move the money into the big iron safe. When they come to ask how much, say that you know nothing. I will say that because of the minister's kindness I shall make a contribution to the cooperative."

"You are always clever, lady," Chou Ma said.

Her mistress climbed into the high old-fashioned bed and Chou Ma spread the silken quilts and drew the embroidered curtains. This bed Madame Liang had brought from the far-away province where Cheng had been governor. There she had lived with him for ten years until the third child, again a girl, had been born. Then he had taken a concubine, hoping this woman would give him a son.

"I will not leave my marriage bed for him to sleep in with other women," Madame Liang had said when she left him.

Chou Ma's voice interrupted these memories. "Shall I leave a light burning since there were footsteps tonight?"

Madame Liang considered. "Leave one on the chimney-piece."

She never used the fireplaces in this house, for even if there had been coal, it would have been unwise to buy it. Luxury must be concealed. When she went downstairs to the restaurant, she wore a robe of cotton over her satin gown. Her age, she declared, forbade the severe uniform of coat and trousers that all younger women wore. The truth was that she could not live without beauty. She had been reared in the midst of beauty, her father a rich man in a rich city. She remembered him as he had been when she was a young girl, restless for freedom from the old ways. At first he had been bewildered by her attitude.

"What have I done, my child?" he had asked her sadly. "Did I bind your feet when you were small? Have I forbidden you to learn to read, although reading is useless for a woman? Have I not said you need not marry the one to whom you were betrothed when you were a child? What now—what now?"

"Let me go to Paris," she had insisted.

So she had been sent to Paris, city of beauty, and there had met Cheng and Chao Chung, the minister whose dinner her chef had prepared tonight, and all those others who in later years had joined the revolution back in China. Beauty had been lost in the disappointment of Sun Yat-sen's failure, from which Cheng had escaped into the governorship of a distant province, and she with him.

And now the conquest of the country by strange new doctrines had resulted again in utter loss of beauty. Ah, here was the soul's destruction! She knew all the arguments: the people better fed, corruption wiped away, bridges built, floods controlled, even flies and rats gone—but beauty was dead. She hoarded its remnants—her jewels, her robes, her house.

In the drawing room there was a Steinway piano that the Brandons had left. She had paid for this and for the house from an account in a New York bank into which, years ago, she had been able to put some of her business profits.

She turned restlessly in the huge bed. Outside the curtained windows shone a full moon such as she remembered hanging in the sky above her childhood home. The memory of it comforted her, and at last she slept.

"WAKE, LADY," Chou Ma called. "I call your soul home to your body. Come home, O Soul!"

Slowly Madame Liang's soul returned, and as she woke, she perceived Chou Ma's anxious face above her. "Lady, it is noon," Chou Ma was saying. "The one from above is waiting for you in the Lotus Room—the minister of foreign affairs, Chao Chung. He is impatient."

Madame Liang knew the dangers of sudden demand upon heart and bone, blood and brain. She lay unmoving until she felt thought alive in her skull. Then she filled her lungs with fresh breath, inhaling and exhaling seven times, and moved her feet, hands, arms, legs, until she was alive and present. Finally she sat up and Chou Ma rubbed her shoulders and her back for three minutes. Once out of bed, Madame Liang moved swiftly, and soon she had washed, drunk hot tea and put on a long robe buttoned at the throat.

"He has come with a purpose," Chou Ma said, setting the last silver pin in Madame Liang's hair.

"Then I must be strong," Madame Liang said.

But she looked fragile and remote when she entered the Lotus Room a few minutes later. This room, kept for special guests, was furnished in a French style, with here and there a fine Chinese piece—a two-tiered table set between delicate upright chairs, a pair of Sung vases, a Tang pottery horse on its own pedestal.

A handsome gray-haired man awaited her, his dark eyes lively and his smile brilliant. He had been reared in luxury and educated in Europe; and although he had given up his past gracefully, she knew that in his heart he was cynical and melancholy. They never spoke of their association in Paris and elsewhere, and these days they met almost as strangers. She approached him with feminine shyness, her usually erect carriage subdued to appeal.

"Ah, Madame Liang," he said, "are you well?" He spoke in Mandarin and the cultivated accent was that of Peking.

"I am well," she said, motioning him to be seated. She seated herself in a somewhat lower chair and looked at him, though not fully, for this would have been rude. "May I ask whether the feast last night was to your taste?"

"Each dish was"—he held up his thumb to express excellence—"superb. But we missed you. When we were drinking wine after the meal was over, you did not join us as you usually do."

"I had a headache," she said.

"And this morning?"

"It is gone."

"Then I may proceed?"

"Of course."

"I come as your old friend," he said in his mellifluous voice, which, she well knew, he could use as an instrument or a weapon.

"I know your good heart," she said gently.

"In a high conference recently your affairs were discussed."

"I am honored," she said, inclining her head, not allowing her eyes to observe beyond the upper part of his uniform. He wore the usual men's costume of black trousers and high-buttoned jacket, but the cloth was the finest English wool and elegantly tailored.

He cleared his throat. "What I have to say, Comrade Liang, is in no way a reproach. It is an appeal—an appeal to your patriotism, to your loyalty to the Party, to your—"

She lifted her head and looked him full in the face. "What do you wish me to do, Comrade Chao?"

He replied abruptly, "Your eldest daughter is to return from America at once."

She hid the sudden rush of fear that clutched at her heart and made her voice calm. "She is in the midst of her research."

"She can finish here. She is needed. We know everything she is doing." And, as if to prove it, he proceeded. "Your eldest daughter, Grace, combines beauty and a brilliant scientific mind. She is a research fellow in botany and pharmacology at the Harvard Botanical Museum. She is also a fashion model, and indeed, we have an exact accounting of her weekly earnings. She sends you no money—"

Madame Liang interrupted. "I need none."

"We know that, so it has been suggested to your daughter that she contribute a portion of her salary to the cause. Our people are beyond numbering. They must be fed and clothed. Our great scientific projects are costly. This has all been explained to your daughter, but she does not reply. It is time she came home."

Madame Liang controlled her trembling lips. "Will this not waste the years she has spent upon valuable medical research?"

"No. As you doubtless know, she is doing research on a certain intoxicating plant. She has spent two summers in the jungles of South America in search of the plant, which there they call cohoba. But we have this plant also, in our own southern jungles."

"But she is gathering together all her knowledge into a book—"

"Our ancient Chinese books contain more than she can find anywhere else. It is for this indeed that she is asked to return. We wish her to compile from their rich and ancient lore modern textbooks that can be used in our new Medical Institute in the capital. Why should her skills be wasted on Western materials when here we have the accumulated knowledge of centuries?"

Madame Liang touched her pink silk kerchief to her lips and tried to answer his smile. "You will convey the news to her?"

"She will be officially invited to return," he said as he rose. "Write to her as a mother. Tell her that we are beginning our greatest era and need young women like her."

"Then she will not live here with me?"

"We will see. Certainly it will be her duty to visit you." Affable and smiling, he bowed his farewell. As she followed him to the door, he suddenly turned. "One more suggestion— do not communicate with her through your usual chain! An important link in that chain was found dead in Hong Kong eleven days ago."

She returned to her seat, pondering what he had said. What part the dead man had played in the "chain," as Chao Chung called it, she did not know. But Chao knew exactly what she had been doing. Her letters to her daughters, written openly, were, of course, read. But she sent other messages—hidden in a scarf, a length of silk—through her widowed sister in Hong Kong. She must devise a letter warning her sister and asking her to tell her eldest daughter to go into hiding. Grace must not come home.

As soon as Madame Liang had this thought she gave it up. Wherever her daughter hid she would be found—and punished. And Grace would not hide. She had been reared to love her country and to be proud that she was Chinese.

It was several weeks before the summons found its way to Dr. Grace Liang at the small hotel where she was staying near the botanical station on the edge of a South American jungle. She had been on a trip in search of cohoba, beyond reach of communication. When she returned to the hotel one night, she saw a bundle of mail on her table.

Travel-weary though she was, she sat down and looked through the letters. None from her aunt in Hong Kong nor from her mother? She was always anxious about her mother, living her precarious capitalistic life in the Communist desert.

No, wait—here was an envelope—only why from Peking? She tore it open and drew out a sheet of thin rice paper covered with Chinese characters.

"Comrade Dr. Grace Liang," the letter began. "You are invited to return to your native land without delay. Our new China has need of its young men and women. You will sail on the fifteenth of September on the *President Cleveland* from San Francisco. Your fare is paid. After arrival at Hong Kong you will leave for the mainland. At the border you will be met by a guide, who will give you a railroad pass to the capital. This invitation is not to be refused. Your mother has been told that you are coming. You may arrange for a stopover of two days in Shanghai to visit her." The letter was signed by an unknown name.

She folded it slowly. Around her the jungle darkness was deepening after the short twilight. She had been expecting the summons. The wonder was that it had not come before. She had known when she chose to become a scientist instead of a concert pianist that sooner or later the summons would come.

She had been only fifteen when her mother had sent her to America to study music. In the girls' school in Shanghai she had shown talent as a pianist, and her teacher, an American woman, had insisted, "You must go to one of our great American schools of music. Perhaps Juilliard, in New York." Yet, when she had finished Juilliard, she had gone to the Harvard Botanical Museum.

"Oh, why will you insist on being a scientist?" her sister Joy had cried. "They'd never force a concert pianist to come back—you wouldn't be productive in the new society. That's why I've chosen to be an artist. In the new society, who wants a pianist? Be anything—anything but a scientist!"

But by then Grace was certain she wanted to be a scientist. And whatever the new people were politically, were they not her own people? Whatever her future was to be, she would be of more service if she became a good scientist.

So she had become a research fellow. And because her

mother might one day need the money on account in the New York bank, Grace had begun to supplement her income by working as a model. Her slim figure, tall for a Chinese girl, happened to be of the right proportions for fashion, and her oriental face—well, she was considered beautiful.

After she had bathed, she put on a silken Chinese robe and ordered dinner sent to her room. It was brought by the silent Indian woman who had been detailed to wait on her. Strange how Asian these South American Indians looked, Grace thought. The Asian strain was surely the strongest in the world, the most prevailing. And now, though her own people were enemies of the Americans who had done so much for her, she was glad she was Chinese.

She laughed softly to herself, remembering her first teacher, an old Confucian scholar. "We Chinese must remember at all times that we are the superior people of this earth, the most civilized, the nearest to the gods. All others are barbarians in varying degrees." In her innermost being she, too, believed that her own people were superior to all others. But wait— were these new Chinese the same?

"You would not recognize our country!" her mother had written in one of her secret letters. "We are ruled now by the children of peasants. Heaven and earth are upside down. Those who were high are made low—or are dead. Those who were low are raised up and they rule. We must wait, perhaps for a hundred years, until the times are set right again."

When she had eaten, Grace went to bed, but not to sleep. Instead she lay awake for hours, her mind busy. Which should she follow, the warnings of her mother and of her aunt in Hong Kong, or the summons she had received from Peking? It was nearly dawn when she finally made up her mind.

She longed for her own country, her own people. Kind as the Americans had been to her, she wanted to go home. And was this not also her duty? China had need of her youth, her Western education in science. Even as a child, Grace had been troubled by the sight of children in Chinese villages wasted by illness or blinded by infections. She had asked her mother, "M-ma, why don't they call the doctor?"

"Because there is no doctor here," her mother had replied.

"Then why don't they go to the American hospital in Peking?"

"They are too poor," her mother had said, "and there are too many of them."

She realized now, lying awake in a distant outpost in South America, that she had never forgotten the faces of those people, her people. She would never be happy until she went back to them.

IT WAS night in the great restaurant. Not a table was empty and the guests were gay. Most were Chinese, but there was a sprinkling of Europeans, Africans and turbaned Indians, a few of them businessmen and their wives, the others diplomats. It was almost like the old Shanghai, Madame Liang thought, pausing here and there to greet her customers at the tables.

In those past days there had been a constant flow of travelers from everywhere on earth. Now, of course, the walls were up. She had protested the walls at first, even to Minister Chao Chung, who had been her friend. It was true that Chao Chung had encouraged her to leave her husband, and her husband had accused her of being in love with this friend, but she had denied the charge. Throughout the years she knew that Chao Chung had spoken the right words in the right quarter, words that enabled her to keep her palatial house and her famous restaurant.

He was here again tonight, at the head of a long table reserved for him and his associates whenever he came to Shanghai from Peking. She paused beside him and smiled.

"I congratulate you, Comrade Liang," he said cheerfully, so that all at the table could hear him. "We have received a letter from your eldest daughter telling us that she wishes to return to her country to help our people in medical science. This is patriotic indeed, but from the daughter of such a mother, I expected such patriotism."

It was the first time Madame Liang had heard of her daughter's decision. Then Grace's letter to her must have been intercepted! The walls went higher and the gates, one by one, were locked.

"Thank you," she said, as coolly as if she had already known what he had told her. Then she turned and moved gracefully among the tables.

She lived thereafter in a fever of expectation. There was no one of whom she could inquire, "When will my daughter arrive?" She dared not write to her sister in Hong Kong or to Grace herself. Nor did she wish the minister to know that she knew nothing. Let him imagine that she had many ways of private communication, some of which he could not discover! Then it occurred to her that he might wonder why she did not write her sister, and forthwith she wrote one of her usual letters.

II

THE DAYS moved smoothly into late summer. There were times when Madame Liang could imagine that nothing had changed in Shanghai. Business continued to be good, her dining rooms were crowded; and the markets were better than they had been since before the last famine. Nevertheless, one afternoon she felt restless and engaged a horse and carriage for a ride about the city.

The sky was clear and a clean wind blew in from the sea. The city did not stand on the shore of the East China Sea but a little way up the Yangtze River, whose yellow earth-laden waters stained the blue sea for miles beyond the coast.

She sat in the carriage, wrapped in a light silk gown hidden under a covering robe of gray cloth. "Drive along the bund," she directed the driver.

How would this city appear to Grace, accustomed now to great American cities? Here there were no cars, or very few, only buses, picking up and setting down their silent passengers. She felt a pang of jealousy for the sake of Shanghai, which she loved. Would her daughter appreciate its present life? Would she remember that once these streets had been crowded with beggars and refugees from famine and flood? Now the streets were filled with other crowds—not the rich, not the poor, not the foreign, but people plainly dressed and clean, and not one a beggar.

On Nanking Road, the great thoroughfare, shops sold many different goods. The carriage rolled onto the bund itself, where there were no shops but the banks that had once held foreign gold still stood. In the old days the bund had been the center of vast international commerce; now it was a park, and along the river's edge were benches and shade trees. "Stop," she told the driver. "I will sit here for a time of contemplation."

While the carriage waited, she sat down on a bench at the other end of which was a very old gentleman. His skin was pale and fine, his hands those of a man who has never worked. But he was no longer rich, for his satin robe was worn and frayed. In other days she would have greeted him, but nowadays one did not greet strangers. Yet when she sat down, the old man smiled and spoke. "Madame, it is a pleasant day."

She gave a small answering smile, then gazed over the river, whose waters were busy with boats bearing three-cornered sails, with ponderous junks and slow barges.

"I can remember when this was the busiest place in the city," the old man went on. "Great ships came up this river, and dockworkers carried loads on their shoulders. And there were beggars and thieves darting everywhere."

He paused, and she murmured courteously, "Was it so?"

"At our age, madame, we remember other days," he said in a low voice. "And let me tell you, if you go behind that part of the city that was once Japanese, even now you will see many poor people—swarming like flies on a manure pile."

She began to be afraid of the old gentleman. "Everything cannot be done at once," she said. "At least the rich are not so rich and the poor are not so poor."

"Give us time," he retorted, "and some will be rich again and some will be poor. It is man's fate."

She rose, bowed slightly and walked away. One never knew who, for a little money, might act as a spy. But what the old man had said about the city stayed in her mind, for she had seen it in all its several lives. Twenty years ago she had come here with her three small daughters, and in those days the world was here—France and England and Japan, each playing its part. The streets had been clean in the foreign concessions, and the traffic swift, controlled by foreign policemen. How angered she had been when she found that she could not take her children into the park. "Is this not China?" she had demanded at the entrance.

"No," the policeman had replied, "it is a piece of England, a bounty after the last Opium War."

Beyond those foreign parts, the Chinese city had festered in a maze of narrow filthy streets and open gutters.

She remembered next another Shanghai, upon which Japanese bombs were falling, but only on the Chinese sections. The people ran out like rats and took shelter in the foreign streets. Then the Japanese held a victory parade and everywhere lay dead Chinese soldiers, the dead of the Nationalist Army left behind when Chiang Kai-shek fled.

Shanghai had lived through more agony. Beautiful girls were sold on the streets for a dollar or two a night, and then even the dollar became worthless and money blew about the streets like wastepaper. The shops were filled with American merchandise, for then Americans were the visitors, but it was stolen and sold in private markets. Corruption rotted the entire city and no one was innocent. So sickened was she that she had welcomed it when the new people laid siege to the city. Rich men and their families fled to foreign countries; those who stayed were butchered in the streets until the people could endure no more and cried out that the war must end, even though victory belonged to the Communists.

And then they came in, the silent army, their cloth-shod feet noiseless as they marched, angry peasant men. Grim as the gray tide of the sea, they flooded into the city and took possession of everything, even to the very soul of man.

"I will return to my home," she said now to the driver. "I have seen enough."

GRACE LIANG entered her aunt's dining room. The house in Hong Kong stood on a rocky hillside, its low Chinese rooflines melting into the landscape. The large central hall faced the sea and the harbor, but the dining room, behind it, gave only a view of the crowded city. Her aunt was already at the table.

"I hope you were not waiting for me," Grace said, taking her seat. "I slept too well. I had forgotten the air here is so mild."

"Sleep while you can," her aunt replied. "You may not be able to sleep so well after you have crossed the border."

They spoke in English, which the servants did not understand.

Her aunt was lifting the lid of one dish after another. "I have been looking forward to a real Chinese breakfast," Grace said.

"There is the rice congee, and here are the small dishes to accompany it," her aunt said.

They filled their bowls and, in deference to good manners, ate for a few minutes without talk. Then Grace put down her chopsticks. "My mother seems to do very well in Shanghai, Auntie."

"You will see for yourself how well she does," her aunt retorted. "Naturally she cannot put in writing what the people endure."

"You really think—"

"I do not think, I know. I spend some hours each day in the refugee camps, where our people go after they cross the border from the mainland. Suffering pours from them. These communes—the children are put in one place, the parents in another. Is this not to disturb the very harmony of heaven and earth?"

"Perhaps they do not believe in this harmony."

Her aunt nodded. "They do not believe in anything that the ancestors teach us. Therefore they cannot endure. It is merely a matter of waiting."

Grace smiled without replying. She had made up her mind to see this new China for herself. On those last days in San Francisco she and her two sisters had met at the Brandons' house for long talks before they parted.

"I do not fear for you. I am glad you are going home," Mercy had said. "Our mother is alone there." She was the strongest of the sisters perhaps, the most talkative and emotional.

"I cannot believe that I have anything to fear from my own people," Grace had said firmly.

Joy had said nothing. She was the quiet one, the youngest, the dreamer, the artist. A small slender girl, she painted in a way that was strangely unlike her, filling enormous canvases with bold brushstrokes and strong colors.

Grace had continued. "Of course I expect to find changes. But our people have always accepted change." She smiled. "I remember an old farmer getting on one of the first airplanes to fly between Shanghai and Peking. He carried a basket of hens on his shoulder. He was not in the least surprised when the plane lifted itself from the ground. One would have thought he had traveled every day by air—with hens!"

They had laughed together with the tenderness habitual to them when they spoke of their own people.

"I miss our people," Mercy had said. "There's something about them that's different from every other people on earth. They are always gay."

They had fallen silent, and then Joy spoke. "Perhaps we shall all be happy together again." An hour later they had parted.

"And now will you go with me to visit my refugees?" her aunt was saying.

"Of course." Grace rose as she spoke, and while her aunt gave directions to a servant, she stood looking out the window over the city. Beyond the mountains, across the barrier, her country waited.

"BUT THESE people have left everything behind them," Grace exclaimed. "It is natural that they are full of hatred."

They stood on a busy street corner in Hong Kong. Tall buildings rose on either side, the new housing provided for the refugees by the British government. On every floor the verandas were lively with fluttering clotheslines.

"But these people are the ones the new regime is supposed to be helping," her aunt replied. "Yet when they escape, they begin at once to live as they did in the old days. They begin to be independent and set up small businesses. See that hillside covered with shacks? That's where they live at first. A refugee family works together, young and old, to build that poor shelter. As soon as possible they move into a two-room apartment in a housing unit. Next they buy a few boxes of matches, a handful of candy, a pound of peanuts—any small thing they can package and sell on a street corner. And they prosper. We're hated all over Asia because we always grow rich from just such pitiful beginnings."

While they talked it began to rain. "Get in the car," her aunt ordered. "We'll drive to the barrier."

The barrier was crowded with Chinese waiting to see who might cross the border today. Grace watched the people push their way into British territory. Many were old, but most were young, and she was convinced she saw keen intellectual faces among them. Why did they wish to leave their country?

She turned to her aunt. "Not all of these people are peasants, Auntie! What will the others do?"

"They will melt into the city," her aunt said. "They will find their friends; they will live in silence, waiting."

"Waiting for what?"

"Whatever your mother is waiting for. There is always change, for better or worse—and I tell you, there cannot be worse. But you will see for yourself."

GRACE WAS restless and eager to leave this crowded island of Hong Kong. "I shall write you everything, Auntie," she said in farewell.

"Write me nothing," her aunt cried in alarm. "You will find answers to all your questions, but I have my own answers."

Grace left her aunt at the border one clear morning and was met by a man assigned as her guide, who presented her with a letter from Comrade Chao.

"We have long awaited your arrival," the letter said. "Linger if you like for a day or two in Canton, observe the masses there and how the ancient crafts have been nourished. You will take the train to Shanghai and visit your mother for two days. On the third we shall expect you to leave for Peking to help in the important medical work for which you have been summoned."

She told her guide she would indeed stay for a day or two in Canton, a city she remembered for its delicate and beautiful crafts, especially in ivory. She had read in Western journals that the ancient beauty of China was no more. Now she would see for herself.

When she got off the train she felt a vague disappointment. She had grown used to the opulence of American cities, of apartment houses circling Central Park in New York, of rich old town houses in Philadelphia and Boston. Beside them Canton seemed a city of meager charm. Here and there a fairly well dressed man rode by on a bicycle or a woman in a neat long gown paused at a vegetable stall. But most of the people were poorly dressed, and many were barefoot. Yet even the poor were clean, she observed. And the streets, once filthy, were clean now too, even in the poor areas.

While the guide attended to her baggage and accommodations, she took a walk around the city. The small shops in which craftsmen had lived and worked were gone. She approached an elderly woman in a neat costume of gauzy black. "Elder sister, will you tell me whether the ivory workers are still to be found in this city?"

The woman stared at her. "The proper address is comrade," she said as she pointed, "and the ivory workers are yonder."

"Forgive me," Grace stammered. "Thank you." She tried to say "comrade," but the strange word would not come.

Yonder was not the street of many houses she had pictured, but a small factory, within which she found the workers and a fine exhibit of ivory pieces. She had always loved ivory, cream-white and hard as bone and yet somehow soft as living tissue. Each craftsman, sitting in his place, was given his material, and he had to study the shape he held in his hands until he saw a new shape, suited to its lines.

She saw the showpieces she remembered, the ivory balls, one carved within another, perfect and free, until there were as many as twenty-six. She saw ivory junks with twisted ropes of ivory, old men and women with ivory wrinkles, and laughing Buddhas of ivory. She saw a landscape carved in ivory that breathed of spring in its blossoms and weeping willows, every detail perfected by a fine electric drill.

"A drill?" she inquired of the carver. "And what if the point slips and your art is destroyed?"

The bronze-faced old man smiled. "It never slips," he said.

From ivory she went to jade and saw how a carver had used the natural color of his jade to portray green grapes, green leaves, gray rock. She saw jade panthers and tigers and small pet dogs, the colors of the stone mimicking natural hues.

She found beauty, too, in the humbler materials of wood, bamboo, and even paper, in which clever scissors had cut intricate scenes of land and waters. She remembered how on feast days her mother used to bid her servants paste on the doors and gates these paper pictures for good luck.

That night she stayed in a Chinese inn and ate such cooking as she had forgotten could be, though the dishes were simple. She went to bed at last, deciding she had seen enough of this city. In her childhood, she remembered, the streets had been gay and noisy, with children laughing, neighbor calling to neighbor, vendors shouting their wares. Now people came and went in silence. A gray city, she would have said, except for the lovely carvings she had seen. In the midst of the new silence something remained of the past she had known, and it was beauty.

THE LAND was still tended—that she could see even from the train window. The fields were green with young rice and every odd corner and narrow space was given over to vegetables, as though the people could never forget how they had starved in other years. Yet even the land was changed. No longer were there separate fields, for boundaries had been torn away. Now the landscape was one great garden of waving green, promising a good harvest.

She longed to ask how it had happened, but there was no one in her compartment whose looks invited conversation. Her silent guide stared blankly at the opposite wall. The other two passengers were young men in the ubiquitous uniform of the country, jacket buttoned to the narrow collar and trousers of the same dark cotton; both were studying small books. She resumed looking out the window.

Instead of turning east toward Shanghai, the train continued north toward Peking. She would leave it at Wuhan, the guide had told her. "There you will take a river steamer for Shanghai. And at Wuhan you will see the new bridge."

She was curious to see this famous bridge, which engineers of half the Western world said could never be built across the wide stretch of the Yangtze River. But first she must see the provinces. In the fields gray water buffalo were pulling the old wooden plows; nothing changed there. No, wait. The hills, once bare except for fuel grass, had been planted with young trees and there were new reservoirs for irrigation. Next she saw farmers scattering a white powder over the fields. Chemical fertilizer! It had been unknown in China at the time she left. This meant the nation had a chemical industry now. Perhaps it was producing medicinal drugs as well.

As they passed through Hunan, the houses were no better

than they had been, but the people were better dressed, their clothes less faded and seldom patched. In this province Mao Tse-tung was born, the son of a prosperous farmer who tried to force the rebellious young man to be a country schoolteacher. Mao Tse-tung a country schoolteacher!

Ah, here were the cooperatives, doubtless! Groups of twenty or so men and women worked together in a wide field. Only in small plots did she see children working; these must be the bits of land allotted to families for their own use.

Another day, and the landscape changed to the red clay, bare hills and ancient villages of the next province. Barley was being threshed on village threshing floors. In the old days, she remembered, many birds flew above the threshing floors, bold in pursuit of the grain. They had been killed on government orders, and too late this government had discovered that without the birds, insects became rampant.

Suddenly she saw the great bridge at Wuhan. She opened the window and looked out. The bridge stood upon eight piers and had three levels—the train tracks, above them a roadway for trucks and buses, and a walkway above that. Slowly, slowly the train crept across the mile-long span. As she gazed on the vast river two or three hundred feet below her, she felt a great pride in her own people. If they could build this bridge, was there anything they could not do?

After a three-day trip down the great river, she stood at last before her mother's gate, her guide, as always, a silent though courteous presence. She dreaded the meeting with her mother and at the same time she eagerly longed for it. Would she find her aged and changed?

"Does my mother know we are coming?" she had asked.

"Assuredly she does," her guide had replied. "Everything is prepared and in order." The mild, colorless little man had been with her now for days, and though he had disappeared once in a while, when she had so much as turned her head, he was there again. Apparently he had orders to watch her every movement.

He knocked on the gate and it was opened by the gateman, a slim old man with bent shoulders. They followed him to the house, where a younger servant in the usual blue cotton suit bowed his head in invitation. "Please enter." In the old days he would have called her "young mistress."

This servant led the way through a square entrance hall, strange to her since she had only once or twice visited the Brandons in Shanghai. Then he opened a door.

"She has come," he announced.

MADAME LIANG was sitting in her drawing room in a large carved wooden chair. Her eyes had been fixed on the door for the last ten minutes. She had been told the exact hour when her daughter would arrive, and she did not doubt that at the stated moment the door would open and Grace would be there. Now she saw a tall young woman, very slim and wearing a soft gray suit. The face was strong and resolute, the dark hair short and slightly curled, the dark eyes calm.

"Mother," Grace said in a low voice.

Madame Liang rose and stood waiting, her eyes upon the guide, who took two steps forward. "Comrade Liang, according to instructions, I have delivered your eldest daughter. Please confirm!"

"I will confirm," Madame Liang said.

He made a short bow, then turned to Grace and said, "In three days I shall return for your journey to the capital." He left the room, the servant closed the door, and mother and daughter were alone.

"Mother," Grace said again. Her impulse was to throw her arms about her mother, and yet she hesitated. Madame Liang moved forward and took her hand, gazing into her daughter's eyes.

"You have scarcely changed, Mother," Grace said. "I think you are a little thinner."

"I am growing old," Madame Liang replied. She drew her daughter to a sofa and they sat looking at each other. At last

Madame Liang spoke. "I want you to know that I forgive them everything."

"Mother," Grace cried, "what do you mean? Whom do you forgive?" It occurred to her now that her mother was not well. And they were speaking in English, she suddenly noticed. Never had they done so in the old days. When her mother did not reply, she asked, "Why are we speaking in English?"

"It is safer," Madame Liang said. But she began to speak in Chinese. "You must be weary. On the train, on the ship, how do I know what hardships you suffered?"

Grace replied in Chinese, not so easily after the years of harsh English. "I have been well treated. My guide saw to that."

"Ah, doubtless," Madame Liang replied. "It was his duty. Let us go to your room." She rose and led her daughter by the hand up the great staircase to the second floor.

"I have put you in the room next to mine. One never knows," Madame Liang said vaguely. "Sometimes there are noises in the night—street noises. It is better not to open the window."

Suddenly her vagueness melted away. "Refresh yourself, my child, then come to my room. Tonight I do not go down to my restaurant. Instead our meal will be served in the sitting room adjoining my bedroom. We will talk. Two days will not suffice for all we have to ask and to tell."

The two women looked at each other with searching eyes, then embraced. In her arms the daughter felt the slight and delicate frame of her mother, while the mother felt the strong tall shape of her daughter. Each knew an instinctive trust in the other.

Their meal was served by Chou Ma, dishes chosen from the restaurant by Madame Liang herself, and Grace declared that she had not eaten such food since she was last in Shanghai.

When the dishes had been removed, Grace said in English, "Mother, what did you mean when you spoke of forgiveness?"

The room was quiet, the doors were bolted, the windows

closed. There was something rare, even precious, in the atmosphere of the small room, and to it her mother lent her own grace. None of the daughters had the full measure of Madame Liang's beauty. Somehow Grace had not expected to see her mother still exquisite.

"I should have to go very far back in years to answer your question," Madame Liang replied. She lit a fragrant cigarette. "I forgive my people," she said slowly, "first, because they are trying very hard to achieve stability; and second, because all that they do and feel and say is the result of history."

Madame Liang smoked thoughtfully while her daughter watched her beautiful wise face. "I will pluck out the heart of the matter," she said. "Through our thousands of years, our weakness has been our pride. We believed, and still believe, that we are the superior race, that our civilization is above any other. While other nations flourished and passed away, our nation continued, the center of all. We knew this, and that certainty has been our undoing. We could not believe that the time had come for us to change because a new power had come to mankind. It is the power of science, first manifested in new weapons. This science was our undoing, and all the wisdom of Confucius could not save us."

Madame Liang looked her daughter full in the eyes. "Our fault was that we put our faith above all else in the wisdom of our good men. Not to kill, but to create, they taught us, was the basis of continuing life. To behave toward others as we would have them behave toward us. Then our good men failed us."

"What do you mean, Mother?"

"They did not see that even the good and the wise are at the mercy of the man who carries the weapon. The old teachings failed, not because they were wrong, but because the world around us was barbarian. Must we become barbarous in order to live?"

She lit another cigarette, the great jade ring on her left forefinger gleaming in the light of the flame. "Yet, even so, we might have prevailed if events in history had not combined against us. I sent you and your sisters far from your own country because I foresaw the combination of events that would bring disaster to our people. I wished you to survive."

"What events, M-ma?" her daughter inquired.

Madame Liang laid her cigarette on the ashtray in order to count upon her fingers. "First, our country was approaching the natural end of a dynasty. The old empress dowager was near death and without an heir. At such times our country always breaks into sections, each section headed by a strong young man, upheld by his own army. One of these men wins over his rivals and becomes the first emperor of the new dynasty—a healthy process, for he is a man of the people and a proven natural leader. But second, suddenly there was no throne upon which such a victor could sit. What confusion, therefore! And why was there no throne?"

Here she put forth a third finger. "Because a young Christian, Sun Yat-sen, and his followers had overthrown the very structure of our government! Your father was his friend and I was his follower, among thousands of the young. We dreamed of a new country, strong enough to hold back the greedy Western people who coveted our land. And family tradition and our age-old civil service kept our people steady while we made the change."

"But why throw away all the past?" her daughter asked.

Madame Liang showed impatience. "Because it was the only way we could take power, or so we thought. We had all been educated in the Christian schools in the West, and our young men could not pass the ancient imperial examinations, from which our civil administrators were always chosen. I see now how wise were those tests, which discovered for our people the quickest and cleverest minds. Did you know that England based her civil service upon ours? And that the Americans took their civil service plan from England, and so from us?"

"Mother, how could I know? I have not studied these matters," Grace said.

"Ah, but I have! What we did not realize was that the people create out of themselves and their own needs the type of government that can ensure peace and order. How, then, could we young dreamers borrow a government from the West? Our people did not accept what we discovered, though for ten long years we struggled to persuade them.

"Alas, in those ten years the Russians destroyed their government and set up another, frail and unsteady, but a structure. And we were in chaos and our leader, Sun Yat-sen, was in despair. Though we had known for centuries that the Russians had designs upon us, we needed to believe, and we who were young believed their young. 'Let us help you,' they said and came with advisers and weapons—and here they are.

"I have led you too hastily, for the Japanese attack came upon us earlier, and the defection of the Nationalists. But you can see the coming together of these mighty events. And meanwhile, two great world wars had weakened the Western powers and hastened the independence of their colonies here in the East, increasing the turmoil. And so we dreamed of the rise of Asia, with ourselves as the leaders, as we had been in the past."

Madame Liang had continued to count off one finger and another until she had arrived at her thumb, and her daughter marveled at the swift clarity of her mind.

"So here we are now," Madame Liang went on. "And without hope of other leaders, our people have lent themselves with whole heart to the new effort. But the real revolution must take place in the hearts of the people. In a few years we are trying to change the thoughts, the habits, the principles of centuries—to make a new people out of the oldest in the world. They are good people, but desperate, for all roads save this one have been destroyed." She looked up. "Tell me," she said, "did you hear any Americans say why they will not have us in their United Nations?"

Grace answered as best she could. "M-ma, it is because they think we are an aggressor nation."

Madame Liang was shocked. "We? But we have fought no aggressive wars in two thousand years!"

"It was because of Korea, M-ma. We sent a volunteer army."

"But that was our duty! Korea is one of our tributary nations and has been for many centuries. It was our responsibility, always, to send a volunteer army if any of our tributary nations was attacked by a foreign power."

"They don't know that."

"Do they not read our history?"

"No, M-ma, I don't think so."

Madame Liang looked astonished and shook her head and murmured, "The Americans—our friends—" To her daughter's shock, she began to sob softly.

"M-ma!" Grace cried. "M-ma, why do you weep?" She knelt beside her mother and wiped her pale cheeks with her handkerchief.

Madame Liang tried to laugh. She said unsteadily, "Very foolish, for I have nothing to weep about—except, somehow, everything!"

"You are tired, M-ma. This day has been an excitement for you, and you have been alone too long. I blame myself. I wish I could stay with you. I will ask—"

"No, no," her mother said hastily. "In fact, it is better for me if you ask no favors. You are needed elsewhere. One must think of our people now—not of a single person."

She seemed so alarmed that her daughter said no more. But why was she alarmed? Grace wondered.

III

"EXCEPT THAT you are living in the Brandons' house, Mother," Grace said, "I could imagine that nothing is changed."

They were sitting at breakfast in a small pleasant room that faced south toward the garden, where chrysanthemums bloomed amid the calm of autumn. Here Chou Ma brought their bowls of rice congee and the appetizers of salt fish and salted duck eggs and a dozen other traditional small dishes.

"Yet everything is changed," Madame Liang replied. She took a small fish delicately between her chopsticks and put it into her congee. "Everything in America is changed also."

Grace looked up surprised. "Why do you say so, Mother?"

"We are told of their poverty and strikes and the revolution of the black serfs! I feel sad for the Brandons. They must think with regret of this house in which they were so happy."

Grace put down her chopsticks. "Mother, what are you saying? The Brandons are very happy. They live in a beautiful house, bigger than this one, in San Francisco. Mr. Brandon is the president of a great bank in the city."

"Then I am deceived! So America is not changed?"

"Only for the better. The black people are asking for their rights and they are being given them—too slowly in some places, but surely. But such disturbance never touched me or my sisters."

Before Madame Liang could reply, the door opened and Chou Ma ushered in a tall Chinese man in a blue army uniform of fine English wool. He put out both hands and his voice, when he spoke, was rich and deep. "You are early risers, comrades! But you, Comrade Liang, are always filled with zeal for the day's work. And this is your eldest daughter?"

He spoke in smooth Mandarin, and Grace, rising to her feet, looked into his handsome oval face and recognized him from pictures as Chao Chung's chief aide. "Captain Li—"

He put up a graceful hand. "No—no—we have no titles now. Even officers in the army are simply 'comrade.' "

"You have breakfasted?" Madame Liang interposed.

"Yes, yes. I too rise early."

Madame Liang gestured to Chou Ma to clear the table.

Captain Li seated himself and beamed at Madame Liang and her daughter. "What a happy day for us all! We have waited for your return, Comrade Liang. Your laboratory awaits you. Your staff is ready. We have chosen some of our best young minds to work with you."

"I shall want to learn, too, and from my elders," Grace said.

An enigmatic expression flickered over his face. "They also wait to welcome you." He smiled.

Grace was aware of an uncertainty in his manner. His eyes did not meet hers frankly, his smile was too ready. Her mother, too, was behaving with constraint. Or was it merely the old-fashioned silence of a lady in the presence of a man?

"A full schedule has been prepared for you," Li was saying. "You will live at first in the hostel for those who enter from overseas—especially from America, where the people know nothing of what is taking place here. It will be necessary for you to empty your mind of all past concepts and prepare yourself for the new. Meanwhile you may begin by writing a full report of your recent work. Our experts will determine what is worth preserving."

She felt a slight indignation. "I can assure you that my work has been done under the most careful scientific—"

He put up his hand. "Comrade, it is useless for you to defend yourself. We proceed according to our own methods. I see it will take time for you to understand."

She looked at her mother, bewildered. The beautiful face was without expression. "Mother," she urged, "you understand I am not defending myself."

Madame Liang smiled. "As Comrade Li says, you need not."

For a moment Grace felt herself with two strangers.

"You have let her stay away too long," Captain Li said to her mother.

"Perhaps you are right," Madame Liang said.

He rose, glancing at the watch on his wrist. "If you will excuse me, I have an important appointment."

"Of course," Madame Liang said.

"TELL ME more about your sisters. You saw them just before you left America?" It was evening again, and mother and daughter were alone in Madame Liang's sitting room. It was a place of mixed decor. The floor was covered with a Peking rug of pale

417

green and rose. The furniture was Chinese except for two comfortable armchairs of rose velvet.

"Mrs. Brandon invited us to stay," Grace answered. "You know she has never forgotten you, but she thinks it better not to write."

"She is right," Madame Liang said.

"You really think so, M-ma? But why should—"

"Come, come—you and your sisters?"

"Yes, Mother. Since the Brandon children were all away at school, Mr. Brandon at the office and Mrs. Brandon here and there the way American ladies are, we had three long quiet days together. M-ma, my second sister wants to come home to China. Mercy is beginning to think that all loyal Chinese belong in their own country. Joy wants to see you, but I don't think she will leave America."

"Let them both stay where they are, unless they are summoned as you were," Madame Liang replied, and fear crept over her face like the shadow of a cloud.

That night Chou Ma entered Grace's room. "I came to see if your mosquito net was fastened."

"It is fastened," Grace replied. "I have not forgotten the mosquitoes of my childhood."

But Chou Ma was in no haste to leave. She came to the bed and lit the candle on the small blackwood table. "Eldest sister," she whispered, "has your honored mother told you of my troubles?"

Grace sat up and smoothed back her short hair. "We had many matters of which to speak."

"And I must not keep you from sleep," Chou Ma said.

"I am awake," Grace said. "If you do not tell me, I shall be sleepless with curiosity."

Chou Ma settled herself on a footstool, her face dark with woe. "I had a son," she said and closed her eyes, remembering. "He lived in the village of our ancestors with his wife and two sons, and had two acres of good land. Then the new people came down on our village like locusts and would not go away. They argued with my son's wife, a good woman but without words to answer them. They tempted her with descriptions of life in the communes, saying that every day she and her family would be given free food, which she need not even cook. And she persuaded my son to give himself and his wife and children, his land and ox, to the commune. Ah me, how can I tell you?" Chou Ma rocked back and forth on the footstool and wiped her eyes.

"What my silly daughter-in-law did not know was that in the commune husband and wife may come together for only one half hour every fourteen days. Then in a small room, with only a narrow bed, they—" Chou Ma coughed decently behind her hand.

"I understand," Grace said. "Tell on, good mother."

Chou Ma lowered her voice. "On the wall of each room hangs a big picture of Chairman Mao, and my son told me, 'M-ma, how could I so much as touch my wife's hand when he watched me with such eyes?' "

"Of course he could not," Grace said, suppressing a desire to laugh.

Chou Ma went on hoarsely. "Each time he met his wife he could not take her, and they became restless and quarrelsome. At last he said to her, 'I will get a small boat and we will cross the river into a foreign country and I will find work.' "

"A clever plan," said Grace, observing that Chou Ma expected a reply.

"A clever plan," Chou Ma agreed, "but by now my grandsons had come to believe all they were taught in school. Their mother led them toward the river one night, after telling them what their father planned. When the seven-year-old saw his father, he cried out loudly, 'Here is the traitor!' At this, comrades swarmed out from the bamboo and carried my son away—to what end, alas, I do not know!"

"What happened to the boy?" Grace asked, her heart racked with pity.

"Oh, him they made into a big hero," Chou Ma said. "The

boys and their mother are still in the commune—and she perhaps a widow!"

"I am glad you told me this sad tale," Grace replied. "I will remember it when others praise too much."

Chou Ma made no answer but stole away from Grace's room, weeping silently.

"Mother," Grace said the next morning at breakfast, "Chou Ma told me her story last night. Can it be true?"

Madame Liang glanced at the door. It was closed. "As she tells it, it is true for her. Another person might tell it in a different way. Chou Ma's son wished to remain an individual. But at this time it is not possible to be an individual. It may even be wrong."

Grace looked at her mother. "That doesn't sound like you."

They were still using English, in unspoken agreement that this was wise.

"Since I decided to remain here," Madame Liang replied, "I try to be an acceptable citizen. I love my country, whatever it is, and I am old enough to know that all things pass. What my people suffer, I will suffer. If I continue to live while they die, it is only because I still hope and I want them—and you—to share my hope." She fell silent, her lovely face suddenly aged.

"Then you didn't send us abroad just to escape?" Grace said.

"No," her mother replied. Madame Liang pressed her lips together. "The more our people suffer, the sooner they will learn what they do not want. We tried our way and it failed. Now these new people are trying another way. But is it the Eternal Way of which Lao-tzu spoke? That is what our people must discover for themselves."

Chou Ma appeared at the door. "Madame, Minister Chao is here," she said in a loud voice, conveying that he was, in fact, immediately behind her in the hall.

Madame Liang rose. "Ask him into the Lotus Room," she told Chou Ma. Then she turned to her daughter. "Will you excuse me?"

"Of course, Mother," Grace said.

The minister stood as Madame Liang entered the room. She bowed slightly and seated herself. Long ago she had learned not to begin a conversation with an official. She had almost learned to think of this man only as an official, except that a memory now flashed into her mind, a moment in Paris when she was on her way to a class at the university, the moment when she first saw him and recognized him as the handsomest man she had ever seen.

"Forgive me for coming too early," he began.

"You are not well," she said softly.

He smiled. "Do I betray myself? I have many burdens."

The man drew down his heavy black brows and began abruptly to speak in French. "You have not forgotten your French, madame? We studied it together in Paris, remember?"

"I forget nothing," she replied in the same language.

"Ah, then I proceed. Your daughter must be warned." He hesitated, glanced about the room and began to speak rapidly under his breath. "At least warn her that for a long time she must only listen. She has been in America for many years and she has learned to say what she thinks. Here there are certain—passwords, shall we say? She is too valuable to lose through—a mistake."

"I understand," she said.

They looked at one another, each remembering a day long ago when he had asked her to marry him. And she might have done so in those dreamlike days in Paris had she not accepted Cheng a few months before. She remembered very well standing by Chao's side under a plane tree, half sorry that she must refuse.

The memory made a bridge between them, for she had never forgotten that he had loved her. Nor could she deny that he still attracted her, with his energy, his sharp analytical mind, his grace of manner. Yet how implacable he was, how dangerous when he discovered a traitor!

He rose. "We understand each other, you and I—we always

have, I think. I would not have you grieve or live in anxiety. Prepare your daughter, comrade."

That night, therefore, the last before her daughter must set forth to Peking, Madame Liang called Grace to her private sitting room. "You must be ready to accept change," she began, "and you will be able to do so if you remember there is no change."

Grace laughed. "M-ma, don't be cryptic!"

"I mean exactly what I say," Madam Liang replied. She lay upon a couch, wearing a negligee of pale pink satin and high-heeled satin shoes of the same color. No one ever saw her feet except Chou Ma. Long ago, when she was five years old, in her father's absence at the imperial court, her mother had wound bands of strong white cotton about her tender feet, tightening them each day for months until she ceased to run about, grew thin and waxen pale. Then one day her father came home and found her sitting on her bed, stroking her wounded feet to ease the pain. What anger then! He had torn away the bandages himself, had wept when he saw the small mangled feet, and then, carrying her in his arms, he had burst into her mother's rooms.

"Did I not tell you to leave this child's feet as they were?"

Terrified, her mother had begged, "Consider, my children's father, who but some farmer will marry a girl with big feet? I do it for the child's future happiness."

This her father had utterly refused. "You will not see that our country is changing! Even I have changed. I wish *your* feet were not tortured stumps!"

Cruel words, for her mother had been proud of her own tiny feet, measuring no more than three inches. But to the child, her father's words brought only joy, for she was freed. To comfort herself now for her disfigured feet Madame Liang always wore exquisite shoes.

"You will be shocked by the changes," she went on. "And you will be rebellious, angry, frightened, unless you remember, steadfastly, that there is no real change."

"Teach me, Mother," Grace said.

"The change is this, my child. Eighty-five out of one hundred of our people are peasants. Those who controlled them are no more—the landlords, the gentry, the literate; people such as you and I sprang from are gone. Ah, what a dragon Chairman Mao has released! What cunning, what understanding of his own people! He is the son of country gentry, those who are called peasants by the literate and landlords by the illiterate, a between-man, one belonging to neither side and to both. But the dragon he rides, my child, will rid itself of the burden!"

Far into the night Madam Liang unrolled for her daughter the scrolls of history, and finally she concluded, "Yet if a ship is well managed, it will survive the turmoil of rough waters and proceed on its way. So it is with our country at this hour. I know that beneath the turmoil there is no change. Our people are what they have always been, the sons of Han, the superior people. Yes, though it is forbidden to speak the name of the great Confucius, I read his words in secret. I feed upon the ancient wisdom."

Her daughter had been listening quietly. Now she spoke. "Mother, how can you remain silent, how can you live as though you approve?"

Madame Liang rose, opened a locked chest and drew from it a book wrapped in a red silk cover. She read: " 'The superior person acts in accordance with the character that has become perfected in him. His is a way of life that can submit to scrutiny on any day. Being hidden means that he is still in concealment and not given recognition, that if he should act, he would not yet accomplish anything. In this case the superior person does not act.' "

She turned the pages and read again: " 'The superior person is inexhaustible in his will to teach, and without limits in his toleration and protection of the people.' "

She closed the book, wrapped it in the red silk cover and locked it again in the chest.

"YOU WILL stay here until you find a place to live that pleases you more," her new guide said. He was young and confident, yet there was about him an air of anxiety.

Grace looked around the room. It was large and decorated in a dull blue. "This looks very comfortable."

Her guide smiled widely. "Here is your bath." He opened a door with a flourish. "In winter, steam heat is provided. Now, since it is only autumn, heat is not necessary." He felt in the pocket of his blue cotton uniform and took out a slip of paper. "Here is the address of the Medical Institute. You are to report at ten o'clock tomorrow morning." Then he bowed abruptly and left her.

She went to the wide window and put aside the curtain. It was evening and Peking lay before her in a glowing map. Rising above the other buildings was one that was new to her—the Great Hall of the People, the guide had told her proudly. She had come to the city on one of the new trains, which had also been a cause for pride. Between stations the floors were always swept and the plush-cushioned seats brushed. At either end of the aisles pots of hardy ferns gave a garden air, and the polished tables shone. When the train stopped, vendors clustered about the exits and cried their wares, as they had done in the old days.

Ah, well, she thought as she looked from the window, I will not be living here for long. A few weeks, she had been told, must be spent in reorientation at the hostel. Then she would find among the low tiled roofs of the ancient city a small old house, walled behind a gate, with a flagstone courtyard and a lily pond, to which she would return at night after her day in her laboratory.

"Comrade," a lad at the door said, "where shall I put your bags?"

She turned. "Leave them, please. I will unpack them."

She opened her purse, but the lad frowned and put up a protesting hand. "It is not our custom now," he declared and marched out of the room, closing the door behind him.

Late that evening, after dinner in a bare, clean dining room, Grace sat down at the desk in her room and began the first of the letters she had promised to her research associate and close friend at Harvard.

"Clem: Outside my window here in Peking the past stands solidly. The Great Square of what was once the Forbidden City, where emperors lived with their imperial households, has been carefully restored. Judging from the little I've seen this first day, I should say that while my people are proud of the past, they take an equal pride in being completely modern. Tall buildings spring up here and there without contradicting the ancient architecture. . . ." She paused. Should she describe her brief visit to her mother? Somehow she hesitated. Finally she wrote: "My mother belongs to the past, yet she accepts the new with faith because the past has been so worthy of faith."

And then, in a sudden change of mood, she altered the scene in her mind. "At this hour, Clem, you are beginning another day—a day different from mine. I see you in the laboratory, working with a microscope and notebooks. Tell me everything, Clem! I love it here, but I'll be lonely— sometimes, anyway."

She slipped the sheet into an envelope, vaguely troubled. As a Chinese, she was too proud to tell even Clem that she was afraid, and, moreover, she did not know why she was afraid.

She was heartened to discover that the water ran hot into the tub and that the electricity, after a half minute of wavering, settled into serviceable light. Perhaps life in this new old country of hers would prove pleasant, after all, or at least comfortable enough to allay fear.

In precise, beautiful Mandarin, the old doctor intoned, "*Ma p'ien ts'ao* is one of two cures for malaria."

Grace opened her medical dictionary and found the English translation. She knew the herb, European verbena. "I have heard of it," she replied.

The old doctor looked surprised. She had already learned

that it was a waste of time to try to convince a Chinese doctor of the old school that Western medicine was of any value. The old doctor tugged at his sparse beard and proceeded. "The name of the disease differs in various parts of our country. It is called 'coldness entering the body,' 'the chill disease,' 'catching small chickens,' 'the venerable old gentleman,' 'the forever recurring,' 'heat enters body,' 'the fever-chill,' 'dumpling in belly,' 'three-day disease' and 'hundred-day disease.'"

She listened, marveling at the discernment in each name for the complex illness of malaria, the varying time schedule of chill and fever, even the description of the swollen spleen in the last stages as "dumpling in belly."

"The cause of the disease," the old doctor was saying, "is well known to be eels. Eels should be destroyed in epidemics of the disease." He scratched his head with a long fingernail and stared at it. "Lice again," he muttered and shook his forefinger in her face. "Do not trust foreign medicine for malaria," he said. "Too much of the foreign bitter powder causes heavy fever of another disease."

She was stunned at the accuracies and inaccuracies of the materia medica of her own country. Blackwater fever was indeed the result of too much quinine. How was she to combine these medical truths and falsehoods into some sort of relation to the science of the West?

It was her first day in the laboratory set aside for her in the great modern hospital that years ago had been the gift of wealthy Americans. The hospital was maintained with scrupulous attention to modern Western medical practice. Doctors and nurses were clad in spotless white uniforms. Yet the old physicians in their long robes were treated with deference.

She had been greeted that morning by a tall, handsome young man in the uniform of the Party. "I am Liu Peng," he had told her. "Also a doctor—a surgeon. You will get instructions from me. Your task is to provide a synthesis of our own medicine and that of the Western school. A great responsibility has been placed upon you by the Chairman himself. If you have questions, feel free to ask them of me." He had then introduced her to the old doctor. "Doctor Tseng, one of our most eminent physicians of the Chinese school."

Her thought was disturbed by a loud yawn from the old doctor, and his breath blew a foul gust to her nostrils. "Now let us talk of acupuncture," he was saying, "the science of the ducts in the human body. There are three hundred and sixty-five points in the body where the ducts rise to the skin. Skin, ducts and inner organs are one system, subject to the changes of yang and yin."

Soon, from a lifetime of Peking dust, he was clearing his throat and breathing with difficulty. He had spoken too long. Grace opened her handbag and produced a small bottle of an antihistamine she had brought with her from America. "Try this, honored doctor," she said.

He shook his head. "Two ways of life cannot be mingled, or the body becomes confused and yang and yin are put out of order." He closed his ancient book. "Acupuncture," he concluded, "cannot be taught in a day. We will continue tomorrow." And gathering his gray robes, he bowed and left her.

Grace walked out onto the hospital grounds. These, too, were scrupulously maintained. A faint haze hung over the city, and though the air was mild, there was a hint of chill beneath. She paused beside a pool where goldfish darted in the late afternoon sun like flashing splinters of gold. Contentment crept through her being. Autumn was a lovely season here in the ancient city. There was no reason for fear—no, not one. She had her work to do.

IV

AFTER A WHILE she left the hostel for her own house, her own, that is, by way of rent. When she had told Dr. Tseng of her wish to find an old Peking house, he had stroked his little beard thoughtfully. "The house next to mine in the Street of the Three Foxes is empty," he had said. "The owner died last week and the family has moved to a commune outside the city." She had gone with him to see it and with no trouble had arranged to move in.

She lingered now for an instant before the red gate, its double leaves hung with two heavy iron rings. Set in the surrounding wall, this gate was no different from those set in the walls on both sides of the narrow street. Yet it seemed special because it was the gate of her home in her own country. Feeling the deep contentment of every Chinese who returns to his own, she pushed the gate open and entered.

Someone had swept the courtyard and at the entrance to the house had set two porcelain jars, each containing a dwarf pine. The central room was furnished with old Chinese furniture of good quality. There she found an elderly servant couple waiting for her.

"At Doctor Tseng's command," the man murmured, bowing. "We are surnamed Wang."

"We can do everything," the woman added.

"Lao Wang and Wang Ma," Grace began, using the old honorifics suitable to their station. At once she saw by the look of fear upon their faces that she was wrong. "Comrades," she amended.

They smiled. The woman said coaxingly, "It is better for the willow to bend with the wind."

"I must learn to bend," Grace replied.

They disappeared into the kitchen and she sat down and surveyed the room. She must buy a few good scrolls for the walls, a landscape or two, and a comfortable chair. No curtains were needed for the windows, however, for their small panes were covered with fine rice paper.

Her thoughts were interrupted by a loud knock on the gate. Lao Wang ran across the courtyard to draw back the bar and she heard a strong male voice, which she at once recognized as that of Liu Peng. "I will come in," he was announcing.

She saw him stride across the courtyard ahead of Lao Wang.

"Please do come in," she said, rising to greet him. "You are my first guest."

"Why have you moved from the hostel without permission?" he demanded without greeting, seating himself in a wooden chair.

She opened her eyes wide as she sat down opposite him. "Must I have permission to move?"

"It is required," he said brusquely. "Otherwise how would we know where to find you?"

She considered this and decided to accept it with lightness. "Here I am! When I am not working at the medical center, I am here."

Suddenly he was cheerful. She even saw the glimmer of a smile in his unusually large black eyes. "Now that I have done my duty," he said, "let us next proceed to conversation. Has the old doctor given you the basic philosophy of our Chinese medicine?"

She shook her head. "Only specific illnesses and their remedies. He is teaching me now about acupuncture."

"Ah," Liu Peng said, "then I will instruct you, philosophically."

"Please teach me," she said.

It was the traditional reply of the classical pupil to a teacher, and he glanced at her suspiciously but proceeded.

"I will outline the basis of Chinese medical philosophy for you. You understand, of course, that while we reject the ancient mysteries, we continue to accept them as part of dead history. Let us proceed therefore with the classical work of the great sage Lao-tzu, a man most strangely modern though he lived thousands of years ago and whose philosophy opposed the formalism of his contemporary, Confucius. He, Confucius, is truly dead, and with him his works. We reject him because he imprisoned our people within his rigidity. Lao-tzu, on the contrary, set forth the flexible principles of Tao, or 'spirit'— the spirit that permeates all heaven and all earth. Tao includes all that is not, and all that is. Lao-tzu describes it this way."

Liu Peng brushed back his short stiff hair, placed his hands outspread on his knees, and lifting his head, he closed his eyes and began to chant, as scholars do, the ancient poem of *Tao Tê Ching*:

> "Silent, aloof, alone,
> It changes not, nor fails, but touches all. . . .
> I call it—Tao.
> Tao means Outgoing.
> Outgoing, Far-reaching.
> Far-reaching, Return."

Liu Peng paused to stare at Grace, as if he had asked a question.

"Beautiful," she murmured, "but I do not understand it."

"And why can you not understand it? Because it contains all that exists within the harmony of balance. What is this harmony? It is contained within the correspondences. And what are the correspondences? The relationships between the five elements: wood, fire, earth, metal, water. These create; they also destroy each other."

He paused, his eyes inquiring again, and promptly she replied, "Explain, please."

He proceeded. "On the side of creation, wood creates fire; fire, as ash, creates earth. In earth there is metal; metal melts to become liquid. Water creates trees—or wood. On the side of destruction, wood consumes water through trees, earth can stop water, water destroys fire, fire destroys metal, but metal in an instrument destroys wood. These are correspondences, outgoing, far-reaching; and far-reaching, they return. Within this circle of creation and destruction man must live harmoniously, in tune with all that exists. This is the fundamental philosophy of the cosmos upon which our Chinese medical lore is based."

"It is difficult to base diagnosis and prescription upon this," she murmured.

At this moment Wang Ma, as Grace would always think of

her, appeared with teapot and bowls. "Honorable comrade," she addressed Liu Peng, "you have talked yourself dry. Please drink tea."

He frowned at her even as he accepted the bowl. "Leave off the 'honorable'! It is forbidden by the new regulations," he said with sharpness.

Wang Ma looked frightened. "Forgive this old stupid! I forgot."

"Then remember," Liu Peng said.

So sharply did he speak that Grace was moved to defend the old woman. "Is it a new correspondence that she has broken, perhaps?"

He caught the sarcasm and a flush rose under the tan skin of his cheeks. "The task of teaching peasants is endless, but everyone, however ignorant, must learn the New Way."

"But is it the Eternal Way?" she inquired slyly.

The question was so impudent, so mischievous, that for a while he did not deign to answer. He set the bowl upon a small two-tiered table at his side and sat frowning and deep in thought. Suddenly he rose and looked her straight in the eyes. "All I have told you is nonsense," he said harshly, and without further word he stalked out of the room and across the courtyard.

It was her first night in the house, and Grace felt a strange foreboding permeate her spirit. After barring her bedroom door, she sat at a table to write a letter to her sister Mercy. Before she put pen to paper, she closed her eyes until she saw her sister clearly, the slim tall figure in the straight Chinese dress, the smooth black hair hanging to her shoulders, the vivid dark eyes, the fresh young color of her skin. Then she began to write.

"Dearest of Sisters: I am now living in a small old house of my own, with two old servants. . . ." She wrote on for an hour, becoming more cheerful as she described her comfortable house and her pleasure in her work, and then put the letter in its envelope. San Francisco—how far away it seemed.

I am being foolish, she told herself. I have not been here long enough. When I get answers to my letters, when Clem writes to me—and she pictured Clem peering through a microscope in the laboratory, the sun glinting on his red hair. O Clem, write to me! I am so far away—

THE SUN was setting in the western sky beyond the Golden Gate Bridge in San Francisco. Mercy Liang leaned against the railing, watching the last rim of gold, and close at her side John Sung was talking. "Hush," she said. "This is the moment. When the sun disappears, it will be rising over our own country."

Silently, they watched the last glimmer of gold sink into the sea, while above the water the white clouds turned to rose. She sighed. "John, we must go back to China!"

He did not reply at once. It was an old argument, yet one upon which in essence they agreed. He was a nuclear physicist, and his country needed him, but he had not been permitted to go to China. "I've been talking again to my senior at the installation, but he gives no hope." He spoke Chinese in a low voice, glancing over his shoulder at the few people passing.

"I had a letter today from my sister in Peking," Mercy told him. "All goes well with her. She saw our mother in Shanghai. She is living quite comfortably in spite of—everything. I want to go home, John. It will not be good for our children to have been born American citizens if we do eventually go back to China."

He smiled at her. A lovely face, he thought. And he loved her, her impulsive heart, her quick speech, her tall slender body. "First we must marry," he reminded her teasingly.

She responded with vigor. "John, you find every time we meet a new way to make me change our wedding date. On the tenth of May we marry. Mr. and Mrs. Brandon are preparing for our wedding on that day."

"Months to wait," he sighed.

"It will give you time to be released from your contract."

"I may not be able to get a release, remember."

"Then we could go to England, and not come back! The Americans have no right to say you may not return to your own people!"

"They don't say that. They are simply working on my clearance before I go into secret areas of nuclear physics."

"You told me yourself that was an excuse. They don't want you to go back to China and work there in nuclear physics!"

"I said I *suspected* that was the reason."

"You know it *is* the reason!"

Passersby glanced at them curiously, and these glances quieted the two. They turned away from the sea and sky and walked to where John's car was parked. In half-angry silence he drove her back to the Brandons' house, where she was staying. For a moment their hands clung. "Tomorrow?" he asked.

"Tomorrow," she said.

They parted, and she went into the house. Mrs. Brandon was in the living room arranging a bowl of roses on a low table. "John isn't staying for dinner?" she asked as Mercy entered.

"I didn't ask him," Mercy replied, sitting down on the edge of a white velvet chair. "We had a—we had something of a' quarrel."

"Did you now?" Mrs. Brandon murmured. She waited but the girl did not go on. "You can't say that much and not tell me what you quarreled about," Mrs. Brandon said in her direct American fashion. "I take your mother's place, you know."

"I want to go back to China, Mrs. Brandon, and John says he won't be allowed."

"Probably not—a top young scientist!"

"Then he should go anyway."

"Against the government?"

"It's not our government!"

Mrs. Brandon left the roses and turned toward the girl. "My dear, that's not very gracious of you. Your mother would never speak like that."

"My mother is an old-fashioned Chinese woman. I am not."
Mrs. Brandon stared at the defiant girl. She returned to her
roses without reply, and Mercy rose and left the room.

That night after dinner when Mercy had excused herself to
write letters, Mrs. Brandon recounted the conversation to her
husband. "It's really not like Mercy to speak so—so belliger-
ently."

"John is a fine man," Mr. Brandon said. "He will do what he
thinks is right. I wouldn't worry. And he'll never be allowed to
go back to China—not under present circumstances."

The affairs of men and governments were beyond Mrs.
Brandon's concern. She fell to thinking about the wedding she
had promised to give the young Chinese couple.

"Where will you go on your honeymoon, dear?" she asked
Mercy the next morning at breakfast.

The girl, looking as pretty as a half-opened rosebud, Mrs.
Brandon thought, replied in innocence. "I would like to go to
England. And John wants to visit some great English scientists." She laughed sweetly. "Even on our honeymoon, I think
he will be a scientist first!"

"The child seems herself today," Mrs. Brandon reported to
her husband that night, "and they're going to England for
their honeymoon."

Mr. Brandon looked up from his magazine. "Hm," he
grunted, "that's odd. The Communist Chinese have an embassy
in London."

"Oh, you like to put two and two together," Mrs. Brandon
said.

"Well, I usually make four, don't I?"

"I suppose so," she said absently.

SIX MONTHS and some days later, Mercy and her husband,
John Sung, were received into an ornate private office in
the Chinese embassy in London. A handsome man in a severe
dark uniform sat behind a vast desk at one end of the immense room.

"I have," he said in meticulously accented Chinese, "already communicated with the authorities in our capital. A special plane will convey you, Doctor and Mrs. Sung, to Peking. There you will be welcomed suitably and assigned to your posts."

"I also?" Mercy inquired.

"You also," the official said gravely. "I suggest that you consider the founding of a new school of music in Peking. We have many new folk songs created by our young people. They should be compiled and written down. To you, Doctor Sung, I would like to say that you return to our country at an opportune time. Our scientists are devising a new hydrogen bomb, of a force superior to any yet known."

"A bomb?" John Sung repeated. "My field is industrial nuclear physics rather than military."

"Industry is useless if it is at the mercy of a voracious Western power such as the United States."

If the official noticed that his guests did not reply, he made no sign. He continued stamping some papers with a large red seal.

In the jet aircraft that night, when the lights were dimmed for sleep, Mercy reached for her husband's hand.

"I'm excited," she said. "Or perhaps afraid."

"Afraid?"

"Well, I know it won't be the same country in which I grew up. My mother's letters are so—strange. So much alike—and once in a year or two a few lines tucked into a gift saying that I am to stay in America. Oh, what will the Brandons think when we don't come back? We'll write letters and explain . . ."

Now that they were beyond return, John Sung felt a chill in his heart. He had left China as a boy with his father, who was the younger brother of a merchant in San Francisco's Chinatown. There John had grown up, dependent on his uncle after his father died. He had not told even his uncle that they were going home to China. For wherever its people wandered the earth, China was forever home.

He fell into a weary sleep, and Mercy slipped her hand from his. Let him sleep, though she could not! There had been no time since the wedding—a beautiful wedding, she thought tenderly, remembering the flower-filled rooms alive with warmhearted generous people. It was impossible to believe that friendship was dead between such people and her own. She glanced tenderly at John. His handsome face looked younger than his twenty-seven years.

"The most brilliant of our young scientists," his employer had said at the wedding. "I predict a great future for him, Mrs. Sung."

The jet trembled slightly and John awakened. They sat silently, their hands clasped, as the aircraft flew across the dark sky—eastward.

MADAME LIANG was in the restaurant when Chu San, her trusted business manager, signaled to her that he had a matter of importance for her attention. Gracefully she drifted out of the room and met him in the small private elevator that Mr. Brandon had installed years ago for his mother, who was crippled by arthritis.

Chu San touched a button and the elevator stopped midway between the first and second floors. Now he could speak without fear of eavesdroppers. "I have just overheard in one of the private dining rooms that the eminent young Chinese scientist Doctor John Sung and his wife have escaped from the United States and are now in Peking."

"Well?"

"His wife is madame's second daughter."

"No!"

"Madame did not know?"

"Not that they were married."

"Madame's letters are being intercepted."

"All letters are intercepted," she said impatiently. "My eldest daughter has not told me that my second daughter has left the United States. If I am not told everything, how can I act wisely? I must leave at once for Peking. You will go with me." She paused and then added, with effort, "By air."

"Madame!" he cried in pity, knowing how much she disliked the modern way of travel.

"No, it is necessary," she insisted. "Tell Chou Ma to pack my bags immediately."

In her eldest daughter's house in Peking, where Mercy and her husband were now living, Madame Liang was seated in the place of honor by the central table. "Because of the servants we will speak in English," she began, addressing her second daughter. "Explain to me why I was not informed."

Mercy answered, half apologetically, "M-ma, we were not sure whether we should come home. John had a good job in America. But we realized that after our marriage, if we had children there, they would be American citizens. It was confusing to me to think that I would give birth to American citizens."

Here John Sung interrupted. "Moreover, I felt that I should contribute to our own country. We need scientists. So we went to England—and just kept traveling eastward."

"Under the protection of our own authorities?" Madame Liang asked.

"Yes," John Sung said bluntly.

She surveyed this first son-in-law of hers. What she saw did not displease her. Tall, handsome enough, an open honest look, direct speech. "I appreciate your patriotism," she said, "but you must also have patience, now that you are here."

The next few days passed in hours of curious contrast. In the evenings the family took their evening meal, waited upon by the servants, as they had been before the great change. In the daytime Grace went to the hospital and continued her studies with the old doctor, while Madame Liang discussed many subjects with Mercy and John. She was especially curious about the Americans nowadays and put many questions to her daughter and son-in-law about them. "Is it possible," she said at last, "that they do not know the injustice they have done us?"

"What injustice, M-ma?" Mercy asked. Now that she was in her own country, she was in a bloom of happiness. She rejoiced that she and John had left America immediately after their marriage so that her first child would be born here in the land of his ancestors, now also the land of their future.

"I mean," her mother was saying, "that the Americans, in breaking off communications after the great change, have violated the law of friendship. For a century the Americans were our only friends in the West. They alone seized no territory of ours, nor made war against us, nor demanded indemnities. Indeed, they modified the demands of others. Yet it seems that they do not value the ancient bond of friendship." She turned to her son-in-law. "Do you understand what I am saying, or have you lived too long among Americans?"

"You are right. I have lived too long among them," John Sung said honestly.

"Then I will explain to you," Madame Liang replied. "An honorable heart does not cast aside a friend because he is in trouble, not even if he changes his nature and becomes a criminal. Between two nations friendship must also be eternal, else the friend is false. What was our crime against the Americans? Is it a crime to change a government? Because of this lack of reason on their part, our love for Americans has changed to hate. I fear for the future! A generation is growing up here that has never seen an American face or heard an American voice. What do they know of Americans except to hate them as they are taught? There is no hate so dangerous as that which once was love."

John Sung listened with the utmost attention, and then he said, "To the Americans, communism is a crime. They will have none of it."

"But why?" Madame Liang asked with true wonder.

John Sung replied thoughtfully. "I suppose because of their own history. Their ancestors fled from Europe to escape tyranny. Freedom was their dream. To them tyranny is endemic in communism. It is not the Chinese they hate. It is the tyranny they imagine."

"Imagine!" Madame Liang repeated. She shook her head. She looked east and west, and then she changed the subject.

Three days later Madame Liang returned to Shanghai.

WINTER WAS melting into spring and Grace had progressed from listening to practice. She attended the clinic several times a week and observed Dr. Tseng's methods. On a certain morning Minister Chao Chung entered the doctor's office. He wore his usual dark blue uniform, and though he looked somewhat pale, he gave his customary smile.

"Ah, Doctor Liang, I offer myself as a patient this morning." He sat down and addressed himself to the old doctor. "Doctor Tseng, I come to you to report that I have felt unusually tired for several days and I have not wanted to eat."

"Allow me to see your tongue," Dr. Tseng requested.

Chao Chung put out his tongue and the doctor gazed at it for a long time. "Now let me feel the pulse in your left hand." Chao Chung put out his left hand. Dr. Tseng took the wrist in his right hand and turned to Grace. "Observe how I press my fourth finger here where the palm parts from the wrist, placing my first and third fingers next to it. I will examine the three pulses here, first pressing lightly, then with medium force, then very deeply." After a long time he spoke again. "Comrade Chao, please extend your right hand."

Altogether his examination took nearly an hour. Then he gave his diagnosis. "You have slowed the rhythm of your heart by fatigue. Rest for three days, and do not use your eyes. I will give you a light treatment of acupuncture and you will feel better."

Chao Chung lowered his jacket from his shoulder and the doctor thrust a needle into two points, one to the left, the other to the right of the nape of his neck.

"I feel better already," Chao Chung declared as he buttoned his jacket.

"It is because the balance between yang and yin is restored," Dr. Tseng told him. He turned to Grace. "I will discourse this morning upon the subject of yang and yin."

Chao Chung paused at the door. "By the way, Doctor Liang," he said, "your brother-in-law—have you influence with him?"

Grace smiled. "No, but my sister has."

Chao Chung hesitated. "We are having some difficulty with him now that his period of tutelage is over. He is reluctant to carry out certain instructions."

"I know nothing about this."

"Naturally! Since he is working in areas where secrecy is essential, you would hear nothing. Tell your sister that he must not be too individualistic."

"But will she understand?"

"*He* will understand," Chao Chung said. He raised his right hand in a gesture of farewell and left the room.

Grace, however, did not understand, and felt his words burning into her brain even as Dr. Tseng's droning voice expounded upon yang and yin.

"You will learn from this ancient book, written three thousand years ago, that there are two kinds of blood in the human body. One is controlled by yin, the principle of darkness, and the other by yang, the principle of light. These two work together, in balance."

She began to listen, for what was this double blood but the discovery, centuries ago, of the blood in the veins and the blood in the arteries? No wonder hers were a proud people!

When Grace reached home at dusk, Mercy met her in the courtyard, smiling with some secret happiness. She locked her fingers with her sister's right hand. "I went to a doctor today, and I have happiness within me!" Mercy said triumphantly, using the old Chinese phrase.

"O fortunate sister!" Grace cried, embracing her.

In the excitement Grace forgot the morning's conversation with Chao Chung until the evening meal was over and she and Mercy were alone in the central room. John had excused himself. He had eaten less than usual and Mercy had been concerned. "I wonder if he doesn't feel well," she had exclaimed.

"Ah, I'd forgotten," Grace cried, and then repeated Chao Chung's admonition. Mercy listened and was troubled.

"What does he mean by individualistic?" she asked. Her large dark eyes were so childlike that her sister was touched.

"He said my brother-in-law would understand," Grace replied.

When she was alone with her husband Mercy repeated what Grace had told her. "Do you understand?" she asked.

"Yes," John said bluntly.

Mercy pressed him gently. "Will you explain to me, darling?"

They spoke in English, as they did whenever they were alone in the night, because the Chinese language did not contain the words of love they needed for communication. But now, in the darkness, she heard sharpness in his voice. "I am a scientist and I have a conscience about my work. Chao Chung is a politician and he thinks only of government and how to achieve its goals. We disagree, that is all."

Suddenly she was afraid. "But, darling, do you think you should disagree so soon—and with so powerful a minister?"

He bit back his reply and did not answer at once. Let her not be made unhappy on this day! It occurred to him that he had no right to make her afraid. And should he put this new life in danger in order to maintain freedom for himself, a dedicated scientist?

"Let us be happy," he said at last. "We have so much to make us happy." He held her close until she was comforted, but he lay awake for a long time. He knew very well what Chao Chung had meant when he had accused him of being individualistic.

He had been summoned early in the morning to the minister's inner private office, a room with soundproof walls and a double-thick door. Chao Chung had been sitting behind a huge desk of heavy blackwood, with Captain Li on his right. It was the first time John Sung had been summoned into the official presence and he had felt vaguely afraid.

"Sit down," Chao Chung had commanded, without his usual smile. John Sung had seated himself in a side chair while his superior studied some papers.

"In reviewing the military possibilities of the future," Chao Chung began suddenly, fixing his intense black eyes upon his subordinate, "it is a question of how we should be prepared to destroy the enemy in case of attack."

John Sung waited. What enemy? What attack?

Chao Chung continued. "We have, it is true, the world's greatest expert in rocketry in charge of our nuclear development, thanks to the foolishness of the American senator Joseph McCarthy some years ago. After five years of waiting, Doctor Tsien was not cleared as a scientist in the United States, and in disgust he returned here.

"However, our military experts agree that pending the full development of our nuclear weapons, we should protect ourselves by more subtle methods. Germs of some sort, or drugs—something that could be used imperceptibly but with deadly effect." The heavy black eyebrows shot up above the questioning black eyes.

John Sung stared steadily back. "Please proceed," he said.

"My own suggestion," Chao Chung said, "is a radioactive poison, poured secretly into the sources of water supply." He unfolded before him a large map. "Here are the sources of the water supply of the United States. It could be done so easily—beautiful, isn't it?" He looked up at John Sung, his face brightening.

"It could be done, of course," John Sung said, aware of his heart thumping in his breast. "But I hope that none of these methods will ever be necessary. There is honor even in war."

To his surprise Chao Chung slapped the desk loudly with both hands. "You have been too long in the decadent West!" he shouted. "There war is a game, with rules, romance, glory, pity for prisoners—all nonsense! War is for one purpose only—to kill the enemy. He who kills first wins victory—the first and the most!"

He was so angry that he leaped from his chair and walked back and forth across the floor. "We hate war! We Chinese are too civilized, too realistic to imagine war is a game! Did not the ancient emperors forbid the use of gunpowder, our own invention, in weapons because such weapons would destroy many innocent people? Centuries ago we understood the principles of rocketry, but an emperor forbade its development, lest weapons so devised kill innocent humanity! Did we create the first atomic bomb and drop it on a city? Did we devise poisonous gas and noxious germs to use in warfare? We, who for centuries have believed war to be utterly despicable and soldiers to be the lowest of criminals, are now compelled in self-defense—" He broke off, choked by rage. Suddenly he stopped at John Sung's side and leaned over him, eyes burning, voice hissing. "Do you know how to make this radioactive poison for the water sources of an enemy?"

John Sung gazed unflinchingly into those furious eyes. "Yes," he said, "I know how to make it." Then quickly, to prevent the command, he added, "But I will not."

Chao Chung bit his lip, restraining himself. It was too soon. This man was still new to his own country. He must be changed before he could be obedient.

"You are too individualistic," he declared abruptly and motioned to Captain Li to lead John Sung from the room.

V

"FRESH TADPOLES coming out in the spring should be washed clean in cold well water and swallowed whole three or four days after menstruation. If a woman swallows fourteen live tadpoles on the first day and ten more on the following day, she will not conceive for five years. She can repeat the formula twice, and be forever sterile. . . . This formula is effective, safe and not expensive. The defect is that it can be used only in the spring."

Grace put down the notes she was studying and laughed.

"Why do you laugh?" Mercy inquired.

It was now late spring and the sisters were sitting under a spreading date tree in the courtyard. Mercy was sewing on a small red satin jacket for her coming child.

"I am reading a formula for birth control," Grace replied, and she read the paragraph aloud. Mercy listened, unbelieving.

"But it's nonsense, isn't it?" she exclaimed.

"It's disconcerting, but it may not be nonsense," her sister said. "That is the amazing fact about our ancient medicines. One thinks them absurd—but more often than not there's an element of truth."

"Tadpoles?" Mercy made a grimace of disgust. "I prefer to follow the Chairman's direction. He said he hoped our people would realize that it is an asset to number seven hundred million. A large population is a good thing, he said."

"And you proceed to add to it," Grace said, teasing.

"I'm proud of it," her sister retorted. She held up the tiny jacket. "I hope it's a boy. I want to be a good Chinese wife. And I don't believe in birth control! It's a means of killing the Chinese people without shedding blood."

"You've been reading my old file of *The People's Daily*," Grace said, referring to the official Communist Party newspaper.

"Well, so I have," Mercy retorted. "I've been away so long, and there was no way of finding out anything while we were in America. Why don't the Americans want to know about us?"

"They are afraid of us," Grace said.

"But we've always been friends. I can't imagine the Americans I knew wanting to act like imperialists," Mercy said. She put down her sewing and leaned back in her rattan chair. It was late afternoon. The midday heat had subsided and the evening coolness was stealing in upon the wings of a slight breeze.

"They wouldn't, of course," Grace answered. "But they

have not yet created a way for themselves—the Eternal Way that our mother speaks of so often."

"Is ours the Eternal Way?" her sister asked.

"I don't know," Grace replied slowly. "I just don't know."

"Because, if it isn't," Mercy went on, "then we are lost, John and I. We have staked our lives, and the life of our child, on the faith that ours is the Eternal Way." She folded the small red jacket. "Come, let us go into the house. It is growing dark."

John would soon be home and Mercy wanted every comfort ready for him. For she had discerned, some weeks ago, a dark mood descending on him. The enthusiasm of his return seemed to be fading, though he was as resolute as ever. He rose early every morning and, after a quick breakfast, went off to work. But he never spoke of his work, and if she questioned him, he gave her vague answers. She supposed that he must be working on secret projects.

When John Sung came home that evening he found hot tea waiting, his bath ready and fresh clothes laid out. He sat down in a low chair in their room and closed his eyes.

"You are tired," Mercy said solicitously.

"Very tired," he agreed somberly.

"Drink your tea, darling." Mercy poured as she spoke.

He lifted the bowl and drank it half empty. Mercy watched his pale face. He had closed his eyes again and she thought she saw a tremor on his lips. Suddenly she was afraid. He was troubled or in trouble. Why would he not tell her that much at least? She resisted the impulse to demand an explanation. Instead, she took up the little red jacket. "See what I made for the baby today."

He took the jacket from her and smoothed it on his knee. "Very nice," he said listlessly.

Now she was really alarmed, and hurt besides. "John," she cried, "aren't you glad we're having a baby? It's—he's—one of the reasons we came home, isn't he?"

He shook his head and handed her the tiny jacket. "Whether

it was a good reason—valid, you know—" He broke off. "I'm tired, Mercy. I'll have my bath and rest a bit before dinner."

He left the room and she sat holding the jacket. Foreboding clouded her spirit.

THE MUSEUM was almost empty. It was a hot July day in New York. A few people moved languidly about the vast rooms, the men coatless and the women sleeveless. Only one man, a Chinese, Joy observed, was dressed neatly in a dark suit, white shirt and pale gray tie. He was standing before a painting, a modern conglomeration of colors and shapes, and gazing at it with complete absorption. She recognized the celebrated artist Hsuan Teng.

Her heart made a double beat. It had been his watercolors, faultless in Chinese technique, but of skyscrapers, docks and all the crowded sights of the city, that had helped her decide to become an artist. Modern in every thought of her facile brain, she had not, however, wanted to paint in oils. Yet how could she express her own emotions, so inexplicably violent, in a gentler medium? Then she had discovered the paintings of Hsuan Teng, who despite the subtlety of his ancient Chinese style could portray the violence and tragedy of modern life in a great city.

She knew that he lived in New York, and the knowledge had influenced her, at least mildly, to leave the shelter of the Brandons' house in San Francisco and take a small room in New York only a few months ago. Whether or not she returned to China, at least let her see all that she could of art before she went.

She approached Hsuan Teng. "Mr. Hsuan?" she asked softly.

He turned and she saw his kind round face. "Yes, I am he."

"I have wanted to meet you for such a long time but I have not dared. I am Joyce Liang. My family calls me Joy."

He had an air of old Chinese courtesy, a grace that reminded her of her mother's friends. How old was he? An indeterminate age. His face was young but there was a glimmer of white at his temples.

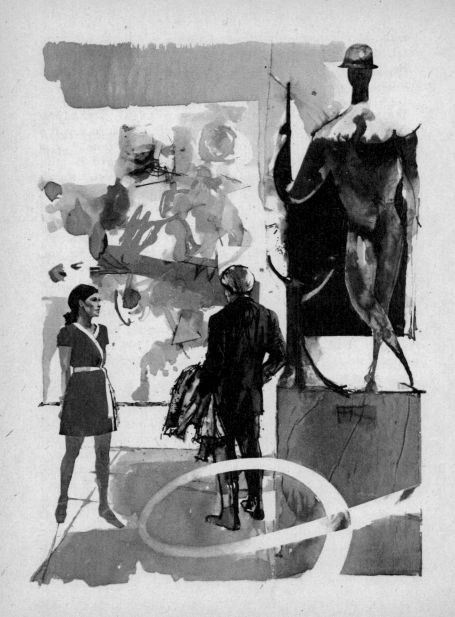

"You are an artist?" he asked.

"How did you know?" she replied.

"Paint under your fingernails," he said.

They laughed, and his small eyes shone. "I cannot resist an artist," he said. "Let us sit down. Tell me what you paint."

They sat side by side on a bench, facing a massive mural of clashing and merging colors. "I can't answer your question," she said. "I paint, searching, perhaps, for what I want to paint."

"It is not easy to find what one is born to paint. Do you know my work?"

"Who doesn't?"

He ignored the intent to praise. "Do you perceive an essence in it?"

She considered and replied, "The human figure is always small—so small that often it is lost. Your painting 'Father and Son'—I had to search the snow-covered landscape before I found them, no bigger than this!" She measured her thumbnail.

"The human figure is always there, is it not?" Hsuan Teng's voice was gentle.

"Always," she said.

"Because man is the essence, however small."

She said earnestly, "I would like to learn from you."

"Why not?" he replied. "We are both Chinese. I will teach you what I have learned."

From this hour their friendship began, the loving friendship of an older man for a young woman, the adoration of a young woman for an older man. And then, inevitably, China came between them and they fell into an argument over whether or not they should return to their own country. She told him of her mother, of her two sisters, and he listened carefully.

"But none of them is an artist," he exclaimed.

"My sister Mercy sings—"

"But you say she went back so that her child might be born in his own country! This is not the reasoning of a pure artist. She is a mother first."

Joy could not deny this, for Mercy's letters now were always of her coming child, and how right she had been to return home.

They had met for a lesson at his studio and Joy was still awed by the huge rooms, three of them opening one upon another, all richly furnished and hung with his paintings.

His gaze fixed upon an old scroll opposite them. "Can you read the Chinese characters on that scroll?"

She blushed and shook her head. "I have forgotten many characters. I think, anyway, I could not read that ancient writing—seal characters, aren't they?"

He nodded. "That's right. Four ancient seal characters. Exactly translated, they are: 'Heart Resembling Gold Rock.' The scroll was presented to me by a society of artists before I left our country. The characters describe the heart of a true artist. Gold, the finest of metals, as firm as a rock! When I am tempted, I hear the voices of my dead comrades, whose hearts were gold but not rock."

"What do you mean?" she asked.

"I mean they are dead," he said sternly. "They died by decapitation for rebellion and by hard labor for daring to criticize the rulers. Now you know why I do not return."

He gazed at her somberly and she was afraid to speak. Seeing her great sorrowful eyes, her tender mouth, he was gentle again.

"No, my child, freedom is the only air we artists can breathe, and wherever in the world the air is still free, that is our country."

He rose and led her about the studio, talking as he went. "In these rooms is the record of my life. Here you can see the best of the paintings I did before I left China. I grew up in a village outside Shanghai. My family was poor, for my father smoked opium. He was kind and quiet. I loved him—and I always saved some of the money my mother gave me for food from her salary and bought him a little opium secretly. He took it and said nothing, and I said nothing."

"Did your mother never know?" Joy asked.

"If she knew, she, too, said nothing." He went on to another picture. "This painting is the last I made before coming to America. A misty morning on a street in Shanghai—a ricksha man pulling his vehicle, his customer a fat old gentleman going to the tea shop."

"All the rickshas are gone now, my mother writes me."

"Ah," he replied, "I daresay there is still bitter labor, nevertheless!" and he moved to the next painting. "But when I reached San Francisco," he went on, "I was enchanted by the great buildings, high above the sea, and the rocks. I painted my way across this vast country, until I reached the eastern sea. Here I live, blending my colors to express the meaning of this city, so beautiful, so hideous, so rich, so dangerously poor—" He broke off and shrugged his shoulders. "Enough," he said. "Did you bring your portfolio?"

"I didn't dare."

"Are you afraid of me?"

"Of course I am."

"I don't understand. I, too, am still searching. An artist is always in flux, always ready for new impressions." He led her to the third room, his workplace, as she could see. An enormous unfinished painting was fastened to the wall and a smaller one stood on a large easel. Both were of a vast theater filled with people gazing at a brilliant stage where dancers moved in an elegant ballet.

"How do you blend?" she asked, fascinated by his nuances of light and darkness.

"I mediate the colors with clear water," Hsuan said, and chose a brush from a crowded jar, dipped it in a bowl of water and applied it to a bold streak of scarlet in a woman's cloak, then blotted the wetness with absorbent paper. The harsh outline softened, the scarlet faded into deep rose and melted into the shadows. "I may do that several times," he told her, "until the shades are exactly what I know is right."

It was the first of many lessons. Joy came to realize at last

451

that it was Hsuan who kept her from returning to her own country, her own people, her mother and sisters. She was beginning to live her life apart from them, and he was her teacher. Nevertheless she could not be with him day and night. He was famous and sought after, and sometimes he went to Europe. Then she waited alone in her small brownstone apartment, and waiting, she began a painting of her own, an abstract, a troubled reflection of her secret indecision. Days passed into weeks and weeks into months, and slowly the question answered itself. She began to love him. If he did not love her, she would return to her own country.

"IF, AS YOU SAY, your younger sister is about to give birth to her first child, I recommend broth made from an old hen, in which the root of ginseng has been brewed," Dr. Tseng told Grace.

Summer was over in Peking and Mercy expected her child at any hour.

"To gain the best results," he said pontifically, "the ginseng root must be dug at midnight during the season of the full moon."

Privately, Grace decided to examine *Panax* ginseng for its chemical qualities. When her lesson was over, therefore, she retired to her laboratory. By late afternoon she had finished her analysis and was about to conclude that ginseng was useless, when the door opened and Liu Peng stood before her.

"Ah, here you are, comrade!" he exclaimed. "I met old Doctor Tseng on his way home, and he said you had studied ginseng today. I guessed you might be making your own experiments."

"There is nothing here to help in childbirth," she declared. "Tannin, bitters, resin, starch and volatile oils—that's all."

She was about to throw the liquid away when Liu Peng stayed her, his hand on her wrist. "Wait—you have missed an element. There should be a little panacin—perhaps enough for healing. There is always something true in our materia medica."

He did not immediately remove his hand, and she remembered noticing his finely formed hands one night, months ago, when he had taken her to an old small restaurant where duck was prepared in the traditional fashion. She had worn a long red brocade Chinese gown with a stiff high collar and no sleeves, one that she had not put on since her return. She had been uncertain whether Liu Peng would approve, for he was politically strict. But that night he had seemed gentle, and as they lingered over wine, he had spoken almost softly.

"I had forgotten how a woman glows—a beautiful woman in a long red gown."

"You don't think it wrong of me?"

"Not when we dine alone in a small restaurant and drink shao-hsing wine with roasted duck!"

From that night on she had surmised what was in his heart and questioned her own. Was there to be something between them one day? He was overworked, always busy, a modern surgeon, fearless and original, she had observed when she had seen him operate, and he suffered terribly whenever he lost a patient.

"Ginseng is bitter at first when it is brewed," he was saying now. "Then it grows sweet. Be careful if you taste it—it's said to be an aphrodisiac." He was teasing her and she made a grimace.

"I don't believe in such things. Aphrodisiacs are only taken by people whose minds are on lovemaking anyway."

"So you don't believe in lovemaking?"

"I didn't say that—" Before she could finish, she heard her name called.

"Doctor Liang, you are wanted in the office. Your sister has arrived at the hospital to give birth. Doctor Liang!"

"Oh," she gasped. "I must go—immediately."

Her nephew, the child of Mercy and John Sung, was born six hours later in the western wing of the hospital. He was a strong child, plump and lusty, and he shouted his anger when Grace administered a sharp slap on his buttocks.

Later his mother, sipping hen's broth and ginseng, smiled at Grace. "I have fulfilled the purpose of my life. I have presented a new citizen to my country."

Madame Liang received the news of her grandson's birth with emotion. She celebrated by dispatching gifts to daughter and child, and then by retiring to her own quarters for the rest of the day to reflect. Fate had sent her a grandson, a portent of tomorrow, and no one knew what he would become, surrounded by great forces whose influence no one could foretell.

IN THE minister's private office John Sung sat facing Chao Chung behind the wooden desk. "You still refuse to develop the secret weapon for use against the United States?"

"I do not wish to work on weapons," he replied.

The minister took up a paper and appeared to be studying it. "You understand you have no right to refuse a command?"

"I have another reason not to enter the area of science where you have asked me to go, Mr. Minister. I am working now in the field of genetics."

"You are a scientist. All scientific principles are the same."

John Sung did not reply. His dark eyes were fixed unblinkingly on the handsome face opposite him.

The minister put down his paper. "And all scientific effort must now be concentrated in the area of defense. We have learned our lesson. A thousand years ago we stopped the development of explosive weapons on the grounds that they were monstrous. Even gunpowder we used only in fireworks. Who could have imagined that the Americans would develop atomic bombs and rocket weapons and all manner of deadly chemicals? You, a scientist, know their secrets. Can you refuse to protect your own people?"

Still John Sung sat in stolid silence.

Suddenly the minister shouted in loud short barks, "I know why you refuse to cooperate with us! You hide a traitorous love for Americans! Our most dangerous enemies! The Russians are too stupid for us to fear! The Americans are not stupid! They surround us with their bases! They must be destroyed!" Chao Chung paused and took a breath.

"Why should we hate the American people?" John Sung asked.

He well knew how dangerous such an inquiry was, but when he thought of America, he saw crowds of forthright, kindly people, ignorant of the world, but curious, and liking to be amused. He could not, to save his life, create anything to destroy them.

The minister was shouting again. "Why should we hate them? Because ours is the only true civilization! Did you ever hear of Sun Wa, who lived three thousand years ago? No? Read his *Art of War*. 'If you are not in danger, do not fight,' he wrote. Now we are in danger! You among all our scientists, you can provide our defense. Do you still refuse?" he demanded.

"I still refuse," John Sung said faintly.

"Then you must be—compelled," the minister said gently.

John Sung rose. "Am I dismissed?"

"Temporarily," the minister replied with sudden indifference.

That evening John Sung entered their bedroom where his wife sat on a low rattan chair, suckling their child.

She looked up at him and smiled. "Our son has gained nearly a pound since we came home."

"I wish you could see the picture you make," he said, sitting down on the bed. They spoke in English, uncertain of listening ears. Should he tell her of the danger? He could not. And would it not be useless, since they could not escape? He would be watched wherever he went. Better merely to continue his work in the laboratory.

Mercy laughed down at the child who had fallen asleep at her breast. "Look at his little hands! Feel how soft they are!"

Forcing his mind to give up its fear, he knelt beside his wife and took his son's small pink fist in his own large palm. He was responsible for this new life. Had he the right, then, to imperil it at the very beginning? Dare he indulge his personal conscience at such cost? He could not decide—not now, not yet!

The new child thrived and grew as autumn turned to winter. The household seemed tranquil enough. Each member fulfilled the days, absorbed, it seemed, in the present.

" 'DRIVE OUT the tiger by the front gate and let in the wolf by the back gate,' " Madame Liang quoted.

Her daughter Grace had arrived from Peking on a visit at the moment when the Russian scientists were leaving China in anger.

Grace lifted her eyebrows. "The tiger being?"

"The Japanese and the Western imperialists," Madame Liang replied. "The Russians are the wolf, of course. But I knew the Russians were not here to stay. I don't know why we have tolerated them all these years. They took Outer Mongolia and Manchuria, by domination, at least. Now let them go."

Grace protested. "But, M-ma, no one else will help us, certainly not the Americans!"

"Let us use our own talents," Madame Liang said firmly. "We will take the lead in science again, as we once did."

"M-ma, I never heard you speak so—patriotically."

"I am Chinese," Madame Liang declared. "I believe in our destiny. We must trust to our own genius, which has in other times brought us back to order and prosperity." She was sitting at her desk in her private office. A large window opened upon the west garden, and across its wide panes snowflakes drifted to the ground. Although it was the Chinese New Year, the city was quiet and she expected no callers, since she made no calls. Except for her business, she lived in total seclusion.

"I suppose," Grace mused, "that we Chinese were led to the conviction of our own superiority because we were surrounded by lesser peoples and did not travel to Europe and America."

"We knew our own superiority before Europe and America existed," her mother retorted. "And do you think there is anything new under Heaven? I trust all to our own people. You remember that when Confucius was asked which was most important to a state—food, weapons or the trust of the people, he replied that weapons and food could be given up, but the state itself would only be destroyed if the people had no confidence in it."

"And have the people confidence now?" Grace asked.

Madame Liang gave her daughter a strange look. "Ah, it is a question—have they?"

Upon reflection later that night in her own room, Grace comprehended a curious similarity between her mother and all other Chinese, and that was their absolute confidence in the superiority of being Chinese. Communist or not, her people still believed themselves the center of the world, and of the human race. She marveled that this could be true except through ignorance. Yet her mother—wise, cultivated, gracious—was not ignorant. Indeed, were these not the very attributes of superiority?

Lying awake in her bed, the cold moonlight slanting across the tiled floor, Grace laughed softly to herself. Could any force, human or natural, destroy a people who believed themselves indestructible and had so believed for thousands of years? Was this not the guarantee of life, the Eternal Way?

Liu Peng sought Grace out the day she returned to Peking. He ran after her down the long central corridor of the medical building and drew her into an empty classroom. "Great news. The Russians are all gone!"

"Since they helped us, perhaps you are rejoicing too soon?"

"What is this 'too soon'?" he demanded. "There cannot be two suns in the sky. Coexistence with the Russians is fantasy. One must always be above. We have always been that one."

"You and my mother!" she exclaimed. "You are using communism as an instrument to express your convictions as a Chinese. Our country never was the center of the world—we only thought it was."

"But of course we have always been the center! The whole world wanted our trade and still does. One by one the surrounding countries will yield again to our influence. Under communism, too, all will look to our leadership!"

He was absurd, medieval, anything but the modern man he believed himself to be. Yet in the vortex of her anger she felt an irresistible attraction. His eyes were brilliant in their blackness, his mouth was firm, he was all earnestness and fire. What was this rising fever in her blood?

"You—you, too, are Chinese," Liu Peng was saying. "I will compel you to understand our people. Yes, communism is our present instrument, but what does the instrument matter if the meaning is the same? Bit by bit what was ours will return to us. All will be harmony under our direction. Without war we will win now, as we always have. Then will come the Great Peace. You and I are not on opposite sides. We stand together." He took her hands in his. "Do I speak the truth?" he demanded.

"Yes," she said, her voice a whisper.

Later, as she worked, she reviewed her feelings. Yes, perhaps she was in love, but how little she knew of the man she loved, and how little he knew of her! Yes, she was Chinese, but a Chinese who had seen the world beyond. Liu Peng knew nothing of the world and desired to know nothing. But he was young, he was brilliant, and he would see the truth when she revealed it.

VI

As SOON AS they were alone in their room John Sung told his wife what the minister had informed him that day. "Tomorrow morning I am to be sent away for hard labor."

Her breath left her. He saw her face grow pale, and her voice was tight and high. "You are accused?"

"Because I refuse to work on poison weapons for use against the Americans." He described the plan to poison American water sources.

"I see that you had to refuse—of course. I am proud of you—but I feel guilty. It was I who insisted that we come here."

She bit her lip; he put an arm about her shoulders and lifted her chin with his other hand. "Each of us serves his country as he sees best. Don't regret." He gazed deep into her eyes. Then, unable to bear the thought of not seeing her, perhaps for years, he released her and sank into a chair. "You must stay with your sister," he said. "Or else go to your mother in Shanghai."

"I will stay here," she said. "I will start my school of music. I must make the time pass somehow!"

Tears filled her eyes and he tried to comfort her. "It is a good way to serve your country." But his voice sounded hollow even to himself, and when their eyes met, she sobbed aloud and flung herself into his arms.

"Prices are higher than one can pay, madame," Chu San said.

Madame Liang sighed. "Heaven has put a curse on us."

The day seemed like any other day. Yet each day, by imperceptible degrees, was worse than the one before. The people, blind with faith and hope, had been led astray. The year before, far-reaching decisions had been made by those above. She had distrusted them and had even dared to make known her doubts to Minister Chao Chung. "We Chinese are not like other peoples who trust to their inventions," she had told him. "We trust to the land."

"We will trust to everything at once," Chao Chung had replied with his usual confidence. "We will make a great leap forward in both manufacturing and agriculture."

As the months passed she had watched in deepening dismay as the heroic peasants strove to learn how to smelt iron ore in small ovens built in their backyards and on their threshing floors. She had watched with alarm as the peasants were herded into communes. Within her own family a blow had been struck. Without a word to her, Chao Chung, whom alone she had trusted, had banished her daughter's husband to hard labor.

"Old Li has come to beg a little food," Chu San was saying.

Madame Liang was eating her own frugal breakfast, but she pushed the dishes aside. "Bring him to me," she said.

The door opened softly and Old Li, a peasant, stood there, blinking and smiling. He had changed much in the years since she had last seen him on his small farm outside the city. Then a ruddy-faced man of middle age, now he appeared thin and ragged and aged.

"Sit down," she said, and to Chu San, "Bid Chou Ma fetch another bowl and a pair of chopsticks." Then she leaned toward him and said softly, "Tell me all you have suffered."

Trusting her, as everyone did, he began in a low voice. "You know me, lady. I am a common man, as were all my ancestors. Heaven put us on the land and there we have stayed. Nevertheless, in our own way, we did well. In my great-grandfather's time we were able to buy a little land. Since then, each generation bought more, until we had seventeen acres. Who would have thought such an age would come upon us that a few poorer than I, whom I hired, would turn against me and call me a landowner and one to be despised? Who would have thought my own sons would desert me?"

He let his head droop. Chou Ma came in with bowl and chopsticks and went away.

"Eat," Madame Liang said firmly. "Hot food comforts also the soul."

Old Li tried not to show his hunger but only after he had eaten three bowls did he put down his chopsticks. "We cannot let down our hearts," he said, "though, in truth, we work our bodies to skin and bone. By day we till the land; in common we plant and reap the harvest. At night we try to make iron. How can we make iron? It has not been our destiny."

He leaned forward to add fearfully, "There will be no harvest this year! Many work, but they are strangers to the land and they plant too deep or too shallow, and the earth refuses to nourish the seed and the seed dies. By next year, lady, all our people will suffer from hunger and lack. By two years from now, the people will be desperate, and then what will become of those above?"

"They will change," Madame Liang said. "They know in their secret hearts that the will of the people is Heaven's will."

"Many people will escape to Hong Kong," the old man went on. "Among them will be this humble man. I have nothing now to sell—no eggs, no fowl, no pork, no cabbage. But what of you, lady?"

"I will stay. I have always stayed," Madame Liang replied.

JOHN SUNG was sleepless on his narrow bed of boards, every muscle aching as though torn from his bones. Yet at daybreak bells would ring and whistles would blow to summon to the fields the peasants among whom he was now stationed. Rough though it was, he was silently compelled to acknowledge that there was an element of rightness in the policy of subjecting intellectuals to hard manual labor. A waste for the time being, he reflected, but a necessity if a modern nation was to be welded out of this vast population of nearly seven hundred million people, most of them peasants.

Centuries of separation between the intellectuals and the peasants had produced a dominating elite that had no concern for their own people and were the chief obstacle to the building of a nation. He himself had never lifted a hoe before.

The light of coming day now crept through the cracks of the wooden walls. Men sat up and stared about them, bewildered by upheaving changes, such as the separation of parents from children, old from young, men from women. They woke up dazed to this new day of hard work and promises shouted by the hoarse voices of the ardent young cadre.

"The production brigade is the foundation of the people's commune! Comrades, you will have your reward! No more famines! No more hunger! Everything for everyone!"

John Sung's reply was silent but steadfast: the great experiment was doomed to fail. Human nature prevails, and human beings think, work and live for their own rewards. Today there were no rewards.

The sun rose to the horizon. Bells rang, whistles screamed, and in the allotted fifteen minutes the peasants lined up. The commanders of brigades and teams shouted, and men and women marched like soldiers to the fields that were no longer theirs. John Sung took up his hoe, one in an endless line.

THE CLOCK in the central room of the sisters' house in Peking read near midnight when John Sung's day ended far in the west of China. All clocks in the entire land marked the same time so that, the Chairman decreed, the country and its citizens would be a single entity, living at the same tempo.

The true time was exactly twenty minutes past six as Mercy entered her home at the end of her workday. She was met by an elderly woman carrying the baby. "The little lord cried not once while you were gone," the woman said proudly. The baby stretched out his arms to his mother and she took him and pressed him to her.

"Were there letters today?" It was her daily question, although in five months there had been only one affirmative reply.

"Only a letter from your honored mother in Shanghai," the old woman told her. She gave the letter to Mercy, who began reading it avidly. Had her mother succeeded or failed?

As I promised, I spoke to one individual of another. He agreed to see what could be done to shorten the period or ameliorate the conditions. Nothing more definite could be exacted. He then commended your music school. It is his wish to make it a part of the National University, lest it be frowned upon as an individualistic effort. I need not tell you that it might be useful in your present situation to do what you can to comply.

Mercy folded the sheet and put it into her pocket. When her

elder sister came home she must not know that Mercy had asked their mother to intervene on John's behalf. A deep division was growing between the sisters. Grace, in love with Liu Peng, could believe no evil of those above. She argued even against her sister's impatience to have her husband home again. Last night the quarrel had become so open that Grace had cut it short by saying, "If we, the daughters of our mother, cannot agree, then let us be silent on the matter."

Now as Grace entered the room where Mercy waited, she was determined to be courteous. They were dependent on one another, and childhood memories bound them together. For a few moments they united in admiration of the healthy little boy who sat on his mother's lap playing with her gold bracelet. It was the bracelet that provided the approach to dissension. Their mother had given them twin bracelets upon their graduations from school in Shanghai.

"Where is your bracelet, sister?" Mercy now asked.

"I put it away," Grace replied.

"Why?"

"I felt it did not suit, somehow."

"Suit the times, or suit Liu Peng?"

"And does that matter to you?" Grace asked, too quietly.

"Not in the least," Mercy responded lightly. "Only—you've changed since you've known him."

"I am not conscious of change, except that I understand our government—and what it does—much more clearly."

"Such as putting its best men to hard labor?"

"The system doesn't allow for exceptions. If John Sung is allowed to refuse an allotted task, who can be compelled to any task? We must work as a single unit. Each man, each woman, fits into a given position. We can't see the entire pattern, but those above, the planners, can see."

Tears welled into Mercy's large dark eyes. "That doesn't bring my husband back to me!"

"We can't think of personal emotions—none of us can."

Mercy was suddenly angry. Her eyes dried. She snatched

the baby and went swiftly to the door. There she paused. "I wonder what Clem would think of you now," she cried. "I can't imagine his even liking you anymore!"

With this she left the room. Grace sat motionless. Clem? They had exchanged two or three letters, then suddenly she had received no more. Had the letters been stopped by some unknown order? She would never know, and the uncertainty had made her stop writing.

Still, she had hardly thought of Clem for months, and she realized that Liu Peng was isolating her from everyone. What had been attraction was now love, an emotion as personal as the one for which she had reproached Mercy. She had had only three recent meetings with him, all in the presence of others. Had she only imagined tenderness in his voice, warmth in his eyes? His words had been few, only directions for her work, but the power of his personality had poured from him in electric waves. She was not accustomed to the extreme control of a Chinese man, and it added to her excitement. How almost infantile Clem now seemed in her memory, ready to take her hand, to parade his adoration, to share his thoughts! She resolved to be more reserved herself, more respectful toward her superiors, and to be more worthy of Liu Peng, she decided to study the philosophy of the Chairman himself. What manner of man was he, this one upon whom the future of almost seven hundred million people depended?

It was a full week before she saw Liu Peng again, and then it was by chance in a hallway of the Medical Institute. He stopped, surprised to see her, and she stopped also. They faced each other, fixed for a moment in the stream of swiftly passing students and bewildered patients, not knowing what to say. She seized upon a pretext—though genuine, surely—for delay. "I want to learn more about the principles of the Chairman," she said earnestly, improvising as she spoke. "What his dreams are, and what he wants to achieve—"

"Read his books, his poems," Liu Peng said coldly.

She withdrew her spirit from him proudly. "Thank you,"

she said, and she was about to walk away when he caught her wrist.

"Stay," he said in a low voice. "When can we meet?"

"Where you will, when you will," she told him. "I live with my sister, as you know, in the Street of the Three Foxes."

"At nine tonight, after work," he said and let her go.

That night when Liu Peng was introduced to Mercy, he reached over and took Mercy's child from her arms. The little boy gazed at him doubtfully and drew down his mouth to cry, but Liu Peng coaxed him with smiles and hushing. Then, holding the child on his knee, Liu Peng began abruptly to talk of the evils of birth control, gazing into the child's enchanting face while he spoke.

"Consider the loss to the nation if this child had not been born! What if his mother had prevented his birth in the mistaken idea that she could serve our country better by becoming the head of a commune or a brigade? Our Chairman is right. We need more people, not fewer. People are our national treasure." His piercing black eyes softened as Grace had never seen them. This man could feel tenderness. He looked at Mercy and smiled. "May you bear many more children," he said gently.

But Mercy seized the moment for herself. "It is not likely with my husband far away in a peasant commune."

"Can that be?" Liu Peng asked Grace in surprise.

"It is true," she said.

He rose and placed the child in the mother's arms. "Then it must not be," he said.

When Mercy left them because the child was growing fretful with hunger, Liu Peng became restless. "Let us go into the courtyard," he said. "The moon is bright."

Grace followed him into the courtyard, and there under a ripening plum tree he began to unwrap a package he had brought with him. "Here are books," he said. "They will tell you about the Chairman—his life, his nature. You will see why we follow him."

This, then, Grace realized, had been the purpose of his visit.

"China can be conquered," she read that night when she was alone, "only when all the people of Hunan province are dead."

This proverb she had heard repeated often by her father in her childhood. He was a shadowy figure to her now, a handsome man, impetuous and passionate as the pepper-loving Hunanese were said to be. That the Chairman was born in Hunan made him understandable to her. Son of a land-owning peasant, he had learned, nevertheless, to read, and his youth had been spent in the fomenting atmosphere of Sun Yat-sen's revolution. She read a poem he had written recently on his return to his native village:

Only because so many sacrificed themselves did our wills
   become strong,
So that we dared command the sun and moon to bring a new day.
I love to look at the multiple waves of rice and beans,
While on every side the heroes return through the evening haze.

She read and reread his many poems and essays and his autobiography, and was deeply drawn to this man. Moreover, her reading gave her endless material for talk with Liu Peng.

One day when summer had passed into autumn and in every courtyard chrysanthemums were in full bloom, Grace felt unusually blithe walking along a tree-lined boulevard near the Great Square with Liu Peng. To the north were the palaces of the past, with their tile roofs of royal blue, vermilion pillars, pink walls and white marble bridges.

She would have liked to slip her hand into his, but such familiarity as one saw on American streets was not permitted here. Nevertheless, she was happy. For added to the joy of her satisfying work was the joy of knowing herself in love with Liu Peng. She was an explorer in all she did, and she must now explore her love for this man who attracted her so profoundly.

It was not easy, for he held himself apart even today, when her longing for his touch was so strong that he must feel its electric demand. But he was only talking—talking—and she could scarcely hear him for the thunder in her blood.

They entered an ancient palace open to the public and wandered through the opulent rooms. His voice went steadily on and fragments caught in her brain: "the unfortunate season—restless peasants—"

When they were alone in a remote wing of the palace, she stopped and turned to him impulsively, unconscious pleading in her eyes. She saw his face flush. Without a word he reached for her and in an instant his lips were upon hers. Nor did he draw back quickly. Joyfully she felt the warmth of his flesh through his cotton jacket and smelled the clean soap smell of his body. Then he drew back, his arms still about her, and gazed down on her.

"I have never kissed a woman like that before," he said. "A man reads of such things—and wonders. Now I know."

"Know?" she repeated.

"What it means," he said.

ON THE other side of the world it was the day of the opening of Hsuan's exhibition in one of New York's leading galleries. Word had flashed through art circles that the famous artist had developed new techniques, and collectors and lovers of art had come from all over the country.

Mr. and Mrs. Brandon, relative newcomers as collectors of Chinese modern art, had flown in from San Francisco and were now entering the doors, their eyes roving over the packed rooms. They were a handsome pair in their late fifties. "I don't see Hsuan or Joy," Mr. Brandon was saying.

"How could you find anyone in this crowd?" Mrs. Brandon asked.

At this moment they were discovered by Joy herself. Though usually she wore Western dress, today she had put on a long close-fitting Chinese gown of apple-green brocade. "Ah! You have come!" She was enveloped in Mrs. Brandon's warm embrace.

"We wouldn't have missed this for the world," Mr. Brandon declared, clasping Joy's hand in both of his.

"How is your dear mother and Grace and Mercy and John?" Mrs. Brandon asked all in a breath, and full of affection.

Joy was instantly grave. "I haven't heard for months."

"The gossip is that things are going badly in our beloved China," Mr. Brandon said.

Joy turned to him. "Oh, what have you heard?"

"Crop failures, drought in some places and floods in others—and failure of the communes."

"Oh, *no!*"

Just then Hsuan pushed his way gently through the crowd, smiling courteously, shaking hands, reaching Joy's side at last. "How good of you to come so far," he murmured, his right hand extended to Mr. Brandon, his left to Mrs. Brandon. "I am so happy—so very happy."

"Hsuan," Joy exclaimed, "Mr. Brandon says affairs are very bad in our country—famines and floods and no harvests!"

"What else can be expected?" the artist said with composure. "Heaven is outraged." He thus conveyed his disapproval of her mention of disasters on such an occasion. Then he turned with his delightful smile to Mrs. Brandon. "Let us proceed to the west wing. I want you to see my abstracts."

His English was grammatically correct, but his accent was his own, the stress often upon the wrong syllable, so that even when he had told Joy last night, "Truly, I *ad*ore you," she had not been sure of what he had said, and then only afterward had grasped the full import of his words. She had been in a complex state of mind ever since. They, master and pupil, had strictly maintained the formality of their relationship, although she had not hidden from herself the passionate nature of her feeling for him. Tonight, when the crowd was gone and they were alone, he would say more—would he not?

"I am trying to catch the world mood as I feel it," he was telling Mr. Brandon. "Realism today is in those particles that are the feelings of separate human beings, surging around our globe and soaring into space. I am trying, through color in motion, to express that surging, that soaring."

Mr. Brandon gazed at the painting they had stopped in front of, a medley of interweaving colors, blending and contrasting, but certainly expressing motion. "A splendid performance," he announced, "but above the heads of most people."

"You think so?" Hsuan asked, a bit dashed.

"I am sure of it," Mr. Brandon said with decision. "Nevertheless, I want that painting. I want to live with it. Perhaps without knowing it, you have expressed the spirit of your own country."

That night, when everyone was gone, master and pupil went to a nearby Chinese restaurant to discuss the day. They smiled at each other across the table. The opening had been a great success, many paintings had been sold (but of the abstracts, only the one Mr. Brandon had chosen) and critics had been respectful. Joy looked at Hsuan's somewhat round face, and he put on his spectacles and gazed at her intensely in return.

"Is something wrong with me?" she asked innocently.

"On the contrary," he replied. "I am merely inspecting the young woman I intend to marry."

She was stupefied by his directness. Her mouth fell slightly ajar. He put his spectacles in his pocket and smiled at her. Then he looked grave and cleared his throat loudly.

"For many years I reproached myself because I refused the marriage my parents arranged for me when I was a boy," he began. "My parents were sad, for they wanted to see grandchildren. But I was hard of heart as only the young can be. Knowing myself to be an artist, I put aside all thoughts of marriage and escaped to America, where an artist can still live in independent peace. It takes much time to find a wife, and I have had no time. First I had to be a success for myself. I am a success. And now, too, by good fortune I have met the wife that I have wanted for so long. She is you!"

Joy wanted to cry out, "Of course I will be your wife! I have been waiting, waiting all these months!" And she wanted to laugh because he was such an individual, so much himself in every circumstance. She wanted to put her hand across the table to him, but so frank a gesture might offend him, so she replied in grave and modest tones, "I will be honored to be your wife."

To her astonishment it was his hand that moved across the table and enclosed her own.

THE MEAGER harvest fell before the storms of autumn. The wrath of Heaven had not slackened during that interminable year when the peasants had been bribed or forced into communes. In rows, thousands upon thousands, they had plowed and planted the rice fields of the south and the wheat fields of the north, but the harvests were scanty. When the rains should have fallen, there was only dry sunshine. Now when the fields of rice should have been golden for harvest, the empty heads bent before the untimely wind and rain. Frost came early and the skies were perpetually dark. Strange rumblings were heard underground and the earth trembled, now here, now there. No one could explain the failure of the crops, for the planting had been done with hope and zeal. Now hope was gone and zeal had died into despair. In vain did the young men who were leaders run everywhere, trying to encourage the doubting peasants.

On a day in early winter of that dark year John Sung sat among the peasants with whom he lived under the thatched roof and between the mud walls of a farmhouse in a western village. Rain seeped through the aging thatch and dripped upon them as they listened to a young leader, his voice cracking, now childish, now manly, so that the peasants laughed, hungry though they were.

"Under the new plan of our Chairman there is equality for all," he was saying. "No more shall there be bitter labor for the peasants and idleness for the city folk. Each commune will work for itself, feed itself, govern itself, each of you sharing the work of farmer, student, factory worker, and soldier."

A dream, John Sung thought, beautiful and impossible. But although he disagreed with what he was saying, John Sung found himself pitying that earnest young man with all his heart. What would befall him on the day he was awakened by truth and reality?

The peasants needed no pity. They would follow the New Way only if their bellies were filled, their bodies covered, and if now and then they could laugh. Their loyalty went no further, for long ago they had lost the power of dreaming. No, John Sung told himself, he did not pity the peasants. They had given up their land, but they could take it back. So long as there was land they were safe.

As he sat on the narrow end of a bench among the others, John Sung looked no different from them, his face brown and lined, his feet bare and gnarled. In his many months among the peasants, he had listened to their talk and observed their ways and learned of his own country from them, who, in fact, represented most of its people. His silence, his wisdom, above all, his sharing of their labor had brought him their trust. By natural selection he had come to be their undeclared leader.

Now that the rain made work in the fields impossible, the young man was at a loss as to how to command and what to assign. He, too, had come to depend upon John Sung, and he turned to him in pleading silence.

John Sung rose to his feet. "Comrade, would it be well for us to twist the old straw remaining and make rope from it? In this way we would not waste our time."

"It would be well," the young man agreed.

When the peasants rose halfheartedly to begin twisting old straw into rope, John Sung lingered behind to speak alone with the young man. "Comrade, we have enough rice for only two days more," he said.

The young man looked at him. "Supplies will come." When John Sung did not answer, he went on. "Do you doubt it?"

"I doubt it," John Sung said.

"I swear—" the young man began but John Sung cut him short.

"You swore that eleven days ago, comrade. You said 'within three days,' but no supplies have come. The cooks in the common kitchen are frightened. 'What shall we do?' they ask me. I can but reply that it is not my responsibility. I am only the head of a work team."

The young man's lips trembled. "Is it my fault that the rains fall at the wrong time?"

"It is not yours nor mine nor any man's," John Sung said. "Nevertheless there should be a plan somewhere. Surely there must be reserves, grain stored against the possibility of famine—"

Now the young man's eyes flashed. "Can you doubt the Chairman? Is he not our father and mother? He plans for everyone!"

John Sung bowed his head and was silent. Though he was a full ten years older than this lad, he had learned by now that youth was in power.

Youth was in power and famine fell upon the country. The people were bitter and angry, for they had been promised that never again would they suffer famine. Yet here were the old familiar pains of starvation and shortage, the old despair of not knowing where to turn. Out of fierce devotion to these humble men and women among whom he had worked for many months, John Sung went from one person to another in the hierarchy above him, quietly seeking advice, until he found himself at last in Peking. Thus on a cold snowy night near the end of winter he stood outside his own gate and beat on it with half-frozen hands. It opened and Lao Wang stood there, peering into the darkness.

"Who are you?" the old man asked.

"I am Sung, the father of the child here."

Lao Wang lifted the lantern so the light fell on John Sung's face. Now he recognized him. "But how thin you are, master!" he exclaimed.

"Many are thin these days," John Sung said. "And do not call me master. I am master of no one—not even myself."

Inside the house John Sung softly crossed the central room and opened the door to their bedroom. A night lamp shed its dim light on the bed and he saw Mercy there, asleep, her dark hair loose on the pillow. In the curve of her arm, his face against her breast, lay the child.

The tears he had not shed for misery now welled into his eyes for joy. These two, at least, did not look starved. As though impelled by his presence, Mercy slowly opened her eyes. She looked for a long moment. "I keep dreaming of you," she murmured.

He knelt beside the bed. "I am here," he said.

She put the child aside and turned into his arms for a long embrace. At last, drawing away to look at him, she cried softly, "Oh, how thin you are. You've been ill!"

"Only starved," he said. "I've been passed on from one level to the next," he explained to her, "until here I am in Peking, with authority to appeal to the highest level."

She was instantly anxious. "But it's dangerous!"

"I can't think of myself," he replied.

"Then think of your son!"

He shook his head. "People are starving." He told her of the peasants' anger and disaffection, hopelessness and rebellion.

"But why have the communes failed?" she asked, bewildered.

"The main reason is that too much has been taken from the peasant and too little has been given him in return."

She covered his lips with her hand and looked fearfully about the room. "Hush—be careful what you say," she exclaimed.

Her words told him what he did not want to know. Even here in his own home there was fear.

He was received immediately in Chao Chung's office the next morning. A hot bath, food and his own clothes had restored him somewhat, although the clothes hung loosely on his frame. And he knew himself changed in many other ways. He was enmeshed in his country's problems and aware of its power. Was he disenchanted? No, on the contrary, he was enchanted by its landscape and by its people.

"I am glad to see you, Comrade Sung. Sit down," Chao Chung said cheerfully. "I have good reports of you. You now are at the head of a work brigade. But I suppose you have come to ask to be released from hard labor."

"By no means," John Sung said. "I have come first of all to thank you for sending me into the ranks of the peasants. I have learned a great deal. Second, I have come to ask for food for our peasants, and more, for a policy that will prevent famine forever."

Chao Chung's heavy eyebrows drew down over his flashing eyes. "The Chairman has thought of everything. The peasants are his children and he is their father. How dare you say there is no policy? Can we prevent flood or drought?"

"Other nations have done so," John Sung said.

He had gone too far. Chao Chung sprang from his chair. "You have not yet known hard labor! You will go to the mines!"

But John Sung could no longer be frightened. "If the Chairman is our father, then who are you, comrade?" he inquired.

Chao Chung could not but admire him. His eyes shone with unwilling amusement. "I am the eldest son, and it is I who send you to the mines."

VII

IN HER loneliness Madame Liang reviewed her life, herself and her family, pondering and reflecting, until the immediate future became clear to her, emerging from the past.

That ancient sage Lao-tzu said, "Throw eggs at a rock, and though one uses all the eggs in the world, the rock remains the same." Never was she more sure of the unchangeable than now, when disasters created by man and nature fell upon the people; when the peasants were compelled to ruin fertile topsoil by deep plowing, to waste fertilizers on rich fields and drain water from rice paddies, changing age-old habits because the printed paper gave instructions unsuited to the time and the place, the seed and the soil. In ignorance they had led the bewildered peasants astray until half-starved people were escaping by the thousands to Hong Kong.

News went abroad, to the nation's disgrace, she knew, because to her surprise she had received packets of foods from her third daughter, Joy, in New York. She herself needed no food, so she had sent the packets to her daughters in Peking. Times were evil and she determined to fly to Peking and see for herself how her daughters and their household fared. The thought that her grandson might be in need of strengthening food was alarming.

When Madame Liang arrived at the Street of the Three Foxes everyone there was surprised and properly overjoyed. It was evening, and her daughters were at home, but her son-in-law was gone. Her grandson was awakened from sleep, and after staring at her for a long time undecided whether or not to cry, he smiled and allowed himself to be taken into her arms. In this amiable atmosphere Madame Liang inquired into the details of their lives.

"We have enough to eat, my mother, never fear," Grace said. "You send us food, and the child has the dried milk Joy sends. Our servants find rice and chicken and eggs."

"And the people?" Madame Liang inquired.

"It is here as it is elsewhere," Grace replied.

She saw a look of fire flash between her two daughters. "Come now," Madame Liang said with authority, "what is between you two?"

"My sister keeps comparing our country unfavorably to others," Grace answered with impatience. "Were she not my sister, I should feel compelled to report her unpatriotic attitude."

Mercy's eyes were bright with tears and anger. "Tell what

you like," she cried. "It is not your country of which you are thinking but of that Liu Peng! You were not so patriotic until you began to love him!" She turned to her mother with a piteous sob. "Oh, M-ma, can you speak to someone and ask if John may come home? You should see him—a skeleton. He came all the way here to talk with someone above, and for this he was sent to the mines! And my sister blames me."

"Blames you? For what?" Madame Liang asked.

The sisters exchanged hostile looks, but neither would speak. What, then, could she do? These were new times and parents were no longer obeyed. She withdrew gracefully, saying she was tired.

As Madame Liang lay on the bed, her active mind recalled every look and word of her daughters and she resolved to do what she had never done. She would send word to Minister Chao Chung that she was in the capital, and he and his wife would invite her to their home. She rose, wrote the letter and sent it by Chou Ma, who had come with her to Peking.

Then Madame Liang rejoined her daughters and the evening was spent in pleasant talk and in reading Joy's letters from New York. When Chou Ma returned with the invitation Madame Liang expected, she did not mention it until Grace was called out of the room by a servant. Then she leaned toward her second daughter and said in a low voice, "Let your heart rest, my child. Tomorrow night I dine with the minister and his wife."

"Oh, M-ma," Mercy breathed. "You can do everything!"

Madame Liang arrived at the home of Chao Chung the next evening. Chao Chung's wife, once a motion-picture star in Shanghai, knew of his early love for Madame Liang but, being twenty years younger, felt no jealousy. She greeted Madame Liang with pleasure and excused herself to supervise the cook.

Chao Chung then invited Madame Liang to walk through the gardens where, in spite of the chill of early spring, the plum trees were in bloom and bamboo shoots were thrusting their pointed heads through the earth.

"It is far north for bamboo," Madame Liang observed.

"Too far," Chao Chung agreed, "but I have sheltered them, as you see, here in a corner. I must have bamboo."

Madame Liang smiled. "What you must have, you will, as always."

"Except in one instance," Chao Chung replied with mischief.

Madame Liang laughed. "Will you never forget?"

"Never," Chao Chung said, his small eyes merry.

"Foolish," Madame Liang said, but gently, for a reminiscent mood was to be encouraged when she wished to speak to Chao Chung not only of her son-in-law but also of national matters. Yet it was too soon.

Later came a moment when the last course had been served and Chao Chung's wife was away with the servants. He leaned back and began to speak in French, a sign of feeling between himself and an old friend of Paris days.

"I have felt for some time, madame, my friend, that you do not entirely approve of all that is now being done for our people. This would not be dangerous except that we are in a period of national hardship and there is a central dislike of criticism, a stage that will pass as we become more secure. We have made mistakes, but consider that the Russians left us without technical aid at the time when we needed it most. That was why we took the Great Leap Forward. A failure? Yes and no. Technically, yes, but our people were awakened to the need for modern industry. And we've realized that our chief assets are the people and the land. The Chairman ordered the people's communes. That is to say, he put the responsibility on the people."

"A failure, was this not?" Madame Liang said.

Chao Chung sat upright and squared his shoulders. "All has been for the best," he declared. "We are no longer subservient to a barbarian Russia. I will tell you a secret—"

He leaned forward to speak low. "The Chairman is the most Chinese among us all. He is not so much a Communist—oh, he believes in communism, but it's his instrument, not his creed. We have only to follow him and under his guidance we shall see Chinese reclaiming the whole of Asia. Not through armies, mind you! We will advise and aid the discontented, and they themselves will be our forces."

Chao Chung paused and Madame Liang felt her moment had come. "There is only one policy I question. Is it well"— she seemed to hesitate—"is it a wise use of the national treasure to send a scientist, learned in Western technology, to work in a mine?"

Chao Chung stared at her, then he gave a bellow of laughter. "O woman," he exclaimed. "How deviously clever you are! It is a waste. Moreover, he has been punished enough. He has learned to work with his hands. I will recall him at once."

"Thank you," Madame Liang said, and as his young wife returned to the room, Chao Chung gave Madame Liang a look in which amusement was mingled with a shadow of sadness.

"You never change, my friend."

"It is true," Madame Liang said. "I never change."

"You are a Chinese," Chao Chung said with admiration.

MADAME LIANG had lingered on in the capital and now the dust storms of the early spring were over and the city was at its most beautiful. One fine afternoon she went to the ancient Gate of Heavenly Peace, from whose base she viewed the great new square, large enough to hold nearly a million people, and the Great Hall of the People. From here she could see the soaring pillars of the Museum of the Revolution. New boulevards, lined with trees, were busy with people traveling by foot or pedicab, bicycle or bus, and now and again by car. Policemen stood in glass-enclosed booths at every other corner. They shouted orders through bullhorns, but the people were orderly and seldom needed their reprimands.

Later, when she returned to the house, she found that Chao Chung had kept his word. While she had been out seeing the city, John Sung had come back to his family by special plane. He met her in the courtyard and took her hand in his.

"You have come!" she cried triumphantly.

"I thank you that it is so," he replied. "I do not regret my banishment," he told her when they had sat down inside the house in the central room. "I have learned very much. I am a good farmer now, and also a miner. But my most valuable knowledge is what I have learned of my own people."

She liked this son-in-law very much, with his large work-worn hands, somber dark eyes, and face too strong to be handsome in any usual way, yet manly and pleasant. Now Grace came home from her work, and with her was a tall young man whom she introduced as Liu Peng, but being somewhat weary, Madame Liang excused herself and went to her room to rest before the evening meal.

When the meal was over, they went into the courtyard and sat down. Madame Liang was given the most comfortable seat, and the two young men, John Sung and Liu Peng, sat on the stone doorstep. The evening was warm after the first day of summer heat. Lao Wang cut open a watermelon and each ate a slice, spitting the black seeds on the ground. A mood of happiness prevailed, first because John Sung was home again, and then because underneath all else was the hope that after two tragic years they were at last on the way to a better harvest.

"Say what you like," Liu Peng was saying, "but after a hundred years of confusion and unrest, we have achieved work for every man and woman, schools for children and two meals a day."

"Which means," Mercy retorted, "that we are all equally poor."

Madame Liang listened, aware of the hostile undercurrents, but proud of her family assembled about her here in the moonlight. They were young, they were handsome, and though Liu Peng was not one of them, she discerned that he might be soon.

"I am grateful for all of you, my family," she said aloud.

"Families are only a means of exploitation," Liu Peng declared suddenly. "Parents treat children as capital assets and children wait for parents to die so they will have an unearned income."

"So now sons spy on fathers and children are sent far from parents," Mercy interjected bitterly. "I shall keep my child with me."

Her sister turned on her. "Many women are glad to put their children into a day nursery so they can leave the house. No, young and old are glad to be rid of each other."

Thus the evening, begun so benignly, broke into noisy fragments. Madame Liang made up her mind to return the next day to her own house where, though lonely, she could live in peace. And John Sung, at his wife's command, the next day rented three rooms in a tall new concrete building on the far edge of the city.

Removing themselves, however, did not bring peace to John Sung and his little family. For the first few weeks all went well. He resumed his work in genetics and was given a small laboratory of his own, and Mercy busied herself with her child and her homemaking. Then one morning John Sung was visited in his laboratory by Captain Li, who presented him with a letter from Chao Chung saying the Chairman wished to suggest that genetics, in the case of the scientist John Sung, should be related to the study of nuclear science, especially the effects of fallout from a nuclear explosion on human chromosomes. It was necessary, the Chairman had declared, to relate all scientific study to some practical end. Neither time nor money could be allotted for the study of pure science.

"It is the wish of those above to consider the talents and the desires of valuable men like yourself, Comrade Sung," Captain Li said. "Only when these run counter to the plans made for their benefit are citizens redirected."

"How am I to be redirected?" John Sung inquired.

Captain Li consulted a paper. "You are to go to the province of Sinkiang. Your work will be there for the next three years, and your superior will be our great expert in rocketry, who—"

John Sung interrupted. "Does my family accompany me?"

Captain Li's black eyebrows lifted. "I believe your wife has been assigned to a new school of music here in the capital."

John Sung sat with his head bowed. "I must prepare myself," he said at last.

"You are allowed three days," Captain Li said and marched from the room.

"I WISH we had never left America!"

Mercy's cry pierced her husband's heart. The child on her lap looked at her wonderingly and drew down the corners of his mouth.

"We could escape—get to Hong Kong, where my aunt would help us. Hundreds of people do," Mercy continued.

"What would you think if I told you I don't want to go?" her husband said, sitting down at the table he used as a desk.

"I'd say that I don't understand you!"

Anger underlay the tone of her voice, and the child slipped from her lap and crawled to a patch of sunlight on the floor and tried to catch it in his hands. Both parents, diverted for the moment, joined in laughter. Then John Sung said, "Our people need us more than you or I can imagine. A deep struggle is emerging in our country. It will rise to the surface the moment the Chairman dies of old age." He had lowered his voice and spoken in English.

"What struggle?" she asked, her voice as low as his.

"The struggle between the ideologists and the experts," he said. "Our national problem is wrapped up in one word—production. The theorists do not know how to organize for it. The experts are merely biding their time. They know that without them there can be no national development. I am one of those experts. Now do you see why I want to stay?"

Mercy was moved unwillingly. "But our son—"

John Sung interrupted her. "Ah, our son! By the time he grows up, ideology won't matter. Men will be chosen for what they can do technically, not for what they think or dream. Our son will see the fruit of what men like me will plant." He paused, remembering the peasants among whom he had worked. "Our people are worth saving," John Sung told his wife. "I will stay with them, and I am proud to have my son grow up here."

Thus Mercy gained strength from him and said she would do her share by setting up the school of music within the National University. "But I will live here alone. I will not return to my sister," she told her husband.

"I PROPOSE," said Liu Peng, "that we live together as comrades for some months before we marry officially."

Grace Liang withdrew from his arms. "Is that necessary?"

She put the question lightly, so that he would not think she was conventional or bourgeois. However, she was deeply shocked. They had been standing in her courtyard on a September day, late in the afternoon. Now he sat down on a bamboo chair while she knelt beside the small goldfish pool and began throwing bits of stone into the water. "But don't you want marriage?" she asked.

"I am not sure. Perhaps if our relationship is good, you know—I'll want it."

"And if I want it now?"

"You'd be foolish. You don't know me well enough."

"But well enough to sleep with you?"

"I hope so."

"But just for sleeping—wouldn't someone else do as well?"

"No. I want to be serious."

He was leaning back, gazing up at the sky, waiting for her to speak. She looked at the large intensely black eyes, the heavy black brows, the surprisingly tender lines of his mouth. She loved him with a deep physical passion. His mind she did not wish to explore, lest she find there something that might prove him less worthy of love than she wanted him to be. Nothing mattered to her except this moment, alone together, and she felt the heat in her blood rise.

He looked at her suddenly, and she saw that he perfectly understood what was taking place within her. Without a word he rose from the chair and walked across the courtyard. He drew the iron bar across the gate. "Now we are alone."

He clasped her right hand in his left hand and together they walked silently into the house and into her bedroom.

MERCY SAT at her piano pupil's side in the classroom of the music school, her trained ear hearing every discordant note while her thoughts pursued their separate ways. Months had passed since John Sung had gone to the remote province of Sinkiang, and his letters were few and dry. She sought to forgive him for what seemed coldness, knowing that he could not communicate the meaning and purpose of his work even to her. Nor could she write him about their child, for other eyes might read of her increasing fear. The child had passed his second birthday and soon, on his third, he must enter a state school to be taught what she herself could not believe: that Americans were the enemy. If she told him that Americans were not fiends, but kind, generous people, he would be taught that she was a traitor.

In her confusion she became a lonely soul, living as she did in a huge new building where all were strangers. She did not see even her sister Grace, who, she heard, had accepted Liu Peng as her lover.

Mercy's music school had begun with eleven pupils, one of them a young man of twenty named Chen. Under Mercy's teaching he made great progress, and she showed him how to write down the music he composed. He found her not only an excellent teacher and a good friend but also a very beautiful woman, and he wove youthful dreams about her, fancies of how someday he would rescue her from unknown danger or even save her life.

Mercy thought of him as one who would someday become a great musician. But would he be denied the freedom to create the music that came from his soul? And would her own son be like Chen, gifted but with no power to achieve the heights to which his gifts entitled him?

At last she concluded that she had done her son an injustice in bringing him to be born here in his own country. So much did her thoughts disturb her that she wrote a letter to her mother, asking her to come for a visit.

"AND WHEN did you last hear from my son-in-law?" Madame Liang inquired of Mercy. Her grandson sat on a small bamboo stool, observing her carefully. She made no overtures toward him, but continued her quiet conversation with his mother.

"I seldom hear from him," Mercy answered. "He is in a highly classified area, though he will not work on weapons that may be used against—"

Madame Liang looked hurriedly about the room, laying her forefinger on her lips as she did so. Mercy fell silent, startled by her mother's gesture. It was at this moment that the little boy left his stool and came and placed his small hands on his grandmother's knees and gazed into her face. She, deeply moved, lifted him to her lap and put her arm about him and felt deep tenderness pervade her.

"What are you thinking, M-ma?" Mercy asked.

"I am thinking," Madame Liang said slowly, "of this child's future. Our people will one day right themselves, but in the transition, how will this child survive?"

Mercy whispered to her mother, "Ah, you see what I fear!"

Madame Liang continued to embrace the child, who rested in peace against her breast. Then she spoke in a low voice. "So long as his father lives, you need not fear. A scientist of his high learning is too valuable to kill."

"Thank you, Mother," Mercy said.

MONTHS LATER, unknown to the world, a moment drew near in that lonely place where John Sung lived among hundreds of other young scientists, a moment when one of the most powerful of modern weapons, the first of its kind in China, would soar into the sky and release its fury. The young scientists, three hundred or so, most of them trained in the country they were now urged to hate, were assembled near the remote spot where the mighty creature was to be released.

John Sung was among those who waited that day in the desert surrounded by high and barren mountains. A delay was announced, and then another and another. Impatience mounted among the spectators. John Sung began to doubt in his heart whether the weapon was ready to be fired, and he was about to return to his own laboratory when suddenly the countdown began over the loudspeaker. He stayed, pressing forward among the others, as the fateful seconds passed.

Alas, that final second never came. Without warning, the huge object, trembling with impatient inner energy, burst of itself into a roar so mighty that the earth shook and the whole sky turned into flame. A rain of fire fell upon the desert for miles around, and in that deadly rain all perished.

CAPTAIN LI mounted the stairs of the National University's School of Music. In his hand he carried an envelope stamped with the seal of Minister Chao Chung. The newspapers had made no report of the desert blast, yet everyone knew that a catastrophe had occurred in that distant place, though its nature remained obscure, for no one dared to speak. Captain Li found Mercy as she was about to leave her office for the day. He clicked his heels and saluted. "Comrade Sung, I have a message. From the minister."

Mercy sat down in the chair behind the desk and slit open the envelope with a narrow brass knife. As Chao Chung had instructed him, Captain Li turned his back when she drew out the paper. She had time to read it once, twice, and then he heard a low long moan.

"Are you ill, comrade?" he called, and when she did not speak, he felt compelled to look over his shoulder.

She sat there holding the paper, her face pale, her eyes black and staring. When she saw him looking at her, she spoke, her voice strangling in her throat. "Do you—do you—know what news you have brought me?"

He shook his head. "No, comrade. I do only what I am told."

"Then go away," she said.

And he, accustomed to obedience, opened the door and left.

When he was gone, Mercy sat for a long time, the white paper crushed in her hand. The pupils were leaving for the day. There were nearly a hundred of them now. Waiting for her husband to come home, she had done her work: she had built a good school. Now he would never come home and her work, too, was finished. She would take her son and leave their country forever.

Yet how could she get away with the child? She would be watched, she would be caught. She would not ask her mother's help. No, no, she must not even let her mother know. If it was discovered that her mother had let her go, what bitter punishment would ensue? She must do the best she could alone.

At this moment she heard a piano. Someone was playing Beethoven brilliantly, beautifully. It could only be Chen, who often stayed to practice after the others had gone. Suddenly she knew what she must do. She followed the music to the room where he was playing and opened the door softly. He saw her face and his hands crashed on the piano. "What has happened?"

She handed the paper to him. He read it twice and gave it back to her. "How can I help you?" he asked, his heart tender with mingled pity and joy. This was the hour of which he had dreamed.

It was almost impossible for her to speak; her lips were dry, her tongue seemed swollen in her mouth, her throat was tight. "My son and I—we must get away—get to my aunt in Hong Kong—go on playing—someone may be listening."

Chen began to play again, soft music that his hands remembered, while she talked under her breath. Her longtime fears for the future of her most talented pupil mixed now with her sudden new plans for her small son and herself. She assured

Chen that in America he could have great success in music and could make riches that, for the most part, he could keep for himself.

Mercy continued her work for a day and, under cover of his music lesson, she arranged with Chen to go with him to a village near the border where his paternal grandmother lived.

"We will fly to Canton," Chen said, his voice low under his music, "but we must make speed before our absence is discovered. The day after tomorrow is a summer holiday. Let us leave tomorrow separately by night flight. From Canton it is a short train ride to my grandmother's village. If anyone asks, I will say we are brother and sister and we are visiting our old grandmother. In the village we will change our clothes to poor ones, and return to Canton immediately. In the morning we will press across the border among the crowd, with baskets of vegetables and fruits to sell."

After further talk, always with music hiding their voices, they arranged the details of their flight, and they were able to do what they had planned. Mercy told her woman servant that she was going to Shanghai to visit her mother for four days. It all seemed easy enough until that moment when she crossed the border, a basket of peaches on one arm and the child in the other. Among the crowd she passed easily into Hong Kong. When she knew she was safe, she turned to see if Chen had followed her.

But even as he had one foot over the line, an officer seized him by the shoulder. "You are no peasant." He roughly snatched Chen's right hand and showed it to those about. "Is this the horny hand of a peasant? Even the handle of a basket makes a blister. Step back, you!"

Chen could only obey, and Mercy, as she watched, felt tears rush to her eyes. Why had she asked this innocent and talented lad to help her? Yet without him she probably could not have escaped. Chen did not so much as turn his head, for he would not have the officer know that he had anything to do with her, lest she, too, be stopped somehow.

Heartsick but safe now with her child, Mercy sadly went her way on foot to her aunt's house, disguised in her rough peasant garments, her face dusty and her hair out of place. She mourned over Chen. If he was not shot as a traitor or put in prison, he would at the very least be sentenced to hard labor in some distant place where no music could be made.

VIII

"Your sister is a defector," Liu Peng said sternly.

Grace waited for him to say more. The news of Mercy's escape had already come to her through the usual servant channels. Grace and Liu Peng had taken their evening meal and were now in the central room.

"Your sister," Liu Peng continued, "has crossed the border. A young pupil named Chen went with her, but he was caught and has been returned here for questioning and punishment. Already he has confessed."

"What does he confess?" Grace asked. While Liu Peng talked, she was constantly aware of his eyes, his extraordinarily expressive hands, the grace of his lithe body.

"He wished to go to America because he thinks there his talent will bring him money!" Liu Peng's voice was scornful. "I cannot understand how a young man can deviate so profoundly after going through our school indoctrination."

"Perhaps the young need a new idealism—perhaps nationalism rather than revolution would appeal to them," Grace offered.

Liu Peng pondered her reply. He had never known before a woman with whom he could exchange ideas as well as embraces. He felt, too, the strange excitement of her knowledge of that great unknown enemy America. And his curiosity grew with his amazement at her scientific skills, for he recognized that her training and techniques were superior to his own. There were times when he resented this and was brusque and cold toward her. But she had deeply roused his love.

He compelled himself to hear what she was saying. "Nations grow as people grow. I am not sure that we do well, moreover, to return at this late date to the early methods of the revolution, such as the recent decision to abolish officer titles in the army and address everyone as comrade, whatever his position."

"But that is to eliminate the consciousness of rank and the hope of personal fame and financial reward," he declared.

"These are necessary incentives—they are what men live by!" she insisted.

"Bourgeois thinking!" he cried.

"Old slogans!" she retorted, laughing.

He was always aroused by her laughter. How dare she laugh? The conflict of their minds spread its heat to his body. He wanted to subdue her, to force her to his will and way.

"You don't know what you are talking about," he shouted, slapping his knees with both hands. "The Chairman has privately decreed a new way to continue the struggle against landlords and rich peasants. If this revolutionary struggle is not maintained, he fears our people will slip into revisionism and even fascism."

"What is this new way?" she asked.

"The young will rise up. The Chairman will use our youth. Rebellion, the ancestor of revolution, is indigenous to the young."

"But I am shocked," Grace exclaimed. "Can you mean that revolutionary talk and indoctrination are to take the place, even in the army, of teaching our men the techniques of modern warfare? Why, it's medieval! No ideology can replace the hard discipline of *learning*. We can't do without the 'experts'!"

"We can't do without the revolutionary spirit, either," Liu Peng said.

"Then that means another purge!" Her face was grave. For the moment she had forgotten him, and this he could not bear.

"Why do we grow angry with each other?" he demanded and rose abruptly. In two strides he had crossed the space between them and she was in his arms. She yielded immediately. Every argument ended so, and in those moments she instinctively avoided what she knew: that she did not respect his mind, limited as it was by narrow revolutionary doctrines.

MADAME LIANG was inspecting her kitchens, the chef at her heels to note her comments and corrections—the immense wooden chopping blocks were not scrubbed white, the cooking vats did not shine as she wished, and the leftovers were not sorted quickly enough for the hungry poor who still came at twilight to the back doors.

Her affairs in order, Madame Liang sat down to a cup of green tea, suddenly feeling old and solitary. Ever since Mercy and the child had escaped, Madame Liang had felt herself under surveillance. Outwardly all was the same. Her arrangements with those above had not changed. For ten years, technically, all that she had once possessed privately had belonged to the state, and this made her, technically, the employee of the state, on salary. In fact, however, she operated her restaurant as she always had and no accounts were formally submitted.

She was now altogether alone, except for Grace, her eldest daughter, in Peking, and she avoided thinking of her because she dreaded the moment of confrontation when she could no longer ignore the situation in which Grace was living. Yet she ought to be content. Her grandson and two of her daughters were safe. Her sister had cleverly written from Hong Kong: "Your second daughter is visiting me for a few days. After that she will return to her sister." The key was in the phrase "return to her sister." Madame Liang knew that Mercy would never return to Grace, since those two were very far apart. Therefore "sister" could only mean Joy, in America. Once Mercy was there, Madame Liang would worry no more, although she might never see her again—no, let her face the truth, she *would* never see either Mercy or Joy again. She would never see even once her son-in-law Hsuan, the great artist. And she had lost her

grandson. Ah, there was the real stab in her heart! He would grow up in another country, foreign to his own people. And it would be a very long time before there could be peace in this distraught country of hers.

Now the ruthless young, instigated by secret permission, were destroying and killing and burning all, in the name of the aged Chairman. In the army there were other struggles, more profound, more hidden. No military heads had appeared in her restaurant for several months. How many had been purged? And there was talk everywhere of another Great Leap Forward, in spite of the failure of the last one. The quarrel between the ideologists and the technologists was reviving. She could only wait in silence for the old Chairman to die, as many others were waiting, so that the people could prevail.

She wondered what would happen if all her generation died and only these ruthless and ignorant young were left. Who would there be then to restore the wisdom of the past?

THE SEASON in Peking was midsummer when Madame Liang arrived at her eldest daughter's house. Her reason for coming was twofold. First, she now knew that her second daughter and her grandson had reached the United States safely. She had this assurance from her youngest daughter, Joy, who had sent a letter to her aunt in Hong Kong, which Madame Liang's sister had hidden in a jar of candied coconut and sent on. In a few words Joy was able to tell that Mercy and the child were safe, that this had only happened through the help of Mr. and Mrs. Brandon, that no one must worry anymore.

"Oh, my mother," Joy had written, "come here to us. You have never seen my husband. I am so happy. I am expecting my first child. Come and see your grandchildren. I think of you all the time. Mother, Hsuan is a great artist, but I am improving. I took a prize for my portrait of you, done from memory. Mother, come and stay with us the rest of your life."

When she had read these words of love, the tears so long dormant came welling to Madame Liang's eyes. Why should she not leave this country of turmoil? For, however long her life, she could not hope to see peace. She was sorely tempted, therefore, to find her way to the United States. Sitting alone in her rooms, she had imagined herself in that other country, peaceful and surrounded by her grandchildren. Then she had thought of her eldest daughter; how could she leave without telling Grace she was going? Upon this impulse she left at once for Peking.

Now she and Grace sat in the courtyard with palm-leaf fans in their hands and waited for Liu Peng to come home, Madame Liang warning herself to behave as though Liu Peng were her true son-in-law. This was not yet the moment to speak against him.

"Perhaps Liu Peng can tell me if it is true that armies of our own people are fighting each other in the south," she said.

"What have you heard?" Grace asked.

"I have heard that in the city of Wuchow on the border between Kwangtung and Kwangsi provinces there is war between those who are for and those who are against the Chairman. Two thousand homes have been destroyed or badly damaged—so I have heard."

"Liu Peng will know," Grace said.

At her mention of his name a silence fell between mother and daughter. Madame Liang broke it. "Tell me about your work, my child."

Her daughter gave a peal of clear laughter. "M-ma, you are so—delightful! Do you think I don't know why you came? But, well enough. Doctor Tseng is an amazingly good physician. He diagnoses with accuracy. He fails only in the crudity of the drugs he prescribes. Somewhere along the way, M-ma, our people refused or were forbidden to develop the techniques of modern science, based on freedom of thought and experimentation."

"Ah, you have the kernel of truth," Madame Liang remarked. "The ancient rulers did not allow freedom to the creator, but neither do the new rulers."

Before Grace could reply there was a knock upon the wooden gate. The old manservant ran to draw back the bar, and Liu Peng entered. He appeared weary, his eyes shadowed under his black brows, and there were spots of blood on his trousers.

He bowed slightly to Madame Liang. "Allow me to change my clothes. I have spent many hours at the hospital today. There was fighting in the outskirts of the city."

"By all means rest yourself," Madame Liang said courteously.

In a very few minutes he was back, however, and Grace poured a bowl of tea for him. "My mother was speaking of science and why our people did not develop modern techniques," Grace began.

But Madame Liang refused to be protected. "And I said that our present rulers allow no freedom of thought."

Liu Peng gave her a piercing glance. "There must be order before there can be freedom," he declared.

This was the burden of the argument that continued for the several days of Madame Liang's visit, though almost against her will she admired this powerful young man. She spent long hours alone during the day, but Grace came home before Liu Peng and mother and daughter had this time together. On one such day Madame Liang brought up the other reason for her visit. "Your sisters beseech me to come live out my old age with them."

They were sitting in the central room, and the rain dripped in a silvery curtain over the door that was open to the courtyard. From the distant sounds Madame Liang had known that there was unrest in the city. She had asked no questions of the servant couple, but once, at noon, when she herself went to the gate to see what was happening, they had laid hold of both her arms.

"It is known that the famous Doctor Liu Peng lives here and so we are safe so long as the gate is not opened," they told her. "Wild young people are everywhere roaming the streets, seeking to kill those who, they think, are rich and do not obey the Chairman."

She had remained all day behind the locked gate.

"Can it be possible that you would think of leaving our country?" Grace exclaimed.

"But if I can do nothing to help, if years must pass before we have peace, if I must live out my life alone, without grandchildren—" A wily look crept over her face. She began again. "And you, my daughter, living as you do with this man. Oh, I can see he is a man of powerful force. Being what you are, a strong woman—no, still I cannot understand why he is not your husband!"

Grace did not reply for a moment. "I will not force him. I can only decide for myself. I will never leave him—"

She broke off to listen. From over the walls came a long wailing scream. There was an explosion somewhere not far off and then the crackling of flames. Grace ran toward the open door, but before she could run through the curtain of rain, Madame Liang caught her wrist. "What can we do against them?" she cried.

"It is of Liu Peng I am thinking," her daughter cried back.

But Madame Liang pulled her into the room. "Think of yourself! Is he more than a man? In this disorder what will compel him to stay with you forever? Where are my grandchildren? They are in a foreign country because their parents dare not let them live here. Where are your children? I ask you—do you even dare to have a child? No, you dare not! Is this order? In the name of our ancestors, is this decency? I will go to America. I give up hope for my own people. Perhaps when I am a ghost I can be born again in peace in my own country—"

She was weeping now, and Grace knelt before her and chafed her mother's cold hands. "M-ma, don't cry! I will be a better daughter to you. I will even ask Liu Peng to—to allow a ceremony at the marriage hall. I'll not be proud anymore. And then we'll have children and you'll have grandchildren on both sides of the world. M-ma, don't think I forget those years I spent in America—happy years. Someday when the turmoil is over . . . Our people are a great people, M-ma—worth everything—even our lives. That is why I stay with Liu Peng—I can't explain—only I know I can't leave him—ever—ever—any more than I can leave our people."

Madame Liang dried her eyes. "I can't leave, either—I was dreaming again. It is true that I helped to create this chaos and I must stay with my own people. I must go home. I will stay there the rest of my life."

"M-ma, don't—"

Madame Liang rose from her chair, pushed her daughter aside and went to pack her box. Sometime before noon the next day she went to the airport, accompanied only by Grace, Liu Peng having sent word by messenger that he had to work around the clock because of the many wounded. There were few passengers on the aircraft, for now it was futile to try to escape. Turmoil was everywhere.

"M-ma, come back to us." Grace clung to her mother's hand.

But Madame Liang shook her head. "Forgive me," she said. "I have no right to reproach you for anything—I who helped to begin it all. Take care of yourself, my child—and forgive me—"

She did not wait to hear her daughter's pleas. She walked resolutely up the gangway, found her seat, leaned back and closed her eyes. She was on her way home.

Shanghai was quiet when she reached it some hours later. It was twilight and few people were on the street. Madame Liang put down her heavy box and sat on it until a pedicab came near, drawn by a very old man. He stopped when she hailed him, and when she had climbed in, he pedaled away in the deepening dusk. At her gate she descended and paid him.

"Shall I wait until someone opens the gate?" he asked after he had put her box on the stone threshold.

"No," she said. "Someone is here."

He lingered nevertheless, yet no one came. She pushed at the gate with both hands and felt a bar across it. Then, by the flickering light, she read the rude words scrawled in red paint on the wooden bar: "This capitalist house must be burned to ash."

Madame Liang turned to the old pedicab driver, bewildered. "My home is to be burned," she faltered.

He could not read but he understood the look on her face. "They have burned many houses," he said.

He waited because he did not know what else to do. He was alone and she was alone. He had never had a house and now neither had she. Where would they go? Each asked the silent question.

At this instant a band of young wanderers came singing down the street, some of them almost children, and they, too, were homeless. Singing their wild song, they stopped to stare at the helpless old persons standing before the barred gate. Suddenly their singing turned to wild laughter. Madame Liang cried out to know who they were, but they only laughed more wildly and swarmed about her. In terror she clung to the old pedicab driver and he tried to shield her with his arms. It was useless. With sticks and stones they fell upon those two aged persons and beat and pounded them to death. When they were dead, those young went on their way again, singing.

OF MADAME LIANG's three daughters, only the eldest was present at her funeral. It was the finest funeral that had taken place in recent years, and all were surprised at the number of people who crowded about the bier. Unknown persons, whom for years Madame Liang had cared for and fed, gathered quietly in the main dining room of her restaurant, which now had nothing in it except the bier on which she lay. All the furniture had been destroyed by violent youths, her personal rooms had been ransacked and her personal possessions robbed. These rooms were now closed. Only the main dining room had been cleaned and made ready for the funeral.

Among the guests was Minister Chao Chung. He laid a bouquet of white flowers beside her and stood for a moment

gazing down at her face, which even in death was beautiful. Chou Ma had dressed her in a rose gown of brocaded satin, which hid the cruel wounds on her body.

What thoughts were in the grieving minister's mind no one knew. Memories of the past, perhaps, and fear for the future? Watching that handsome and sorrowful face, Grace could only wonder. How much of her mother's life she had never known!

Though Liu Peng was at her side, suddenly she felt alone. The love between them had been intensified by this death, for Liu Peng, divining her loneliness, had been more than usually tender toward her. Yet, though she had passionately defended him even in her thoughts, now she wished that the bond between them were not so tenuous.

When Madame Liang's body had been consigned to the earth, Grace returned to the house on the Street of the Three Foxes. All was the same there, and yet nothing was the same. Even her love for Liu Peng was not the same.

Now that her mother was gone, she felt a responsibility, a duty toward her. Madame Liang had been sustained by faith in her own people; it was as though that beautiful woman, so steadfast, so silent, were transmitting that faith to her daughter in some unknown way. With this spirit of her mother Grace felt strong, and she became so resolute that Liu Peng was aware of a change in her that he could not understand.

Thus days passed until one night she declined his lovemaking. He flung himself out of the bed they shared and shouted at her, "What—have you stopped loving me?"

She lay looking at him, her hands clasped behind her head. "I love you more than ever," she told him honestly. "But it is true that I have changed. I am more than a woman in love. I see now that ours has been a halfway sort of love, reaching no farther than two persons here in this house. Sooner or later it will die unless it grows, and it will grow only as we grow enough to sustain it. I could go away and live in peace, as my sisters have done. But I choose to stay—not only because of you . . . I choose as my mother chose. I have faith in our people. Liu Peng, I can't live as we have been living. I want you to marry me. I want your children. I want to live in the old way—husband and wife and children—"

Liu Peng listened stubbornly. "And what if I refuse?"

She looked back at him as stubbornly. "Then we part," she said firmly. "I have my work to do and I will do it."

"You don't love me," he muttered.

"I love you and something more," she replied. "I love—" Here she broke off, smiling, but with tears in her eyes. "Will you marry me?" she asked, not demanding but so winsome that he could not resist her.

Yet he would not yield easily. It was not his habit to yield. And while he was silent, struggling against himself, she considered him most tenderly. A powerful, willful, impulsive man; a man of strong emotions, an honest man; a man with infinite capacity to grow, a man who could go astray for lack of knowledge, the son of a peasant, a man of the people—ah, that was he, a man of the people! She loved him for being what he was, and because she loved him, she shared her mother's faith in others like him.

He spoke at last, gruffly, as though he were angry. "I will marry you because I cannot live without you. You are bourgeois—but I cannot live without you. If you must have children, then have them. I cannot live without you."

She laughed and pulled him down until his head was upon her breast, and she cried out in the midst of her laughter, "Oh, how I love you!"

ACKNOWLEDGMENTS

The condensations in this volume have been created by
The Reader's Digest Association, Inc., and are used by
permission of and special arrangement with the publishers
and the holders of the respective copyrights.

The following works by Pearl S. Buck, originally published by
The John Day Company, are reprinted by permission of the Pearl S.
Buck Family Trust, Harper & Row, Publishers, Inc., and Methuen
London, Limited: ·

THE PROMISE
Copyright 1942, 1943 by *Asia* Magazine, Inc.; renewed © 1970, 1971 by Pearl S. Buck.

PAVILION OF WOMEN
Copyright 1946 by Pearl S. Buck; renewed © 1974 by Janice C. Walsh,
Chieko C. Singer, Richard S. Walsh, Jean C. Lippincott, John S.
Walsh, Edgar S. Walsh, Henriette C. Teush and Carol Buck.

A BRIDGE FOR PASSING
Copyright © 1961, 1962 by Pearl S. Buck.

THE THREE DAUGHTERS OF MADAME LIANG
Copyright © 1969 by Pearl S. Buck Foundation, Inc.

ILLUSTRATION CREDITS

Frontispiece: Illustration by Hodges Soileau

A Bridge for Passing

Page 322 (top): Karsh of Ottawa/Woodfin Camp and Associates
and by permission of the Pearl S. Buck Family Trust

Page 322 (bottom): By permission of the Pearl S. Buck Family Trust